ZAPATA ROSE IN 1992
& Other Tales

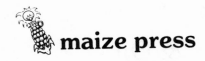 **maize press**

general editor
alurista

distributed by
Bilingual Review/Press
Hispanic Research Center
Arizona State University
Tempe, AZ 85287-2702
(602) 965-3867

ZAPATA ROSE IN 1992
& Other Tales

Gary D. Keller

 **maize press**

ISBN: 0-939558-11-4

Library of Congress Cataloging-in-Publication Data

Keller, Gary D.
   Zapata Rose in 1992, and other tales / by Gary D. Keller
      p. cm.
   Includes the four stories from Tales of El Huitlacoche plus three new stories.
   Contents: Papi invented the automatic jumping bean — The Mojado who offered up his tapeworms to the public weal — The Raza who scored big in Anáhuac — Mocha in Disneyland — Hidalgo, adventure capitalist, sallied forth to aid the Third World — A Chicano FBI searching for Carmen Loca in ¡Sal Si Puedes! — Zapata Rose in 1992.
   ISBN 0-939558-11-4 (paper) : $12.00
   1. Mexican Americans—Fiction.   I. Title.
PS3561.E38534Z3   1992
813' .54—dc20   92-12551
                                                     CIP

PRINTED IN THE UNITED STATES OF AMERICA

Cover design by Lynn Nees, Bidlack Creative Services

Back cover photo by Conley Photography, Inc.

Acknowledgments

Four of the stories in this collection originally appeared in the following publications:

"Papi Invented the Automatic Jumping Bean" (original title, "The Man Who Invented the Automatic Jumping Bean") in *Bilingual Review*, I, 2 (1974), 193-200. Reprinted in *The Pushcart Prize, II: Best of the Small Presses*, ed. Bill Henderson (New York: Pushcart Press, 1977). Also in *Best of the Small Presses*, ed. Bill Henderson (New York: Avon Books, 1977).

"The Mojado Who Offered Up His Tapeworms to the Public Weal" in *Hispanics in the United States: An Anthology of Creative Literature, Vol. II*, ed. F. Jiménez and G. Keller (Ypsilanti, MI: Bilingual Press, 1981), 13-27.

"Mocha in Disneyland" in *Hispanics in the United States: An Anthology of Creative Literature, Vol. I*, ed. G. Keller and F. Jiménez (Ypsilanti, MI: Bilingual Press, 1980), 57-74.

"A Chicano FBI Searching for Carmen Loca in ¡Sal Si Puedes!" in *Bilingual Review*, XVI, 2-3 (1991), 197-210.

(Acknowledgments continue on last page of book.)

Table of Contents

When one significant section of the community burns with the sense of injustice, the rest of the community cannot safely pretend that there is no reason for their discontent. —*Waitangi Tribunal* (New Zealand)

So, pues, I'm just a vato loco man
but if we have our way again
we'll ask for 'Miliano Zapata's rise
stake him out in pater-frater's guise
cause if we have Zapata
We'll never again need Zapata
　　　　—*El Huitlacoche*, "The Urban(e) Chicano's 76"

Something is afoot in the universe, something that looks like gestation and birth. —*Pierre Teilhard de Chardin*

Papi Invented the Automatic Jumping Bean

My dad invented the first authentic wormless Mexican jumping bean with an empty Contac capsule and a ball of mercury he siphoned off a store-bought thermometer. He did it for potential profit in Ciudad Juárez in 1953 in a high-rise complex that the government built for el pueblo out of prefab concrete and reinforced plastic girders. They named it Huertas de Nezahualcóyotl after the Aztec poet-king.

It was a big seller all over Mesoamérica. I saw it in the heart of Aztlán, through the frosted glass of a candy store window in Alamogordo on Christmas Eve. Big novelty! All-purpose wormless jumping bean! Never dies or runs out on you! Works on body heat! It was in one of those candy stores that the Coca Cola company moves into in a heavy way. They put up all your signs for you. They tack up tantalizing murals of cheeseburgers and coke. Above the counter the name of the store and the proprietor is in lights with two psychedelic Coca Cola imprints on either side, like Christ between his thieves. They only let you sell Coke.

I saw them in the hands of esquintles on the Mexican altiplano and even in the capital. The jobbers on Correo Mayor sold them by the gross to the peddlers, hustlers and other street people. Years later on one of my wanderings I spotted them in the renowned Quetzaltenango market in Guatemala. An old Indian woman in her shawl had them stacked up in symmetrical mounds like frijoles pintos. She looked like one of those sibylline old indígenas from whom one might expect sage or psychedelic advice. I questioned her. "Mother! What do you sell here? Mexican jumping beans?" But she paid me no heed. She sat there, mute and sassy, receiving the indrawn vision.

Not that my old man made a centavo from his invention. That

day in '53 he came home from across the border with only about fifteen Delco batteries in his pickup. Competition was getting brutal. And what with the invention of aluminum cans . . . He had himself two Carta Blancas, scratched himself here and there; then came an inspiration. From the souvenir shelf he took the miniature Empire State building that he had bought on Times Square after the War (fighting for Tío Sam was the thing to do in those days) and carefully removed the thermometer from the tower. Then he came out of the john with a Contac capsule that he had emptied. He split the thermometer and tapped the jelly-like mercury. He made a ball from the mercury and slid it into the capsule. He held the capsule tight between his palms. He looked like he was hiding a cigarette butt from the vicissitudes of the wind. Then he let it go on the table. Mother of God! Did it jump! My father, who was fond of scientific discourse (he could expound at length about the notion of sufficiency in scientific theory), explained that it was the heat of his palms that turned the mercury to frenzied bubbling and made the capsule bounce and teeter as if there were a drunken worm in it.

Two days later he produced a refined version with the capsule painted pretty like an Easter egg. He showed it to his compadre, Chalo, who knew a jobber in El Paso. ¡Qué amigazo! They went to see the jobber. The jobber went to see a plastics manufacturer, a man with great metal presses and centrifuges to force molten plastic into little cavities.

There were endless delays, boredom, abulia. My father quickly got fed up with waiting and decided to invent something else. He put together a plastic submarine out of a Revell box, bored two holes in it and filled them with hoses. He pumped air in and out with a hand pump. The sub went up and down "like magic." With the other pump he fired a dart-like torpedo out of the submarine's hulk. The ship was not a total success. A little rough water in the bathtub and the sub would roll over like a dead bullhead on the Río Grande. "It's the balance," my dad said. "The balance has to be perfect. The tolerances are too fine. After all, plastic weighs nothing. You'd have to be a real engineer to solve it."

My father didn't consider himself a "real" engineer. He was smart enough to know that he was some sort of claptrap genius and also to know that he had no credentials. Maybe he considered himself on a par with a "jailhouse" lawyer. He used the adjective "real" like a scourge and a vision.

About six months later we spotted my baby sister, Conchita, playing with one of those merry, lifeless beans. My dad turned from his domino game and glared at her, with malevolence. "Where'd you get that!"

Conchita began to quiver. "I traded it at school for two clear marbles!"

"They have them at school!"

"Yes."

"Everybody has them?"

Conchita nodded.

And so it was finished with the automatic jumping beans. Except for the malestar that it left in my father's gut. He didn't really care about the royalties that he had fantasized over. He just wished more people knew who the real inventor was. We never talked or told anyone else about it. We made ourselves forget.

That was one thing I couldn't tolerate about my father. We were witness to a succession of unprincipled ruses that were played upon my father's person to the discredit of the family honor. Part of it was that fatalism characteristic of Papi's generation, that passive resignation and acceptance of "reality." That was difficult to stomach, yet certainly not unique; it was the norm, therefore tolerable. To this my father added a boundless and totally unfounded faith in people. He was an ingenue, a trusting child, a father to all his charges. And what's more, men, including confidence men, had confidence in him.

How my old man had faith! And he'd been in and out of so many operations. He had scoured the Southwest for old batteries to haul across the border to transform into lead ingots and sell back to the Americans; he had stamped out Jesus Christs on metal plate, struck Virgin Marys from rubber molds, learned the ins and outs of libraries in order to invent a process to detin cans; he had set diamonds, manufactured brass buttons for the armed forces, designed costume jewelry, set up a nickel-plating bath, run a route of gumball machines, managed a molino de nixtamal for tortillas, bought a chicken farm (without having read Sherwood Anderson), gone to school at the Polytechnic, bred rabbits, trained geese to be industrial watchdogs, raised a family and invented the automatic jumping bean. He trained scores of young men in the techniques of lathes, presses, files and baths. He was able to initiate not a few followers into the mysteries of the electro-mechanical creed. But after his accident with the sodium hydroxide he shut himself in. Now and then one of his former disciples would come over with a sixpack to pay his respects. These men would be foremen at the mine at Smeltertown or supervisors of the toaster assembly line at the Magic Chef complex. Papi was pleased with his pupils but he used them as case studies— fox and crow style—to prove his point that my brother and I had to get college degrees as engineers. "There's no other way," my dad told us continually. "You have to have a passport."

In some circles my father was considered a soft touch. The chicken farm went broke after my father hired an holgazán with no experience "y unos huevos de plomo." A year after he convinced el patrón to get into the detinning business, everybody was privy and there were eight detinners in Juárez alone. Besides, they started coming out with the aluminum can. The geese functioned beautifully but he couldn't convince enough people to accept the idea. The War was over and nobody needed brass buttons. After a while his eyesight wasn't so good and he couldn't set diamonds. The big companies didn't like the idea of him moving into religious jewelry, so they muscled him out at the retail level. The United States customs officials raised the tariff on lead ingots. The gumballs got all sticky inside their machines in the Juárez sun. Somebody invented the automatic tortilla press and nobody needed raw corn dough. He never was able to graduate from the Polytechnic—after eight years of going at night he was doing an isometric drawing of a screw and he stopped and said he wouldn't. We ate lots of rabbit and someone went ahead and manufactured automatic jumping beans without informing my father.

I spent five years in college; for three of those I tried to be an engineer. Go be an engineer! Get thee to an engine! My father would pin my shoulders to the wall and lecture me with manic glee. Me and my younger brother would not only be engineers— but metallurgists! He feared for his poor Mexico-Americanized sons, alloys of detinned beer cans. Appreciable schizophrenes. Unable to speak a tongue of any convention, they gabbled to each other, the younger and the older, in a papiamento of street caliche and devious calques. A tongue only Tex-Mexs, wetbacks, tirilones, pachucos and pochos could penetrate. Heat the capsule in the palm of your hand and the mercury begins seesawing and the capsule hops. Those were his sons, transplanted, technocratic, capsular Mexican jumping beans without the worm. He believed in education and a free press. Would society listen to reason?

My father liked to walk in the barrio and as hijo mayor it was my privilege to be at his side. We'd walk down the main drag, past the chicharronería ("sin pelos, ¿eh?") where the pork rind hung to dry, and past the molino de nixtamal where at six in the morning you could queue up for the masa that came out like sausage from the funnel and was molded into a ball and sold like a pumpkin on a scale. Invariably we'd look at what was doing at the movies but we never went in. It would be either a Mexican flick like *Ustedes los ricos* or *Nosotros los pobres* with Pedro Infante or Jorge Negrete, or a World War II gringada with Spanish subtitles. John Garfield scowling like a Protestant moralist with a tommy gun emerging from his vientre. We would wind up at my father's favorite tortería, El Mandamás del Barrio. My dad would have a short beer and I'd wolf down some nieve de mamey. Then followed a half-hour rap between Papi and the braggadocio owner, don Ernesto. They would share their mutual entrepreneurial visions. Going home my father could become very moody. He would compart his frustrations and his hopes. He made me feel like a true varón and I would listen to and guard his words jealously and, from the time I was twelve, with intense anguish. My father usually couched his ambitions in terms of money or some other material objective (dólares vs. dolores). But it was transparent even to a youngster that his true goals were more intangible. He spoke of handing down an inheritance or heritage to his sons, a patrimony, a family business, the establishment of a new order. This pleased me. What I feared was his attribution of responsibility. His resentments had become self-directed; he blamed himself for his failures, he knew he was a brilliant man and yet, somehow, his objectivity about the physical world had become perversely countervailed by a totally immoderate estimation of his position in it. Perhaps it was his pride and hunger for recognition that accounted for his overweening hunger for blame. Even his accident at the detinning plant he figured, along with the insurance companies, as some "act of God." My father had no sense of being suppressed; he believed in his freedom of action to a degree that, at the age of twelve, imbued me with fearful trembling for my own personal accountability. He pressed his sons hard on the school issue. School didn't matter to him particularly as a medium of factual knowledge (much less wisdom); he pushed it on us as a means of attaining the necessary credentials—un pasaporte was the term he used with blind naiveté for the connotations of his choice. School, or rather, graduation and the diploma were a passport into America. It permitted the bearer to travel the road royal.

One evening, as usual, my father was questioning me with meticulous detail about my schoolwork. I told him that tomorrow I would have to crucify a frog. It was for junior high biology and sad and dreadful. For two weeks Maestro Rodríguez, a maestro fiercely loved by me, had been methodically outlining with a piece of yellow chalk on a slate board the life mechanisms of the green frog. I had committed the life to memory, consuming him organ by organ. Tomorrow I was to force him open. After the frog was dunked in anesthesia I was to nail him to a piece of plywood. That was the crucifixion part, his little limbs completely distended so that the torso would be exposed to the public, scientific eye. A disturbing image which my father relished; a frog pinned like a man or boy with arms and legs stretched out on the edges of a raft, belly up on the infinite green sea . . . And then I would use the stainless steel razor to cut the frog into twin symmetries. I was to remove and label the liver, the heart, the brain. I was required to identify the optic nerve.

That evening my father had more than one short beer at El Mandamás del Barrio and I had more than one nieve in order to sweeten my mouth. We were troubled and enchanted by the imagery of pollywog martyrdom. When we went home my father was more moody than usual. He looked like a sullen, pathetic victim. The honor in his jaw had softened and he almost seemed to be pouting. He transmitted to me an uncontrollable trembling and a fear for my life and integrity. The most dreadful thing was that none of it could hinder me or make a difference. In the morning I would put on my blue school uniform and go to my biology class and do what I must do.

One day in college when I was staggering around the stacks and fell across Jung's *Psychology and Alchemy*, I had an inkling of what my papi's metallurgy was all about. Alchemy: The transformation of dross into gold and the fashioning of the gold into a higher, purer meaning. The goose that laid the golden egg. Out of your ass, man! I spent three years in college dunning the physical world for a sense of reality. I learned all about the acids, bases and salts. They took on a moral connotation for me. But I never could get much realization from the natural world. I preferred reading a novel or loving a woman. At that time my father was semi-retirado. His face had been disfigured by a geyser of caustic soda when the detinning bath blew. For over six months something had been going awry with the bath. Every three or four weeks there would be this awful rumbling and out of the tank ten feet long by ten feet wide would spout a geyser of boiling caustic soda and tin slush. My father was very concerned. The workers were coming on the job with heavy rubber tarpaulins close at hand. There was muttering that this was hazardous work and they should get a raise. My dad walked around with a yellow pad; he kept scribbling numbers. Every day he dropped his plumbline into the foul-smelling tank and took a reading of the solution level. He was convinced that the variation in the buildup of incrustation at the bottom of the tank had led to substantial variations in temperature within the solution. When the temperature differences became too extreme: the geyser effect. He advised that the tank be drained and that the incrustations be scraped from the bottom so that the solution would receive uniform heat. But el patrón wouldn't hear of it. There was too fierce a competition for the scarce tin cans. If they were out of business for two, three weeks, they'd never get back on beam. What they had to do was plumb the tank for all it was worth and when she blew, ¡que se joda! If necessary they would go back to old batteries and lead ingots. One day my father was standing over the tank with his plumbline. He looked like a little bronze boy fishing in a vat of vaporous split-pea soup. Suddenly, without warning, the physical world spat up at him. He took a sop of alkaline base right on the head. Very funny! Just like Laurel and Hardy. What the hell, there's only a finite number of tin cans anyway. Besides, my dad would never have to worry anymore that he was being discriminated against merely because he was Hispanic.

After the accident Papi mostly stayed at home, although he was known to beat it out occasionally to Chalo's for un partidito de dominó. He gave up his vocation as a subpatrón, a teacher, trainer and overseer of men. He claimed he wasn't up to breaking in new men with his face disfigured as it was. He wouldn't be able to face the chisme and derision of resentful ingenues. He had taken it on himself and it made him lose his confidence. Now and then he'd get an inspiration and rush to his closet, which he had fashioned into a shop, and work over a virgin hunk of metal with his press and files.

Chalito and I went to college, where after many peripeteias I eventually majored in sociology. In the afternoon my brother and I ran the gumball route for el patrón. In our pickup we wandered through all the good and bad-ass neighborhoods of El Paso and Ciudad Juárez. Everywhere we stopped a horde of expectant esquintles descended on us. "¡Ahí vienen los chicleros! Dame un chicle, ¿no?"

My old man made it easier for the gumball business when he invented some kind of corn oil to spray on the gumballs so they wouldn't stick to the glass or to each other. On the other hand, it was our solemn duty to fix the charms to the glass sides of the machine so they couldn't fall down the gum slot and requite some grimy-pawed tot in his vision of hitting the gordo from a magnanimous vending machine. My dad even discovered that it was easier to give the storeowner's 15% cut of the sales by weight rather than having to count out all the money. Some storeowners were not so certain, however, about the reliability of mass in the physical world and they needed constant convincing that weight and count were equivalent. Every once in a while they'd "keep us honest" by making us count the money too.

It was a tolerable life and when I graduated from college my father was present in his dark blue suit and dark tie (the combo he reserved for a funeral), feeling proud and tender and somewhat ill at ease about his scarred, reprehensible face. He poured me a tequila with his own hand and made me lick the salt from his own wrist. "You've made something of yourself!" he told me. He was not too sure about the nature of these "social" sciences but he was confident that the degree would satisfy the contingencies of the "real" world. When he died, perhaps from boredom, loneliness and a thwarted imagination, he laid a heavy rap on me. He said I was the oldest and therefore I inherited the responsibilities. I should see to it that the family was kept intact, go about the unfinished business of establishing some solid, familiar enterprise, a patrimony.

If I did not forgive my father his naive belief in his omnipotence then I would have succumbed to his logic and in condemning him would validate his credo of an ultimate, personal accountability. The vicious circle; the double bind. It is better to forgive him and lay the blame on a myopic, racist society that would have granted a white Anglo of his talents an adequate station in life. This position too has its fearful hazards for it alienates me from my father's vision and his wishes. Pater noster. His love for and exuberant response to the world pose a momentous challenge. His younger son made it as an engineer. He works for General Dynamics where he helps design submarines.

He was a man who inspired confidence . . . I prefer to fix him as he was when I was twelve. It was long before the vat full of sodium hydroxide had turned eccentric and he was at his height of virility and joy. One golden afternoon after school I went down to the detinning plant and peered through the fence at the scrap metal yard. The yard was one square kilometer wide and filled to the brim with brilliant metal. It was a splendid day and my father had decided to do some physical work with his men. He sported a magnificent Zapatista mustache. He had taken off his shirt and his bronze chest and arms rippled with muscles as he dug into a mound eight feet high of shimmering scrap and filled a massive wire cage. He looked like bronze Neptune with his trident or maybe like a revolutionary poster of an industrial worker emanating joyous aggression. The workers were laughing and marveling as he filled the wire cage in six minutes and then attached it to the crane that hauled it to the tank of caustic soda. I wanted to go inside the yard but I was fearful because Papi's trained geese honked militantly at me from the other side of the fence. At that time I was about the same height as these ferocious bull geese and a week earlier one had pecked me on the cheek. Neither the bruise nor the moral outrage had healed. Finally the geese became distracted by a stray dog and I made a dash for it. My father greeted me with delight as if I were a creature unique, a novelty. We went to the furnace where they melted the batteries. He knew the furnace fascinated me. He let some of the molten lead down the channel and into the ingot molds. Molten lead does not look base at all but rather like fine Spanish silver. We inspected the artisans who fashioned the soles for huaraches out of old rubber tires. We checked out the rabbits who also lived in the yard. There was a white fluffy one I enjoyed petting and laying on certain prepubertal fantasies.

During the break the young macho workers would place a narrow board ten feet long by ten feet wide across the steaming and bubbling vat of caustic soda. The brackish vat looked like a place on Venus where Flash Gordon might land and the machos liked to reassure themselves by walking over the board they had laid across the corrosive brew. My father did not approve of this practice. As a man of responsibility and devout observer of the physical world he believed to the utmost in the principles of safety. Unfortunately the young workers did not share his sense of caution and they played their little game. That day they invited a brand-new worker to walk his way across the board, just in order to verify his machismo. This worker did so without the slightest hesitation. He walked across once and was rewarded with the promise of a free beer. He walked over again and received another free beer. He was supremely confident. He went over again and stumbled into the vat. The worker had heavy rubber boots but before he could catch his balance he went in over the knee and the solution filled up his boot. The workers were hollering and my father came running with a fire extinguisher filled with neutralizer. They got the worker's boot off and a patch of skin from the man's calf came peeling off with the boot. My father foamed what was left of the leg and wrapped a blanket around it.

The ambulance seemed to never come. For me and perhaps for others present the young worker had somehow been transformed and transported to an inhuman category. He was no longer like me, he was something alien, revolting and mortifying, something with which I could no longer identify. But my father held him in his arms and comforted him. The young worker was in such intense pain and shock that he could not scream. He whispered to my father if he would be short a leg. My father was too committed a realist to deny it. He clenched the young man's hand in his own. He talked to the worker about the dignity of work. He told the worker that the leg didn't matter, that maybe he wasn't el patrón but he was el subpatrón and after he was well he would see to it that there was work for him.

My question is: Why wasn't Papi recognized as the inventor of the wormless bean and other joyous novelties?

The Mojado Who Offered Up His Tapeworms to the Public Weal

¡Oyez, oyez! ease your wearies and you shall learn about the case of the State versus the hapless, peripatetic mojao, a surely woeful account in the main—a sucker mojao who slipped across the Bravo stepping stones in a snorkel, flippers, and a toy-store trident—but not without socially redeeming values as well as intimations of brave third worlds, indeed a tale with certain exuberant dimensions of H. Alger-like mobility to which all we citizens of this good nation still (or ought still) respond.

First let me alert you to my editorial intentions. This account as first told to me meandered worse than the Río Grande itself and I mean to edit it. Moreover, I shall want to focus on the moment of conversion, with its sepia qualities of the old print or Far West photo, of the pícaro who once he is scourged and brought to escarmiento (that of course is the moment when our mojao offers up his tapeworms to the public weal) takes to clean living and his place as a far-seeing subject of the State. And it's a totally true story too, I heard it firsthand from a gentlemen—digo un gentilhombre—known as one el Rompeculos, in the Trailways station in Earth, Texas. We were casual fellow travelers killing our drudgery as we languished in Earth waiting for the express to come in and take us straight to Ajo, Arizona, and then to San Diego (San Dedo to those who know it well) with blessedly brief pit (piss) stops in Muleshoe, Needmore, Bronco, Humble City, Jal, Wink, Pecos, Boracho, Eagle Flat, Tornillo, Socorro, Chamberino, Bawtry, Bowie, Cochise, Mescal, Pan Tak, Suwuki Chuapo, Quijotoa, Tracy, and Why. Among the ceaseless hours of waiting and the Chili Dogs, wet and dry burritos, and the juicy jujubes, we took to snorting, piston-like, shots of translucent Pancho Villa tequila (haven't you tried that brand? It's sold exclusively in liquor stores across from bus stations and strictly in $1.99 units), alternating them with swallows of homemade terra-cotta-colored border-town sangrita which one of my companion's amigas had brew-mistressed, tempered with chile pequín, and measured out for Rompe in an ornate onyx flagon.

"Why do they call you Huitlacoche?"

"I choose to call myself that."

"I know it as something to eat. A mushroom or fungus that grows on corn."

"I know him as a boxer I admired some years ago who being a poor Indian became wealthy with his fists and returned wealth to the poor."

"Oh, him. I remember him. Didn't he once fight in the Mexico City bullring?"

"Yes."

"Good."

"Why do they call you Rompeculos?"

"I choose to call myself that. Basically because I'm an arrogant chop buster."

"Good."

This Rompeculos, a muscular brute perhaps about 40 years old with a tattoo of the Aztlanense eagle gorging itself on la ser-piente, who as my narration will definitely prove had the gentle, inquisitive sensibility of a schizoid poet, was a sometime hauler of Coors beer along the desert floors and byways. Contrary to what the inside covers of matchbooks so gamely enthuse for ingenues, he really had learned to master the big rigs, and was used to making significant bread—when he worked at this han-dle—hauling 6000 cases of Coors in a 14 wheel semi and an extra 8 wheeler in tow. He was, of course, a sometime contrabandist, this being the borderland, after all. As for trucking though, as he put it, the "blow job" could get to you. He'd be driving down the Waco run and in the dead night of desert air, all by his lonely, with only a pinup of Sylvia Pinal or María Dolores or Flor Silvestre above his shield to keep him company—Dios es mi copiloto—when suddenly one of those 99 bottles way in back would blow. That's it. They would have been all shook up by their tripping and suddenly he'd hear one blow and a few minutes later another would pop its cap and gush forth and five big ones down the road it would be a third coming to climax. I guessed then that the beer, that was his problem. But I was mistaken. At any rate, here he was, a little down and out in Earth, Texas, precisely where I was.

"What'cha here for, hombre?"

"Well, I needed some chavos to continue my studies at the uni."

He looked at me cross-eyed, like el pícaro that he was. "You a college kid?"

I got very sullen. Being a brutish sight myself, and a higher education gridironist, I felt an occasional prerogative to be temperamental. "I'm not a kid. I'm back from Nam."

" 'Ta bien. What do you play, middle linebacker? You're huge enough. You here on a bandit run?"

"Something like that. ¡Pero de mala muerte!"

"They fucked you over, ése?"

"Yeah, man. I was supposed to score enough Irapuato green to get me through my junior year. I came down all the way to the central altiplano y pues nada, puro pedo."

"Shit, man. En Irapuato, puras fresas. Ese, that's all they sell there, strawberries. And even be careful with those man, cause the top berries look real good and plump como los besos de una vieja salada but down below they're all huangas and overripe. No, ése, to Irapuato for fresas and to Morelia for morelianas and to Guanajuato, de tan alta alcurnia, for camotes (camo te vienes, camo te vas, camote te meto por detrás—they don't call me Rompeculos for nothing), and to Veracruz for huachinangos, not to mention huapangos, and to Aguascalientes for the best goddamned cockfights you ever saw in your whole life, digo, la feria. But for mota, man, you've got to get way up high, see? Up in the foothills around Toluca, up in the mountains by Amecameca where you can see prince Popo copulating with princess Ixta. Up high, ése, that's where the mota is, Toluca green."

"Oye vato, thanks so much for telling me this shit now that it can do me no good. Aquí pues estoy en mero rasquachi eating pecan chunkies on the bench in Earth, Texas."

"Aw, don't worry about it, ése. Supposing you did score, then you would have had to move your stash across the border. A tenderfoot college vato like you. Who knows what might have happened. You could have ended up like that jerk in the movies, the Midnight Express. It can happen. I'm telling you cause I know." Rompe scratched his head and squinted. "Let me give you some advice, Huitla. Forget about the foliage, it's pure risk man, especially if you're not enchufado into a border brokerage. Next time you come down, run a few parrots. Más vale."

"Parrots? ¿'Tas loco?"

"I'm telling you, man. Pound for pound they'll make more money for you than marihuana. You can buy parrots on the streets of Laredo for maybe 25 or 30 dollars. You know what they go for in San Antonio? Three hundred big ones! A little further inland, say Kansas City, seven hundred, no más. And with a parrot you've got fluidity. You take your investment to any good pet shop y ahí no más, they exchange it for currency, just like at the bank."

"I don't know, vato loco. I wouldn't buy no parrot but for sure I'd buy a lid of mota."

"That's because you don't know birds, ése. They're the only ones that will accept a human. You can raise a pigeon and it'll do acrobatics but you can't get one to crawl on your finger or hop on your head. The parrot alone will tolerate human companionship. People love them because they become like humans. You teach them to talk, to sing. They've got perfect pitch. I've got one myself. It sings strictly songs of the Mexican Revolution. You know, *Adelita, La Valentina, el 30-30.*"

Finally the Trailways bus arrived. Feeling very tipsy we lurched our way to the Earth men's room to empty our bladders. Then we boarded the bus, picking seats up front where it was less bumpy.

Rompe continued his sermonizing. "All you do is douse their bread with a little tequila and take them over the bridge in a sack under your seat or donde sea. And if you get caught, ¿qué importa? At most a fifty dollar fine, if they even bother. Cause nobody takes parrots seriously, not even the customs agents. With marihuana they can catch up with you 500 miles north of the border. But pericos! ¡Qué ricos! Once they're across you can't prove a damned thing!"

"You're making me sad, Rompe. Real sad. You know how I'm going to spend this summer? Breading shrimp at Arthur Treacher's or grating that foul cheese they use at Taco Bell. Puta madre, and the worst was that my cucaracha conked out in the sierras. It did, it slipped a rod and I had no lana to get it mended."

"So what you do man, you junk it? What's the matter, don't you guys get a football scholarship?"

"Yeah, they throw us a bone, but college is expensive, especially for a Chicano b.m.o.c."

Rompe shrugged his head. "So where's your cucaracha?"

"What could I do, they wouldn't even buy it, a car with U.S. plates in Mexico. Finally some wool brokers in Chihuahua city gave me some lana for it, mostly for the radio although they claimed que tenían modo de arreglar lo de las placas."

Rompe laughed. "I know that Chihuahua wool-gathering crowd, they're enchufadísimo con la aduana. For sure they must've cleared five hundred, maybe a grand on your fotingo. What year was it? What model?"

I just looked at him aggrieved and drank maybe two fingers worth of tequila.

Rompe looked me over as if for the first time, con sospechas y cautela. "You studying to be a doctor?"

"¡Esos! I hate those fuckers."

"¿Pues qué?"

"Poet. ¡Pueta! A nomad."

"¿Poeta? What kind of career is that? You're a strange guy, Huitla. And your name is as strange as you. ¿Qué tú haces? You eat magic mushrooms? ¡Hay que vender la mota y no esfumarla!" He had a big poet's belly laugh, a shot of Pancho Villa's best and a good swallow of fiery sangrita, settled back into his pullman seat and told me this tale about a woeful friend of his: un mojao.

Now, this story meandered up and down into every backwater and eddy like the Río Bravo itself. I mean, please don't think that I'm going to bore you with the sort of river flotsam he laid on me— the bit about how this mojao once managed a molino de nixtamal, overseeing the mixing of the corn with water and slaked lime in order to produce the gruel that would then be ground into masa harina while the benditas queued up at 6:00 a.m. for their supplies, or how he landed an RFP from the Yuma, Arizona, CETA to offer a crash course to ex-junkies on how to train geese to be industrial watchdogs for the junkyard business (meaner than junkyard dogs! was the program's motto), or how during one period he painted watercolors of cherubs, madonnas and 31 types of chirping birdies on birch barks for los turistas, or how he seduced the wife of el mero chingón jefe de la Falfurrias migra, or the sweatshop he labored in that produced synthetic blue pellets supposed to look like genuine turquoise in order to imitate the jewelry of the Santo Domingo Pueblos, or all those other border conceits. No, none of that, but I must declare, some of this pueta's story—it was like you are panning the Río Bravo for precious substance and all you come up with on your plate is dead catfish after toxic catfish and suddenly there's this clunker, the fabled nugget that made the Golden West—well now, that is something to polish and assay. So, Dios mediante, I would like now to focus on this meandering mojado and that golden moment when he redeemed himself in the eyes of his Anglo overseers through the ordained intercession of the therapeutic tapeworms that thrived in his infected bowels. Let us make a beginning y ahí va de cuento.

Erase un mojado pero muy mojao. According to his cuate el Rompeculos, who knew this wet from the very start and, it could be claimed, dogged him at key intervals like the cartoon angel of good conscience, he was born in the massive wheatfields of Sina-loa, labored in those fields with all-told thirteen brethren (and sistern?) reaping the wheat from wither our daily tortillas are pat-ted and fashioned to fill our panzas with cheese and bean burritos. Nothing out of the ordinary, this young, rude, clever, robust, and fearfully ignorant country chamacón, living his days and labor-ing mightily in the breadbasket of northwestern Mexico, a plains mozalbete who knew no further than Guamuchil to the west and Mocorito to the east. This life was—how can I convey to you the idyll of laborious ignorance?—the bliss of unremitting and un-selfconscious routines, an agrarian, Skinnerian utopia (as Keats put it, to think is to be filled with sorrow), until one day, it was about puberty or maybe a bit into it already, he found himself re-turning the coa to the long white stable of the latifundio and came upon his two older sisters lying on their backs in the straw with their skirts up and their comely legs spread, each with a hand-some caballerango on top doing a flopping dance like contrin-cantes in a cockfight or partners in a horizontal jarabe. Stead-fastly he shut the door on the intrusion into his vida. Pero, ¡ay maldito! ya se le entraba el gusanito de las dudas. A dirt road traveling true through the wheatfields was no longer merely a dirt road but a segmented trajectory over time. It was a vector with a retrospect and a prospective future. The signals of nuestra vida natural suddenly took on a new semiotic. What was that arboreal warble that correlated with a young peon's erection? and that long fastidious mutter of oxen that harmonized with a mancebo's inchoate brooding, and finally, passionate resentments? As Rompe judged it, in that establo parpadeo our young mojao had eaten of nuestra manzana del saber and ultimately—as every mojao must feel so deeply in order to be mojao, that is, genuinely driven into border waters—tasted the notion of class.

One day our mojao was musing and chewing his emotional cud by the fire in his adobe home. The firelight made a suppurative dance on the caked wall and ultimately on the breast of his younger sister Consuelo, and for the first time our pre- and proto-mojado looked upon his sister and himself with foreknowledge. There was young Consuelo, whose breasts rose like certain rivers in times of flood—a natural and irreversible consequence of the springtime or of puberty; poor Consuelo, suddenly and without warning tears streaming down her golden firelit cheeks, her rising, yearning, uncontrollable pechos.

And our mojado knew direction. A triptych the first panel of which put in place the prior conducta of his two older sisters, those very traitors to rural vida who long since had departed flamboyantly on the backs of potros negros, the made mates of mustachioed caballerangos, the kind of varones machos that the Sinaloan wheatfields so proudly boost and supply with field machetes of tempered steel. No longer would his vida contain within it the dulcet periodicity of the three nights a year, el Día de los Muertos, la Nochebuena, el Domingo de Gloria, when these loving archangels would with infinite care fashion festive tamales and fill them with ground walnuts, with coconut, pineapple or strawberries, and feed him, madonna fingers to chamaco mouth. They had been carried away by the implacable, migratory wind and he knew in that moment that he would never see them again.

In the second retable he saw Consuelo, who grew to beauty by days, by discrete moments before the fire that lit adobe walls and the slanted morning sun that illuminated swaying, bread-bearing grasses. Growing to beauty her pechos swelled hopelessly, advertising themselves against her will. She suffered and he suffered with her the bodily rackings of pubertal premonitions, the foreknowledge (and the foreskin) of carnal perdición. He knew this, saw it transmitted from his meaning-laden gaze to the eyes of his dear unsuccored sister, her campesina's eyes, so unused to manifested extremes of feeling, now clouding before revealed truths, a break in the stoic line of her lips. Finally a peasant's sigh issued from inside Consuelo, a sigh patterned on those she had heard from time to time emitted by peasant women who sit in visitation of their loved ones in the camposanto.

And el viejo saw this too, "viejo vivo," chuckled Rompe as he recounted this all on a bus that opened up on the Earth to Ajo trailway like a farting jogger in the clear—"porque más sabe el diablo por viejo que por diablo."

"Yes," said Rompe, who gave high marks—a poet's premium—to those who know even though they cannot act upon what they know. "Los que saben, saben, the viejo just looked up from where he was resting, rose to his haunches on his petate, looked at his son, el mojao sin todavía serlo, with a knowing, señorial air, and then at Consuelo and her heaving, autonomous breasts and said, '¡Ay Consuelo! Parece que tú vas a ser el Consuelo de los hombres.' "

And then, as if this axiological and ontogenetic proposition had been mustered at great physical expense, el viejo crouched back into the adobe shadow, only his eyes visible as brooding points.

And our pobre mojado looked first at his inconsolable sister, for whom the mandates of rural honor and vergüenza would dictate the most vigorous sibling defense of her virginal status, and then at his father, pater noster, nuestro señor de todos los mojados, a man who had conceived and raised a robust and nutrido prole, who had always operated within the narrow orthodoxies of the code of the countryside; now only his eyes were still driven, some message for our mojado in them surely of laissez faire, a blessing of mobility (outward if not upward) from our father of the wetbacks, our viejo who had been a proverbial Sinaloan template of a villano en su rincón but for whom no Lope sang paeans of rustic praise, no Fuenteovejuna had risen in defense, no reasoned alcalde had intervened against mustachioed machos and their brandished machetes, no Zapata had offered land much less liberty, no Villa, no Orozco, no Obregón had risen a dedo meñique much less offered an arm, not even a Demetrio Macías to offer a fatalistic appreciation of the inertia (punctuated by staccato and unavoidable all-be-them clearly heralded catastrophes) of his wheatfield peonage.

Now to the third retable, himself down low, his member perniciously rising like a volcanic promontory—¡un Paricutín!—from the humdrum llano, an icon erect in the latifundio, feeding itself on the sorrowful solace of autonomous breasts and the acquiescent despair of worn-out lives, generating libido, as must be the case of any mojao who is truly a mojao, from motives that give impetus to the transgression of taboos. Our mojado knew then in that moment by the shrinking fire of his peon's hearth, in his own swelling, robust sex that was foremost (and foreskin) an act of wet defiance to the social and filial orders, that he would be departed in the morning, onto the dirt road that would become a dusty tar ribbon to Juárez (city in turn founded in the name of a mighty rural leader and iconoclast), there to mingle with a veritable ragtag army of wets recruited from the countless villages, hamlets, and milpas of the sovereign interior of México. This was Juárez before the maquiladoras and the pleasing rhetoric of the Chamizal, where certain women were paid pesos or dollars to do dirty deeds with donkeys.

As I sorted out this torrent of words which gushed forward from el Rompeculos and doubled back into prefixed rhetorical rivulets, I was at once caught in the web of this hip and coarse narrator, and tugged by a certain anxiety. This man did not fit clearly into the slot or stereotype that I had fashioned for him.

"Did you go to college?"

"Hell no! ¿Y por qué lo preguntas?"

"I don't know. You seem so awfully knowledgeable. Are you claiming that your mojado friend left home because he was aroused by his sister? What am I supposed to think? That he became errant to maintain the fiction, or perchance more poignantly, the reality of his sister's chaste honor? Or what?"

Rompe chuckled. "Don't exaggerate, poeta. On the other hand a mojado must cross waters to be truly one, isn't that so? And don't ask me again about college. ¡Qué college ni que college! I am a citizen, and a leading one, I might add, of the Third World. Try to understand that. You come down to our world looking for some pin money to carry you through a semester—¿y qué? This is not México. This is not the United States. This is a third land, a band or contraband 2000 miles long and 200 miles wide. It runs from the sand dunes of Matamoros to the seacliffs of La Jolla. It's run by its own logic and psychologic; it cooks up its own Tex-Mex food, concocts a language called pocho, musters its own police, la migra. Its felons are sui generis. Where else can a guy get busted for running double yellowheaded parrots, dealing in transnational lobster and shrimp or smuggling flasks of mercury and truckloads of candelilla? Its city-states hang on each side of the frontier, tit for tat, Tecate and Tecate, Calexico and Mexicali, San Luis and San Luis, Gringo Pass and Sonoyta, Sasabe and Sásabe, Nogales and Nogales, Naco and Naco, Columbus and Palomas, Laredo and Nuevo Laredo, Progreso and Nuevo Progreso, like brother and sister—forgive this somewhat Malinchesque although not unjustified analogy—copulating in the night with one eye over their shoulders making sure that faraway parents are not spying.

"While it may pay tribute to remote power centers—Washington, Distrito Federal and other humbug—this borderland, which I will now christen on this pathetic Earth to Ajo express as Mexérica, functions like a satrapy. No borderline here but a wriggling membrane that soaks in produce and spits out product. Its city-states own themselves and are committed almost totally to their own introspective, autistic symbiosis—more appropriately to the relationship of the shark and the pilot fish, the yucca plant and the yucca moth, or the commensalism of the beneficent tapeworms and their human host.

"And the currency. That is what is most peculiarly wet. More than the transnationalism or the transgressions, it's the transactions. As a country we are most like a Wall Street, a brokerage. Power seekers, power brokers, and the impotent; all cross this river, where there is a river. We have dealers in orifices, in euphoria, in human futures and orange juice futures, in man's labor, in the fruit of women's labor, in Christmas tree ornaments, silicon chips and semiconductors, and toothpaste. A friend of mine is the biggest 'importer' into Mexico of fiberglass drapes. This is a world that makes a market in sadists and masochists, in siervos and señores, in capitalists and wild-eyed revolutionaries . . ."

"And vatos locos too, right ése? Wild-eyed poets, exuberant truck drivers?"

"Yes, Mr. Huitlacoche, them too, as well as b.m.o.c. Chicanos. Do you know how far we have branched out? Do you know how much certain labor-intensive industries depend on us? I'm not talking about hotels, mister. I mean steel and petrochemicals! Do you know how much San Antonio depends on us; hell, do you know how Chicago depends on us? We are branching out mister, we've opened up consulates or dealerships—en esta tierra son la misma cosa—in El Salvador, Nicaragua, Bolivia, Colombia, Perú, you name it, if it's impoverished and still retains some minimal level of aspiration, we've got a presence. Hell, I could show you a store on Laredo's Convent Street. A modest, unimposing grocery, where they sell more Tide, Pet Milk and Kool-Aid than anyplace else on this earth. When I read about the developing world, the Third World with its massive infusions of people and currencies, its Aswan dams, its World Banks, I am amused. This is a Third World. Dollars are changed into pesos, pesos to dollars, it is a barterworld and a borderworld, the only frontier on earth where the truly poor commingle with the well-to-do inhabitants of the richest, most spoiled nation on earth. This band, this contraband, my nation Mexérica, Amexica, is a fulsome place of economic growth. It is also a cloaca into which drains the commingled phantasmagoria of the richest and the poorest. And I am one of its citizens and self-adumbrated bards." Our rompeculos of the mojados then chortled, downed another two fingers of Pancho Villa and slumped into his seat.

We had been on the express for over six hours and it was a very dark vehicle that sped us to the first reaches of New Mexico. Most of our fellow crew slept fitfully. Here and there one could detect buzzing patches of conversation.

"Tell me then, Rompe, what happened to our young mojao when he reached the wicked city?"

Rompe yawned. "Nothing special. He didn't stay young too long. He learned. He became borderwise and shed his fieldish ways for fiendish ones. From what he told me I figure he was a mite stupider than most. One huckster convinced him to run the river on his own. This poor stupid mojao had saved maybe 60 to 70 bucks as a result of long hours of toil painting little angels and doves on almate bark for the gabacho tourists, and he threw his lana to the coyote who donned him up with a snorkel, flippers, a diving mask, and to add irony to injury, a little trident made of plastic that mocked King Neptune's sovereignty. Then he gave him a copy of one of those 'secret maps' that abound in the Golden West, pointing to everything from treasure to choice bends in the river, and set him off to swim the Río Grande. Except that in that place and at that time of the year the water was so low that he lost his huarache—I mean his flipper—across the stepping stones in the water. Here our mojao was, in the dead of night, dressed up in his sporting-goods store best, slipping over the dead bullheads beached on the riverbed stones. And all the time the officers of la migra are waiting in their cop car, trying so hard to muffle their laughter that they're shitting. You see, it was all a set-up. A cruel practical joke. When wettie gets over to the other side they flash a beam on him and fall down in mirth. One by one the officers go to relieve themselves by the river. Then they apprehend their delincuente, fleece him of his garb and throw him back across the border. When el mojao gets back to the cantina all his acquaintances are clued in."

"Hey hombres, here comes el indito!"

"The one who dressed up like the Creature from the Black Lagoon!"

"He just got back from el coloso del norte!"

"What's the matter, Macario? You look all wet!"

"Oye, indio triste, lend me some money from what you made pizcando melones!"

The "Mojado According to Rompe" follows a different story line from there, and then it turns again and takes a third direction. What seems to be clear though is that this ése of rural honor, perhaps partially because of the warped joke, turned to re-enacting the role of mojado, emerging baptismally from the Río Bravo time and time again. For one, although he was as clever and adroit as any, he refused to learn much of the English language. Moreover, basing himself on the Mexican side of the river he sought out opportunities that required continual round-tripping. That's apparently how Rompe met our mojado: they were working double yellowheaded parrots plus an occasional scarlet macaw. This became a big bull market around the time that the Baretta television show peaked. Buyers competed to bid up parrot futures to unprecedented river highs.

Rompe and the wet would go down into the interior and dicker with the Indians who trapped parrots in the coastal jungles. "Make them young," they told their Indians. "For every young parrot you get a premium because those are easier to train. The maldito older ones are so wild, all they want to do is bite off an index finger." From the jungles of the interior the parrots traveled by fotingo to the Río Bravo. Rompe and the mojado would feed them a little bread soaked with pulque so that they would get drowsy and then they put them in a long flat cage that went atop a raft of inner tubes. Y pues, así no más. Facilito as Tzintzuntzan. They ran the river and picked up their van on the other side. From there to the parrot jobber who had orders on account from all over. There were birds for Houston oilers, Dallas bankers, Wichita ranchabouts, Norman, Oklahoma, academics and Chicago fashion plates.

In his prime our mojado was a grand sight. Dressed in a cordobés hat, finest Mexican leather hand-tooled boots, a Spanish bolero vest, with a superb pawn bolo tie fashioned from an old serpentine Tarahumara arrowhead studded with forty pieces of turquoise, he would find himself from time to time in Rosa's Cantina, lunching on short ribs soaked in red chile and catching up on the latest news from the Third World commodity market. When the city's Visitor and Convention Bureau decided to shoot a promo film he landed a bit part as the incarnation of Old Mexico. He looked like a Casasola sepia photograph of a 1910 Mexican revolutionary.

After sauntering to the post office or the telégrafos to wire some money to Sinaloa, he might, when business called for it, pack some clientes from out of town into his Winnebago and drive down to the zona de tolerancia where each bar had its own prostitutes licensed and medically supervised by the municipal authorities. Lots of college kids would be there mixed in with truckers, oil hands, ranchers, salesmen, other whatnot, and especially políticos. Our mojado didn't like to go there much. He didn't like the way the gabachos used the place as their pigpen. It seemed that a gabacho could be a faithful one-woman husband and church-going Elk or Moose in the coloso but once he crossed the border he figured he could paw, puke and otherwise make a fool out of himself with impunity. They were right. One night a well-heeled, distinguished looking black dude was trying to get laid. The hooker turned him down flat and suggested he try a lesser club down the street. It seemed that the management didn't cotton to the girls taking on black customers cause a class joint like theirs could start losing their gabacho clientele. El magnate

was stunned. Jesus Christ, it was the last place in the world where
he was expecting discrimination! He had to convince the puta that
he was really a Puerto Rican grown up on the continent who had
never learned Spanish. That made it o.k. and flushed with pride
he paid his money and together they went on back.

Just one problemita. Anonymity was the virtuous precondition
of transriver entrepreneurship in Mexérica. Or to paraphrase
Heraclitus, a bandit oughtn't step into the same river twice. Our
mojado began to earn himself a pretty big handle. While he had
always stayed away from the aguas mayores, flesh and leaves
in their various formats—these, under any account, being con-
tolled by conglomerates of certain orders—even his long position
in aguas menores was eventually compromised, and even under-
mined, by his air of haughty and driven defiance. A rural, Calde-
ronian curandero of his propia honra, this mojado arrogated and
amalgamated notions of robber bandit and Robin Hood even
though he was riverwise enough to "know better." So then, while
at the beginning his transgressions, when uncovered by the border patrol, were punished by the customary petty fines and slaps
on the wrist—who really gets fired up about smuggling parrots
or the prime ingredient in chewing gum?—his wet attitude of
villano pero honrado quickly began to impress an indelible mark
on the crowded, bored and hurried courtrooms where novelties
could quickly be seized upon to alleviate the crushing monotonies
imposed by the blur of contraband cohorts that filed past the
judges' gavels. Similar was the attitude of the law enforcement
community, some members of which apparently began to call him
epithets like el superwet, el mojado en ajo, et alia. Our mojado
noticed that his capture rate, which had an initial background
level approximating a random walk, had risen off the charts to
the point where at the close of his career it was more like an
águila/sol tossup. He was worried, business was badly down, and
his familia, now living in better quarters in Culiacán, began to
voice remonstrations over larga distancia. But in misfortune too
our mojado soberbio reveled in his own way, coming out of the
bends in the river with parrots in his arms and an air of fever-
ish anticipation (la migra ¿sí o no?), reliving in each crossing the
river renaissance, this our San Juan Bautista, guardián de todos
los mojados.

What is clearly apocryphal, claims el Rompeculos, yet certainly symptomatic in its being attributed to our bedeviled and vain-glorious mojado en ajo, was the so-called "wet warranty," which made its presence known for a few years around the time that Chrysler, G.M., and others promoted it in a different economic sector. The way it worked was that for a certain insurance pre-mium the exporter of a commodity could in effect guarantee de-livery of goods (or their dollar value) across the border irre-spective of confiscations, water damage, dust storms, or acts of God. Indeed it was the "wet warranty" that destroyed el mojado's brokerage, which, given his high capture rate, could not afford to reimburse suppliers at any reasonable premium. Ni pedo, some insensitive souls blamed the new market circumstances on the arrogant mojado who indeed, while not a conceiver of the warran-ty, had, in a paradox that operates elsewhere in México (vid. Partido Revolucionario Institucional), attempted in a certain sense to institutionalize what had always been conceived as a peripatetic roll of the bones. Contrabandists began to mutter darkly (this, by the way, was during the period when Joe Columbo organized the Italian-American Civil Rights League and paid so dearly for his gesture) about the new affront to the truer days of caveat emptor, of river skullduggery, even as they had to comply with the economic writ of the period.

"Maldición. There are too many coyotes desgraciados who are making an effrontery of the perils of the river!"

"Precisamente. These pendejos are giving too high a profile to our dealerships."

Our mojado, like so many other Mexican revolutionaries and freethinkers over the decades, took a cue from caution. One moonless night, making sure he wasn't being tailed, he packed his personal belongings and drove to a place way upriver—a hardship spot with steep banks and a dearth of landing places, but one that also claimed the advantages of few sensors and virtually no patrol. He ran the river for one last time, never to return again.

Our mojado quickly descended from his comfortable bour-geois life into the vast anonimato of the undocumented worker. In a sense he wanted it and needed it that way. He shaved his Zapata mustache, cut his hair a different way, and took a humble job sorting remnants at a blue jeans manufacturer with an in-famous reputation for its abuse of illegal aliens. He felt safe there;

he blended in. He cut off relations with everyone, even his family. It would only be a few months, he felt. His only connection was with his compadre, el Rompeculos.

Clearly la vida was softening up our pícaro for a spectacular conversion. Those forces of fate that redress Tex-Mex hubris were conspiring against our San Juan Bautista on two juxtaposed fronts. One was that the border entered into one of those sporadic periods when potentates in Washington become "deeply concerned." El mundo tightened up. There were delays on the International Amistad bridge for three and four hours. The United States Army Corps of Engineers busily installed a "tortilla curtain" to keep out illegal aliens, a reinforced steel mesh wall supposedly incapable of being cut but which was riddled with holes by sunup. The Border Patrol issued a list of persons it wanted to nab for high questioning, or rather, to pin some delitos to; payment was offered leading to the apprehension thereof, and our mojado made the list. His person became of some value and soon a co-worker in the remnant division of the factoría developed a certain inkling. The other factor, according to Rompe, must have been the "Huevos Whateveros."

"Huevos Whateveros," I asked him. "What the hell are those?"

"Third World food," said Rompe. "They're delicious. Let me share my own recipe. Take the remains of the last few nights of Mexican meals—chilaquiles, pico de gallo, frijoles refritos, ruptured enchiladas, a foresaken chile relleno and so on—and lard them into a deep frying pan. Add sufficient stewed tomatoes to obtain a brew and on top of this bubbling riverbed crack open as many eggs as called for, yolks intact. Over a low heat grate some braided Chihuahua cheese and sprinkle with as much cilantro, green onion, and epazote as coraje would prescribe. ¡Qué rico!"

"My God!"

"Well it probably was the huevos whateveros that gave him the tapeworms. After all, you can't use ingredients that are too stale or you run certain risks. At any rate, one day I received an emergency call from the mojado. Come at once! Can you believe it, the bridge was so tight with migra, aduana, fiscales, and the rest of that riffraff with their sniff hounds going through the gabachos' dirty underwear that I had to borrow my neighbor's water wings from his pool and cross the river that way. When I got to the mojado's I was confronted with a grotesque scene. A bull-necked, rednecked Texan with a name like Bubba was directing his skeptical, Spanish-surnamed migra underlings who were gingerly stepping over the wet's vomit as they pulled on each of his arms. El mojado was pleading to be taken to the hospital. He was in the throes of calambres and slumgullion upchuck. The mojado's pet parrot (and if truth be known, only true companion over the years) was hysterical, ranging at full blast from the famous aria from *Figaro* to *La Cucaracha* to multiple pocho groserías.

"Hi there occifer! Where are you taking my compadre?"

"Haul off, scudsball! I'm taking this border bandito off to the slammer! He's on everybody's hit list, the Border Patrol, the Texas Rangers, the T-men, Batman and Robin, you name it. He must be a mastermind behind some Bolivian cocaine ring. Do you know how many times this shitheel has been up the river? Thirty-six count'em convictions, thirty-six!"

"Aw, come now occifer, don't hyberbolize. You know he's small potatoes. Why get so excited over a few lousy parrots that bring so much delight to lonely suburban housewives or a bargain basement lobster dinner for eight? Besides, I'm not asking you to let him go or nothin'. Put a ball 'n' chain on him for chrissakes but get him over to the hospital. If he's D.O.A. at patrol head-quarters our trade association is going to hold you strictly to ac-count." Rompe looked severely at the two Hispanos. "I see you two Judas-lackeys have gotten wetback barf on your Gucci loafers."

The scene at the hospital was no less poignant. The migra overlord stood fidgeting in the wings and growling into his walkie-talkie. The internist was chattering excitedly with the hospital administrator while Rompe sat with the mojado who, one hand on his underbelly, was in a state of stoic dejection.

"¿Por qué están tan excitados?" the mojado asked.

"No sé. El médico anda discutiendo con el jefe del hospital. No sé de que se trataría. Quizá de la migra."

"No, eso no es. Ha de ser que voy a morir al momento." The mojado was quickly becoming convinced that he was an accelerat-ed terminal. A fitting dénouement for the life that he had lived.

The internist came over to the Mexicans. "Mr., uh . . . Mojado. It's not serious at all what you have. All they are are tapeworms.

Taenia saginata to be exact. They're fairly common in some parts of the underdeveloped world, but not at all common around here. Actually, they're pretty valuable. . . ." The internist looked disarmingly at the wetback. "I mean, not really valuable, but useful, experimentally useful."

The mojado looked at the doctor with incomprehension.

The internist turned to his compadre. "Go on, Mr., what's your name, Mr. Rompeculos."

"Diz que tienes gusanos. Diz que no te hacen daño y a lo mejor valen más que todo el oro de la mina de El Dorado."

The mojado brightened up measurably. He thought the worms in his body must be along the lines of Ponce de León's fabled elixir if they were worth their weight in golden nuggets.

The internist smiled ingratiatingly at the mojado. He made a little wriggling motion with his index finger as if it were a cutsie worm. "Sí, Mr. Mojado. That's right, el gusano."

The mojado smiled back and reciprocated with the same wriggling finger. "Oh, yes, meester doctor . . . the worm."

The internist turned to Rompe and explained the conditions of the barter. It seems that the hospital could put fresh specimens of taenia saginata to excellent use for their medical students. Fresh, living specimens—these would be so much better than mere mounted fantoches. Their medical students could be so much better prepared in the field of contagious diseases. Mr. Mojado would be doing a genuine service to society, a true charitable donation to the public weal. And incidentally, the doctor and the hospital administrator noticed that Mr. Mojado was having a bit of a problem with the Immigration Service? They were prepared to vouchsafe for Mr. Mojado, offer him a job on the spot as a matter of fact, nothing too strenuous of course, they couldn't . . . put any strain on their valuable flesh and blood test tube. All Mr. Mojado had to do was agree in writing to let them have . . . access to his tapeworms. They would do the rest.

By now the redneck had gotten very un-red. Images of a nice bonus and a commendation that had been dancing in his mind's eye were going under like a bloated, toxic catfish sinking into the Bravo for a third time. "Say here, doc, what do you mean about this felon being a worm factory or some kind of one-man maquiladora? This here border bandito's a known major criminal with 36 convictions and he's gotta be taken to justice. No way is he gonna be gainfully employed except maybe at the rock quarry!"

"Not true, not true!" shouted Rompe. "Worst he ever did was cross the river with a soused-up parrot. He's a fine citizen, sends all his income over to Culiacán where he's got a sick old father and twelve brothers and sisters."

"Well now, Mr. Bubba," said the hospital administrator. "I'm sure we can accommodate every one in this regard. We certainly think that your apprehension of this rascal should go recognized, and we'll help you see to that. But now that we've got him, let's give him some meaningful social role. Think, Mr. Bubba, this gentleman here, Mr. Mojado, can perform a vital function in the service of the public weal. As a matter of fact, and I'm sure you're not aware of this, your own chief of the Immigration Service is a patient of our head internist here, Dr. Buggy, whose helping him along with the duodenal ulcer that this frustrating wetback situation has brought on to him. Don't you see, it's with the experimental data that fellows like Mr. Mojado can provide that we may gain a real breakthrough and help you patrolmen out with medical solutions!"

The mojado had suffered another stomach spasm. Having no food left in him he had expectorated a small portion of phlegm mixed with blood. The hospital administrator snapped a finger and a silent indocumentado came out with a pail and mop (all the orderlies were wets, they were the only ones who could "afford" the pay). The doubled up mojado moved to face the internist. He pointed to his underbelly. "Is pain!"

"Oh, we'll take care of that, Mr. Mojado. Soon as you sign up with us we're going to give you a superb medicine that will control your tapeworms so that the pain will be just about eliminated. We need to control your supply of tapeworms, don't we sir? That's the essence of experimentation, isn't it, observation and control!"

"¿Qué dice?"

"Dice que si firmas te quedas aquí con una medicinita y si no te dejan morir de gusanitos hideputas o te llevan a la pinta o las ambas cosas a la vez."

"Dile que firmaré. Pero que me ayude. ¡Que me ayude!"

"He says he'll sign. But help, auxilio, socorro, amparo!"

"Mr. Mojado, I'm so glad that you are cooperating. I knew you would. I could tell you wanted to be of service to the community. Now, whenever you defecate, Mr. Mojado, you know, move your bowels (the internist made an indicative gesture with his hips), do so in a special vessel we'll be giving you. You see, the tapeworms are nested in your fecal matter."

"¿Qué dice?"

"Que tienes que cagar en una olla."

"¿En una olla?"

"Sí, es muy importante."

"Está bien. Lo hago. Con estos dolores cagaría en los cojones del Buda si fuese necesario." The spasm was easing and the mojado felt a little better. He had heard the word "fecal." It sounded like a place in the Yucatán where some time ago he had bartered for parrots. "¿Qué es, 'fecal'? El médico dijo, fecal."

"Es la caca."

"¿La caca?"

"Es la caca, es la mierda. Quieren que tú cagues en una olla para pizcar los gusanos que van a estar horadando en tu materia excremental."

The mojado was stunned. "¡Ay, fuchi!" He turned to the internist and pointed to his butt. "¿Fecal?"

"Sí, señor," the doctor replied and shyly patted the wet's ass. "Very valuable!"

"¡Mierda!"

"What's that, Mr. Mojado? No comprendo."

"¡Caca!"

The doctor looked quizzically at the mojado, then at Rompe and back at the mojado.

The mojado screamed at the top of his voice, "Eshit!"

The internist blushed. "My, señor Mojado! You do speak pretty good English after all. I think your English is much better than my Spanish!

Burn out. The last six hours on the bus together we spent in a restless hush. A half hour in front of Ajo, Arizona, the sun had risen over the desert. There is no finer color to the desert, no finer air than that of a desert dawn. We were by the Organ Pipe

Cactus National Monument and here and there the sun shone through the giant flowering saguaro cacti and through the iron-wood trees that seemed like dwarfs in comparison.

"You'll be off this bus in minutes, Rompe, and into a cup of fresh coffee. That'll be nice."

"Yeah, Huitla. Appreciate passing spirits and gas with you. There is one last thing I ought to tell you though."

"What? That you are the mojao?"

He looked startled. "How'd you know that?"

"I guess it was your impassioned grasp of details. Also, a no-name mojao. Más sabe por viejo que por diablo, right?"

"God damn!" He punched my arm affectionately. "That's right, you clever college vato."

"You still into tapeworms?"

"Hell no! Those nasty little critters! I got out of that indentured servitude some years ago. Learned English real good—I'm even a resident of the coloso now. I mean, I'd never become a U.S. citizen, but I'm strictly legit. I've seen the re-Hispanization of the deep Southwest over these two decades or so, the demographic effects of migration, the palpable result of raza versus Anglo birth rates, the Hispanic changeover of officials ranging from mayors to county clerks and police officers. I used to think that it all meant the reconquest of the Southwest by the Republic of México, gradually and in evolutionary increments. Now I realize it's another thing, a new patrimony that is more than the mere sum of its parts, the Third World." He laughed. "Maybe we ought to join with you college intelligentsia vatos and call it Aztlán.

"That would be fine with me, Rompe."

"Yeah, but it would be quite an undertaking, wouldn't it? Students and river runners, hand in hand? We'll do it quiet, in desert stealth, right? No use building up big recognition. A rep could be bad for this border. Although, I don't think anything except maybe a totally East German goose-stepping mentality could put a real lid on the Bravo."

"What about the family back home?"

"Good, ése. Consuelo's 32 now and she's still not married or anything. Isn't that grand? She's thinking of taking her dowry and entering el convento. Never in our maddest dreams did anyone in our family figure that one of us could have the lana to enter the Church. Or maybe she'll marry after all, maybe to some gente de bien, alguien de villarica. It's her choice."

The bus was pulling into the parking lot of the Ajo Cantina and Grille. Rompe whispered in my ear, "You know what I'm really here for? I'm into running cactus. It's strictly part time, but it's real good bread, a seller's market. I've got a bandit run going for two 60 foot saguaros. Got a big rig loaded and waiting. I understand some outfit like Bank of America or American Express wants them for the front office grounds. Hay que cumplir, ¿verdad? Hell, cactus—pound for pound there's more money in them than coca leaves. And nobody, and I mean nobody's gonna bother you about a cactus. What's the worst it's gonna do you? A few stray thorns in your paw?"

"Wear heavy gloves, ése."

"Now you're talking, vato habilidoso. ¡Cógelo suave! Ai te huacho."

He walked out of the Trailways bus with his cocky air of rustic indio vergüenza and coraje.

I thought as I sat back in my seat, immediately missing his camaraderie, that they had taken much from the Rompemojado. They had taken his loved ones, his puberty, his sense of honor and of shame, his indio way of life, his mother tongue, and the very fruit of his bowels. But they had given him uniquely new family ties, a sense of coraje and varonía, a novel-fashioned lengua, a Third World identity and a river baptism in fire. Add up each column, then, and call it a waterworks wash.

And then, finally, there was the matter of the fecal matter—the aguas mayores. It's not every hombre who can claim his turd as a deduction to the common weal.

The Raza Who Scored
Big in Anáhuac

I thought, being raza, that this was my tierra. You know, roots, ¡qué sé yo! Now I think maybe I'm just another extranjero, one who crossed the wrong-way river.

I came down to learn stuff. Junior term in Anáhuac. At the Universidad Nacional Autónoma—the student movement—¡la revolución estudiantil!—I met and befriended Felipe Espinoso. He helped me with my notes because, speaking frankly, my written castellano isn't the best. "Language loss" is what some professor once muttered to me when I tested out at Cal State. Felipe was curious about Chicano ways. He called me "güero valín, the Mexican in preppie polo shirts." That made me laugh and I would kid him about the same Yucatecan guayabera that he wore every day that I knew him. We were both attending the same course, Theory and Practice of Mexican Social Class Structure, taught by tal profesor, one Maximiliano Peón, who alerted us at once to the fact that even though his remuneration was not enough to cover the gasoline that the trip cost him, he was proud to be teaching this course at UNAM as a servicio to the youth of his patria.

From the profile Felipe reminded me—it was an uncanny, almost perfect likeness—of a Mayan head in Palenque, a bas-relief with the prominent Mayan nose and receding forehead that I had pondered over in an art book at the Cal library. I had always wanted urgently to visit Palenque. I used to think about its gothic arches and cornstalk glyphs when I was just a kid, working behind the counter at the Taco Bell, baking cinnamon crispas. Now I found myself in Anáhuac, peering into the eyes of a Maya.

Felipe pressed me hard on Aztlán, and pleased with his avid interest, I was proud to tell him about the meaning of César

Chávez' black águila in a white circle, of vato and cholo, the Sleepy Lagoon riots, the finer points of pachuquismo, the fate of Reies Tijerina, the difference between an acto and a mito, Los Angeles street murals, and the old Operation Wetback of the '50s and the silly Tortilla Curtain que parió.

In turn, I queried him about the political peripecias of Vicente Lombardo Toledano, the pastimes of Siquieros when they threw him in the Lecumberri lockup, the subtleties redounding in the national diversion of deciphering every six years who the PRI tapado really was, the new malinchista movement of contemporary Mexican feministas, what Buñuel had really meant in *Los olvidados*, and why Cantinflas had plastic surgery done on his notable nose.

One afternoon after class, at the tortería which surely has the best crema in the valley of Mexico, La Tortería Isabela la Católica, only a few minutes from the University library which is a living historico-revolutionary mural, I confided in him a Chicano hope for a binational carnalismo. We were both brought to tears and to a heartfelt abrazo de correligionarios, not to mention compinches.

In class Felipe Espinoso was quiescent. Weren't we all? In our aula there were over 80 where there should have been 50. The earliest got seats, the next earliest, window sills, then came those who pressed along the walls until the door could no longer be opened and the half dozen hapless laggards who either missed the lecture of the day or tried to catch a semblance of the proceedings from outside, through a window. The University had been built for 120,000 almas; there were over 260,000 in attendance. Classes had been scheduled seven days a week from the earliest morning until midnight.

During the days approaching registration, Indians trod in from the valley, from the mountains surrounding the valley, from the plains beyond the mountains which circle this Anáhuac. They filed down the mountain roads, dog-tired, without chavos or any other material resources, spurred on by an implacable will for wisdom and upward mobility. Alentados perhaps by rural maestras de escuela they came for the term to UNAM where tuition was basically free. They traveled the roads in huaraches made from the rubber of discarded tires, slept where they could, in attics, hidden in obscure recintos of the university, in the swimming pool when there was no water, waited resignedly for a seat to study in the hopeless library that could no longer accommodate the push of the masses, begged or hustled for the term's nourishment. I have seen this drive that cannot be stemmed by any earthly privation or police state curtain at my heartfelt border, across which God's innocent children slip into the promised coloso of milk and miel, and I genuflect before these campesino multitudes and each day relive their fierce, steadfast resolve, share their dusty anger, revere their pursuit of self-improvement.

Halfway into the course, Felipe made a pronouncement. "Güero, I thought I liked Prof. Maximiliano Peón. I no longer like him. He is a deception. He is pequeño burgués."

"He comes out here for nothing to teach this unwashed horde and untouched rabble, doesn't he?"

"Sure, he comes out, and punctually. He's all subjectivity and nineteenth-century retórica, spouting about the incontrovertible objective realities of Marxist-Leninist revolutionary materialism. He's a living contradiction, a comfortable gentilhombre, an hidalgo of the professorate, all immersed in bourgeois pieties and comforts, drunk with arriviste parfums and amaretto and frangelico liquors. But to assuage his sotted, corrupted soul, to aggrandize his smug persona, to allay his midnight anxieties— because he knows well that his kind and his class would be first to the paredón in a genuine revolution—he sacrifices salary and comes out here to provoke Inditos de Lerdo Chiquito so that they may march to revolutionary beats, so that they may be mowed down by imported burp guns. Yes, he'll watch it all on his Magnavox in the parlor. He'll be hoping that he's hedged every bet, that he'll come out triumphant no matter who wins the partido."

I should confess now that Felipe was a fanatic for the Jai Alai and he had taught me to be a fanatic. His frontón imagery troubled me. Of course it was what everybody tried to do at the Jai Alai, bet on the underdog when the price was low and hope for the score to turn, then bet again on the opposing team at good odds and sit out the game a sure winner no matter which team won. . . . I protested, "But I love his Spanish! My God, his command of language!"

"¡Coño! Sure you do. You're a poor, hapless Chicano—a güero pocho boy who has never had the opportunity to study your mother tongue with any formality or system until now. Don't be deceived. It's all Porfirian sophistry and pedagogical petti-foggery. He doesn't even speak Spanish anyway. He speaks Castilian. And these poor, ingenuous indios—I include myself here, once a poor simpleton from Quintana Roo—who also are mostly tonguesmen of Zapoteca, Huichol, or whatever, they are mesmerized by this castizo buffoon who wishes to provoke their action for lost causes so he can feel assuaged for having 'done something about the Mexican social class problem.'

"This is wrong," he went on. "Let us have a revolution in Ol-meca, or Chichimeca, or Náhuatl even, or Mayaquiché. Anything but the Porfirian castellano of the Mexican empire and the simper-ing sleight of hand of the crypto-revolutionary."

So, then, Maximiliano fell from his pedestal. But who or what to replace him with?

The Virgin of Guadalupe's day was approaching. We were tertuliando with other left-leaning student intellects at a café in the slanting sun on the Promenade of Institutionalized Revolu-tion, near the cathedral. We could see a pilgrimage approach-ing like marabunta down the wide promenade. Felipe told me that tonight would be a fine one to be at the Jai Alai. Probably he should take all my money and his too and bet it on the main partido.

"Why is that, Felipe?"

He turned to the Promenade. "They will be betting heavy." The pilgrimage swept down the Promenade, eighteen campesinos abreast, marching in for the novena. There were delegations from Tenancingo and Tlaxcala, Acámbaro and Acatlán, Pátzcuaro and Pachuca, and even Pénjamo and Tzintzuntzan. First the crests of cyclists congruous to paramilitants. They had plastic virgins tacked to their handlebars and wheels and pennants that saluted the breeze of their own making. Then came legions of dusty benditos, huffing and chanting the Ave María, each village headed by a priest and an icon. Then down the Promenade of Institutionalized Revolution came herds of goats and turkeys and aggressive geese, bullied by trotting boys and mongrels. The peddlers followed too, hawking tostadas in green or red sauce, sweet potatoes in carts with piercing steam whistles, guava and cajeta, mamey and mango ice, jícama in vinaigrette. Jesting and cursing in the militant sun the pilgrims marched and peeled corn husks, smearing the tender grain of their elotes with colored sauce. On the special earthen track, the last kilometer to the cathedral doors, the supplicants came by on bloody knees, bearing the indrawn vision. In the courtyard they were doing Amerindian dances against the slanting, sinking cathedral walls. Precisely every ten meters hung white metal signs with red letters neatly stenciled: It is strictly forbidden to urinate against these holy walls.

That night at the Jai Alai with all our funds in hand I worried and became a little drunk. Felipe doubted too and wondered if we oughtn't be at the cockfights. "On nights of the novena the Indians come to the cock arena and wager nuggets of gold that they have dug out of the countryside."

"But here too the galleries are filled with countryfolk. Besides, Felipe, we are fanatics for the Jai Alai. We know nothing of cockfights."

"True enough. All I know of the cocks is that they use one straight and one curved dagger. That's all I know. It's a question of breeders and other intimate variables." Felipe sighed. "Whatever happens tonight, we cast our lot with the people."

"Sure," I said. Right then I felt muy raza, muy Mexican. "Sí, con el pueblo." But immediately I started to wonder. "Do you think the games are fixed?"

"Who would fix them for the poor to win?"

"Maybe the government. On orders of the authority."

"I wouldn't put that beyond the authorities. A devious scheme to enervate the pilgrims. But no. Why should the government subsidize the gambling vice? Besides, it doesn't happen all the time. It's just . . . a pattern. We must realize that by probability we stand to lose. But the odds make it worthwhile. A handsome wager."

"But I don't want to lose, Felipe. If I lose I will have to eat pinto beans all month. I'll have to return to Califas."

Felipe laughed. "Come now, compis. It's not every day that a vato loco can wager with the people with a firm hand. Maybe the match is fixed every night before the pilgrims make the final march to celebrate Tepeyac. Just to brighten the Indian's firm belief in the miraculous. But no, I don't think there's any question of a fixed game. It's simply the milieu, those days when the campo and the aldea come to court, the Indians packed in the galleries, hiding behind masks. I think it's a spirit that descends on the Jai Alai court. An ether which comes from the galleries and penetrates the players."

"Perhaps a revolutionary spirit?"

"Yes, but lapped up by the gambling vice the way mole is contained and dammed by corn dough. The inditos make their way up to the galleries expecting the supernatural."

I laughed. "What would Gramsci think of this, Pablo Freire, even the barbudo Carlos Marx? Could they construct a paradigm pa'l fenómeno?"

"Hard to say. It's too early in the course."

"You're right, Felipe. On a night like tonight one should be a Jai Alai fanatic. Have you seen all the grenaderos about?"

"Yes. They've even brought a contingent in from Atzcapotzalco. I'm sure there are two in front of every pulquería, every brothel, every revolutionary square, every Ateneo in Mexico City."

"How many do you think there are at the University library, underneath the mural?"

Saturday night at the Palacio de la Pelota, El Frontón México. The Jai Alai court was stretched and wide, bounded by three rock walls. The open end was strung with an immense steel net protecting the spectators from the missiles. Occupying the choice seats in the middle of the stands were the vested ones, Arabs and Jews, gachupines and wealthy Mexicans who played the favorite and lapped up the chiquitero money.

There was a roar from the crowd. The intendant and four huge Basques with long straw wickers bound to their wrists entered the court. They marched single file and solemnly along the wood boundary line. Then they turned and faced the crowd, placed their wickers across their hearts in salute, and gave the slightest of nods. There were whistles, jeers, and enthusiastic applause. The players broke rank and began to practice up. It was two mean frisky bucks playing against two stooping esthetes.

Felipe studied the program. "This match is a timeless syndrome: youth versus experience. Only a poet or saint will win this."

"Well then," I asked. "Who do we bet on?"

"It doesn't matter, güero. The team that falls behind and permits the chiquiteros to bet their pittances. We will bet on the underdog, the people, and their expectations for a miracle."

"I like that, Felipe. A higher logic. I may be a vato loco but you are a vate loco. A meta-wager and a melodrama. A dialectic that ends in a materialistic. I like the pastel money of México. It's easier than the hardened green of the dólar."

Redcaps called the odds out, which were an even 100 red versus 100 blue, and the match to 30 points began. The fierce bucks dominated from the very start and as the score mounted in their favor the odds dwindled, 50, 30, 10 to 100. From the galleries there was a steady projection of sullen mirth.

I saw an Olmec-looking type call out, "That old camel should be playing marbles with his grandchild!" and a striking mestizo who looked the prototype of Vasconcelos' raza cósmica imprecated a few times and then said, "Get him a pair of roller skates . . . and a seeing-eye dog!" Rejoined a weasel who looked more like the critics of Vasconcelos who coined a raza cómica, "No, old fool! Bring him Sancho Panza!"

The score was 20 to 12. The redcaps had become bored and sat in the aisles kibitzing with their clients. The guards, instead of standing straight up, were lounging on the very net that bounded the court. And the sharks filed their teeth or counted their fistfuls of wagers on short odds or nonchalantly cracked sunflower seeds. That was when we bet most of the money credited to us for a month of studies and livelihood on the underdog at 80 to 1000. The sharks were glad to take our money. "No lo hagan," a concerned bourgeois gentilhomme advised us. "You're just going to make a tiburón happy. ¡Que el partido se va de calle!"

A portentous occurrence. The Jai Alai became like the opera buffa. The old artistes made two points and there was an ominous silence. The redcaps got up from the aisles but called out few odds. There was almost no betting. They were waiting—the galleries and the short money, seven, eight thousand strong—for another mysterium. The intereses creados squirmed up in their chairs like weasels. This point—it was taking too long, too many volleys! The great and turning point came in like high tide and the redcaps quieted nor scuffles nor coughs but the pok of the rubber and rocklike sphere impacted and spread upon the front wall and the long, retrograde arc of the orb obfuscating in spotlights, the skim of wrists along the green middling and the crack of stone's conjunction with straw. Rolando, the stiff yet still graceful elder, scooped up the ball on the short hop and propelled it swan's neck thick on the middle so it angled sinuously on the low wide front, bounced within the far outside wood and spiraled into the netting. The galleries were ripped wide open with Amerindian joie de vivre. The men or beasts within tore asunder their poses and stepped outside themselves. The promised sign! I turned to Felipe. He glowed with cherubic ecstasy. I held his head like a son. The redcaps called out odds: 40 to 100, make it 45, no, 50 to 100. Red and blue tickets passed countless brown hands. The aisles writhed like serpents. We bore the manic coaster to allegorical heaven.

It was like the Westerns too. The well-off villains in their business suits and gold pocket watches presenced their reserved finale. They put away their pepitas and pistachios and their eyes popped and jaws hung awry. "Cover!" they begged the redcaps. They wanted to cover, to hedge. The God-fearing rested easy. None of us doubted the outcome. Social and poetic justice would be done.

Rolando was all about, luxuriating in his renaissance, his regained nerve.

Soon we were winning! The young bucks leaned against the wall and slowly sank to the floor, their innards chafing, their tongues flapping. Holding his wicker high above him like a torch, Rolando traversed the court with the stately mockery of a cere- monious bullfighter. Caught up in the euphoria I began to scream a confused litany of mythic templates. The eagle, the serpent, the nopal, the thunderbird, the ¡Sí se puede!, la MECHA, el Anáhuac, Aztlán, all jumbled in the same olla. Felipe and I em- braced. "¡Vamos a ganar! ¡Venceremos!"

Then, an inexplicable alteration of events. The elders loosened up—¡que se aflojaron!—got tired, and permitted the youngsters to come back. The game tied up at 29. The ultimate metaphysic! Peepee was drawn from the caved-in bladders of many. The galleries lost their nerve and hastened to hedge their spleens. The sharks and businessmen, anxious to reduce their losses, covered the Indians and bet all the Rolando they could. The red- caps shrieked out the odds, 100 even, 100 pesos, pick'em.

I grabbed Felipe. "Los indios have lost their nerve and are seeking insurance. ¡Tienen los huevos en la garganta!"

"Me too!"

"Let's cover! If we do, we win either way!"

"No way," Felipe said, "let us ride!"

I was in a swoon. "Oh, God! All that pastel!"

"Are you with me?"

I squeezed his hand. My knees were buckling. His face was mauve and bloated. "God, yes!"

I am an innocent, I thought. The ingenuous fanatic. For the moment I loved him so I could have given him my life.

The ultimate point began.

Rolando served the ball, a giveaway straight to the opposing frontman. We should have lost, instead the ball dribbled obscenely out of the unnerved wicker.

"We won!"

The young buck climbed and clawed the net in a twist of fury. Futile as Bergman's squire.

I turned to Felipe. "You won! You knew the old boy'd do it!"

He didn't seem terribly happy, though. He pointed at Rolando leaving for the dressing room, wiping his brow amid hosannas. "It took a lot out of him."

I felt funny. Felipe and I split the money, 50-50. The devalued pastel wad of Mexican money barely entered my pocket. I had more in the wallet. There were bills in my shirt pocket. Child supplicants stood willfully at the exit to the Palacio. I emptied coins into each calloused hand.

"Don't do that," he said.

"Why not?"

"It's bad form. It makes you look like a gringo."

"I know that. It's only because tonight I've scored big."

"No, never. You'll spoil them."

To win money: that was not enough. Felipe was still angry, knotted up by the match, and slowly I became angry too. It was not enough on the eve of the Virgin's day, despite the magnificent catharsis. Why? No más por no más.

Felipe had been silent while we lined up and collected our bets. Now he almost whined. "Now we must go and fuck some woman. I know a brothel, not too far."

"I don't want to fuck some woman! I'm too buoyant. I want to keep my money. Not tonight, Felipe. I'm too worn."

"Pues sí, compis. That's the way we do things here. The night won't be complete. El rito del Jai Alai se lo exige."

"I thought you were a poet, a mystic, and a left-leaning intellectual."

Felipe cursed a lot about shitting in the milk of the Virgin and all that folklore. "If you win, you've got to go. Don't leave me to my designs."

"What's this brothel like?"

"Perverse! What güero can claim to have known México without having visited its muchachas?"

"What do you mean, perverse?" I asked him hostilely.

He grinned. "Authentically perverse."

La Madama Lulú's was not perverse. It was repulsive, y me pareció muy típico. Two grenaderos sat on the sidewalk in front of the brothel. Some político or máximo chingón was fucking his brains out. Their carbines lay on the pavement at their sides. They winked at us as we went in. The brothel bureaucrats sat us on an overstuffed Louis XVI and the whores lined up and flaunted us all petite soirée fête in stained miniskirts. "¡Vamos a hacer beibis!"

I didn't have the huevos to choose so the most entrepreneurial of their lot plopped on my thighs and fondled my member. Soon, having been kneaded like a croissant, it began to acquire that mauve, belligerent feel. "Ven aquí," she coaxed. She took some of my salmon and sandía-colored money and gave it to the bookkeeper. The bookkeeper gave me a red poker chip. Then I had to give the poker chip to the porter who meticulously opened the door to a broomcloset cubicle and handed me a roll of toilet paper. We went inside. I didn't give a shit anymore. ¡Qué carajos! I was resolved. Yet suddenly I realized I was fucking a perfect stranger.

Later we were famished. The high was worn and it had turned cold and raw. There were pilgrims wandering the street, like strays. Felipe and I went to an all-night estancia where they cut newspapers into napkins. We had steaming hot caldo tlalpeño. We had machitos, finely minced tacos of bull testicles sprinkled with aguacate and cilantro in piquant sauce, sympathetic cannibalism. We washed it down with Carta Blanca. Felipe was quiet and grave. He looked frightened. I couldn't fathom what he was thinking.

I kept drinking. After a while I asked him, "Why don't men

and women do anything or go anywhere together in this country? Why are the men in the plaza and the women en casa?"

"They do go out together," he protested.

"Sure, to a té danzante at five in the afternoon."

"Those are appropriate hours. I'm sorry that we are not as advanced as your civilization."

"I've told you before, Felipe. It's not my civilization. Shit, I just live there. Don't blame me you sent out a fuck-up like Santa Anna to do an hombre's job."

"Here we still believe in the novia santa."

"You do?"

"Sure."

"I mean you, Felipe Espinoso from Quintana Roo."

"Why not?"

"It seems muy raro. I bet. The novia santa. It goes well with la casa chica."

"Don't insult me."

"I'm sorry. You have a novia waiting for you?"

"Sure."

"Where?"

"In Tulúm. It's small."

"Sure, I know it. There are ruins there. Hay presencia del pasado."

"Tienes razón."

"And how long since you've seen her?"

"The six years I've been here at the University. I take a course and a course and a course. Como tu work-study, right?"

"Not quite. You're going to marry her?"

"As soon as I graduate."

The night was cool and Mexican. Stars appeared like wishes. It was very still, soon it would be early. We walked with our hands in our pockets and our faces down, steadfast in the drunken ambience. We came to a park. The coconuts and the palms were still and etched. Some campesinos with no place to go were trying to sleep on the benches that they had arrogated. There was suddenly a clump of grass in front of me. I plopped on it. The grass tickled my nostrils. I giggled.

"Get up!" Felipe sounded alarmed. He pulled me. It seemed like someone else's arm.

"¡Viva la revolución!"

"Be quiet, won't you!"

"What do you mean, quiet? Is this a police state? ¡Viva la revolución! ¡Viva la virgen de Tepeyac! ¡Viva Tonantzín! Let every good fellow now join in this song, Vive la companie. Good health to each other and pass it along, Vive la companie."

"Get up!"

"No, you come down. Down to my level."

"All right. If you quiet down."

I laughed. "Where I live they say Mexicans—that means Chicanos of course, not you real Mexicans—were made to pizcar tomates because they're built low to the ground. What do you think about that?"

He flashed his winning grin. "I'm curious about your Chicano ways."

"Well. When are you going to graduate?"

"Soon, if you keep quiet so no one steals my money tonight."

"Did you walk to Mexico City from Tulúm?"

"Well, no. Actually, I got an aventón."

"And were you like the indios that come streaming in from the picos and the valles around registration time?"

"Most assuredly."

"And did you live like them, begging, and hustling, and working?"

He smiled. "Well, nobody gets to find much work in this city."

"So then?"

"So I'm still hustling. Only I'm an advanced student now, senior class."

"¿Qué me dices?"

"I'm sorry, güero. We were playing only with your pastel money."

"Only my money? But I saw you pitch in your share."

"That was merely sleight of hand."

"I see. So then, at 29 up, you weren't really that nervous."

"Oh, I was very nervous."

"Yeah, but not as nervous as me."

"No, I wouldn't think so."

"No, you wouldn't think so. After all, for you it was win or tie."

"Something like that."

"And you don't feel bad?"

"I feel very bad. I need for you to know how bad I feel, even now, after winning, despite winning. Not only the money, but my life's dream, enough to live on so that I can take a full course of study and graduate. Porque, compis, tú eres mi cuate, ¿sabes? O, como dicen los tuyos, soy tu carnal."

"How can you say this shit to me now? Do you know I'm debating whether or not to kick your fucking head in?"

"Pues, ponte chango, carnal. Pa' la próxima más aguzao, vato. Porque ya aprendiste. That's what Buñel meant in *Los olvidados*. Like they say in these parts, más cornadas da el hambre que el toro."

"Don't hand me that pestilent shit. You simply hustled me. I'm just as poor as you. You knew if I lost that match I would probably have had to drop out and return home. Either that or starve."

"And you're not used to starving. Sure you're poor—I realize that. But you work. As a stock boy, at Taco Bell, as a piss pot polisher. Lo que sea, entran los chavitos, haga cola para el financial aid. You're poor like Cheech and Chong. We use the same word, poor, but we don't mean the same referent. I mean devastated, a nullity without the remotest identity."

"Why are you telling me all this stuff now? You won your ticket. Why couldn't you have just let me keep on thinking you were a fucking prince?"

"Pues, por pura vergüenza. You may not believe it: allí en la casa de putas, where much profound Mexican thought takes form, I thought about it long and hard. But you deserve more. You are a fine fellow, very young, ingenuo, and my sense of shame and your need to know, they joined forces. It may not be as pretty as pastel illusions or the half breed Virgin who showed herself to the cosmic race, but I felt I owed you the truth. Por eso bajaste al Anáhuac, ¿no?"

"And besides, you have enough money now, ¿verdad? You've got your graduation ticket and you can give up your contingency pigeon, right?"

He looked crestfallen. "I'm sorry. Los malos hábitos are difficult to overcome. I want to go to school intensively now and graduate and no longer do what I used to have to do."

"Well, I guess the course is over. It's been . . . well, it's definitely been a learning experience."

"Get up, güero, please."

"Why should I? I want to sleep. Here, entre las palmas."

"They won't let you sleep here. Some grenaderos will come by. They'll take you to the station and keep the pastel money which you think is so much softer than the dollar."

The grass began to smell of manure. I got up.

On the ninth day I discovered I had contracted the gonk. That was quite a letdown. The same day the pilgrims returned to the countryside and the grenaderos abandoned the University library with its revolutionary mural. I watched the campesinos as they trod out of the capital. The drunken revel was over and so was the holy fervor. They were tired, broke, bearing loathsome lesions on their knees that peered out of their trousers, which had worn away in their penitent sojourn to the Virgin's sanctuary. They looked like a crestfallen army in retreat. They resembled those Vietnamese multitudes on the run that we used to look at, guilt-ridden and repulsed, on the evening news.

When the last of the campesinos and their geese had moved on I could then cross the Promenade of Institutionalized Revolution to the barrio pharmacy where they were caring for me. All my money seemed to be dissipating in penicillin and in little luxuries to assuage the discomfort. Every day I walked sore and open-legged to the pharmacy and pulled down my trousers in the back room. The attendant, una celestina fea y arrugada who looked like the incarnation of gleeful disapproval, would put the needle in.

"How many cc's are you going to give me?"

"You need a million cc's this time up."

"No chingues. You'll have the needle in my bun for over five minutes. It'll be an hour before I'll be able to move my leg."

"¡Cómo que no chingues! That's what *you* should say to yourself, güerito. ¡Porque chingue y chingue y mira el resultado! O como decimos por aquí: Quien se acuesta con pulgas . . ."

"Spare me the dénouement. Let's get it over with. Look, why don't you just give me 500,000?"

"You want 500,000? I'll give it! You know how many machos come back here three weeks later, open-legged and bawling because the pus is back again and dripping out of their putrid chiles?"

"God no, give me the million. Anything."

"Here it goes, y no chilles, ¿eh? güerito valín. Porque como sabes, tú tienes la enfermedad de los meros machos." She began to laugh with great moral gusto. As my leg turned numb I realized that in Mexico the man wasn't always in the plaza and the woman only en casa.

It was just a few days before my term was up and I was to return to Califas. I bumped into Espinoso in the library.

"Hola, vate loco."

He looked embarrassed, almost searching for a space to slink into. "Hola, vato loco. It's been some days since I've seen you."

"Well, yes, I've been spending time at the old farmacia. I got the gonk, thanks to you and your macho ideas and your disgusting putas that you believe are sensuously perverse."

"Well, I figured. I got it too. La mierda de gonorrea is epidemic here."

"Well, that's the best fucking news I've heard all week!"

"You think so? You want to reenact the Alamo here in the library? Fuck it, man, be happy it's just gonk que se quita con penicilina and not what they say you get on the other side of the river, herpes. Let me tell you something, güero, and this is God's truth. Since I've been here, six years in this hostile valley, that was the first time I got laid."

"Not enough billetiza, right?"

"Right. It wasn't a financial priority."

"Sure, you didn't have a sufficiently dumb gringo to hustle big enough at the Jai Alai. Well, you must be busted by now what with shots and poultices and all. Here, let me stake you again— what the fuck, the Chicano baboso never learns." I flipped out a pink and canary bill with the likeness of Venustiano Carranza and stuffed it in his guayabera pocket.

"I'll accept it as a wedding present on behalf of my novia and me."

"Yeah. I was sure that you'd accept it o.k., Mr. Savoir Faire."

"I don't mean to hurt you, güero valín. But, ¿sabes lo que tú eres . . . en el fondo?"

"No, Mr. Maya. No idea what I am en el fondo. But I'm sure you're gonna tell me, Mr. Sabelotodo."

"En el fondo tú eres . . . ¡turista!"

Time softens the sense of injury and lets the little nostalgias form the veins and lodes that make the past palatable. If I had an address to write to, I would have sent him a card or something. But there was no address, maybe the empty swimming pool, o como dijo esa noche, una nulidad sin identidad remota, and barring that I would find myself in the State library, which seemed like an unsullied cavern, to sit and ponder, open the page in the art book to the Palenque man, frame ideas, sometimes talk silently to the stone head.

When you give meaningful events the profound reflection that they require, the many details that you missed in the ongoing come into relief and give a new bent to the hurt. In the labyrinthine library of my soledad I uncovered and relived the discreet portents and signs. How he envied and admired attributes that I didn't remotely realize. Güero, he called me, though in this country I could not remotely pass for fair. And my blue jeans and knitted polo shirt were such a center of attraction, the ballpoint pen that contained three cartridges, red, black, and green. Finally, I gave it to him. The way he liked to introduce me to girls on the campus—girls, I conclude now, who were not his friendly acquaintances as I had thought at the time, but barely accorded him the minimal courtesies of fellow studenthood. He would introduce me, I realize now, with a touch of the panderer, and how they would take to the exotic Chicano, the güero valín with a rather hairy chest who maybe reminded them in his knit shirt of some phantasm image they had conjured in their head, a Robert Redford, well-heeled, privileged and native in Spanish. You were waiting there, Felipe, furious and sotted with envy, bridling your lust—how you must have kept so much venom under wraps—hoping that I would puncture the maiden ethics of niñas bien, maybe score, maybe there would be a scrap of carrion in it for you. For you hadn't been laid in six years!

How you queried me, Maya, about so many things like routes and rivers, fences and sensors, coyotes and pollos. Were you trying on Chicano, my friend? Were you speculating on the North? How proud you were, como un tío paternal, when you arranged a little public trial for me at the tortería, bade me eat the chile más pequín de la tortería. And when I passed your little test and won a round of student applause did you not say, see, he's no gringo now, he's earned his bones. But it was nothing! I've been eating those pequines my whole life!

Now I feel so mortified that I could have confided in you—

¿qué?—after two or three days of acquaintanceship at most, such intimate yearnings as my whole carnal hope for Mexican-Chicano compañerismo. ¡Qué ingenuo! Now I know, máximo peón, that even in oppression, even if there are only two oppressed peas in a constricted pod, they will disaggregate into an oppressor and an oppressed, a siervo and a señor, a leader and a led. That is the nature of oppression and of the oppressed, the theory and the practice. That they know only what they know and act on what they know, a great chain of oppressed people, a great daisy chain of being that leads not straight to St. Thomas' sandía-hued heaven, but low, up and down picos, down and up valleys, across llanos and even across rivers where the current runs in opposing directions. Yet, truly escarmentado that I am for having so readily and unselfconsciously confided in El Otro, that moment in the tortería, that heartfelt abrazo over tortas de lomo . . . How is it that two oprimidos of such divergent estirpes, of such varied formation, could have, if just for a transitory term, communed? I cherish that shared governance of perceptions even though to obtain it requires a racking sojourn into memories filled with penitence and humiliation. And I think of a passage in Hemingway where it is observed that where we are weak, there nature surely breaks us, and if we fare with good fortune, and go on the mend, there where we were weak we are now the strongest. And although in the end it's all the same for nature will break us, definitively, it will not be at the junction where once we were weak and now we are strong.

Amigo, I don't quarrel with your many truths nor the intensity of your motives. Of one thing, no cabe duda, I am poor like Cheech and Chong—thank God for it, bless that level of poverty that still subsidizes the notion of humorous solutions.

Well yes, there is one perception that I quarrel with. ¡Yo no soy turista! In truth you were the tourist, amigo, as well as the tour guide and the conning lout. A most engaging and eager one, the way you genuinely investigated my nature, but like any tourist, even an enlightened and avid one, you compared the landscape by a self-same standard. Your sense of the picturesque, the empathetic, and the offensive were all measured out in the same pastel currency. But the estranged is different from the tourist. It is his lot to wander forth, to cross rivers that flow up course, seek out his own image in the dubious landscape of the other, search for a currency that isn't there. Por supuesto, the Chicano needs to gaze into smoky mirrors that reflect no peer. Know this, venerable Maya head that has perdured for 1200 years on a coated ivory page in a slick art book in a State library: I am strong where I've been broken and I'm not prepared to cave in.

Mocha in Disneyland

When you are swinging in the Swiss Family Treehouse in the midst of a starry Anaheim night, listening to the random baying of Disneyland's hounds as they go through their militant patrol, then there is ample time for musing. Mi tesoro de la sierra madre is sleeping snugly at my side. He is only naked and damp in the blanket I had the foresight to pack. I am rather glum though, for having swum the channel between Tom Sawyer Island and Fantasyland under the eye of Disney's futurizing moon, fleeing the insistent baying of increasingly proximate patrolhounds, not only my clothes but even my tobacco has become waterlogged, not to mention the forlorn wrinkles and curls on my padded leather pipe. The child, like a plush panda on his father's back, his arms resolutely round his father's waist, we bobbed like apples in the cold black waters of this festive themeworld. Now, thank God for it, five hours until dawn in Disney's kingdom, there's ample time for musing.

I remember that they used to call us café con leche. A brown person and his white querida strolling the barrio, or better yet, white astride his moto, fumando mota, white thighs and wacky white kneecaps flashing in the motorwake. Those were halcyon days: the miniskirt and unreconstructed integration. Los vatos were eyeing us with unconcealed envy. I was proud. "Orale, ése, ahí vienen, el café con leche. Hey man, I hear you're playing middle linebacker for State!"

The other morning I opened the post and saw Pancholín's scrawl on the verso of a Knott's Berry Farm postcard. I become tense when I get mail from my kid. I know it's going to basically govern my day. "Dear Daddy. I hope the cut on your cheek and the itsy-bitsy one on your nose is better now. I never see you much. The Creature Cantina you sent me se me rompió. I still love you but you're low on my loving list. First comes my mama, and then, Socorro, and then comes kitty-gato. Then comes YOU. Stephen comes to visit us a lot and stays over all nite. I love my mama all the way to the last number of counting. I love you too, but not as high. Pancholín."

That's what I get from beddy-bye, Kid Cappuccino, el mocha, the fruit of coffee with milk.

Well, that's it then, I thought, we're going to the beach. Only not there, because that muscle-bound oaf, Stephen, with his wriggling tattoo and his bionic pretensions probably lives with them both in a lean-to on muscle beach. I'll find someplace. I'm fed up with computing and permuting the parameters of bilingualism and wearied by the Feds with their ungracious timelines and audit trails. "You've never missed a deadline," my wife once said to me, "and it will kill you." Weird Hispanic Person. (Did you ever hear that joke: What's a Dry Martínez? A Mexican with a vasectomy!)

Actually it's not true at all. I've missed my share of deadlines. Lately, more than my share. I find the angst of impending loss flowering at the side of my self-correcting typewriter. I peer into the stereoscope for the hundredeth time and pass the experimental design:

PIE	PIE
DIME	DIME
COME	COME
HAY	HAY
ONCE	ONCE
SEA	SEA

One stimulus is going into the Hispanic eye, the other in the Anglo. The data base is moving under me like quicksand. This is something like mal de siècle. Frankly, I don't know if it's mala fe, or merely mala leche.

I have a lab assistant who is very practical, and this is an invaluable asset. "Plain Jane," she calls herself, "the Carpenter's Dream Girl." I abhor this sort of gabacho masochism but in her somehow I tolerate it, and even empty my soul.

"Why don't you send for Mocha and have him down here

with you for a few days? Show him a good time, take him out to search for fauna, maybe even go down to Disneyland?" She's mixing coffee in a beaker. We do everything by sterotype in my lab, you know, by the book. It helps me with my identity problem. God knows, I'd wear a white lab coat if I could get away with it. Or maybe one of those grand white chef's hats? But the students would never stand for it. They'd laugh me out of Hilgard Hall. As it is, the minute the temperature goes down a mite I put on my three-piece corduroy suit with leather arm patches and light up a briarwood, padded leather pipe.

I look at her with a sort of ironic leer, the kind that masks the sort of hope you find in certain brown-skinned Catholics in Vegas, who think that with the drunkenly solicited grace of God, they can, in one definitive roll, come up with midnight at the Circus-Circus. "How could I even consider taking a couple of days off now? Aren't the Feds already muttering darkly about audit trails and figuring maybe we jerked them off for a hundred grand in computer upchuck?"

"Bah, come off it, Huitla. You're the senior Chicano in the State system! With any luck at all the auditors'll find that unauthorized trip to Tahoe and the University will have to bump you up to dean."

I laughed. She's right about that. A little embarrassment could be a great help at this point. I could leave behind the miasma of unsynthesized detail and move into the upper reaches. The deanship! A passport to the acme of thought.

"There you go then, schmendrik, it's settled."

"But wait. I can't take time off from my classes. You know I never run out on my students. I'll have to wait 'til the trimester break."

"You don't teach on Friday, do you? Take a three-day blow. Have you ever read that Hemingway tale? You could use a three-day blow. Shit, I'll even fill in for your Friday afternoon tutorial. You better decide quick before I change my mind."

Now we've come implacably to what is really the gist of the matter. I look at her as if she were a creature demented. "What are we talking about? You know I've already had him during this trimester. That's the condition of the Consent Decree. I'm surprised at you, Plain Jane, your own gabacho judge imposed that condition. 'Look here, Huitla, once every trimester you get to have your son. That's plenty for your kind.' "

She chuckles. Pours milk into her coffee and eyes me like a shrewdy. "Well, maybe Linda will be cooperative. She just might look upon it differently this time. Circumstances do change, you know. Maybe she could use something of a healthy transition, seeing as how Stephen appears to have moved in."

Thanks, I needed that fact of life rubbed in my face. But I sure was pissed. "That California fruit fly, muscle bound maricón, hijo de la gran puta, mother-fucking no-good scum bag, hijo de un perro chirifusca. ¡Me cago en la leche que te han dado! ¡Me cago en tu estampa! ¡Me cago en el padre que te hizo! ¡Me cago en tu madre puta! ¡Me cago en tus muertos! ¡Me cago en la mar! ¡Me cago en la mierda! ¡Me cago en la porra! ¡Me cago en los cojones de Buda!" etc., etc.

Two weeks later I was at Linda's doorstep in Ventura. "Did you pack enough underwear for Kid Mocha this time? I don't want him to end up being a big chief gray pecker again!"

"Sure thing, perfesser. Can I get my A now?"

Pancholín bit my hand. "I'm no big chief gray pecker! That was for you, cukkamonga!"

"Ow, stop it. STOP IT! Look at my hand."

He swelled with glee. "Let me see it, Daddy. Are the teeth marks rising in your skin yet?"

"Look," said Linda. "I've got a couple of pieces of chicken in the refrigerator, some hardboiled eggs. I'll pack them up for you."

"No, don't bother."

"Why bother, right? They'd just compete with the junk food on the road."

"Sure. Taco Bell, Wendy's triples."

"Yeah. Burrito supremes. 'Hot and juicies.' "

"How come you're being so forthcoming?"

"I'm always forthcoming, Huitla. Too much so, that's how I get into trouble."

"I bet you could use these three days."

"I could use these three days."

"Is it that serious?"

"Not really."

"So it's that serious, huh? Mocha, go away. Play with your molded plastic toys. You heard me. Beat it! Scrambola!"

"Don't be a heavy, Huitla. Don't make me weary. It's as serious as it's ever going to be. It's not serious."

"How could you ever get mixed up with a tattooed beach bum like that?"

"You're really fucked up, you know that? He's only got one tattoo and it's on his arm. You make him sound like he came out of a Ray Bradbury story. Jesus Christ, why did I tell you about that tattoo? I suppose I get what I deserve."

"So when are you planning to get married?"

"I'm not thinking along those lines. But if *you* need a wedding ring I've got one you can have."

"Sure baby, thanks for the offer. Deep down you always thought I was basically your standard Hispanic troglodyte, didn't you, Linda? I mean, your typical A-frame Chicano structure, sure, with a veneer of Taco Bell and Lawn King dabbed on, an overlay, a glaze so to speak, a doctorate in scientific observation and measurement and the three-piece corduroy social life of the university, but down in the nitty-gritty, a romping pleistocene el macho."

"God save me from this. You promised, Huitla. You said you'd come up here and take Pancholín for a few days and give me a chance."

"Yes, I did. I'm sorry."

"We fell in love, we got married. And it was fine. But it didn't work out forever. There's no need to do this . . . this exercise in self-doubt and mortification. There was nothing . . . It was nothing that you point to on a good-bad scale. Just a lack of adjustment. A misfitting."

"Sure, like a tailor who messes up. You've told me a hundred times if you've told me once. A marriage that was a poorly tailored suit. Besides, who am I to complain of tattoos, didn't I use to drive you through the sal si puedes on my Harley Davidson?"

"That's right. Your skull and bones cycle."

"Sure, you remember that. Mostly I remember your knees, flashing white in the window panes of parked cars as we'd motor by. Jesus Christ, what woman wears a miniskirt on a motorcycle? ¡Y gringa! And los vatos, café con leche is what they called us. Hey man, here comes the strong coffee and his side of cream.

Remember how they'd make those barnyard kisses? I'd get pissed. Ya estuvo, ¿no? Maricones de mierda. All fall down!"

"Huitla, come here. Sit down, I want you to know . . . and not because this is so serious, because it isn't. It's just the first, you know. And you need to adjust, and Pancholín too. But the odds are one day there will be a serious one. I want you to know that I loved you, and I still love you. It wasn't you or me either for that matter. It wasn't culture or race or your personality. I love you, but we couldn't . . . we couldn't live together forever after. Life is just not like the fairytale. It was just a misfit. You've got to believe that. It's really true."

"You mean, we were just too different?"

"Yes, too . . . like jigsaw pieces that don't really fit. They look like they fit for a while. But then you go back to them and they don't."

"Well, you're right there. Life ain't like no fairytale. That's for sure. That's for fucking sure. What odds do you think Lloyd's of London offers on mixed marriages?"

"Very low, I suppose. But that's got nothing to do with us. That's not what did us in. Besides, we were only a partially mixed marriage."

"Partially mixed! What in the hell are you talking about?"

"Well, we're both Catholic, aren't we?"

"Oh, sure, you in the Loew's Paramount in downtown St. Paul converted into a cathedral with orchestra, loge and balcony seating, and me in an adobe chapel in the high sierra where you don't bother to distinguish between the Christian godhead and the true Quetzalcoatl! Tell me, you remember our trip to Turkey and Greece? Do you agree that we conceived the kid in that Asian watering hole somewhere on the road between Homer's Troy and St. Peter's Ephesus, or do you still maintain that an accurate backwards extrapolation of the days proves that conception was while waiting for the damn plane to be ministered at the Roadway Motor Hotel on 42nd Street almost under the gray West Side Highway and the New York docks?"

"I see that's still bothering you."

"Yes, you might say it's paradigmatic."

"Well, have it your way, you can invent your little creation myth if you like."

"No, seriously. I want to know your objective thinking on this matter."

"You know what I think. I'm sorry it disappoints you, but I was counting. That was my count. You should understand that. You're a researcher."

"Oh sure, a count is a count. How come when I count I go back to the ottoman in Balikesir?"

"That's because you don't make the full count. You refuse to add in the days that I was actually late."

"How do you know you were late in bearing? Couldn't it be my way, that we conceived two weeks later?"

"That's romantic Huitla, and mythical, but it's just not true. I was late. He was holding on for dear life. Inside me."

"Well, you're right there. Life is no fairytale. That's for sure, for fucking sure. You're always right, Linda. A total misfit. A marriage like a poorly tailored suit. Except for el mocha, let's call it a wash."

Finally, we are on the open road, shuttling down Highway 1. Coming up is Las Tunas beach. I know this area well. I used to own a bike.

Pancholín is playing tensely with his fingers. "Is there really an Order of the Golden Carp, or are you just making it up like the rest of your stories?"

"I never make up stories."

"Oh yeah? What about your dumb dromedary?"

"My dromedary is real."

"Then how come I can never see it?"

"You've seen him in a zoo. Also a Bactrian. But you haven't seen *my* dromedary because you don't believe in my beautiful dromedary and you only abuse him. You can only see him if you believe in him."

"That's what you always say. I bet your dromedary is not so beautiful. I bet he's ugly. I bet he's got poop on his bottom."

"No wonder you can't see him."

"I want to see him. Bring him here. I'll give him a punch right in the hump."

"No way!"

"I do believe in him! Hey, dromedary, listen! I believe in you . . . I believe in YOUUUUUU . . ."

"He doesn't believe you."

"That's what you always say. You don't have any dromedary. And there's no dromedary that spies on me at school and tells you what I do. You've got a dromedary, all right. It's in your head. That's all that it is. A dromedary in your head, but it's not real. And that goes for your golden carp too, and all your other cukkamonga made-up stuff."

"My dromedary told me you were playing in front of the school with Rick the other day and you lost your shoe in a pile of leaves and you had to go around without a shoe like a barefoot contessa until the assistant principal took you out at lunch period to find it."

"How did you know that?"

"My dromedary told me."

"Where was he?"

"Looking at you and Rick from behind the jungle gym."

"I bet Mommy told you."

"No, she didn't."

"Yes she did."

"No, she didn't!"

"Yes she did! She told you and not any silly dromedary what if it's real only lives in a zoo."

"Does your mommy know what you and Rick were playing in those leaves?"

"No."

"Well, I do."

"What?"

"Star Wars."

"How'd you know that?"

"Not only Star Wars. You were playing that you were in the garbage compactor."

"Who told you that?"

"My dromedary. He was a witness."

Pancholín became quiet. He pondered the facts. "I bet you just figured it out cause you're smart. You're a pretty smart daddy but you've got dromedaries in your head."

"You don't believe me?"

"I only believe in dromedaries when I see them."

"Then you can't see my dromedary. Because you've got to believe in him first. Then you can see him."

"Stop teasing me. Mommy says you're always teasing me!"

"She said that? Look, I'll tell you what I'm going to do. I'll let my dromedary drive the car. I'll take my hands off the wheel and he'll drive."

"You mean he's here now? Where is he?"

"In my lap."

"I can't see him." Pancholín carefully probed the space above my lap with his hand. "I don't feel a thing."

"Naturally. How are you going to feel an invisible creature? He's an ethereal dromedary."

"What's he doing?"

"He's getting ready to drive the car. He smells of desert spices, of myrrh and frankincense. He's just got back from the Sheeba shuttle. Okay, drom. Do your thing!" I took my hands off the wheel.

"Look, Dad, the car's moving!"

The car went straight for a while, then it began to veer off the road. I took back the wheel.

"Boy, some dromedary. Your camel drives just like a drunken dromedary."

"I think he did okay."

"You would. You're always sticking up for him. How come you always stick up for him?"

"I think he did pretty good for an animal with hooves. You should be grateful that you've got fingers and thumbs to grab. How would you like to drive a car with hooves?"

"Hmph! Why don't you stop here so we can go out on the beach?"

"You want to go for a swim?"

"No, I want to have a wrestle right on the sand."

"You think you're pretty tough, don't you."

"No, but I can sure beat you up."

"Oh yeah, tough guy?"

"That's for sure!"

"Only because you pull hair. That's no fair. No pulling hair. Then we'll see."

"What about you, cheater-chiter? You're always giving me lamb leg. That's no fair either."

"All right then. Maybe we'd better not wrestle. Your mommy's right. I tease you too much."

"Aw, c'mon Daddy, please. Please? I wanna wrestle."

We drove some more. You could see the beach and the gray waves curling like tongues from time to time off the road's enticing angles.

"Okay, punk," Pancholín said, "you've asked for no hair pulling, you got it!"

Immediately I veered off the road and down a sider. We parked tilting crazily against a sand dune.

"Oh boy! A wrestle!"

"Wait a second!"

"What?"

"I forgot something. Let's see your fingernails."

He hid his hands behind his back.

"No inspection, no wrestle."

We sat glowering at each other for a while. Finally, he showed them.

"Jesus Christ! They're worse than Dracula's!"

"I swear I won't gouge. I swear it on dromedary poop!"

"No way! Either I cut your nails or no wrestle. Do you know what my students said to me last time I came into class with my face all scratched up by your claws? They accused me of wrestling with a coed!"

"You can't cut them. You cut them too close. You stink! You make me bleed! I want my mommy to cut them!" He was teary, working himself up into a froth.

"Then forget it, punk. I knew you'd chicken out somehow."

On that note he gave in and presented his claws for trimming. I took the clipper from the glove compartment and worked as quickly and carefully as possible. He winced with every clip although it surely didn't hurt. When it was over he inspected each finger solicitously for blood or for tender pinkness.

"C'mon, Oedipus, time for the beach. Last one there is a squishy tamale. You gonna put on a bathing suit or you want me to throw you in the water with all your clothes on?"

"Don't call me any names, you little son of a bitch. I'll rip the hair out of your head."

The Wrestle is a formal ritual. It contains elaborate rules of redress. There is ample provision for the conjuring up of allies such as bumble horrors and Spider Man, Darth Vader, or in the father's case, the Cisco Kid. There is also occasion to act out favored roles, to bring into service such useful adjuncts as force fields, laser rays, karate chops, or when on a beach, fistfuls of plentiful sand. The overall composition generally follows the sonata form. There is, for example, the initial exposition of the characters of father and son, replete with situation-specific bragga-docio and a variety of feints, dodges, ruses and ploys, and even an occasional scuffle. The development stage is often signaled by ritualized contrapuntal verbal abuse whereby the antagonists are serially baited and goaded with a variety of epithets derogatory of wrestling valor such as Chicken Chartreuse, Chicken Chow Mein, punky Cukkamonga, el moco verde, el grande de pavo, esquinkel (*vid.* esquintle, Nahuatl), kid moco, el creepo, nothing but a pigeon, *et alia*. At this point physical contact begins to in-crease in intensity and range and becomes characterized by a variety of holds, locks, grips and pins, together with rabbit punch-es, bites, kicks, tumbles, karate chops, hair-pulling, gouging, scratching, and pinching. Soon, immersed in this embattled frenzy, one is wont to seek the succor of allies with supernatural or mythical powers. Or better yet, to become one of these transcen-dent beings oneself. "Ha, ha! And now punk, Dr. Precision is going to get you with his horse needle!" With respect to deep narrative structure, The Wrestle often takes its cue from the earlier lore of Westerns. The father is conscious of this, the son is unaware; yet they play it out orthodoxly, even as the surface language reflects the faddish advances of the space age. The good guy (white hat, never a Meskin, except maybe for the Cisco Kid) is beaten up mercilessly while at the same time tormented like Christ on his Calvary (harking back to an even earlier lore), un-til the inciting moment. This pivotal point in The Wrestle is repre-sented by an outrage above and beyond all previous outrages incorporated into the ritual. Thus the crucial element of the out-rage gives to The Wrestle a certain open-endedness, a sense of heretofore unexamined peril, a quality of advancement or additiv-ity, in what otherwise might be considered a closed and self-con-tained system. On the occasion in question, the outrage is exempli-fied by the father (the bad guy) holding the son (the good guy) upside down over the surf, and threatening to throw him in fully clad, moreover actualizing the threat by occasionally dunking the good guy's head into three inches of surf while firmly holding him like a seven-year-old Ulysses, by the heels.

Once having somehow "miraculously" broken the outrage, the good guy, swollen with righteous indignation, a moral impera-tive highlighted in vehemence by the intensity of the very travesty of the outrage itself, takes heavily to task the bad guy, who is thrown from bound to bound and torn limb from limb. Hence we proceed to recapitulation; it is the child overcoming his daddy, all the time assuring him he's nothing more than the Chicken Chartreuse, el punko green snot, grande pavo esquinkel, double deer-crossing with three-in-one oil, high rating on the turkometer, that he has claimed for the daddy all along. Closure is achieved swiftly enough, about four or five times after the daddy issues the incantation, "I give up!" and often with a culminating fistful of pulled hair and a boot in the ass.

We didn't get in until late that night what with The Wrestle, and after that a swim and some chow at a roadside dump called the Doggy Diner. Even Pancholín, who isn't particularly fond of the sedentary life, wanted to rest and muse and ponder. He took off his socks and inspected his toes with a sort of inquisitive-ness that reminded me of the days when he was just a baby and first discovered them. "Think there was any golden carp in that ocean we were swimming in?"

"Naw. Carp is a freshwater fish."

"Well, maybe there was some silver carp in there. What about silver carp, are they freshwater or salt?"

"Silver carp? There aren't any silver carp. Just gold. The golden carp is a fish that once was a god. The other gods were sick to death of the sinning of their people and they turned them into carp to live forever in the river, but there was one kind god, who was so saddened by this, and so afraid for his people, that he asked that he too be turned into a carp to be near them and look over them. This is the golden carp."

"And who were the people, Daddy?"

"The people, Pancholín? They would be . . . the Chicano people."

Pancholín smiled broadly. "Like me, right Daddy? I'm a Chi-cano person."

"Right, like you."

"Only I'm not only a Chicano. I'm a gabacho too."

"Yes, only that's not such a pretty word. You don't have to use that word."

"Well, Chicano isn't such a pretty word either. Some kid up at school called me a lousy Chicano half-breed so I had to beat his ass. Only he was a pretty tough turkey. He was a grade higher."

"Chicano is a nice word for Chicanos. And that's what counts."

"And gabacho is a nice word for gabachos, and that's what counts."

"Only it doesn't work like that. Chicanos call Chicanos, Chicano. But gabachos don't call each other that. Gabacho is a word that Chicanos use for gabachos."

"Don't Chicanos like gabachos?"

"Sometimes they do and sometimes they don't."

"But they don't always like them?"

"Naw, not always. Hell, Chicanos don't always like Chicanos."

"But you're Chicano, right Daddy? And Mommy is gabacha, right?"

"Sort of. I don't like the word you're using."

"Never mind that. You used to like each other a lot. Now, you don't like each other that much."

"But it's got nothing to do with what kind of people we are. We just didn't fit well together."

"But how come Stephen stays over all the time? Stephen's a gabacho, right? Why doesn't Mommy love another Chicano, like you?"

"Would that make it any easier? Your mommy says she still loves me. She just doesn't want to live with me anymore. We still love each other. Besides, she's not in love with Stephen. She told me so this morning. She told me it's nothing serious. Besides, there's not so many Chicanos in this world. We're few and far between. Besides, she loves you, doesn't she? And you're Chicano, right? Besides, I don't like that word, gabacho."

"Okay, then, big shot professor. What word should I use?"

"Use a word that they use for themselves, not one that we use for them."

"Well, like what?"

"I don't know, there's plenty of them. Like white."

"White? You mean the color white?"

"Sure, your mother is white, isn't she?"

"Yeah, she's not only white. She's pure white like a glass of milk."

"And I'm more like coffee-colored, right?"

"Yeah."

"And you, you're a color that's like when you mix coffee and milk, right?"

"Yeah."

"Well, there you go. You're all set."

He thought for a while. "The guy in school, you know, the one who gave me a popeye? He was black."

"Hmmm. Well, he's got his own problems. I can see why he might not like Chicanos. He's a special case."

"Yeah, maybe." Pancholín thought about it some more. "Isn't there another word for gabacho, instead of white? I don't think that word works so good. Only with Mommy because she's really white, the whitest thing that ever lived. Nobody else I know is white. There's plenty of gabachos around who are red looking with red noses or yellow looking, kind of brown, and black and chocolate."

". . . and green and purple too, right kid? Okay, here goes another one for you. Gabachos like to think of themselves as American."

"American? But you're American, aren't you? And you're not gabacho."

"Yes, but I'm Mexican-American, see the difference?"

"Then what am I?"

"Well, you would be Mexican-American; American-American. See what I mean?"

"I'm not too sure. Is there another word?"

"How about Anglo? There's another one for you."

"Anglo? Nah. That's not right. That's when two lines come together. They make an Anglo."

"No, you mean angle. I mean Anglo."

"Are you sure?"

"Well, maybe when I grow older I'll use Anglo. But you know what I think I want to do now?"

"No, what?"

"I want to use gabacho. But I want everybody to know I don't mean it nasty. I even use it for myself."

"Okay, then. It's settled, at least for now. It sounds like your daddy when he was young. He used Mexican, but he wanted everybody to know he was the faithful Mexican, the one that saved the sheeprancher's daughter, and not the perfidious one that . . . uh, did her wrongful harm."

"I'm sleepy, Daddy. Can I sleep here on the couch?"

"I'll carry you. I've got your bed all made."

I put him in the bed. He stretched out his hands and I bent down and kissed him.

"I love you, Daddy. A lot-lot."

"I love you too, pumpkin, all the way to the last number of counting."

"When I grow up I'm going to college and become a professor and learn all about words."

"You know what?" I said to him. "I think you've just made my day." Only I wasn't sure if he heard me because Pancholín falls asleep so fast.

About 7:00 a.m. Pancholín was in my room, making weird noises. He wouldn't wake you up exactly, he knew he wasn't supposed to disturb his daddy. But he'd play in the room. First, he'd start with a whisper. He'd re-create intergalactic battles and summon the Incredible Hulk and Wonder Woman to his side. By 7:30 the whispers had given way to loud zaps and rata-tat-tats as ray guns and stun pistols reverberated from the legions of molded plastic figurines that were propped strategically around the bedroom.

"You want breakfast?"

"What you got?"

"I've got Rice Krispies. I've got Cheerios. Take your pick."

"You mean you don't have Count Chocula?"

"You know I don't keep that sugary garbage around. Your mother lets you eat that stuff?"

"No."

"Well, then?"

"I was just asking."

"Boy, when I was your age all I got was a cup of black coffee and a stale bolillo. Then I had to work all day hunting for tin cans and scrap metal."

"That must have been funnnnnnnnnn. You know what? I want both. Rice Krispies and Cheerios all mixed up. Say, Daddy, do you think we could send away for this magic ring? Only two box tops and twenty-five cents."

"I've got something better than that for you." I opened the top drawer of the chest and took out my Phi Beta Kappa key. "See this!"

"Wow! It's gold, isn't it?"

"Sure!"

"Is it pure gold? Or is it just gold on top like what rubs off?"

"Pure gold!"

"Wow! What is it?"

"It's the sacred key to the Order of the Golden Carp."

"Is that what I get if I make Carp First Class?"

"None other."

"And what am I now? A tadpole, right?"

"Right. But if things go well, by tomorrow you'll be a Carp First Class."

"What are you, Daddy? What class carp are you? Second? Third? Ninth?"

"No, you're going the wrong direction. First is the highest of the classes. Me, I'm a . . . a Goldfish Supreme."

"Is that the highest?"

"Oh, that's definitely the highest. As a matter of fact, I'm one of the senior carps in the system."

"Oh boy, the highest number of counting of carps. What comes after Carp First Class?"

"Well, uh, there's Star, and then, Life, and then, Goldfish Supreme."

"But why a goldfish? I thought you was a carp!"

"Yeah, well, I am. Goldfish is another word for carp. Only it's the secret word. You're not gonna tell anybody, are you?"

"Naw. I won't tell anybody, except for other carps. Who else is a carp, Daddy?"

"Who else? Well . . . uh . . . all the Chicanos. All the Chicanos who make the grade that is. If you ask one and he doesn't know what you're talking about then you can be sure they've passed him by and he's nothing more than a Chicken Chartreuse esquinkel."

Pancholín fell down laughing. "Right! Right!" Then he turned serious. "What about Mommy? Is she one?"

"Well, not exactly. She approves of them though. She's a corresponding member of the academy."

"Why don't we start up a Silver Carps? For mommies and girls."

"Not a bad idea. Maybe we should bring it up in August. You know, on the convention floor."

"Tell me again, Daddy. What do I have to do to be a Carp First Class?"

"Well, lots of things."

"Like what?"

"Lots of things. You'll find out as we do them. But every First Class Carp has got to do these two things. One, he's got to find a treasure. And two, he's got to spend the night out-of-doors, in a scary place."

"Yikes! And we're gonna spend it on Tom Sawyer Island, in the old cave!"

"Right you are, none other."

"Yikes!"

"You're not scared, are you?"

"Naw. You'll be there, right?"

"Definitely."

"Think there's any bats in that cave?"

"I'll have the dromedary scare them away."

Pancholín looked at me dubiously.

"Think there are any snakes in that cave?"

"Naw. Snakes like to snuggle into little holes and crevices, kind of like kitty-gato does. Caves are more for big game like wolves and bears."

"Yikes! Maybe the six wolves all live in the cave."

"What six wolves?"

"You know. The wherewolf, the whatwolf, the which, the when, the why, and the whowolf."

"Oh, those guys. Those are just made-up wolves. Those are wh-wolves. They wouldn't be in Tom Sawyer's Cave."

"I thought they were real wolves! You see, you make up everything! I know the wherewolf is real. I've seen him on T.V."

"So it's real if you've seen it on T.V.? Never mind that anyway. We've got to get ready." I brought the gear that I'd stowed away for the outing. "Think we've got everything?"

"Oh boy! A flashlight! Can we make animals with our fingers against the wall of the cave?"

"Hey, that's a great idea! We'll do all kinds of fun things."

"Wanna see my rabbit? I make a beautiful rabbit. ¡Mira qué precioso!"

"Not now. In the cave."

"You know what? You're missing one thing."

"What would that be?"

"A weapon."

"Nah, we don't need a weapon. We'll vanquish any enemies we may encounter with our bare hands."

"Suppose they've got dogs?"

"Dogs at Disneyland? Nah, they wouldn't do that."

"Why don't you pack some hamburger with sleeping drugs in it? If some dogs come around we'll give them a little snooze." Pancholín chortled.

"Pretty good idea. Only I don't have any sleeping drugs and who wants to carry around some smelly old raw meat in a knapsack all day?"

By 8:00 p.m. we were on our last legs. We had done it all, especially anything that whirred, whipped, whirled, whined, whistled or whizzed (six wh-'s over Disney) including the Jungle Cruise, Star Jets, Grand Prix Raceway, 20,000 Leagues Under the Sea, Snow White's Scary Adventures, Dumbo the Flying Elephant, The Mad Tea Party and Mr. Toad's Wild Ride.

As darkness came upon us Pancholín grew more and more apprehensive. It was a typical syndrome of his so I didn't pay it that much mind. We went back to the locker where we stowed away the knapsack and we got it out.

"Daddy, you remember those hippos and alligators on the Jungle Cruise? That's not the water around our island, is it?"

"Not at all. They keep those big lugs out of the way of the paddlewheeler. Besides, you're not scared of those silly guys? They're no more real than your Creature Cantina or Luke Skywalker. Giant hunks of molded plastic, that's what they are."

Pancholín was dubious, very dubious.

"Well my man, the last vessel moves out in five minutes. Which will it be, Tom Sawyer's Rafts or Captain Fink's Keel Boats?"

Pancholín sighed. "We might as well take the Keel Boats. They look safer."

On the boat he began whimpering and rubbing his eyes, all the while making a herculean effort to hold in the tears. "Do we have to spend the whole night on this silly island? I'm cold!"

"Pancho! Be quiet! You want everybody to know our business? My God, it's the hottest night in the valley. Besides, I packed a blanket."

"Are you sure there's no bats in that cave? Maybe dogs go in there and pee on the floor."

"They don't let dogs in Disney's land. No way."

"Well, we're not supposed to stay in here after dark. What'll they do with us if they catch us?"

"Maybe they'll throw us in that pirate's dungeon over in Adventureland."

He started whimpering some more. "You're always teasing me. Why don't you stop teasing me?"

"I'm sorry. I tell you what. We'll go to the island and visit Fort Mark Twain and fire the rifles and explore the caves for bats. If you want to stay, fine, and if you don't, pues, ¡qué carajo! ¡Fuímonos!"

"And if we go, do I still get to have the Order of the Golden Carp?"

"You know I can't do that. But you can always try again next year when you're a bigger boy."

Pancholín sighed again like the weight of the world and his culture was on him, but by the time we had explored each and every path on the island, each crevice and cave or mine shaft, each sharpshooter's niche and the secret tunnel out of the fort, he was singing a different tune, like I figured he would.

"This place is neat! Can we sneak up to the lookout after everybody leaves?"

"Maybe, if it seems safe."

Soon enough the bell came for the last raft to leave the island. We slipped away and hid way in the bowels of Old Jim's Cave, "quiet like mouses."

"Ya se van, ¿verdad?"

"Pues sí, gringos mensos. ¡Que aquí hay dos chicanitos escondidos de deveras!"

"Papi, ¿ya nos podemos salir?"

"Todavía no. Mira, aquí voy a tender la manta. Acuéstate un ratito. Vamos a hacer animalitos con la luz del flashlight. Ya te diré cuando podemos salir a regir la islita."

"Yo quiero ser el rey. No, mejor el principe. Que tú seas el rey."

"¡Andale pues! Pero por ahora quietito como si fueras la momia de la cueva de Drácula."

We must have been playing in the cave for at least an hour or two. It was so quiet and peaceful. We had ventured out and filled up two pillow cases I had packed with leaves and grass. We were all set. I even considered making a fire, but then thought twice about it.

"Do you want to know why I tease you a little?"

"Yeah. Why?"

"Because sometimes we play in a way that we're like brothers. You know, I had lots of brothers. And we teased each other a lot. I teased them and they teased me. There was Pancracio and Curro and Tecolote and Joselito-Joey and . . ."

"How come you don't still tease your brothers?"

"Never see them anymore. Curro's been dead 15 years now. Tecolote's designing hydraulic screws for the space project, Pancracio and Joselito still hauling scrap metal . . ."

"How come I don't have any brothers?"

"You were going to have some. Your mommy and I were planning to, but we didn't get the time."

"Why would you tease your brothers?"

"Because they teased me."

"Well, I don't tease you, but you still tease me."

"I guess so. The trouble is, once you're a teaser then you're always stuck a teaser. Es un vicio como cualquier otro. I'll try not to tease you so much."

"You'd better. Cause if not maybe I'll pull some more hair out of your head. Why'd the cops shoot your brother?"

"¡Qué sé yo! I wish I knew. Some cops don't like people who look too dark. When you're an older boy we'll have to talk about that more. Ley fuga. Or maybe cause they figured they couldn't pin a rap on him in court."

"What's a rap?"

"When they say you've done something wrong."

Then we heard a sound from outside. We heard it again, a dog barking, a little closer.

"What are we going to do?" Pancholín asked.

"Jesus, I wish I had that poison meat." I packed up our gear. "We've got to make tracks."

"Daddy! Let's go to the Tree House. We'll be way up in the tree. Nobody'll get us there."

"That's a damn good idea. Only one problem, we've got to get across this channel. Look, you wait here! I'm going to swim across and untie the raft and bring it back here."

"No way! If you're swimming out of here, I'm swimming with you."

I could see he was determined. "Look, I'll just be back in a minute. You don't want to get soaked. I'll be right back with the nice dry raft."

"No way!"

"You're going to come with me in the water?"

"Uh huh!"

"You swear to God you'll never tell Mommy!"

"I swear. I swear to God and hope to die."

The dog barked. It was too close for comfort.

"Yikes! We've got to get out of here. You grab my waist real tight. We're going to walk in the water. No heroic stuff now. Nice and easy, walking in the water. That's right, nice and easy."

Halfway across the channel, I asked him, "Feel any fish nibbling at your leg?"

"No. Do you?"

"No, but if you do, don't worry. They're friendly carp."

"Okay."

We were on the other side in a jiffy. We hid in the wooden boathouse where the customers queue up for the rafts. We peered over the rim. Two patrolmen were coming, one from each direction. We ducked down into the shadows of the hut.

"Hey, Bud," one said to the other, "you on again tonight?"

"Yeah, third night in a row Disney sticks me with the grave-yard shift. See anything exciting?"

"What's to see? Minnie Mouse's underpants? Say, Bud. What's the matter, somebody over in the central office don't like you?"

"I don't know. Maybe so."

"You better watch over your old lady, Bud. Somebody in central's got you on graveyard duty." The guard walked away, chortling all the while.

Bud stopped and lit a cigarette. He flicked the match our way and cursed Donald Duck's mother. Then he moved on.

Once they were gone we could hardly suppress our mirth, even soaked as we were.

"Can you believe that? Can you believe it!"

"What a guard, Papi! ¡Qué loco! He looks up Minnie Mouse's dress! ¡Es el más grande de todos los guajolotes!"

While Pancholín wasn't looking I planted on the ground a silver five-peso piece, un Hidalgo that I had gotten as a present when I was a kid and which had been rattling around the bottom drawer for three decades. "You know what? I think you must be the bravest kid in the valley. I've got a mind to buck you straight up to Star."

"Star! Wow! But I haven't even found a treasure."

"Gee, that's right. That's too bad. Say, what's that silvery flashing thing?"

"Look, Daddy. It's a silver coin." Pancholín grabbed for it. "It's the biggest silver coin in the world!"

"It sure looks like it. What does it say?"

"It says cinco pesos."

"Do you know what that means?"

"Yeah, five bucks."

"Yeah, but it means it's Chicano money. It's a Chicano treasure!"

"How did it get here?"

"Maybe somebody originally buried it here for good luck. Or maybe . . ." I look over to the water.

"The carp, right Daddy?"

"I don't know."

"Maybe it's the carp that shot it up here out of the water."

"I don't know. Let's go look."

We looked into the water, long and hard. There was nothing. We looked and looked. Then there was a ripple out in the channel.

"He's out there all right," Pancholín said. "The carp that looks out for Chicanos." We both shivered with that incisive sense of revelation that only young children can experience.

"Okay," I said. "We're moving out to the Swiss Family Tree House."

We crossed the lighted walkway into the unlit bosom of shrubbery, first one, then the other, like guerrillas on assignment. Carefully we made the journey to Adventureland. Then over the puny fence and up the staircased Swiss Family Tree, platform by platform and tree-room by tree-room to the topmost platform. We took off our clothes and hung them to dry. Pancholín wrapped himself in the blanket. We looked down from the treecrown on the Magic Kingdom. Main Street was all lit up and so was Cinderella's Castle. Above, starry heavens capped the sultry night and in the channel prescient carp bided the golden dawn. All was well in the valley.

"Ready to sleep?"

"Yes. I love you Daddy, all the way to the last number of counting."

We hugged and kissed and Pancho went to sleep and I sat up looking out from the tree, thinking warm thoughts about the great chain of being, especially of my father who during one period of his life raised geese to be industrial watchdogs and the way he carried on the day I got that fellowship, my mother in the background, biting her fingers, scared to death and with reason, because I'd be breaking the cycle of tirilones, pachucos and pochos, with their papiamento of street caliche and devious calques, and emerging into the alienating, mainstream Other. God knows, even she had no inkling then I would fall in love with and marry una del otro estirpe. And the walks we took in the barrio past the chicharronería ("sin pelos, ¿eh?"), past the molino de nixtamal, past El Mandamás del Barrio, a beer for my father and a nieve to sweeten my mouth. My father with his moral paradigms, the Chicano Aesop discussing the virtue of geese. "Never take for granted other persons or animals, you must always work toward them, make great effort, is like fine art, a ritual of love." He rolled up his sleeve. "You see this scar on my arm? You see that, the patrón made me go and get it stitched today because it didn't want to heal. You know Doña Jacinta, the big she-goose? She's the one I trained first, she's been with me as a watchdog now for over four years. And what a fine guardian she is. She will hiss like a siren and peck out the eyes of any stranger unless she's well leashed.

But last week I got careless. Who knows what I did, walked in this manner instead of that, failed to greet her in my usual soothing way, had on a funny hat, most of all I forgot that she had just hatched goslings who were under the wooden stairs. Before I know it, peck, peck and my arm was damn near sliced off before she recovered form and hid herself in shame. But it's my fault, I say. I tell the patrón I well deserved this moral lesson, because love is not a cheap commodity. It must be won time and over again."

As often occurs with me, moral quandries rise up from their repressed bottleneck and beset me just as I fall asleep. I remember thinking that on the one hand it was deceitful to have fixed a false mythos on Pancholín with a silver Hidalgo, on the other the fix or rather feelings were real, and as Thomas Merton had once said (I paraphrase), mysticism was nothing more than the concerted return to the childhood condition of feckless faith. Ultimately it was good, I thought or dreamt, to care or feel deeply.

"Hey, motherfucker! What do you think you are? Some kind of tree house owl?"

I woke up groggy. The sun was just over the barranca and in my eyes.

"Say, these brown boys are in their birthday suits."

"Look, gentlemen, we got lost in the cave over on the island. We heard some dog barking and we swam over here."

"Yeah, I bet. Just who the hell are you? The Frito Bandito? And while you're answering, stick out your hands for these cuffs."

"I won't do that."

"What do you mean, Pancho? You won't do WHAT?"

"Take it easy, fella. I'm going to put on my clothes now, nice and easy. Then I'm gonna go with you just where you say. Don't get my son riled up."

"¡No te dejes, papi! ¡No te dejes!"

"You're gonna do what I tell you, boy, and that means these sturdy cuffs!" The guard raised his stick menacingly.

"¡No te dejes, papi! ¡No te dejes!"

The other guard looked through my pants and my watery wallet. "Say, Bubba, take it easy on this sumbitch. He's some kind of perfesser. We'd better get the P.R. man."

"¡No te dejes, papi! ¡No te dejes! ¡No te dejes! ¡No te dejes! ¡No te dejes! ¡No te dejes!"

"That was some fool thing to do!"

"Oh yes, I'll grant you that. But it did have its culminating moments."

"I bet, Mr. Macho. I know, you used to own a bike. What's the matter with you, anyway? You going through a premature climacteric? You getting hot flashes?"

"Maybe so. I'm quijotesque. You're never going to believe this, but it was my hispano way of expressing my great love for you and our son."

"How flattering. Getting booked for trespassing and indecent exposure just for us. Next time spare us the flaco favor."

"Kid Mocha, he was magnificent, you know that? I'm thinking of bucking him straight up to Star in the Grand Order of the Golden Carps."

"Swell! That's great. On his police record let it read that he proceeded straight to Star in the Golden Carps!"

"You're not going to believe this, but you know what started it? His toy, se le rompió. Gabo's deluxe, all Star Wars shiny with fourteen blinking lights and seven discrete functions. And a grand total of six D-size alkaline power cells just to run. What to do? What to do?"

"What in God's creation are you talking about?"

"I'm talking about the unconditionally secure toy." (The ultimate toy, with a self-replenishing warranty. Poor shook up child, all your toys seem to give prematurely.) "Stuck with a bad daddy, and not enough of him at that. Reminds me of Woody's old joke about how bad the food is and besides there's not enough of it. Linda, please don't go to the judge."

"I won't do that. I won't go to the judge."

"Bless you. I'll be good from now on. So help me God, I'll be good."

"Yeah, I bet you will."

"I will, I will! Swear to God and hope to die. From now on I'm the faithful Mexican. Wait and see. Is it serious?"

"What?"

"You and the tattooed man."

"About the same."

"With you everything is always, about the same."

"That's right. I haven't gotten to your point of hot flashes yet. What is Disney going to do?"

"Disney's not half bad. Anybody who could do a Bambi can't be all that bad."

"Are they going to prosecute you?"

"I don't think so. I think we'll sit down together and sign some sort of Consent Decree. Otherwise it would be poor press to go after me, don't you think? 'Weirdo professor and son booked for spending night in Disney Tree House?' I don't think they would want that kind of attention. God knows, on that basis tomorrow night they could have a hundred stowaways. There'd be people sneaking down the plastic hippo's mouth."

"I hope you're right. Supposing they do prosecute? What'll the University do to you?"

"To me? They'd probably make me a Dean. It would be an affirmative action. The University's so dizzy, who could tell? A Disneyland of the mind, to paraphrase a poem I know. Who could tell, with a little student rallying I could end up . . . God knows, look what happened to Hayakawa."

"Yeah, I've heard it. You used to own a bike, and now you're the senior carp in the river. Some success story. Somehow your circumstances and Hayakawa's don't seem quite comparable to me. Non Sequitor, Huitlacoche."

"Well, then, what about tenure? I've got tenure."

"Does it cover moral turpitude?"

"A little flashing in a tree house? There's a moral here for sure, but it ain't turpitude. Look, I'm trying to figure out what I did and why I did it. Get a researcher's handle on it, if you know what I mean. I had fallen low on the loving list. Low on the ratings. This is California. Everyone's for a guy on the comeback trail. All I wanted to do was place a little higher. To rise a bit in esteem. Perhaps to be loved all the way to the last number of counting. That's all it was. It was an affirmative action."

A Chicano FBI Searching for Carmen Loca in ¡Sal Si Puedes!

for Robert Coles

Deputy Ernesto, who in fact preferred Don Ernesto, had escorted the Chicano FBI agent and the sheriff to their car and now he was returning to her house on the fringe of the grove.

With each plodding step the deputy took, Natividad's anger took firmer hold. Once so repressed, her anger now often punctured her veil and stood beside her like a soul sister. This frightened her. It was *her* anger, Natividad supposed, yet it felt like a sister with her own voice. This scared her because la rabia was not a controllable woman, and the key to survival in Mercedes, Texas, was control and restraint.

Natividad's anger mostly focused on go-betweens. There were so many in Mercedes and they were so necessary: brokers, coyotes, alcahuetes, pleaders, panderers, lenders, court jesters, brown crew chiefs who worked for white foremen, all the possible bridges between the mundo raza and the alien, Anglo nation. Her anger focused on those who greased the skids of this cross-cultural world, who made intercourse possible. If only these middle enchufados were cut out, her raza could live completely within themselves like a tribe of happy Kickapoos.

Natividad knew that out there hiding in the orange grove Dominguito was surely spying on them with shame and ire. Ernesto wasn't a bad soul as far as alcahuetes go. Except terribly chatty, parlanchín, querulous, and over the years and the babies and the desengaños Natividad had come to treasure silence as bliss. Ernesto was the brown deputy of a repulsive Anglo sheriff who was so stereotypically redneck he could have emerged from a bad movie. But that's the way it was in the Valley. The sheriffs got their cues from drive-in Westerns. It used to be worse. Ten years ago an Anglo sheriff would have had no use for a brown deputy.

"¡Ay, la Nattie! ¡La Nattie!"

The mother said nothing. Her face was quite impassive, as if she were confronting an Anglo.

Ernesto glanced around, or rather sniffed, as if he were a cartoon dog taking "a bite" out of crime. He felt vaguely disquieted, although he couldn't quite put his finger on why. In the room there was a television, two chairs, and three beds where some of the children slept. The floor was gray concrete and there was a small Mexican throw rug in the middle. In one corner of the room was the little sanctuary with icons of Christ the King, the Virgin of Guadalupe, and el Niño Santo de Atocha. The girls had hung their dolls there too, on hooks. The dwelling was so typical in its spare furnishings, nevertheless it was extraordinary. It was, he suddenly realized, its spotlessness. It was clean beyond all expectation in this little dust bowl on the border. And in that cleanliness Ernesto sensed the defiance and the ire of the mother.

Still she looked at him inflexibly.

He repeated himself. "¡Ay, la Nattie! ¡La Nattie! I wonder what that FBI really wanted? We hardly ever get FBI down here and even then only for drug-related matters." He assumed a confidential tone. "You know, Nattie, I don't think I've ever spoken with a Chicano FBI before. You know, the FBI's going to A&I now. He told me he just stopped here to talk to us, to you, that is, on his way to A&I. Says he's got to protect some Chicano professor who's going to give a fiery speech. The professor is going to say we gotta protect Spanish. Imagine what this state's coming to? Even got to protect Spanish! Are you sure you can't help him?"

"How can I help you?"

"Always so polite, la Nattie." Ernesto sighed. This was a wheedler's stock in trade, Natividad knew. They sighed, they snorted, they laughed or winked, they patted a man's back. All to say, "It's okay. I'm one of you. Soy raza. So now tell me what I want to know and what you want to keep a sacred secret."

Ernesto wiped his nose as if there were dust, although that was quite impossible in Natividad's kitchen sanctuary. "Well, to tell you the truth, I'm back because I'm not sure it's all been said. Pues, I'm back because the sheriff told me to come back. Told me to be sure that's it, if the truth be told. I want to be square with you, just need to do my job."

"Do you want some naranjada?" The routine was so set she could do it in her sleep, maybe in her grave, the devoted mother. Yet, standing beside her was la encabronada, la rabiosa unspeakably incensed, barely under wraps, a dog that is muzzled but straining hard.

The deputy grinned, openly relieved, grateful for la apertura. "For sure! My God, it's gotten hot here in April. Besides, yours is the best orangeade in the county. I always go straight for it at the church bazaar." He thought to reward the mother for her cooperation, or more accurately, to pay dues, which was correct procedure for an agent provocateur. "You know what the FBI said? He said, 'When you see la madre again, tell her I'm sorry I came and disturbed her. Tell her, it's okay. I won't come and disturb her again.' "

"Instead you came."

"Yeah, I guess, Nattie. He's an important guy. And raza too. It's nice to see raza all dressed up, an agent of the federal government, ¿que no?"

She poured naranjada from a Mexican jug that was painted with bright orange blossoms. She pushed it to him. "Para servirle."

"You know, Nattie. You told him nothing. Nothing at all."

"I don't know anything."

"Is that so, haven't heard from her in three years? That's not like Carmen. She was a nice girl, brought up real nice, like all your children. All the others have turned out real nice. And she, she didn't have such a big problem did she? Maybe a little shoplifting. A little something here and there. You know, some youngsters, they get defiant for a while; then maybe they settle down."

With those words, uttered unselfconsciously by the deputy who only meant to put her at ease, poising himself to pry some information from her, Natividad turned ashen, her step faltered.

"If I knew something, I would have told him."

"Why so?"

"Because she did something grave."

"Yeah, I guess she did. What was it?"

Natividad didn't respond.

"Really, Nattie. They didn't even tell me what she did. Not even in a ballpark sense. But you know, don't you?"

"Less than you."

"Was it border stuff? Drugs? Or was it . . . political?" Still she didn't answer. Ernesto sighed. Then he overstayed. He drank too much orangeade, chattering easily, incessantly, his words like grain filling out a silo, sort of amiably nudging, here, there, and back again. Then he had to use the bathroom. Even as he asked very solemnly and was accorded this privilege, it angered Natividad to the core. The brown deputy in her bathroom, surely poking into their medicine cabinet, prowling and sniffing like a galgo. Finally he came out.

"Did you need an aspirin?"

The deputy smiled sheepishly. "Not really."

"Next time you need one, tell me and I'll get it. I know where they are."

"I'm going now, Nattie. Please let me know if Carmen comes around or makes any contact at all. Also, I'll probably be back."

The mother nodded docilely and la rabiosa, hidden by her side, bared her teeth.

Once he was out of sight, she took her broom and began to sweep vigorously, removing the dust of the intruders. Her first calculations turned to el jefe. She flirted with not telling him. But that wasn't right. Also, Ernesto would come to him soon enough, probing, sniffing like a galgo detective. She feared the father's foreseeable anger at this unexpected violation, the shame of the inquiry. She identified with these feelings, too. They both would feel so pleased if they could be utterly at peace in a world of their own.

Sí pues, all this was foreseeable. Natividad's daughter, la Pili, now ten was turning the way Carmen had turned. At ten, eleven, the mother had realized Carmen's indomitable spirit. So dangerous, so noble, she identified with it often, to her great chagrin she probably fostered it, because in fact the mother was becoming angry too by then. Angry and weary and thinking thoughts or spinning presences out of herself and seeing in the little girl an indomitably defiant portrait.

"Why are you so angry? ¿Qué? ¿Qué?"

"She insulted me, Mother. My own name!"

"Your name! ¡Por Dios!"

"She said I'm just like a little puta in an opera. That I'm loca and flirting with all the boys. She said I'm named after that girl, Carmen, who is loca y puta and walks around with a thorny rose in her mouth!"

"¿Qué loca? You're named after Carmen, Texas. The little town on the Río Bravo. Carmen, Elsa, Donna, Mercedes, Santa Rosa, Santa María . . . these towns are all here in our county, all towns named for women y santas, and your grandmother ¡que Dios la bendigue! was also named for that little town of Carmen where she lived all her life. And your grandfather who lived his whole life not once wearing shoes so that pebbles were embedded in his very soles."

"I'm not going back!"

"You must. She's the only teacher in the fifth grade."

"Well, I'm not!"

"Of course you are. What does she know of our world? Or even Carmen, Texas. She's Anglo, gabacha."

"That's right! Gabacha! That's why I'm not going. She wants to hurt me!"

Carmen glared. She was seething, even at ten, eleven. Natividad had heard of wild cacicas who rode with Villa, Carranza, the revolutionaries. Not rieleras, but cacicas with double cartucheras crisscrossing them.

"No," Natividad said with all her maternal authority. "This is what you must do. Show them nothing. The Anglos can call you what they want, but if you give them nothing, they cannot enter your soul. They own nothing. ¡Nada! ¡Mierda!"

"No!" she said defiantly. "I fight for myself!" And then the little girl—after all she was just a little girl—broke down and wept tears of self-pity and pura rabia. Natividad had gained anger, or perhaps the legitimation of anger—for anger has its own natural wellsprings—in those days with the prepubertal Carmen. Give them the Indian visage, the impassiveness of Cuitláhuac or the decorous Hispanic solemnity.

Natividad felt dry and she tasted the orangeade and with a shudder she relived that prepubertal halcyon of her daughter when at the same time she would remonstrate with la Carmen and foster her defiance. Natividad dreamed too of las cacicas—the ones she had heard tales of, how they fought the revolution, and thought to herself that probably the only time las cacicas would have given their foes the indecipherable Indian visage was when they had them up against the paredón.

Later la Carmen turned to sex, pop music, petty thievery, and all manners of gabachería. She was the alien, gone to the other world. That formidable, repulsive world Natividad refused and yearned only for the power to turn back on itself, renegar. A mother of nine children now, she saw each one forming in her womb, emerging, and growing to strong definition. The mother loses one to la vida mala. Está bien, pues. The others, most of the others are turning out right. A mother still loves the lost one, surely. There is no understanding, merely a glimmer of recognition. A mother is left with the scourge and the exemplum. There is this formidable dread, a sense that she may have sinned grievously by contaging anger within her onto her daughter.

El jefe was inside her, cutting and slashing like a Nicaraguan jungle fighter—contra or sandinista, da igual. When he was fired up with shame he made splendid sex. That was the way it was with the machitos in the Valley who had to soportar un sin fin de humillaciones y vergüenzas, ¿que no?

La madre lay with el padre often. Men were like that, urgent, and she obliged without coaxing and out of respect for God's wishes and what is natural. In truth, she liked the sexual episode, particularly when she could lie passively, her mind tickled by her body and in a flight both fantastical and philosophical. Natividad felt that in the sexual episode there was entry into the visionary riddles that unmask their days in this world. But for men sex had a different value, a more violent one, surely. For the state of consciousness for which she used sex as port of entry, they required alcohol or drugs, and that could only debase the experience.

La madre once confided her philosophy of the sexual episode to a man. It was the one and only time, to the priest during confession. She also admitted to her exhaustion at the end of the day—at that time there were six children, a seventh on the way. The father had scolded her for her self-pity, a kind of pride he had told her, the sin of sins.

She had fought back. She had defended her right to complain about her own life. She even wondered out loud how the priest would be able to manage her daily cooking and washing and ministering to the children.

The father had become agitado and she was contrite, trying to make it less grave. He was determined that she would never again challenge his authority. "Don't you know you are speaking to God? I am merely the intermediary between you and Him!"

"I am sorry, padre."

"Why do you keep becoming pregnant if you feel children to be such a burden? God sends us souls and He places them in the bodies of infants who eventually are born. But to *seek* children; that is lust and pride as if with each child you had evidence of God's good graces. It may be that a family with one or two children has been graced by Him as much as a family of eight, nine, or ten children. If a woman is weighed down too much by her children and this causes her to become rude and insolent in a church, when speaking to a padre, perhaps she ought to examine herself very carefully."

Then after a considerable silence, the father had said, "Is it that you and your husband enjoy sex too much?"

"I don't understand, Father. We do what is natural out of respect for God's wishes."

"Sex is only a mere prelude to conception, birth, the presence of a child, who has to be nourished, both physically and spiritually."

"I know, Father."

"Well, don't forget. Recall that you are the vessel, an instrument of God's miracle of creation."

"Yes, Father."

"And before I absolve you, I want to turn again to your arrogance. Don't you know that in your protests and your quarrel and defiance of me that you have defiled confession?"

He waited for her to respond, but she wouldn't. The silent moments passed painfully. She wouldn't respond or let him enter her soul. Maybe if the father had been raza, but he wasn't. She gave him the impassive visage.

El jefe had come to the moment of the curses and weird sayings. It was a sort of losing of control, a prelude to the eye-tippling totality of orgasm. Especially when he was fired up by anger and humiliation, he would talk strangely of violence and revenge to unnamed or barely referred to entities.

"Take it," he muttered under his shortening gasps.

"Ahora, la muerte. The blood. Blood . . . el perro."

Her body tingling pleasantly, her eyes tightly closed, la madre was in her mundo, far away from her husband and his perros y muerte. Thinking of God. Not really thinking of Him but reveling in her insight that she thinks of God often, talks with Him often. Natividad believes Him to be with her. But she knows that she has no right to expect more of Him than any others do. We all make mistakes and He has to judge us. That will happen in the very distant future. Not in anyone's lifetime. The mother is certain that in a thousand years we will be no closer to that future judgment. She told the father that one day and he laughed. "You are wading in the priest's river." The father said that God only knows when. "It could be tomorrow or after the millennia when the fiery stars have been reduced to embers."

"I'm sure it wouldn't be tomorrow, padre. The only thing certain tomorrow will bring is washing. More clothes to scrub and put out for the gulf wind to dry."

The father had looked annoyed. Then he broke into a laugh.

Natividad knew that Ernesto had noticed. In cleanliness there is defiance. Her house the cleanest, her sheets the whitest, just as her naranjada was the sweetest and thickest. We are poor, she thought, but we take good care of ourselves—the best we know how and can afford. She may have gone to school for just a few years but her parents taught her to be gente decente and respectful of God. Can many of the Anglo landowners say as much for themselves?

Father was having it. His panting was shorter and shorter. Natividad was redoing the vivid dream she had some days ago; the one she had confided to Pili yesterday. She was dead and her shadow had fled her body. Suddenly she laughed in the middle of the dream. She realized that she was not dead but merely dressed in her bed sheets, like those on the clothesline that the hot wind from the gulf had been whipping up that morning. She woke up and told el jefe but he waved her aside, "Don't make more trouble for yourself, we already have enough." She didn't want to confide in the priest, so she told Pili, as she might have told Carmen at that age. She opened her heart to Pili and Pili to her. Pili asked if she was anywhere in the dream. No, not to her memory. Pili was disappointed, as Carmen would have been. The little girls wanted to be in the dream too. The girl told her that God was probably whispering to her when she was asleep. He was telling her that if she did a good job every day, she'd be all right. La madre wasn't sure she understood what the daughter was telling her. She is no longer a child, the mother knew. Now suddenly in the midst of el jefe she thought she understood. The girl had said—was it Pili or was it Carmen?—en eso da igual, "I hope the sheet you were wearing was clean. Not a single spot on it." Cleanliness that purified anger, anger turned to productive work—toward God—to cleanliness, she thought. Her little girl had revealed her own mind to her, she thought, just about the time that father concluded his travels, lost all control, all sense of time or space, or even of his eyes which would be rolling back into their sockets. Soon they would both be sound asleep under the blessed sheets for the rest of the night, in their own world with their ancestors, their children, and their kind.

Dominguito waited for the Anglo foreman to come with his truck and take him to the fields. It was Saturday and he worked all day. Domingo was thinking about la Carmen who had made so much humiliation for the family. He had been hiding in the grove—donde las toronjas—straining to hear what the Chicano FBI and the sheriff were saying. He thought he heard them say Carmen was very bad, but maybe he had invented the words out of their muttering.

Domingo remembered his older sister as a wild one. "Es una exaltada," the priest had said shortly before she had brazenly gotten into trouble. A group of girls—of exaltadas—had stolen an Anglo boy's car, driven it wildly, run over a pig, and in the futile swerving run into an irrigation ditch and ruined the car. Carmen had gotten into trouble and became all the more defiant as a result. Domingo was too young to be at the hearing, but what she had said to las autoridades was lore among the children. They said she was a punk, a rebel. Look at her hair, her clothes. No, she said, she was not a punk, at least not an Anglo punk, and not a Brit. Her people were Aztecs, she said, with studied pride. She had merely added a little color to her pre-Columbiana.

Now these autoridades had come and defiled their home, made shameful inquiries. Domingo had spied on them, confused and angry at the violations of his home. The strange Chicano FBI from a different county, the white sheriff, and the Chicano deputy who served as go-between.

Domingo had a cousin who now lived in Detroit. Come to Detroit, his cousin had written him one Christmas on a lovely card. "Every Chicano must make a pilgrimage to Detroit once in his life. It is where the Chevy is manufactured." The cousin was always saying things of this sort. Not unlike Carmen in that way, Domingo thought. His cousin had once said that they needed an Emiliano Zapata here in the Valley. Domingo's father had gotten upset and said the United States can beat anyone. Maybe the cousin was right when he said that the weak can beat the strong if the weak are right and the strong are wrong, but he was helpless when the autoridades came to get him. His cousin and his friends, they liked to get together and say that if you knew what was wrong, you were on the right road, and you'd be better off pretty soon. But that's not what happened. The sheriff just came and told his cousin he had to go to jail. He never even had a trial. They told him they'd already tried him and he'd been found guilty. Then, when they let him out of jail, he left for Detroit. Left for good. Domingo didn't want to leave. He wanted to be with his family.

Domingo didn't think raza would get far in Texas. He didn't think raza would get far anywhere in this backward county that a lot of raza had named ¡Sal Si Puedes! This is an Anglo county, even though most of the people in it are Mexican. You have to be an Anglo to be President. He had hoped Jesse Jackson would win someday. A lot of people in the Valley had supported him and worked hard for him, but Anglos ran everything. Maybe if the Mexican government had the atom bomb, then maybe the Anglos would be more careful about what they said and did. Domingo's teacher said that he and his friends were not "natural students." He wanted to raise his hand. He wanted to ask her what she meant. He wanted to walk out. But then he would be in trouble. His father would punish him; his mother would be upset. The priest would tell him not to defy his betters. That's what happened with Carmen and teachers. They said she flirted, like a so-called Carmen in the theater or the movies. They had made fun of her, these teachers, even her name. And then eventually his sister was gone. They hadn't heard from her for three years.

The Anglo foreman talked about his name, too. The foreman had him doing errands. It was a promotion from the fields, a position of responsibility. Sometimes he called him "kid" and sometimes he called him by his name. He once told him that he liked the name, Domingo. That because it meant Sunday, it was halfway toward being in a state of grace, but that he wouldn't give one of his sons a name like that because people would get the wrong impression. They'd think his son was a Mexican. The foreman was always claiming that he had a tough job, "keeping the Mexicans in line." But then he would look at Domingo and tell him that he was different because he did what he told him to do right away.

The Anglo liked to talk bad about Mexicans. He'd told Domingo the same caca ten times, that Mexicans aren't smart and so we do the harvesting. But he claimed Domingo was better than most Mexican kids. His father was better too, who after twenty years had risen from a farmhand to driving a pickup for the growers.

The foreman's truck barreled down the road and turned in, deliberately creating a cloud of dust. The foreman honked the horn repeatedly, even though Domingo was leaning against the ancient fig tree right in front of the house. Then, just in case anyone had any doubts, the foreman gunned the motor several times. The boy moved on the double to the truck and got into the cabin. As soon as he got in they were off, the red light that the growers installed on the truck's crown churning round and round.

The foreman eyed Domingo severely. "Your family's got troubles?"

Domingo wasn't sure if the foreman was asking him a question or if he was going to give him bad news.

"Well?"

"Yes, sir."

"It's that punker sister of yours who went off?"

"Yes."

"What she do? Roll some big shot?"

"Nobody knows. I don't think she did anything too bad. The sheriff was here with the FBI and they wanted to find her. But they said it was okay."

"Yeah, I bet. They say he's a big shot FBI, which is like a contradiction for a Mexican as far as I'm concerned. Big shot Mexican FBI!" He snorted. "What do the newspapers call that? An oxymoron? So what did he say?"

"Nothing."

"Nothing? Came all the way to your little hovel!"

"He didn't say much."

"That's not what I heard."

"What did you hear, sir?"

"That he's a big fucking Commie. That right in your little house over there on the edge of our orange grove he preached some Commie bullshit propaganda. Some shit straight out of Karl Marx's Commie Red Book. And now he's gone to A&I to protect another Chicano Commie who's going to give a speech and tell us how to live here on our own land. Mouth frothing up like a mad dog. Can you imagine that, out to rile all the Mexicans and turn them against the English language and the Christian faith! And our government goes and gives him a badge!"

Domingo said nothing. Inside he was smiling but also his heart began to pound. He was thinking of a Hollywood movie where a black came into a bar full of rednecks and said, "I'm your worst nightmare! A nigger with a badge!" But he was also thinking of one day when he had seen the foreman become enraged at some Mexican farmhands. He had worked himself up more and more. Suddenly, it was as if Domingo were no longer trusted and was one of them too, one of the farmhands. Finally, the foreman had taken out his revolver and shot in the air. He cursed and raved and shot once in the air, his bullet punctuating his words. This is it, Domingo had thought. He was going to die at the side of the grove and fall into the ditch. His blood was going to ooze out of him and spill into the ditch. He had cast a sidelong eye at the others. They were looking down at the ground impassively, giving the Indian visage. Eventually the squall had blown over.

The foreman drove off the road and onto the shoulder. He came up to a telephone pole. On the pole was stapled a poster:

Movimiento Estudiantil Chicanos de Aztlán

Texas A&I

Prof. Estevan Galarza

Speaking on the Bilingual/Bicultural Reality of the Southwest

And the Need to Defend Non-English Language Rights
in the United States

Beneath the title was a drawing. One figure looked suspiciously like John Wayne, the other like Emiliano Zapata. They were smiling and shaking hands and their free hands were around each other's shoulders. Gingerly, the foreman unclasped the poster and studied it intently for a while. Finally he said, "Unbelievable, the Commies are all over the U.S. even after they've almost kicked them out of Russia," and he put the poster behind the seat in the truck cabin. It looked like the foreman was going to study it a little more, maybe save it for whatever reason.

The foreman went back to his truck. He took out the flask of Jack that he kept in the truck and got back into the driver's seat. He took a long shot. He gave the bottle to the boy. The boy wiped the mouth of the bottle with his shirt and the foreman laughed. "Shit, I ain't got AIDS. Or is it white you don't like?"

The boy took a long one. It burned good. He knew that the foreman was going to gossip now. The foreman liked to tell him about his family in excruciating detail. He liked to talk about the grower too and his family. He liked to talk mostly about sex and family politics.

Sometimes about the sheriff, the growers, and the Mexicans and external politics.

Domingo found it quite extraordinary for a mere boy like him, a small and undernourished, quiet, poor, badly educated Mexican, to be privy to information, gossip, stories, and secrets. It also amused him. He thought of his grandmother who used to say that mice bother no one, and so let them enjoy their crumbs. When the foreman would tell the boy every secret he had, he would always say that it was only Domingo he could trust, because the boy didn't make any difference. Just another Mexican kid. Domingo duly nodded his head.

"I guess it comes in waves," the foreman said. "I got a temper too, you know?"

The boy nodded quietly.

"Damn bitch. She's run away again." The foreman was talking about his daughter. His daughter had run away and she came back without a husband, but she had a baby. Then she had run away again and left the baby with the foreman and his wife, and then she came home again with another baby. "Oh, she'll be back," he said. "For the gravy train. That's for sure, sure as the goddamned gulf wind. And you know what?"

Domingo certainly knew what, but he wasn't going to say.

The foreman looked at him, took another swig, and gave the bottle to the boy. "Exactly! Another baby. I told my wife to get ready 'cause any day now . . . she'll be back with a third. Pigs. The three pigs, that's what they are. Better give me back the bottle." The foreman took the bottle and drank. "One day I'm going to go out and find the three pigs that made my daughter have three babies. I reckon one day I'm going to go out and find them. And I'm gonna get 'em!"

"That's good," Domingo said.

The foreman looked surprised. He hadn't expected any commentary from the boy. "Are you high?" he said.

"Maybe."

The foreman laughed. "High on Jack! We're gonna get 'em. Harvest a little hairy kiwi fruit here in the Valley. Right?"

"Right! Bring 'em to market!"

The foreman slapped his knee. "Six kiwi in a box, like the Fruit of the Month Club! That's good. Yes, it is, my god. Nothing keeps me going better than thirsting for revenge. Isn't it?"

"Yes, sir. Nothing better."

"A Chicano FBI. Shit, that makes me want to puke!"

Now it was time to work. The foreman wanted Domingo to count the baskets the men had filled. He wanted to go over to the field north of Elcouch and remind some of the men that they were slow and that the foreman wouldn't give them too many chances. Domingo hated going up to the men—grown men and family men too—and telling them that. He didn't want them to blame him. Usually they would look over his head to the truck and curse the foreman. Domingo would too, but he would tell them to smile while they were cursing because the foreman might be looking and might catch on. A few weeks ago, he was talking with a crew of the men and they said he was beginning to look and sound like the foreman. They said he was an Anglo in sheep's clothing. Tears had come to Domingo's eyes. One of them felt sorry for Domingo and patted him on the back and told him not to take them so seriously. The foreman had his back to them and he was shouting at one of the farmhands. He always had reasons to shout. Domingo had thought to himself that they could rush him. They could tackle the foreman and throw him into the irrigation ditch and if he came up for air they could push him down, all of them so that no one would know what happened to him, not even the sheriff. He'd stay down, maybe. Domingo reckoned he'd stay down for sure if they filled his pockets with heavy stones.

The foreman drank hard all day. They tore around the fields and he let out tirades and every time they got back into the truck, he took the opportunity to go for his Jack. Domingo wondered what it was. The big shot raza Communist professor? Or the big shot Chicano Communist FBI? The two pigs (maybe three by now) who had entered his daughter and established a lusty, lasting presence? Or maybe the grower had dressed him down. Could be anything. Anglos were hard to figure out.

It was dark when they headed back. Finally the foreman seemed relaxed. He had already finished one flask of Jack Daniels. He had the second in his free hand as he tore comfortably down the country road, his red light churning on the crown of his truck.

"No wonder that scum-sucking Commie comes down here to recruit us and turn us against our God and country. We're all Mexican here."

Now Domingo knew the deepest secret. It was the grower about whom the foreman often complained bitterly for the humiliations he received by his autocratic hand.

"I'm just a Mexican to these scum-sucking growers. A white nigger!"

He snorted. "Just as you guys are brown-skinned niggers. We're all niggers. Might as well join up with Jesse Jackson for all the respect I get. He gets all the money, I make shit for the work I do. You see his jet plane? Fuck! A jet plane he's got comes roaring out of the fields and groves.

"I asked him for a raise yesterday. You know what he told me? Oh, you're worth it, for sure. You're real important to me. Essential. But I can't do it. The other growers would be all over me, skin me alive. There'd be no end.

"Can you imagine that? The crap he told me! It is crap and the same that I tell your people when they come asking. Isn't it?"

Domingo nodded.

"Shit, fucking A. A white, orange-sucking spic, that's what he's got here for sure. Poor white trash."

The foreman began to calm down. "I'm tired," he said. "Twenty years at this, just about as long as your dad. I think we come on about the same year, him as a farmhand, me as a foreman. Hell, he's advancing faster than me! When you're a white nigger, you're on top of the brown but below the real bosses. You're just in between and you've got to dance on your toes all the time. If you smile in front of Mex, they'll think you're a pushover for sure. Then the boss comes and rants, you've been too easy on the Mexicans, you're letting up, losing respect. Shit, then he goes back in his air-conditioned mansion and serves himself up a mint julep. There's no way out of this. It sure sucks. Only in America!"

The truck came to a lurching halt. He was home. "Get the shit out, kid. You make sure you keep your mouth shut." He winked expansively. "Like you always do."

"I'm going to forget it, like always. That way I can't remember it." It was a sort of ritual, an incantation that Domingo repeated one way or another time and time again to put the foreman at ease.

The foreman squeezed his shoulder. "You're the best of them. So's your dad. He's a good Mexican, hard working, responsible, brought you all up good, except for that punker girl. She was bad seed. Hell, eight out of nine, that's pretty good. Someday you'll make crew leader, report directly to the foreman. You'd do a good job. Everybody needs a leader, don't they?"

He waited and stared at Domingo until the boy knew he had to agree.

"That's right. Everyone needs a leader."

"See you tomorrow, same time. Tomorrow's your day, ain't it, Domingo?" The foreman laughed at his bilingual pun. The truck tore down the dirt and lurched heavily onto the road.

Domingo thought deeply as he walked to the house. He thought that the foreman wanted to teach him things, wanted to more than his own teachers. The point is to balance his hatred toward the foreman and his compassion, Domingo thought. He's a bad man, but once you know him you feel sorry for him because of his troubles. Once the foreman told him that his wife would fall asleep right in the middle of his sentence. She would just lower her head and he'd have to pinch her to wake up. He thought of getting a cattle prod and bringing it home. He changed his mind. He thought of using it on some of the men and women in the fields. But then he might get into trouble because nosy people from the outside sometimes come around and look for trouble.

"Have you ever said anything bad about me?"

"No."

"Never?"

"I don't know anything bad about you."

"I don't believe you, you lying chicken-hearted greaser."

Domingo had just looked ahead, his heart pounding.

"Shit! I know I'm no good." Tears were in the foreman's eyes. He looked like he wanted to whip himself, to scourge. He started calling himself all the bad names, many of the ones that the farmhands called him.

Domingo was surprised at how well the foreman knew himself, the bad side.

Every night when he got home from the fields, Domingo reported to his father. This night he could tell his father was also preoccupied with what had happened the day before. "Did the foreman interrogate you?"

"Yes, but I told him I knew nothing."

"Good. He accepted that?"

"Yes. He was upset about the professor coming to the Valley and stirring up la raza. He says the Chicano professor is a Communist."

Father smiled. "You wash up and do your things right away. Tonight we'll watch the late news on television and see what happened at the university at Kingsville with the Chicano professor."

Domingo felt pleased, honored at the prospect of sharing the program with his father. He turned to wash but his father spoke again. "Did the foreman say anything about the Chicano FBI?"

"He said he was a Communist and he was protecting the professor who was a Communist and he said that the professor was going to foam like a rabid dog and say things that come out of Karl Marx's Red Book."

"Está bien. The FBI, the sheriff, and the deputy, Ernesto, talked with me today. They interrogated me for a long time. Then the FBI said that the professor told him that, 'We live in a new and different time; the old has died and the new is not yet able to be born.' I told him I don't know anything about that. I don't know anything about Communism. Perhaps he should ask the priest."

Domingo stood by respectfully.

"Have they taught you anything about this in school?"

"No, only that we have to fight the godless Communists in Nicaragua who want to destroy all church and religion."

"What do you think he meant?"

For some reason, the three pigs came to Domingo's mind, the ones who had come and gone and left babies, or were almost about to come and leave babies. "Maybe it's about babies, maybe the professor's wife was to have a baby, but lost it. Or maybe it's that a new kind of baby can be born. You know, with better science."

El jefe weighed the thought. "It could be that," he said. "It could be something else."

The television coverage of the speech and the political rally was very short, but it affected Domingo measurably. Watching it with his father, everything assumed new gravity and resonance. They were not permitted to actually hear the Communist Chicano professor, but they could see that he gave a speech before a filled auditorium. The voice-over explained that he talked about "the rights of Spanish and the Hispanics" in America. What most impressed Domingo was the enormous rally of students, workers, and farmhands that the news covered and the bold placards and slogans that the people carried. His eyes scanned them with pleasure.

Down with U.S. English!

Respect the Treaty of Guadalupe Hidalgo!

¡Ya Basta!

¡Viva la huelga!

You can't scare us, we're joining the union.

It's outrageous to work for slave wages.

I'm bilingual, bicultural, and by myself.

¡Muera Noriega, Viva Sandino!

Sanctuary for Political Refugees!

A spokesman from the Jesse Jackson organization was interviewed and he thanked the people of the Valley for their work and support of the rainbow coalition. "Keep hope alive," he said, and then in Spanish, "¡Sí se puede . . . en Texas! We'll be for you in 1992!"

The camera turned to some Mechistas. They were boisterous, singing "De Colores." It was so unusual to see boisterous Chicanos in the Valley on television.

"Look at them," his father said, admiringly. "Parecen tan . . . robustos."

When the news was over, Domingo and his father had a conversation unlike any they had ever had before. Domingo realized that it was the combination of events, the humiliation at home, the outpouring at the university, that led to such release: una sacudida de conciencia.

Domingo suggested that if all of the mexicanos in Texas were to stand and unite to express their readiness to die rather than to submit to indignities and bad pay and bad conditions, then the Anglos would stop and be forced to cave in.

Yes, his father agreed, that would be so, but it could not happen. Even if we're stronger than the growers and their foremen and their sheriffs, even if we could outshoot them or wrestle them to the ground, then thousands of others would come, the Texas Rangers— los pinches rinches—and the United States Army and the Air Force. We'd be helpless. Suppose the sheriff was desaparecido; they'd send in a replacement and if he disappeared, they'd move in with soldiers and maybe tanks and helicopters. If we kept fighting, before long we would end up in jail, and not here in the county, but al norte where the Anglos were not few but way outnumbered us.

But if the government did this it would be like declaring war on its own people. Surely Mexico would stand up to the Anglos and help us. All Latin America.

Anglos are tough. We can't win against the Anglos; they have jet planes and atom bombs. If Mexico thought to fight on our side, the United States Air Force would quickly take care of Mexico. Besides, here it's bad, but the Anglos, as bad as they are, have built up the Valley so that there is work for us. The people who live in the villages across the Río Bravo are worse off than us. No work and no one cares if you starve.

But what about the revolution? The teachers are always talking about the American Revolution. They say that the English were bad and that finally the people in Boston and Philadelphia and places like that decided to fight, even if they didn't have an army. And most of the people were against the English and they won. Hadn't Domingo's cousin said if the raza decided basta, no more gabachos treating us like dogs, we could beat them? The foreman says that the Anglos need us more than they ever let on. He's an Anglo and he knows the growers because he's always around them and he hears what they say. When the foreman has drunk too much he spills out what he has heard when the growers drink too much!

Well, there was a revolution once in Mexico and now the government is a little better. It's true that the people that are on top don't always stay on top. And it's happened in Cuba and in Nicaragua and maybe in El Salvador. But then those were Communists who are against God—and who knows, are things better in those places for the poor? Probably not. The Mexican government of today is better than the old government, but it's not so good if you're poor. Mexico is going badly. Mucha droga, mucha corrupción. Maybe there's going to be another revolution in Mexico. It's more likely in Mexico than it is here. Because as bad as it is here, if you cross the border and see how our people live in Mexico, you feel lucky you're living in Texas.

La madre entered. She had been in the kitchen and she heard part of the talk. La madre said that we have a better house than our people across the border, and we have electricity and a television set, but this is not our country and Mexico is, and the people in Mexico have their own country, and that's better than electricity.

"Do you remember the two brothers, the Kennedys?"

"Of course," la madre said.

"Do you remember how we taped their pictures, first the one and then the other, to the wall, next to the icons of La Virgen de Guadalupe and Cristo Rey?"

Of course, she remembered. Those were days of hope and enthusiasm. Even in the language, the feelings. The word Chicano, which before meant someone not worthy of respect, a hell-raiser and a rústico, now came to mean a proud Mexican who stood up for himself and his rights. And raza and carnal and huelga. And Aztlán.

But those days went unrealized. Like mayflies who live for a day, the brothers—Anglo benefactors—had come and were gone, shot down by plotters. And slowly their photos moldered and peeled off the wall—they had come and gone.

"But hope has not gone. Nor rage nor defiance. You saw those Chicano boys cantando la victoria on the television?" She was surprised by her words, the anger had come straight up. Mostly she was surprised by her choice of words. Chicano was not a word they used in their home.

What about the union, then? In California they have a union, a heroic leader, César Chávez, who is almost a saint. A heroic woman leader too, Dolores Huerta, who is not afraid, even though they've assaulted her. Now they want a union here that will work to better our conditions. If we all join, nothing can stop us. And we'll have the union.

This thing of the union has been around twenty years and to no avail. One of the crew chiefs who talked union—he's in jail this very minute. The jail where the Communist professor would go if he chose to stay in the Valley for more than a couple of days. They called this crew chief a drunk, although he doesn't drink much, and they said he was a bad troublemaker. There's no room for a union down here, except if it meets in the jail where all the members will be put by the sheriff. Maybe in Detroit where Domingo's cousin lives, maybe in California, although even there César Chávez has fasted so much that now he's so weak he's ready to collapse, and to little avail. The grape growers were winning there, even in California, despite Chávez. Fasting all the time, and to no avail. Maybe there was this brief moment years ago, when mayflies flitted into the sun for one day, when union seemed a possibility. But now they've closed that apertura and only kids in college can safely boost a union.

One by one the father had pinned back his enthusiasms and drawn him into an ever-tightening arc. Curiously, Domingo felt exhilarated. Political talk, talk of breaking free, argument was rare in his house. The professor, the authorities, la Carmen—all this he thought would have led to humiliation and gloom, anger trapped in the lower depths. Instead, his father seemed so animated in his resignation.

"¿Es que no hay esperanza?" Domingo blurted out in mock desperation fueled by his excitement. "Didn't you see the TV? The marches? Isn't there some hope?"

The father straightened up in the chair. He told his son that he had spent his whole life in the Río Grande Valley. He had risen from a farmhand to crew chief and now he drove one of the pickups for the grower. He knew the Valley, knew who owned what, who had power, and who was utterly without power. He did not want to deny his children a future. He believed that their lives would be better than his own. But hope has to be guarded and maybe balanced with cynical despair. He told Domingo that we should expect nothing to change very much. Things will get better, little by little. Not quickly, but little by little, working hard, saving, advancing. The Anglo won't let it happen quickly, they will resist, but his son's life will be better, richer than his own. And Domingo's son in turn will do better, much better.

Domingo felt the weight of decades of oppression on him. He was unwilling, unaccepting. He was too excited by events to consider such a wait and to give the events that excited him the impassive visage. He sensed in his father a profound embarrassment. His father wanted to give him more, to stir his enthusiasms, but he was too honest a man, or perhaps too cautious, too fearful to give him false hopes. He remembered years ago overhearing a conversation between his father and his uncle.

His uncle had asked, "What shall we say about the Anglos to our children?"

His father had looked tired, hurt, baffled. "I don't know," he had responded to his uncle. "I can take anything, *anything* except a talk con los hijos—to have to tell them what it has been like to be a migrant farmhand."

But Domingo realized he was not tired, not now. He was young! This was the essential beauty and justice of life. The old become tired and the new are born into the land. Just like crops, the seedlings. His blood stirred, his enthusiasms. He was dreaming and musing all the time. One time he thought he would lead a garrison to the Alamo and take it for us. Another time he would catch a ride, a succession of rides and be in Canada. He would find land and make it grow crops. He would be away from every grower in the Valley. He would forget about sheriffs and the Texas Rangers after all.

"Sabe, padre," Domingo said solemnly. "I think the Chicano professor wasn't talking about making babies at all. I think he was talking about something here in the Valley. About something growing here in the Valley, like what we saw at the university today. I don't know what Carmen did but I think it was important. The professor was maybe talking about our lives in the Valley. You know, padre, Carmen was a rebel, defiant. She wasn't just a punker, a Mexican dressed like a punk Anglo with green hair. She called herself the Aztec punker. She must have done something important because she captured a lot of attention. She captured a Chicano FBI's attention who came from far away just to talk to her."

It was late and the father's bones ached from ten hours of tearing across the fields and groves. He weighed this option that Domingo proferred as well. Most of all, he thought about Domingo. Es vivo el muchacho, he thought. The boy didn't do well in school, but that was of no account. No Mexican children did well in school. Es vivo, muy vivo el muchacho. He weighed Domingo's option back and forth. A Chicano professor, a Chicano FBI, really, such strangeness, almost unimaginable. "That too is a possibility," he conceded, finally.

Hidalgo, Adventure Capitalist, Sallied Forth to Aid the Third World

> ### In Memorium
>
> Celina Elba
> Julia Elba
> Ignacio Ellacuría, SJ
> Amando López, SJ
> Ignacio Martín-Baró, SJ
> Joaquín López y López, SJ
> Segundo Montes, SJ
> Juan Ramón Moreno, SJ

Before all else they were human beings, Salvadoreans, who
tried to live honestly and responsibly in the midst of the tragedy
and hope of El Salvador. This may not seem adequate praise
for glorious martyrs, but it is where I want to start, because
living in the midst of the situation of El Salvador, as in any
part of the third world, is before all else a matter of humanity,
a demand on all to respond with honesty to a dehumanizing
situation, which cries out for life and which is inherently an
inescapable challenge to our humanity.
—Jon Sobrino, SJ, *Companions of Jesus: The Murder
and Martyrdom of the Salvadorean Jesuits*

In trying to do good, Quixote does harm, to himself chiefly,
but to others too. He faces the activist's dilemma, accepting
responsibility for promoting justice, but learning that the very
act of redressment distorts right and wrong; his human
perceptions will ensure that action turns out badly. Quixote
refuses to face what Cervantes saw as the basic contradiction of human effort: man may not be God. To presume
to try is madness. Yet he is impelled to usurp God's function
by the God within him. . . . the vision must still be sought
in life, for it is the act of striving that confirms his divinity.
Without such a vision and, more important, without its active
prosecution, existence is sterile, man a stone.
—William Byron, *Cervantes, A Biography*

In a place in the upper Midwest, the name of which we needn't concern ourselves with, the river meets the majestic lake, and no more than a mere hundred years ago it enraptured French trappers with its turbulence. Now in this spot stood the national headquarters of Adventure Capitalists, Ltd., founded by Jorge Hidalgo/George Knight. With branch offices in Washington, New York, Houston, Los Angeles, Mexico City, Buenos Aires, but also counterintuitive places like Colón, Panamá; Truchas, New Mexico; Aracataca, Colombia; Klail City, Texas; Tamazunchale, México; Caguas, Puerto Rico; and the founder's hometown, National City, California, Adventure Capitalists (AC) projected a powerful and idiosyncratic image.

The capitalist partners had their peculiar ways of evoking the company's time-space. Guns n' Roses, the head of the highly important hot salsa division, liked to quip, "¡En Truchas, ponte trucha; en Caguas, cuídate de grandes aguas!" Clearly, the company was different from other capitalist ventures in at least two ways.

Have biculture, will travel

was their lema; nobody did them better in Hispania. And the other way? Each partner tithed for the poor. In fact, it was a precondition of company employment.

On the eve of his supreme salida, we find the fabulously wealthy, workaholic Hidalgo reviewing an advertisement on behalf of one of his many pro bono projects. Slated for the usual suspects, *Barron's, Business Week, Forbes, Fortune,* and the others, it read:

200,000 people were crippled by sharks in the streets of La Paz last year

Loan sharks. Every year, hundreds of thousands of shoemakers, *artesanos,* bakers, and street vendors are financially crippled by them. That's why we have created *Acción Latina.* We provide hardworking men and women with otherwise unattainable, fair-rate small business loans. Thanks to this program, people who only one year ago would be unable to make a living or even to keep their families whole, today have paid their loans back in full and have been given a chance to better their lives.

More importantly, they've been given back their dignity.

All it takes is for you to believe them. Send *Acción Latina* a contribution today.

Adventure Capitalists had conceived the project and put $5 million of its own funds into it. The company was pressing the buttons of every likely contributor. More than that, the AC people were taking personal responsibility for making it happen.

Chez Hidalgo was a penthouse atop the region's most recent erection, ambitiously named Renaissance Tower. It was furnished for success with fine teaks, leather-bound tomes with in-sewn silk page markers about knights who quested for the Grail and paid allegiance to their damsels, bins of econometric analyses, newspaper clippings from around the globe, and statistical packages from the Institute for Econometric Modeling. Adventure Capitalists had its share of beautiful people. Palest hue some of them, the color of Galician vinho verde. Brown carnales, others, the most delicate mole poblano. The partnership went in for spanning extremes; in fact that was the inciting premise, the cash vaca. "Ebony and Ivory" and El Piporro's "Natalio Reyes Colas" were piped into the elevators.

Don Jorge was congruent to the company he had founded, having spent his life in adventure of one sort or another. Born close to the San Diego naval station in National City and seasoned by friendly brawls with sailors, in his adolescent years he began as a hauler, then as the wheels, finally as the brains of a Chicano family-run, border-crossing chatarra operation. In the 50s, tin cans, lead batteries, and the like had vastly different rates of exchange depending on the country they were situated in, and so Jorge learned to straddle the border, just as much later, with puts and calls, he straddled the bond, commodity, currency, equity, and gray markets.

As an adolescent our Chicano capitalist hadn't anticipated going to college, but the 60s and equal opportunity of access took a chance on him, and it was good. Although, as he put it, he was a "nothing-ness" in secondary school, he turned out to be a superlative college student and later, as an alumnus, a catch of considerable collegiate pride and value. He had already donated six digits to alma mater for raza financial aid by the time he entered into his culminating, defining adventure. His was a double major, econometrics and existential philosophy; then to the halcyon days, the founding of Adventure

Capitalists which specialized in big deals of the third kind: high margin, low profile activity in the gray market. Ni pío ni pao, pero a veces plomo; he was wise, sleek, and lean. Yet, Hidalgo would probably be the first to tell you, in hindsight, that he was not really prepared for the forthcoming salida that unbeknown awaited him.

"Don Jorge! Gary Gnu's on the horn!" called out Hermelinda del Pimental. She had the looks and dash to be a fashion model and the pedigree of stoop laborers. She thought her parents might have taken their name from the pepper fields in which they worked, but Hermelinda didn't specialize in picking; instead she had completed a Ph.D. in applied mathematics, disserting on the topic of chaos theory within international finance.

The Midwest was a migrant region: lettuce, beets, and cherries punctuated by one-trick cities that specialized in smelting, rubber, glass, or biggest of all, motors. To these acrid cores of industry some of la raza who had originally embarked on the leafy, fruity, beety harvests were peeled off and permanently affixed. In her family's transhumance 12 years ago, Hermelinda's intellectual qualities, will-power, and strength of character had come to the attention of AC, which was committed to developing young talent. It had started with an outstanding field report by a Carmelite nun who ministered to migrants but free-lanced for the company. "Del Pimental: a peppery bundle of energy with a great heart and all the brains you require. She's woefully undereducated, in fact, tabula rasa. Full of promise, my highest rating." A review of the field documents by the AC forecasting and human resources committees resulted in a scrawl at the bottom of the dossier in the hand of La Malintzín, senior partner in charge of human resource development: "tabula rasa: convert to máxima raza." A decision to commit was entered, a budget line allocated, and a personal file generated, and a hard closer was summoned to the family to separate Hermelinda from the migrant stream—a Jebbie, associate headmaster of the finest prep school in the region. AC found it effective to delegate highly delicate negotiations of the transcultural kind to black robes and white collars. After the customary to and fro, Hermelinda signed on for full freight with a $50,000 bonus paid directly to her family in lieu of the migrant income they would lose. She started forthwith in the seventh grade (seventy-hour week featuring the most rigorous instruction, tutoring, graceful comportment, as well as a full regimen of martial arts) and was supported through the doctorate. Now, 12 years and $362,000 later, voilà, the newest junior partner! That's what AC, "have biculture, will travel," was about, the long wave, la acequia madre, the big picture, the deep thought, the gallant gesture, Saint George (Jorge) and the Dragon, locating the lost progeny of la llorona, whatever it took. Of course, to maintain its human investments the company required sizable profits. The partners saw to it; they had luscious cash flow and an extraordinary balance sheet.

Hidalgo turned his attention from the *Acción Latina* advertisement and focused on Gary Gnu, one of their long-standing and best customers, albeit a complex and difficult one. With Henry and the other motor moguls behind him, the Gnu was an eight digit guy, minimum; he simply didn't bother with lesser deals. Therefore, Hidalgo gave the Gnu's noblesse its due oblige. However, Hidalgo wasn't surprised that the Gnu would be on the horn. It was another one of those midwestern cycles where the sky was falling down on everyone's head.

He touched the phone speaker: "Jorge Hidalgo here. How now, Good Gnu?"

"George, I've got something for you to fix your lance on."

"I didn't suppose you'd be calling to sell me charity tickets to the predator's ball. As you know, we're here to serve. And we're always pleased to read your prospectus."

Adventure Capitalists aspired to be a legend in its own time, the McKinsey and Co. of the gray market. It wouldn't commit to any old venture, but when it did commit, it got the job done, no matter what it took. Known for its effective use of both arms and letters (arms were not denied one whit of resources nor even the most experimental of technological innovations), the company went half the distance alone on what the partners called "Cisco" charisma. Of course, those cognoscenti who followed adventure capitalism were wont to point out that adamantly independent, minority-owned and operated AC didn't have the sort of wire with the pontifex maximus of venture that some of its friendly competitors could boast of, the federal Company itself, but of course, boasting on this point would be counterindicated. While that might be, did any of the competitors tithe for the poor? Only AC did, and that created a certain je ne sais quoi, a creative tension, and a genuine idiosyncrasy that had ramifications even in the field.

Gnu made his trademark cackle. Why else be called Gary Gnu, kiddie TV curmudgeon? Although, after seeing some of the things he had pulled over the last two decades, Hidalgo thought he might be more aptly named Gary Gilmore, just as Gnu once told Hidalgo, straight to his face, that his name was really Hideputa. That was Gnu, a sweetheart. "Actually, George, I meant more in the order of you personally being engagé, not just some of your partners, although I'll concede your people are all summa cum svelte and modish."

"And competent, Gary. As you well know. I think I may be getting a little stiff in the wings for field work."

"Humbug, Knight. It's those brats you've gone and sired. What you people call mocosos and esquintles. And all the money you make. For Christsakes, you seem to be on every corporate board or blue-ribbon commission on the scanner."

"Gnu! I commend you for your expertise on Chicano culture. But as you well know, I'm just the token Chicano, the mere supernumerary soul and conscience of corporate America."

The Gnu, as was often his habit, paid not the slightest attention to Hidalgo's counterpunches and proceeded with his sermon. "Children and the boardroom. Not the paths of proper adventure capitalism, since they induce a certain infelicitous conservatism and a taste for creature comforts more in keeping with those who work with actuarial tables than those who soar with the condors."

"Gnu! I'm amazed that you would criticize conservatism of any stripe! This truly is a new side to your gnuness."

He cackled again. "You're likely to see five new sides out of me; I'm becoming pentagonal." Then, although on the telephone, Hidalgo envisioned Gary Gnu drawing himself up as he did when he would utter one of those nonnegotiable terms of engagement. "If we go with your firm—and Knight, let me observe that we're discussing potential sole-source status—you're out of here no later than Monday a.m. Headed south, I might add. To the Third World."

"There is no Third World, Gnu."

"How so?"

"What was the Second World no longer is. Nonesuch."

Gnu laughed. "Quite. If only the inhabitants of that demimonde would have the prescience to see it your way. Instead they seem bent on wrangling over who owns the Black Sea fleet and the happy bombs. In any case, in recognition of your analysis, I'm upgrading the whole geography of your field ops to Second World status. That quantum leap should make you all happy, servers and serviced alike.

But you're still our man in the Deep South. Of course, given the urgency, we'll be delighted to pay the customary premiums and we'll even pay out of our own pocket your so-called 'tithe,' that smarmy welfare tax you eccentrically impose to the utter detriment of your tribe! Your so competent employees ought to find that quite satisfactory."

"Actually, Gnu, I believe it might corrupt them. We are likely to let you pay the tithe since you are so idealistically inclined and we'll have the employees match it. Doublemint, double your pleasure and so good for the soul."

"Yes, yes, quite." The Gnu apparently couldn't be bothered. He was on a mission, determined to let it all hang out. "And I should note that our prospectus, as you sweetly put it, includes 2% off the top for lubrication. You can keep any residuals on that, no pre-audit, no receipts, no deposits, no returns. That's the deal and I need to see you, say, in 15 minutes."

"My, my, Gnu, we are in a hurry, aren't we? Obsessing about the honorable Japanese? Have they and the frogs already chartered a Concorde and set up shop in situ while we're picking dingleberries out of our arses? Is it that, gnorious Gnu? But I tell you, I'm starved. Compañero, I'll break bread with your company at the London Chop House."

"That pit of public profile! It'll have to be a back room. I'll have my secretary arrange it. I wouldn't want Henry to wander in as he's wont to and make inquiries." Gnu cackled again, but in great good sport. "If I'm going to give you Henry's money, better that misanthropos be unaware that we are dealing with your kind."

"My kind, the energizers, dear Gnu? Or do I suspect it's my kind, the newly Second World people of base bronze and not of gold or silver?"

"Don't get freaky on me, my friend. I don't pretend to be a Platonist, and Henry, other than having inherited the genial gene for the lug wrench, well, he knows shit, preferring to go strictly on his family instincts which are based on 5,000 years of unalloyed prejudice."

Known to Anglos on the periphery by his handle of convenience, George Knight, those in the barrios, rancherías, milpas, and fincas whom AC benefacted knew him more intimately by his baptismal name, Jorge Hidalgo. Others, knowledgeable of Spanish and of the competitive nature and high stakes of gray ops, claimed, as Gnu had once fustigated, his true placa to be closer to the anti-knight-errant, the ungenteel polar, Hideputa. The founder, CEO, and primum mobile Adventure Capitalist had in common with his senior partners—professionals with handles like Trader Víctor, la Dolores de los Dólares, Guns n' Roses, la Malintzín, el Oso Polar (a bear-market specialist), la Cacica de los Debentures, el Capitán Veneno, Sor Juana (truly the conscience of the joint), El Carnal Espiritual—a brilliant egocentrism, immense soberbia only rivaled by an equally dosed, Hispanic-flavored vergüenza, sharpness of wit, relish for a higher, unmundane sphere of activity, conspicuous consumption, extraordinary philanthropy, hedonistic outlook, and willingness to work endlessly in search of high profit. For these pícaros ricos, capitalism was merely necessary, but not sufficient. They considered themselves a select cofradía, verily, a knighthood. Each in his or her own fashion had been wounded by the slings and arrows of the American netherlife. Each had experienced discrimination, often outright racism, and had experienced it in the tenderest years. Nevertheless, each had emerged stronger from the maelstrom.

For Jorge it had come early enough, arrested 10 times and treated like brown border detritus by the time he was 14—he had been tall for his age and enterado—for petty smuggling of scrap metal and driving with a phony Mexican driver's license. Crossing the border an average of 350 times a year, the Hidalgo family liked to move from station to station before the border guards got tired of merely throwing the book at them and started to throw punches instead. Sometimes the Hidalgos were too slow on the rise. Even from the first, Jorge was always very sensitive about his teeth, at least those that were left in his mouth versus those that hadn't made it across borders. As soon as he started earning money he would go to Beverly Hills to where the actors dentisted, just to perfect his grin and bear it.

Don Jorge had likened his own woundings, his rites of puberty as they were, imposed by American and Mexican border authorities alike, to his favorite passage in Saint Teresa de Avila where the seraph twisted its fiery pike in the genuine organ of the soul, causing in the pain, so intense, so physical, in fact much like a roto-rooter reaming, the vehicle of mystical transport.

> He was not tall, but little; very beautiful, his face so flaming that he seemed to be one of those highest angels who are all afire. . . . I

saw a long old spear in his hand and there seemed to be a little flame at the tip of it. This he seemed to plunge into my heart repeatedly, until it reached into my very entrails. When he drew it out, I thought he would draw them out with it, and it left me utterly afire with a great love for God. The pain was so great that it made me moan over and over, and the sweet delight into which that pain threw me was so intense that one could not want it to stop, or the soul be contented with anything but God. It is not bodily pain, but spiritual, though the body does not cease to share in it somewhat—and even very much so. Through the days this went on, I acted like someone driven out of her wits. I did not want to see or speak to anyone, but only to hug myself with my pain which, for me, was a greater glory than there is in the whole creation.

How just like Hidalgo/Knight, who lived in the interface of Anglo-Hispanic irony and sought, body and soul, to reach out and bind into himself these contraries, that he would choose, in college-educated hindsight (after all, he had never even *heard* of her until college), to identify his worst beatings and intensest hugging of pain with Saint Teresa's mystical ecstasies. There was not so much disrespect or iconoclasm in this choice, although there was certainly much wry irony and épater le bourgeois, as could attest anyone who ever heard him discourse on the subject. Rather, Hidalgo felt a genuine sense of matchedness. Hadn't Hidalgo's beatings like Saint Teresa's piercings created a sort of Passion that eventually resulted in prodigious productive energy? The deepest element of this mysterious identification with the experiences of the santa lay in Hidalgo's posttraumatic realization once in college that at the time he underwent his border beatings he had done so with a full sense of acceptance. Truly, at the time, without the slightest hint of irony or self-consciousness, he had accepted the physical as good for his soul. It was wrong, his smuggling batteries and tin cans across borders, and it was good and right to be punished for it. Bless the Lord!—or in those cases, the burly guards who rather delighted in being His instrument.

So then, Hidalgo emerged from college one step removed from his simple self, recollecting that simple, unquestioning post-pubescent Passion with more sophisticated political, bicultural, academic, and other comprehensions. Perhaps as a result, Knight had some difficulty with the concept of a personal God, some doubts and possible obsessions along that line, although he considered himself a respectful if not reverent kind of vato. He would certainly "like" to believe if at all possible—wasn't this, after all, the modern condition? Beyond that, he acquired the greatest respect for the zeniths of both Anglo and Hispanic culture; and as well, a great morbidity tempered by a biting sarcasm for the nadirs.

Surely it must have been similar for each partner, Don Jorge reasoned, in order to have made what was close to an all-consuming commitment to Adventure Capitalists. Each wounded before the age of reason by the infamous undersword of American racism, which curiously enough turned out to be simultaneously a brush with the six-winged seraph who guards God's throne with sacred ardor. Each precisely where wounded, there he or she would be most overtly cauterized and healed, abnormally strong although lustily scarred. The capitalist search for the Holy Grail, conceived in the night of Tenebrae, grimmest night of the soul. Maybe Hidalgo wasn't quite ready for the adventure that was in store for him, but he wasn't exactly an ingenue either.

So then: normal, garden-variety venture capitalism was Caliban to these Ariels. The AC men and women of arms and letters avowed a knight-errantry. They would right wrongs. They would succor the poor, the helpless, the oppressed. They would slay the dragon and even turn its own fire against it; and it would be fun and profitable, a deadly but merry quest. They were patriots. They genuinely believed in the democratic system, in the efficacy of capital formation and the economic model that was its consequence, in the civic resources of the state, and in the call to public service. These latinos were gov jocks from the Harvard K-school, Wharton financial modelers, technology transferers from Stanford. They were also latinos, the first generation educated in the high wire, formerly exclusive act of Wasp dare-to-aspires. Above all, they were latinos y latinas who defined themselves as the loyal opposition. Loyal and opposition: it bridged the gap and tied the edges together. José Vasconcelos had claimed of the ultimate biculturality—the condition of mestizaje and la raza cósmica, mostly imposed by forced miscegenation—that por mi raza hablará el espíritu. These partners in ventures worked to make that spirit carnal and to help the so many less fortunate carnales and carnalas whom in their errantry they encountered to be able to speak with spirit.

The London Chop House was a power place, much too public really for Hidalgo's line of work, but he favored it simply because a

Chicano silk suit in the public rooms was so counterintuitive. Hidalgo was known to mess with the maitre d's head by going back and talking caló with the dishwashers. Today was no fun and games, however; he merely confined himself to plunging lustily into the thickest veal chop available in the Midwest. With it, he sipped the finest, fiery calvados made in Normandy from a huge Baccarat goblet at his side. "My applesauce," he confided, his Latin mustache glistening with fine veal oils, to the aghast Gnu, who despite his adventurist patter practiced perfectly gracious Wasp manners. Now Jorge was down to the bone, which suited him fine. To his unindicted co-conspirator's consternation, he lifted the bone to mouth and did a bravura. Gary Gnu (who actually had some insipid, forgettable gringo name he was almost ashamed to use like Johnson or Carter) refused to acknowledge provocation. His was all expeditiousness and dispatch. Clearly, he was obsessed with the honorable Japanese, Hidalgo guessed, whom Gnu was probably envisioning as already halfway to Buenos Aires, Ile du Diable, Manaus, Kool-Aid-rich Guyana, and whatever other places this salida was going to take them, while here where the river made rapids as it merged into the lake everything was still in the Gnu's Gnanus and they merely dickered about getting a few good operatives on site.

The Gnu straightened up in his chair. "This is it, the big whiffer."

"Christ on his calvary, eh? Going gets tough, tough get going. Any more clichés? Sporting of you, bloke. Bloody nippers! Is that about it, Gnu?"

"I'm not going to joust with you, Hidalgo. This cycle makes or breaks us. The Saturn is totally uncertain, and what is worse for us who claim fealty to the Midwest, actually moot, irrelevant, as it sits in moonshine and cabbage county, Tennessee. Ford, GM, Chrysler—Christ, not to mention Caterpillar, John Deere. Have you looked at that piece of shit they're now calling Navistar? It sits square in the Dow Jones and no longer makes any difference to the average one way or another, no matter how high or low it goes. Irrelevant!"

"I take it that knowing the price of Navistar is integral to this deal. I should have brought our short specialist along, Oso Polar."

"It's part of it. U.S. AID could use a lot of little Nasty Stars or caterpillars, although they may not know it yet. But forget Ursus Major. We're going so far along that you might want to involve Guns n' Roses instead. I can't tell you how dimly I take to that little ditty they now say every time the industrial cycle goes down the slippery slope, 'Last one to leave Michigan, turn off the lights!' Have you seen the negative cash flow? Harumph! Chrysler, they won't even report sales on a 10-day basis any more. It's strictly month to month."

"What's the Western world coming to? Tradition, sir! Even the 10-day sales report takes it on the chin."

"Don't bait me, Knight, I implore you, I'm deadly serious. And I know you're committed to our region of the country. That more than anything is why I'm here to pitch you our prospectus."

"Fine, you've softened me up. Now for the kill. You were always the hardest closer in the business, Gnu."

"Quite right, George. Don't forget that you want to be on the winning team. We have a grand tour of the great developing South lined up for Adventure Capitalists, Ltd. It's 80 days around the hemisphere. You'll go everywhere, including where no one has dared to go before, with our best and final offers. These incentives will knock the huaraches off our clients. We want market share and we will do whatever is necessary, even sell at a loss."

"Right, and make it up in volume."

"I'm not kidding, Knight. Let me show you the ways. For starters, we've built in that 2% lube I mentioned to you, right off the top. And you've got full discretion. We don't need to know details. We're going back to original propositions, the unmoved mover, the unvarnished capitalist. Who's to stop us, the Trans-Ural-Uzbek-Siberian Humpty Dumpty? Don't ask me how we're getting around the gov reg shit. Does that sound like any American corporate posture you've ever heard of since robber barons like J.P. Morgan and John D. Rocke-feller began to feed themselves with silver spoons?"

With that Gnu launched into his prospectus. Hidalgo did not dwell on the content, which seemed to him a sorry pastiche, alter-nately plying the usual levers of high greed and scapegoating the Japanese, the Huns, even the kimchi-eating Koreans and the sorry frogs. Anybody who connected wheels to an axle. Then appealing to regional loyalties—the upper midwestern patria chica that somehow Gnu fancied would stir patriotism and matriarchism in Hidalgo. By the time Gnu was done one would have thought they were living in Michoacán, not Michigan. It was hardly the pitchman's content that struck Hidalgo—he would rather have bought a Lexus—but the tonic qualities were notable.

Hidalgo made it his business to know the muscle tone of the marketplace. Each Sunday, from a formal podium accompanied by overhead transparencies and the finest Jerez de la Frontera drawn from a 500-year-old cedar cask, he delivered a weekly neuropsychic review of the market for the partners. Adventure Capitalists believed in a "full" work week, Saturdays and Sundays included, regularly closing only for Christmas, New Year's Day, and the 16th of September. In addition, employees got their saint's day off, or alternately, they could take December 12th, Our Lady of Guadalupe, as a holiday. The Sunday briefing was one of Sir Jorge's highest satisfactions. He was able to elucidate the elusive strands of both arms and letters and to alchemize them into company policy.

A few Sundays ago he had advanced the theory that of the three sectors of the brain, the primal stem, the rational cerebral cortex, and the limbic system, it was the latter that fueled marketplace decisions. Basing himself on regression, biological *and* statistical, exponential smoothing, and a rigorous rotation of variables, he had concluded that for the short-term investment decision, the primary stimulus was the drive to relieve oneself of the proprioceptive disturbances associated with one's current market position. In the limbic form of mentation the sense of the present becomes superordinate over all other personal time-spaces and physiological relief overcomes all other value sets. Or to put it in terms to which even Donald Trump could relate: "Marketers buy or sell primarily because they want the pain to go away."

As one of his prime clients, Hidalgo also made it his business to understand the Gnu. He had the benefit of a close relationship with the man for almost 20 years, and he had paid generously for intelligence, which he had studied closely.

The Gnu was strictly striped-tie Ivy of post-World War II vintage. Attitudinally, he had been formed just before the 1950s stage of the civil rights movement. At Adventure Capitalists, for heuristic purposes Standard American Time was divided into pre- and post-Brown versus Board of Education. Nothing counted quite as much as that watershed. On the other hand, Tiempo Chicano obeyed the long wave, emerging from both Western and Amerindian prehistory and beginning, on the one hand, in the Nahuatl calendrical cycle well into Quinto Sol with Quetzalcoatl, and on the other hand, 1492 by the Gregorian calendar. The Gnu was the scion of one of the first prominent bean-counting arrivistes who had wrested control of the American auto industry from the hands of the wild-eyed, forged-wrench beasts and visionary tinkerers who had founded it at the turn of the century.

Until the Japanese had become prominent, the father had administered motors on a so-called "firm cost-accounting basis." During that post-war period when the Gnu was in college, the industry moved international, which meant primarily Europe or the more "stable" and accessible parts of the former British empire such as South Africa, Australia, and New Zealand. The Gnu's father had been noted in the industry for smoothing corporate volatility in income and announcing profits and orderly dividend increases for a record 15 straight years irrespective of the actual fortunes of corporate war. Whether the company actually made more profits or less did not affect the primacy of submerged international transfers of funds. While the industry in fact had been subject to extreme cycles over that 15-year period, the accountants had made use of cash flow in and out of foreign subsidiaries and of the flux in international currency exchange rates to manipulate the balance sheet so that their now multinational corporation seemed to be engaged on a rock-solid, permanent, gentle but exciting slope of 6% annual growth. It was the best of all Eisenhower worlds and the financial fixers emerged supreme.

The Gnu, on the other hand, reflected his own industrial formation in the 60s and 70s. He shaped what he could control and idolized what controlled him. In contrast to his father, he believed passionately in the Mammon of cycles. How couldn't he? And in militant entrepreneurship. His training in the industry had reflected the conventional, pedagogically correct apprenticeship of the Wasp automotive aristocracy: a beginning in a lowly and messy capacity in the paint shop followed by planned three- and six-month progressions and promotions up the line. While on one level he had moved with the times, there remained a recalcitrance to move out of his class. In fact, Gnu felt it was his right to rely on an inner circle of white male friends, confidants, mentors, and mentees. At first blush this would seem contradictory, for he had a brilliant mind and he was known for his intense intellectual curiosity. He had made it his business to learn a great deal about other cultures, mostly of the developed world, but also of out-groups. He had taught himself Spanish and not only had mastered the standard register, but with the aid of Chicano dictionaries and people like Jorge Hidalgo, se defendía in the vernacular and the most charged elements of Hispanic political and business argot.

But at best it was all anthropology to him and in his worst moments unabashed tourism, exotica, a Brit studying the *Kama Sutra*. Hidalgo met that type repeatedly among the Ivy set. They relished the other culture at the cerebral level, though ultimately they felt too awkward and ungainly to genuinely participate in it. They ended up mere observers. Hidalgo concluded that the condition was a limitation of monoculturalism; they lacked the ability to genuinely move outside of themselves and, to use Saint Teresa's term, morar in the cultural space of the other.

The last few years had been unkind to Gnu just as they had been unyielding to the auto business. On the other hand, working the counterpunches in gray territory, they had been stellar for Adventure Capitalists, on whom the Gnu had become, it would appear, uncomfortably dependent for making certain kinds of international deals.

So the Gnu had felt painfully squeezed in recent years. Certain critics had begun to see his role as having evolved to that of the grand panjandrum in charge of manufacturing excuses for the industry. He had been seen not infrequently in media makeup on center stage in partnership with senior officials of the UAW, hamming up a Japan-bashing minstrel show for the delectation, if unfortunately not the edification, of the most xenophobic elements of American society. The bean counters were not happy: a straight-up, pin-stripe, right-on guy with impeccable pedigree thrust out of the comfortable penumbra into the circus tent, gooning it up, braying into microphones, and stuttering over teleprompts. Worst of all, publicly consorting with glorified union stewards at media affairs the political equivalent of tractor-pulls! Sponsoring Toyota-bashing rowdies with hammers and beer bottles in their hands. That was no way to manage a career. The Gnu secretly agreed with his critics, but then again, one does what is necessary. In short, Hidalgo concluded, Gnu was not the loyal opposition, he was simply loyal and likely to always be no matter what befell him. Thinking about Gnu made Hidalgo worry about his own bona fides, which he was prone to do anyway under all sorts of associative provocations. Hidalgo reminded himself to reread Sartre's exposition of the "faith of bad faith."

Although they had been dealing with each other for almost two decades with mutual respect and even affection, Hidalgo judged that the Gnu still considered AC to be essentially alien, an object of anthropological 'observe and measure' fascination, a fauna highly evolved from its native culture, but for the purposes of subcontractual or vendor statuses something akin to a source of last resort. The problem for Gnu was that recently the military-industrial complex he represented had been so battered in the Latin American market that there were few entities other than AC to which he could turn. Hidalgo found it ironic that these people who had done so well under quasi-monopolistic conditions were withering now that the marketplace had become filled with international competition. His conclusion, which he often threw into Gnu's face, was that American corporations believed in capitalism but didn't really understand it. Instead of taking capitalism to its logical conclusion which would include, in the Latin American theater at least, bringing Latinos into the innermost circles because of the cultural, political, and social advantages this would reap, if anything the Wasps had retreated into their bunkers. While Gnu alleged agreement with Hidalgo, he claimed a level of enlightenment not to be found in his associates. "Hell, these wrench-luggers who invented the assembly line are still holding on to some degree, especially at the command and control level. They're know-nothings and I can only play with the cards that I'm dealt." The long string of failures in Latin America, notwithstanding the successes achieved through AC, had caused added tensions between the organizations and even in the personal affections of Gnu and Hidalgo.

This had not always been the case. In the early years, acting out of what Hidalgo believed to be the impetus of noblesse oblige, Gnu had gone out of his way to foster and encourage AC. Yet at a certain point, one evident to the industry by the usual financial and status-referential measures, Adventure Capitalists, Ltd., reached the age of its majority. About that time, Gnu's ardor cooled noticeably. In fact, several years ago, in the last truly superb zenith of the motor business before the stock market heart attack of 1987, word had gotten back to Hidalgo. Gnu, in a notably loose-lipped moment, had ventured the opinion that Adventure Capitalists had unduly taken advantage of its distinctive Hispanic-focused status to have "milked the industry for all that it was worth." The remarks had wounded Hidalgo in his amor propio, and things had really never been quite the same with Gnu, although, of course, they continued to banter and collaborate on projects of overlapping interests. Hidalgo considered Gnu's remark to be almost exclusively based on cultural dissonance since AC had performed superlatively for the manufacturing inter-

ests that it had contractually represented. Hidalgo judged that the
sorry but far from uncommon truth was that the blue-blooded Gnu
was not and could never be totally comfortable with Hidalgo and his
cofradía. And vice versa. As long as the Latinos were under the wing
of the Gnus, the latter could obtain enormous ego gratification from
seeing the little brown brothers and sisters succeed. But when that
same enterprise sought to attain peer status . . . Well, Hidalgo
chalked up the restructured relationship to the natural tensions of
the semiopen but racially constrained marketplace. It was a rather
common phenomenon in Hidalgo's experience that racially inspired
animus rose to percolation when a minority enterprise's rise to
power reached the point that it outgrew the niche predisposed to it
by its original white patrons and even competed with them in the
marketplace.

The Gnu's prospectus having been completed, Hidalgo sipped
again from his goblet of calvados and eyed him with feigned
amusement.

"Well and good, Gnu." But you've failed to mention Central
America. El Salvador, or for that matter, Nicaragua. Some little
whippoorwill tells me there's a big fraction of your passion in them
thar jungles!"

Gnu smiled slyly. "I figured you'd mention it."

"What is this, the SAT? In El Salvador we're talking about the
second leg of the ley agrícola, dearly departed Duarte's legacy
strongly committed to by U.S. AID, World Bank, IMF, as well as
other federal worthies with exceedingly deep pockets. The first leg
went okay given the potential for Salvadoran horror, but that was a
cosmetic expropriation and distribution to the campesinos of holdings that were in excess of 500 hectares. Let's face it, in a miniskirt
like El Salvador, latifundias of that dimension are an oddity. But the
second leg, now we're talking about the breakup and distribution of
parcels that will mean goring the ox of the boys who are sponsoring
the right-wing death squads."

Gnu looked at Hidalgo/Knight with wry amusement. "But we're
merely focusing on the challenges. Oughtn't we keep our eyes on the
prize?"

"Ah, yes. The flip side, our eyes on the piñata. A big market,
especially by the standards of the currently zombielike U.S. construction and agricultural equipment business. If we include the
commitment that's building up to Violeta Chamorro in Nicaragua,

there's potential for selling Central America every backhoe in America that our real estate and construction businesses have declined, deferred, or defaulted on. And that's a mess of backhoes."

"Quite. And the nicest thing is that it can all be wired. You know how I've spoken out against the artificial maintenance of such obsolescences as currency and checks. My dear, sainted father would have appreciated this. Here good old American money can simply be transmitted from federal and international accounts into ours."

Hidalgo enjoyed Gnu's double entendre, obliquely introducing the wiring element. Clearly the guy must be totally obsessed with the honorable Japanese, even in a market where they would appear to be little more than a nuisance factor. "Yes, in war-torn Central America as opposed to the more open markets further south, wiring is of the essence. IMF, AID, the way they like to work is sole-source vendor. They're quintessential bureaucrats. Price is no object, but they hate to fill out forms in quintuplicate, although they want you to. And of course, no thought here of giving good federal greenbacks to foreign concerns; the sole source will have to be an American. So our competition would be limited to maybe four or five sources, Nasty Star, Cat, John Deere, a couple of also-rans."

"That's right, my friend, we all have an abhorrence of quintuplicate; actually, it's the pink and the canary forms we abhor. So we're talking sole source right down the line, down to the last cog who you guys decide is just the right one to lube."

"Since we're talking about a 2% lube, what's the gross on this— are we talking 10 digits here?"

"Gross to the max, compadre. Over the term, absolutely 10 figures, and probably high nine in the near. What's 2% of a bil, a cool 20 mil? What you do with that money is your call, no deposits, no returns, no receipts. And, my friend, it's right off the top; you haven't even started to charge us overhead yet, much less an 'honest' ten percent."

"True enough, but we've also got to talk armor. I'm going to need a mil for lead-laced salsa. This could be mucho peligroso. Departed D'Aubuisson may be toast, but his progeny are our Frankensteins, and in Salvador, even though it looks like we're supporting the regime's own ley agrícola, in fact we're going against the sovereign. They'll be interested in landing us make-it-happen dudes into the next century same time they're smiling like Cheshire cats to the appropriate congressional committee."

"I don't dispute your analysis, dear boy. No problemo. A mere mil, a very reasonable figure. Just do me the gran favor, my friend, to stock up on Ben Gay for your stiff wing. Take an extra satchel of the stuff. 'Cause it's you down maracas way or it's no go. We can't delegate this one to your pretty people who the only Red Hot Chili Peppers they know is some funky band that plays heavy metal to the dismay of Tipper Gore."

Hidalgo didn't bother to quibble. With a lube requirement like that, it would take someone who had 20 years' experience swimming with raza of various cultures and diverse palm-greasing styles. On a smaller deal Guns n' Roses could have been the field op and he would be the headquarter honcho. On something like this, they would have to flip. "I'll tell you, esteemed Gnu, you could find a dozen capitalists to work through Brasilia or Caracas, but El Salvador, Jesus, all they use hefty bags for is to place stiffs in garbage cans. I wouldn't touch this shit if we weren't on the side of the angels on this one, you know that?"

"Of course I do, that's why I've come to you. Because you believe in this agricultural reform shit and all the tingling pan-Latino goodfeelings that come with it. You'll work extra hard to make it happen, won't you? Just for moral and economic ideals. And we'll sell maybe half a bil in Salvador and Nica alone as a result. Besides, you have a soft spot for old Duarte, if I'm not mistaken, ineffectual dupe that he was. But after all, a Notre Dame boy, in fact Father Hesburgh's personal protégé, what?"

"Right on all counts, Gnu."

"With what I pay for backgrounders these days, I ought to be. Jesus, what softies you Catholics are. I should write a book. In fact, one day I will write a book, the memoirs of the last successful Wasp in América. The last one who made it without having to do salsa. And of course, where that bozo Duarte failed, you have the ego and the wits to succeed, in his name and the name of all the Panglossian Latino goodfellas. You're not going to let surrogates for sushi-heads and kimchi-eaters implement the agricultural reforms of the most needy Latino garden spot in all of Eden, now are you?"

"Right again, Gnu. Especially about my big fucking ego. Except for the part about being a Catholic. More like a Catholic wannabe."

"Stuff it, Knight. If you're gonna quote me more Saint Teresa or Sartre like you've been doing all these years, I swear I'll puke. So then, do we have a deal-o? Let's face it, the window is open and somebody's going to get to climb through it. It ought to be you. I always come first to the very best. I do my homework, I make a realistic offer. In your case, it's both bread *and* land. Here's an opportunity to continue to consolidate your aspiration for secular sainthood status *and* earn a sizable fraction of a bil, for you and your partners to dispose of in the deplorable little ways you see fit." Then Gnu, who was absolutely gaga about Brazil, went into a little ditty.

> Rio, Rio
> Rio by the Sea-o
> We've got to get to Rio
> and we've *got* to make time!

"I want to go back and have a summit pronto with my staff, not only the ink pissers but the lead wielders. I'll get back to you."

Gnu called for the bill, which he started going over in that insufferable accountant's way, like it was something personal.

Hidalgo mentally reviewed the deal and its nuances. The whole thing had this characteristic gnuesque quality. Although wrapped in an aura of high jinx and high profit, collapse of the Second World opposition and a corresponding brave new world of untrammeled business practice, Hidalgo sensed it was wanting in truth, perhaps even wanting in sincerity. He sensed danger.

It had that recognizable, double-hedge stink. It was a straddle all right, puts and calls on the same pony. On the one hand it would appear that Gnu and his higher-ups were figuring that they had already lost this one to some other entities which probably had gotten out of the stall months ago. So, what the hell, give it to the Knight. If by some fluke they came out okay, pocket the money and prepare for the next engagement in a new theater. If they didn't, well, it proved that even U.S. Latinos couldn't make it in an "unfair" trade market, especially in the deep southern cone, without the wiring of federal agencies. Then management and the unions could push the Michigan senators into fast forward and really pull the nippers, the Huns, the frogs, and the kimchis by the short ones. Minimax, a no-lose position. And for Adventure Capitalists? It was the same old shit; sole source was really a euphemism for last resort. Give the spics a chance to use their pointed shoes. Maybe they'll spear a few cucarachas in the corners. Anglos can't use a blade like them bandi-tos. Anglos are too "sporting." Sure, for AC it was maxi-min. The day the AC lost a biggie like this one, well, it would go down at motors like 'Miliano Zapata suckered by a white gift horse at the Chinameca hacienda. The whole irony in this, Hidalgo thought, was that the day his community finally got into a position to give free-market capitalism a genuine probe, these fucks had their minds fixed on protectionism.

Even though he had seen this matrix time and time again, Hidalgo felt trapped. The bottom line always prevailed. Ten digits: with the residuals off that, he could provide residential mortgages for every family in Tzintzunztán, Pojoaque, and Aibonito and still give a fabulous bonus to every employee of AC. How could he even toy with turning something like this down? So, as usual, he would need to be the well-trained seal, spinning a ball on his nose while jumping through a flaming hoop and slapping his flippers for an extra morsel of fish. Like those articles in women's magazines that he used to read as a teenager while scavenging the local dumps for lead and tin. "Why young mothers feel trapped!" But why feel bad? At least he had analyzed it right, and that was the best part of the game anyway. Besides, Gnu was certainly obliged to those he represented to strictly give Hidalgo only the information that he required to get the job done. Yet sensing Gnu's possible mala fe and falling increasingly into a deep mood of mala leche, Hidalgo gave Gnu a parting shot. Later he was to mull it over with regret, but at the time it nicely indexed the amourodious quality of their relationship. He made a joke using the one person who was truly verboten in the Gnu pantheon.

"I hear the automobile workers are boosting Iacocca for president yet another time."

The Gnu looked up from the Chop House bill, startled. Having taken considerable psychological precautions, he had managed not to have heard the name of Iacocca in public for ten years.

Hidalgo twisted the knife. "President of Ford Motor Company, that is." The Gnu was unable even to muster a smirk, and Hidalgo bathed him in comradely derision.

*   *   *

Hidalgo calculated time in El Salvador according to the horology of atrocities and catastrophes. He had been to El Salvador several times in the period after the nuns and Catholic laywoman had been raped and murdered and before Ignacio Ellacuría and five other Jesuit priests had been executed and had their brains scooped out and placed at their sides. But not since. The last time he had been in either El Salvador or Nicaragua was a back-to-back trip to both republics several weeks after the four U.S. Marines were assassinated in San Salvador in June 1985.

The death of the Jesuits had profoundly affected him. He had known Ellacuría professionally through his participation in a mission to El Salvador that had interviewed a number of Salvadoran professors and arranged for them to go to the United States to earn Ph.D.'s. He had had an engrossing discussion with several of the marked Jesuits about ethnicity in El Salvador and about liberation theology. Ethnic divisions in El Salvador and other countries in Central America like Guatemala typically pitted the indios against the españoles and the ladinos, the regional word for Hispanicized mestizos. In El Salvador in 1831, the indio Anastasio Aquino rose up against both, telling his people that they should expect no quarter from either the ladinos or the españoles.

The case of Anastasio Aquino and his insurrection led Father Ellacuría and Hidalgo to a discussion of redemptive violence and how it contrasted mightily with evil violence. As expounded in *Freedom Made Flesh,* Ellacuría had suggested that the methods of violence did not determine its sinfulness, but rather that sinfulness depended on whether the violence was perpetrated in the cause of justice or injustice. Ellacuría had pointed out to the Chicano that in Jesus' time, "take up your cross" had a clear political meaning, for the cross was the punishment that the state inflicted on guerrilla terrorists. Ellacuría had decided that the salvadoreños were called to take up their crosses, whatever the political consequences, in the struggle to put flesh on the freedom that had been bestowed upon humankind by Jesus Christ.

Upon his 1985 return, Hidalgo had sent Father Ellacuría Raymond Padilla's classic 1973 *El Grito* paper, "Freirismo and Chicanizaje," taking the time to underline in magic marker the passages that described the analogies between Freirian conscientización, praxis, and love and dialogue and the raza's chicanización, el movimiento, and carnalismo, as well as the Chicano scholar's concept of chicanizaje, a double mestizaje born once in New Spain and Old Mexico as the result of the conventional forced miscegenation of Mexican

Indians and Spaniards and reborn in the United States in the forge of Anglo-Hispanic bilingualism and biculturalism.

Having learned that there was no scanning electron microscope in all of El Salvador for academic or research use, Jorge had arranged for the donation of one to the Jesuit-affiliated Universidad Centro-americana. The microscope had been mostly paid for, anonymously, by Adventure Capitalists.

The calculatedly brutal murder of the priests had shocked Hidalgo. When he first received the information from the telex he had broken down and wept. Subsequently, intelligence sources pointed out that, unlike the circumstances of Archbishop Romero, whose increasingly strident criticism of the 1980 junta led to his assassination, Ellacuría had voiced unexpected support of Cristiani's efforts to restart the peace process. There was speculation that this was among the reasons why far-right elements killed him.

For weeks Hidalgo brooded. He had in his possession high definition photographs of the cinder-block dorm, plainly furnished and filled with shelves of religion and philosophy books. He could make out the titles of some of them: Pope John XXIII, *Mater et Magistra,* Pope Paul VI, *Populorum Progressio;* Paulo Freire, *Pedagogy of the Oppressed;* works by Gustavo Gutiérrez; Leonardo Boff; Pablo Galdámez; Hugo Assmann; Ernesto Cardenal and his brother Fernando; Monseñor Romero; the Quaker pastoral worker, Phillip Berryman; Jon Sobrino, who had been a member of the Jesuit community and would also have been murdered except for his being out of the country. . . . AC soon learned that the commando unit alleged to have killed the priests, part of the Atlacatl, had strong ties to the United States. The two commanders of the unit were both graduates of special courses that had been given at Fort Benning, Georgia. Moreover, the unit had been in the process of taking a training course conducted by Green Berets only two days before the assassinations. While there was no suggestion that the Green Berets had any previous knowledge of the plot, the case only exemplified again what Hidalgo was to highlight three years later before the world press: the folly of American military policy in El Salvador and many other parts of the world.

At the time of the murders of the Jesuits, Gorditor, Hidalgo's favorite AC armor man who was later to accompany him on the hemispheric salida, probably said it best when he heard the details. "The right-wing salvadoreños are laughing at Washington. They are telling us they will do anything they like as long as they fight communism. This atrocity is what eight years of American policy has accomplished!"

Hidalgo thought of himself as a humanist and a warrior; his posture toward death was above all that of the stoic. He sought to live by the classical maxim that to fear death was to die a thousand times rather than merely once. He agreed with Saint Isidore of Seville's observation that it is better to die well than live badly, better not to have been at all than to be a wretch. Moreover, Hidalgo had experience with murders that encapsulated a message of terror. The wound that the murder of the Jesuits caused in him was not related to death per se nor even to the horror incited by the flamboyant, unnervingly arrogant, and grotesquely staged act of terrorism by the Salvadoran military. Ultimately, the death of the Jesuits struck a blow at Jorge's patriotism, at the Chicano's self-identity as a loyal American. That the U.S. policies of aid and abetment of the Salvadoran government, including the military and its many terrorist arms, had been a considerable factor in this and 75,000 like assassinations in El Salvador grieved him profoundly as an American.

When Gorditor learned that he was to accompany Hidalgo to South America including El Salvador, he warned Hidalgo very bluntly, using caló for special effect, that he needed to be extra cautious to compensate for his Salvadoran-incited emotions. "Vato, óyeme, que te hablo en Siria, you really got to make yourself hard as stone over there. Ponerse chango, ¿que no? You know, good Samurai."

Hidalgo laughed. "I should have you talk to Gary Gnu. He would feel vastly relieved that you are borrowing a page out of the Japanese Good Book. The time has clearly come for us to mime them!"

Hidalgo left to Gorditor the technical details—silencer, no silencer, thickness of bulletproof vests, and so on. The salsero had a dilemma. Who might they be up against, particularly in places like El Salvador? The right or the left? The left was apt to have a potpourri, including American weapons purchased clandestinely or captured from the Salvadoran military. They would also have plenty of AK-47s or their clones, which the 70s and 80s had documented to be the ideal arm for untrained insurgents and guerrilla forces, even though it was an unsophisticated weapon compared with the American M-16 assault rifle. Having been manufactured by most countries of the Communist bloc with national variations on the basic design, there were an estimated 35 million of them floating around world-wide, the most prolific firearm of all time. The right, however, would be better trained, often by the Green Berets, and would have the M-16.

Gorditor himself selected for the South American mission the M-16A2 in the smaller, more compact and mobile version, designed for use by special forces or paratroopers. It was a lightweight, gas-operated shoulder weapon capable of semi-automatic, full automatic, or three-round, burst-control fire, using 5.56 mm (NATO) ammunition. He took along a couple of shotguns as well, loaded with #1 buck with 16 .30 cal pellets, deadly even at 15 or 20 yards. For a handgun, Gorditor selected the Combat Grade Government Model of the COLT MK IV Series. He carried it "cocked and locked" and claimed it to be the fastest and most accurate of any handgun available for the first, aimed shot. Hidalgo favored a foreign gun that the United States government had decided to adopt; it had been a controversial decision not to "buy American." On the new Italian Beretta 92SB-F in 9mm Parabellum (NATO) caliber he had engraved the traditional Latin Parabellum motto that around the beginning of the century manufacturers and individuals often put on their guns, SI VIS PACEM PARA BELLUM, 'if you desire peace, prepare for war.' Hidalgo also liked to take a substantial book on a mission. He chose Sartre's *Being and Nothingness*.

Gorditor had a lot of names. This was appropriate for someone who was in the red hot salsa line of AC. Gorditor's real name apparently was Rodrigo Safos. A lot of AC people demurred even on that, claiming that he had changed it so that he could brag that those who went on a salida with him had the distinction of adventuring "con Safos." Hidalgo found the speculation amusing but didn't dig into Safos's placa. Safos had been with AC for over 15 years through the direct intercession of Hidalgo, who had heard about him through border sources. What Hidalgo had learned was that while Safos might not be college material, on the barrio streets and border outposts he was as fearless and tactically versed as one could be. On the other hand, if someone didn't take affirmative action he soon would be top dog for some slimy border operatives. AC took affirmative action. Hidalgo enjoyed going with him on long bouts; he loved to talk caló and caliche with him. Most of Jorge's brothers and sisters and sobrinos and sobrinas were like Safos, not college-educated types but workers, farmers, or service people, but none of them would have the luxury of time nor any of the requisite technical skills to spend 80 days in the field with Hidalgo. With Safos it was reliving lo pachuco but in a rarified, high-tech, brown-faced 007 atmosphere; pachuquez, but with all the boring parts cut out. Yes, they might have a fine old time.

This business of the Gorditor had been Safos's doing. About ten years ago in the "earlier days," on a deal grayer than usual, they found themselves in the midst of some potentially hot salsa. Behind the bulletproof panels of a van they were waiting for a showdown with the man. It could go either way, pío o pao. Just to relieve the scary boredom, Safos said, "Let's just say I'm your Gorditor."

"You mean that fat fuck who iba con Cisco?"

"Not exactly."

"I know the character well. Even the actor, our family, his family. He was border raza from Tucson. Real name was Ysabel Ponciana Chris-Pin Martín Píaz. His best make was *Stagecoach*, but his more typical role was a raza sellout. His character fought loyally for pure-blooded Castilian Caucasians. His placa was white inside, not brown, the Ur-Tío Taco. As far as he was concerned, raza were all canaille."

"You're shitting me."

"I'm not shitting you, calabaza head."

"I've seen the movies too, you know. He was alright. A little fat and a little funny but pura raza."

"Forget that panzón pendejo. How about you can be my Carnicero Bucher and I'll be your Santo Enmascarado?"

"No, no, I can be Chanoc and you can be El Vampiro."

"Are you kidding? I'd rather be El hombre lobo and you can be Capulina."

"¡Capulina, maricón de mierda! Don't insult me like that! How about I'll be Chicano grueso calibre and you'll be El chicano justiciero?"

"Well, now you're making a hell of a lot more sense. That almost fits."

And so on into the night they went over every bad churro and género chicano movie they had ever seen on either side of the border (and they had seen them all), seeking their identities as injustice fighter and sidekick in Hollywood or Churubusco celluloid kinesis, while they waited for a possible shootout with the man. But over the years the handle of Gorditor stuck after all, possibly because it encapsulated something of the sweet and sour wistfulness of chicanada, part parody, part bitter reproach, and the rest a sincere exercise of seeking self-validation in the gringo makeover of his identity. It was the same sort of logic, Hidalgo thought, that brought raza over in droves to Taco Bell and the other chains to eat deracinated Mexican fast foods that went down so easily with almost nary a non-Anglo afterthought.

When Hidalgo explained his "Taco Hell" analogy to Gorditor, the latter thought about it for a moment and laughed. "I don't know about that, vato loco. Speaking for myself, I don't frequent that pit. I'd rather opt for the real salsa. In my line of business, too much Taco Bell or Hell or la chingada and I could end up cinnamon crispas."

When that particular mission of a decade ago was accomplished successfully, both Rodrigo and Jorge celebrated with a visit to a National City tattoo parlor, one of the best in the business having catered to sailors for generations. Jorge came back with a brand-new, wavy-framed polychrome C/S on his wrist, bigger and better than the couple of miniatures he had barely afforded when he was an adolescent.

Jorge's wife, Marta, had a conniption. "Pendejo, look how you mutilated yourself! Don't you have the slightest sense of reality? Are you going to live the rest of your life in a selfish, romantic sleepwalk?"

Jorge had known this was coming and he had prepared a set piece, feigning shock and consternation. "But I just wanted to re-affirm my carnalismo with Rodrigo after such a perilous mission! You know, you never totally leave the barrio."

"Pendejo and machista both, then! What do you think the kids are going to conclude about what you've done to yourself?"

"Well, just that one never totally leaves the barrio. It's our culture."

"Then wear a Zoot Suit and a gold chain. Don't mutilate your body."

"¡Ay, Marta! That's just a fashion statement. I wanted to do something real with a genuine fellow homeboy."

To make matters worse, just to audit and certify Hidalgo's statement, his oldest son, then 12 and attending the most yuppie preppie school imaginable, not without its Chicano-alienating aspect, took to wearing a dangling silver crucifix from his earlobe, which he had bored through for the occasion. The Hidalgo household was in an uproar.

*   *   *

Around the hemisphere in 80 days!

The mission was progressing approximately the way it had been envisioned and staffed out. They had been all over the southern continent, conferring with pin-striped bean counters and the most merry, gracious businesspeople imaginable, quite a few of them not appreciated for their reliability, however. They conducted most of their business over food and entertainment; consequently, they had been eating like pigs.

Chilean pastel de choclo, meat pie with a topping of fresh ground corn for crust, and escabeche de gallina, pickled and garnished chicken. Up the coast to Peru where, despite the claims of Mexicans and others, the locals had invented the original Latin American version of ceviche (the stuff is good in the South Seas as well). It's a different taste to the Mexican palates of Jorge and Rodrigo, a different fish garnished with a different chile, the Quechuan ají. Then a fine arroz con pato, braised duck with rice and plenty of fresh cilantro. To drink, the pisco from the local vineyards and the port of Pisco. Jorge likes it with the thick brown local bitters called algarrobina, and Rodrigo downs it in the form of the now internationally famous Pisco Sour. Argentina for matambre, "kill hunger," a flank steak marinated in vinegar and seasonings, stuffed with vegetables and hard-boiled eggs, or a carne con cuero, beef roasted with the hide on, served maybe with a little chimichurri, the Argentine spiced parsley sauce. In Brazil the feijoada completa of course, washed down with some good batida paulista that combines the Brazilian sugar-cane brandy cachaça with fruit juices. A little moqueca de peixe, sardines wrapped in banana leaves and grilled over coals. Then belt down some of that cachaça straight, forget the fruit juice.

And engaging in world-class tourism. Was this working hard, or hardly working? They were regaled to a Peruvian harp concerto on site at Machu Picchu by the Andean Indianist Conservatory. In Venezuela they visited the Indian stilt houses in the waters along the banks of enormous Lake Maracaibo, the region where the greater part of Venezuelan oil was being pumped up. The houses and the indígena way of life that went with it struck Hidalgo and Safos as essentially the same as when encountered by Alonso de Ojeda and Amerigo Vespucci in 1499, which had promoted the notion among those first European explorers that they had encountered a novum mundum "little Venice," una venezuela. In Belem a priest who had founded a music school for abandoned street children had his orchestra and choir perform Beethoven's Ninth Symphony in Portuguese. In Panamá they took time off to travel to the island of Ailigandí in the San Blas archipelago. There they presided as guests of honor at the grand opening of a new branch of *Acción Latina* that would work to ensure that the Cuna Indians had sufficient resources to continue their tradition of mola-making. To commemorate her appreciation for his efforts, a Cuna woman with a fine brass nose ring presented the Chicano Knight with a genuine syncretic treasure, an antique mola in finest reverse appliqué, colored in lime, strawberry, banana, pearl, celestial blue, regal purple, and deep black, depicting the original 1901 composition of RCA Victor's "His Master's Voice." The early mola-makers had been entranced by the "talking dog" and the musical sounds produced by early wind-up phonographs. They also appreciated the composition of numerous corporate logos and added them to their traditional repertoire of religious imagery, Cuna lore, myths and legends, and other designs.

The Cunas were still doing great work, those who had not been corrupted by quick-make hustlers. *Acción Latina* would help maintain artistic integrity as well as establish an orderly market. Going through the finest corporate specimens, Hidalgo hunted for some that might charm his business associates. He found magnificent Shell Oil and Mobil Oil molas, McGregor brand clothing, Reynolds Aluminum, Viceroy and Kool Cigarettes, Krupp Industries, Peter's Cocoa, Parrot Safety Matches, Hitachi Televisions, Chiquita Bananas, Cinzano Vermouth, Canada Dry, Peacock Flour, Smirnoff Vodka, Bolívar Rum, Anheuser-Busch Beer, Singer Sewing Machines, the Statler Hotel, the International Lion's Club emblem, "God Bless America," Santa Claus, and Kellogg's "Tony, the Tiger."

After 40 days and 40 nights on assignment, Gary Gnu had presented himself in Rio de Janeiro to encourage, coach, and brief them. Gnu loved that city in the absurd, nostalgic way of the Carmen Miranda 30s and 40s that even then had been pure Hollywood schtick. The Gnu wore a white suit and white panama hat to lunch, and when he started going through his briefing all Hidalgo could think of was Alec Guinness and the vacuum cleaner that had been billed as a high-tech threat in *Our Man in Havana*. They had lunch at a restaurant with a magnificent terrace and Hidalgo spent the meal looking past Gnu at the favelas and the 100-foot statue of Christ perched on its great pedestal atop Corcovado mountain. Christ in the distance and the hillside abodes of the poorest of the poor framed the Wasp in finest white linen. The Gnu went on about how much he loved this city by the sea during carnival and Hidalgo pondered how the bill for that one lunch could probably have covered a square meal for everyone living in abject poverty on one of those mountainsides. Finally he decided to shut Gnu up in his subtle way. "Say Gnu, have you heard that the abandoned street children have become an immense problem in this country? They wait outside restaurants for the patrons to come out and then they stab them and take their assets from them."

"Really? I never heard of that."

"Well, you only go to five fork restaurants. You have to descend to the two and three forkers, where they put signs up cautioning you to look to your right and especially to your left when you go out. Yes, it's gotten so bad, and I'm not kidding you here, that they've actually set up right-wing death squads to shoot les petits. They claim they're doing it for the economy; the tourists have been staying away like mad."

Well, as Gorditor likes to say, ¿qué se va a hacer? You do what you can, ¿verdad? And the pagarés and deberés were mounting up, sector by sector, country by country, deal by deal. With a little luck in San José, Managua, Teguci, and Salvador, they would probably make the nine digits, at least in letters of intent. And the tithe off that would represent, to paraphrase liberation theologists, a hefty "preferential option for the poor." The pervasive poverty of Brazil penetrated into Hidalgo's pores and got him to thinking that maybe they could spend some money on the lowest of the low, like the garbage pickers. After all, Don Jorge had a special affinity for dump artistes dating from his adolescent days as a border scrap hog. AC had already experimented with some success on the border at Ciudad Juárez, organizing the Sociedad Cooperativa de Seleccionadores de Materiales (Socosema). São Paulo, Mexico City, and other urban centers could use something like that, a fairly operated garbage picker's cooperative, but they'd have to break the back of the mafufería and caciquismo that prevailed in the garbage dumps in order to organize the pickers effectively. That might require too much hot salsa for the company to handle.

Then to Nicaragua; Hidalgo and Gorditor considered nacatamales to be among the tastiest treats in this hemisphere, so moist when wrapped in banana leaves and the masa filled with simple, honest fare. And the art naïf was probably the best in the hemisphere, outside of Haiti, of course. Hidalgo aspired not only to medieval but renaissance status; he was expert on art naïf and had helped to curate a notable exhibition of same at El Museo del Barrio in New York City. In Nicaragua he purchased a small acrylic signed by an unknown, Carlos Marenco, from Masaya, a town close to the city of Granada on the Lago de Nicaragua. The budding art entrepreneur who sold it to him explained that the work was extraordinary because the artist worked with a magnifying glass and did everything in most subtle miniature. "See this amaryllis, that bougainvillea? Only with a magnifying glass and the tiniest of brushes is he able to do this."

Hidalgo felt extraordinary warmth as he looked at the work. In its fashion it was every bit the peer of those Gauguins and Rousseaus that were in the Musée d'Orsay or that the onerous Japanese were bidding into the stratosphere. It was a procession of the Virgin set in a tiny, pristine hamlet just like the ones that were being destroyed by the various Central American wars. The thatched and tile-roofed hamlet, a mere half-dozen structures, had everything, a sorbete stand, chickens, a rooster copulating with a hen, a dispensary of nacatamales (but only on sábado y domingo) a rosary peddler, and a chorizo, manteca, and mondongo dispensary. The Virgin's procession was graced by fireworks handlers, a five-piece brass, woodwind, and percussion band, and villagers headed by a stooped matriarch with a long rosary hanging almost the length of her cane. La madre smiled beatifically despite her obvious difficulty with walking. The aged woman, pained but happy, seemed to represent the authority of cultural continuity, and in appreciating her simple leadership of the peasant procession, Hidalgo was reminded of a famous passage in William Faulkner's 1950 Nobel Prize acceptance speech. No wonder Latin Americans appreciated him so. "I believe that man will not merely endure: he will prevail. He is immortal not because he alone among creatures has an inexhaustible voice but because he has a soul, a spirit capable of compassion and sacrifice and endurance . . ."

In the far left background of the painting a strapping lad was entering an outhouse, in the far right foreground another lad was urinating, and on the banqueta of the nacatamalería knelt some devotees of the passing Virgin borne on her own platform by five lusty villagers. There was a place for everyone and everyone was in place; yet in the back of the village was this almost surrealistic phenomenon, a painting within the painting—or perhaps a movie. Under an awning decorated with flowers and plants, the image depicted the Lago de Nicaragua in the foreground and in the background an immense volcano carpeted in its lower parts with flowers yet spouting fire and smoke at the cratered pinnacle. Hidalgo interpreted the volcano as symbolic of time and the furies. Most of the larger painting was idealized picturesque, the eternal, edenic, agricultural donnée of the Nicaraguan countryside. Yet in contrast to the foregrounded village was this telescoped painting deep within, a florid volcano harking backward in time to an earlier donnée—a pre-Christian one, Hidalgo presumed—a majestic volcano that predated and prefigured the village, a volcano for all seasons. At the same time, he thought it probably stood as a proxy for the hell that Nicaragua was undergoing. It was volcanic revolution and civil war.

The brush strokes were extraordinary. They appeared to be governed by the esthetics of parsimony, of acrylic frugality. In order to save paint, the artist had created his work on the thinnest layer imaginable. And yet, nothing had been spared with respect to the variety and vivacity of color, the intensity and detail of the composition, and the light which seemed to diffuse the painting from an omniscient source. This was a hamlet lit by the eyes of Nuestra Señora.

"So, then," Hidalgo asked euphorically, "What distinguishes this artist is his technique of the magnifying glass?"

"Yes, most assuredly," the humble stand owner explained with satisfaction, definitively passing over the extraordinary iconography, the symbolism, the composition, the use of color and of paint, the brush strokes, for the circumstantial value of what would seem to pass for "high tech" miniaturization.

Hidalgo chortled with delight, thinking to himself that this was naïf from within, naïf from without: not only the painting in its execution, but in its appraisal. With great enthusiasm he launched into a Socratic dialog with the art seller, pointing out a little stroke here, a nuance there, a certain iconic theme not to be overlooked. The seller responded in kind, no doubt fueled in part by an increasing conviction that he had a live prospect. They both emerged convinced that they had reviewed one of the masterpieces, all this confirmed by a solid sale of same to Hidalgo, whose esthetic ardor had caused him to engage in a purely nominal exercise of the required regateo. When it was all over, the piece nicely wrapped under his arm, Hidalgo felt such giddiness; surely esthetic discourse and honest commerce did not get better than this.

Nicaragua's attractions consisted of not only nourishment for the palate and stimuli from the palette. Physically, Managua seemed to Hidalgo almost identical to the place that he had visited in 1985. The city was like a bald guy or perhaps the conventionally viewed friar's pate, the center razed by the earthquake of December 23, 1972, and never rebuilt, leaving only a few isolated structures unscathed like the Inter-Continental Hotel. Nevertheless, the city grew plentifully on the margins, like robust hair around a smooth crown. Politically, of course, the city had changed radically since his last visit. Despite the obvious potential for violence, Managua excited him immensely.

Even then, in 1985, the city had an excitement that contrasted mightily with San Salvador. At that time, the Contras were relatively far away at the front and the capital was militarily secure and filled with notable people and happenings. For one, the place was full of internacionalistas from Sweden, the Netherlands, West Germany, and the like, engaging and earnest young people with whom Hidalgo enjoyed entering into polemical discourse, lustily defending his philosophy of humane, welfare capitalism. They would have none of it. They had that system at home and they were trying to escape it. They considered Hidalgo's whole concept of humane capitalism to be oxymoronic. The internacionalistas of 1985 tended to be nondoctrinaire Marxist sympathizers; often they were militant "greens" who denounced the West's wasting of the environment. Hidalgo wondered what these folks currently thought about the revelations of the East: the environmental devastation of East Germany, Bohemia, and great parts of the Soviet Union. Hidalgo remembered one earnest Dutch youth who unrolled a poster in order to joust with him. It graphically depicted twice over, once with the caption "Capital of culture" and then again, "Culture of capitalism," the same view of a banal street, crumbling structures, filth in the gutter, a scene bereft of any positive aspect whatsoever. Jorge, who had been to Eastern Europe and to Cuba, tried to convince the youth that the variety of culture and the diversity of city streets were infinitely greater anywhere outside of the entrenched Eastern bloc, even in horrid and squalid places of the repressed Third World, but to no avail. Now, of course, in light of what had become apparent to the entire globe, that proposition would meet with no contest.

Then there had been those very impressive Hispanic intellectuals with lovely beards and handlebar mustaches who had poured in from all over the Latin world. They looked so benignly bohemian, like Pancho Villa or Miguel de Unamuno in studious spectacles. Chocolate brown poets à la Rubén Darío, barbas blancas de chivo courtesy of Ramón del Valle Inclán. Here and there a wilder look, Che Guevara hair flaring to the winds from under a Basque boina. Although he didn't know it at the time, Don Jorge was to "rendezvous with destiny" with the same sorts later in San Salvador.

In 1985 the conference rooms at the Inter-Continental would be filled to brimming in the afternoons with ponencias of one kind or another. And when the day's disputandum was done, these dashing revolutionists with an endearing intellectual bonhomie traveled down the Managuan avenues quite handsomely in their vaguely 19th century anarchist outfits in the company of beautiful Nicaraguan women who for their part tended to dress in spanking-new, well-pressed, green military uniforms, with those notable red and black sandinista bandanas. And everyone had lovely books under their arms, works like Ernesto Cardenal's *El evangelio de Solentiname* and the *Cantos de amor y guerra* by the so-called guerrilla priest, Gaspar García Laviana, who had died in 1978 with a rifle in his hand and a cross under his sandinista bandana in a skirmish with Somoza's National Guard.

In 1985 Hidalgo had enjoyed promenading down some of the streets that dated from colonial times. In the Somoza period they had housed smart shops, but in 1985 they were redolent of idealistic government offices like the Commission on the Preservation of the Coffee Flower and the agency dedicated to the Fostering of the Fresh Water Fish of the Lagos de Nicaragua. He had to visit the Office to Conserve the Nicaraguan Artistic Patrimony in order to purchase timbres to remove from the country a few pieces of patently touristy wood sculptures that he had purchased, what the cultural anthropologists had come to term "airport art" or "Art of the Fourth World."

All this frothy excitement of 1985 had been rounded out by the American hippies. Where had they come from, and why had they flocked to Managua? In truth, American youth were everywhere in the world. He had witnessed them one summer camping out by the thousands on Omónia Square during the repressive heights of the Greek junta of the 1970s. These Nicaragua-touring hippies of 1985 wore the insignia of the 1960s, the worn and torn blue jeans with flowers and peace signs on their buns, the tie-dyed T-shirts . . . perhaps they had inherited them from their parents? The locals as well as the earnest European internacionalistas who were doing gainful voluntarism were disgusted with the Americans. They had entered the country with next to nothing, not more than the minimum 60 U.S. dollars required by the government in order to exit the airport. Once in Managua, they acted as if they were flat broke except for their stashes of drugs, which they consumed conspicuously. They spent their time panhandling for basic sustenance and soaking up the sights with a naiveté that Hidalgo found somewhat charming, something akin to Cheech and Chong's original night club act that the pair had transposed to *Up in Smoke.* "Hey man, this is it, the revoluuuution!" The sandinistas considered them the despicable offal of the corrupt, capitalistic American culture.

Nevertheless, despite so much local color, the most notable thing in 1985 if one went into the Managuan barriadas on the rim had been the mounting disgust and anger of the common people, who complained constantly about their inability to get medicine, or often, basic food, much less shoes or soap. It appeared that all the daily neciedades of Communist life as Hidalgo had witnessed it in Europe and Cuba affected the Nicaraguan common folk, underscoring Hidalgo's resolute conviction about the superiority of capitalism despite its obvious, egregious defects. Of course, Hidalgo had readily conceded to the Sandinistas during their business discussions that Nicaragua was laboring under immense hardships engendered by the U.S., including the embargo and the secret support of the Contras, and so the country was not one of the clear-cut cases.

Now Gorditor and Hidalgo reviewed a Managua with yet a different, fascinating complexion. With the utter collapse of the so-called Second World, at least as epitomized by the former Soviet Union, here possibly lay a clue to whither the new world order. The city was like no other place. The Sandinistas, not without strong pressure, had nevertheless agreed to relinquish power. The Sandinistas themselves were made up of different groups, including the comunidades eclesiales de base, the "grassroots Christian communities" or "Christian Base Communities." Currently even what had been the most Marxist elements of the left wing were wrestling with which politics and economics they wanted to embody. They appeared to have ruled out both Marxism-Leninism and regaining power by military means. Ortega Saavedra was spending much of his time on international salidas, playing diplomat in the Middle East and elsewhere. Some sandinistas were talking about creating a democratic political party under the banner of "humanistic socialism," which was yet to be defined. Tomás Borge, the only surviving charter Sandinista, was trying to establish himself as a celebrity interviewer for foreign newspapers and magazines. He was asking $10,000 to do articles on such figures as Fidel Castro or Muammar el-Qadafi. Some of the younger sandinista directors were out of the country, enrolled at the Harvard K-School, the UCLA B-school, and the like. Hidalgo took notes to pass on to his team of recruiters who visited colleges looking for talent. Others, such as Bayardo Arce, was trying to run the sandinista broadcasting empire like an efficient business. Jaime Wheelock Román, the former Minister of Agriculture with whom Hidalgo had been singularly impressed in 1985, was now in charge of moderating the upcoming party congress. And on the other side of the political spectrum was Violeta Barrios de Chamorro, who took the mantle from her slain husband Pedro Joaquín Chamorro and was propelled by her political skills and by events into the presidency. It was an exuberant place. It could go either way, centripetal or centrifugal. Hidalgo hoped that Cuba would wrench open soon, not only for that unhappy island's own sake, but for this place's as well, to make the grand experiment cleaner and sharper.

Finally, it was time to go to El Salvador.

From the international foreshadowing of Nicaragua to Central America's cesspool, El Salvador, the smallest, most overpopulated of them all, and seemingly the nastiest, most vicious and retrograde as well. Well, perhaps not, Hidalgo thought ruefully, even El Salvador could not quite equal the decades of Indian genocide going on in Guatemala. El Salvador merely got all of the attention. There were so many deplorable places, he really couldn't rank any of them, including El Salvador, worse than second.

From Managua to San Salvador, on the miserably maintained plane belonging to TACA, principal airline of Central America, with its torn seats and its abundant upholstery stains of dubious provenance, Hidalgo took out and perused Sartre's *Being and Nothingness*. It seemed like an apt read preliminary to entering the Salvadoran province of reality. He had been going over the book every few years since he had been introduced to it as an undergraduate. In his mind, *Being* had come to represent something like a reproach, but one that he had yet to fully grasp; so he was periodically compelled to take yet another whack at it, particularly at points in his career when he felt a certain level of mortal or moral danger. Hidalgo had concluded that, simply because of the inherent perils of living and bridging the Anglo-Hispanic bipolar, no Chicano, no matter what his political identity or socioeconomic status, could take lightly Sartre's exposition of bad faith, particularly the distinction between "bad faith" and its ontological alternatives—on the one hand, "sincerity," and on the other, "cynicism." Hidalgo reviewed them again in *Being and Nothingness* and he also went back to the obscure footnote on "the process of self-recovery of being that has been previously corrupted," which Sartre called "authenticity." Then he turned to what he considered one of the densest mysteries of existential psychoanalysis, the section on the "faith of bad faith." Sartre began by endorsing the popular concept of mauvaise foi as a lie to oneself, but then immediately proceeded to separate the phenomenon from garden variety lying and from traditional psychoanalytic notions of the consciousness that is duped by the unconscious.

> The true problem of bad faith stems evidently from the fact that bad faith is *faith*. It can not be either a cynical lie or certainty—if certainty is the intuitive possession of the object. . . . How can we believe by bad faith in the concepts which we forge expressly to persuade ourselves? We must note in fact that the project of bad faith must be itself in bad faith. I am not only in bad faith at the end of my effort when I have constructed my two-faced concepts and when I have persuaded myself. In truth, I have not persuaded myself; to the extent that I could be so persuaded, I have always been so. And at the very moment when I was disposed to put myself in bad faith, I of necessity was in bad faith with respect to this same disposition. For me to have represented it to myself as bad faith would have been cynicism; to believe it sincerely innocent would have been in good faith. The decision to be in bad faith does not dare to speak its name; it believes itself and does not believe itself in bad faith; it believes itself and does not believe itself in good faith.

Hidalgo noticed that as a college undergraduate he had written on the margin of this passage with what seemed to be sophomoric self-assurance all the more frustrating because it was now disconnected from memory or context: "Just like Sartre, Miguel de Unamuno points out, el Quijote dice, 'Yo sé quien soy,' pero el Don Juan dice, 'Yo sé a quien represento.' " He read and reread both Sartre's passage and his own bold scrawl of 25 years ago joining it to Unamuno, Don Quixote, and Don Juan with perplexity and disquiet, as if the answer to a profound antinomy were at the point of revelation, yet remained tantalizingly ineluctable.

God pray, this was important! Clearly Hidalgo, who was an exemplum of homo quaestor if ever there was one, did not want, upon examination of his state, to find himself residing in bad faith. Only good faith would do; but damn it, the categories themselves were so elusive! Turning up from his reverie and the conundrum, he looked out the window of the plane and found that they were preparing to descend into the jungly bosom of El Salvador.

"Bad vibes," Safos whispered to Jorge as they entered the queue to undergo the usual airport formalities. "I've got them from the minute we began flying over this stinkhole. Let's go back to lovely Managua, the bald friar city."

"Seguro que sí, Gorditor, but as you always like to say, ¿qué se va a hacer?"

As they waited interminably for the luggage to come down the belt, they spied down the corridor a couple hundred solemn Salvadoran males awaiting "processing." They had been picked up mostly in Los Angeles and deported back to El Salvador in an American plane. They were quiet and they looked like they were down to their last cigarettes, and after that maybe they'd begin a howlin'.

Then there was the pandemonium at the ticket counter as they left the airport. Everybody in the world seemed to be wanting to leave El Salvador, and their idea of how to accomplish this was to create funnels of clamoring people at each ticket and baggage station.

Gorditor jabbed Hidalgo in the ribs. "Looks like Detroit on Devil's Night. Maybe these desperados are all trying to ride the iron bull or something."

The worst, though, were the U.S. marines, a driver and two guards, fully armed with rifles cocked, who had come with an armored vehicle to escort them to the Sheraton Conquistador in the capital. After they got in the armored van, one of the marines mellowed out. "Shit," he said. "This armor is just for show. If they really want to get us, hey, no problemo. One bazooka placed in the growth at the side of the road. Barabim, baraboom, barabam and we'll be home fries right on the highway."

"I'd rather be a homeboy fry, my friends. Why would they want to off a couple of lousy businessmen?" Safos said.

"Beats me. Except we kinda heard you're a pair of spooks under pinstripe camouflage. They seem to keep wanting to kill us marines, especially if they catch us drinking and helping their lousy economy. They just like killing out here. My pa had some dogs that after a while we found would go out on the prowl and kill hens and shit. Vet said you got to off these animals because once they get a taste of hunters' ways, there's no coming back. And that's exactly what we did. I call it mercy killing, at least from the perspective of the farmer and his livestock."

Then they went down the interminable highway, the growth crowding the asphalt even on this main lane, and Sergeant Mellow took to pointing out the landmarks.

"About here is where they grabbed those nuns. Remember that?"

Jorge couldn't bear it anymore. "Yeah, we remember that, you asshole. The guys who did that are the ones you're defending and training how to kill."

"Well shit, nobody knows who's good and who's bad around here. They say it ain't half political anymore anyhow. Especially now since there ain't no Marxism left. It's all Hatfield and McCoy shit anyway. Or maybe good priest, bad priest."

Jorge was fuming. He was pissed and he was also slightly scared. Driving down this jungle road, even though it was the main drag, with marines as escorts, they were sitting pretty. And these marines, they reminded him of the dumbfucks motoring upriver in *Apocalypse Now*. Finally, he lost it. "Who told you dumbfucks to pick us up anyway? We'd be a hell of a lot safer in an inconspicuous taxicab. You're the ones they want to off!"

After that, they drove in silence to the embassy. Jorge felt bad. He had no business insulting these sad sacks who were just doing what they were ordered. But at least now it was quiet, blessedly quiet except for the fume-belching trucks that were chugging from the airport to town loaded to the max.

A good 100 yards from the embassy approach the marines stopped the vehicle. At the same time enormous concrete truncheons rose from the earth to block the armored car. New marine guards searched Hidalgo and Safos and sent the van to the pound. The last 100 yards were on foot. Except for secure vehicles, nothing was permitted close to the embassy.

The embassy in San Salvador was this big sugar cube of dark-tinted glass. It was as boring a tinted cube as you could think of; it looked like maybe a telephone circuit-booster substation off I-94, actually not even that exciting, a medical-arts building inhabited by practices and practices of dentists and chiropractors. Except that around the glass cube they had built Osaka castle. A full-metal jacket that included a wall with four turrets, one at each cube corner, staffed with machine gunners. To get into the embassy itself you went through a second full-press search and through maze doors similar to a Popeye's Fried Chicken in downtown Detroit, where you've got to contort your hands to give the attendant the money, and they contort your thighs and slaw back to you. Except it was their whole bodies going through the S-maze, not just junk food.

Inside was the damnedest thing. There was no natural light at all. Everything had been sealed tight, and on the corridor walls hung wallpaper in the form of forests and ponds, waterfalls and meadows swept by wildflowers, and small, benign animals: squirrels, bright red cardinals, owls, and peaceful doves.

They talked to the economic chargé d'affaires. "Why ain't there no natural light in this fucking tomb?" asked Gorditor. "God, how I wish I was back in Managua! It's so relaxed in the embassy that the guards look like they could sack out in hammocks. The only hint of antagonism is those big blowups of Sandino's 1930s telegrams to the U.S. on the approach road."

The chargé was a jovial dude. "Shit, you're right, man. We try to get to Nica whenever possible, it's almost R&R, especially compared to Teguci or Guatemala City. Here, almost every night there's some drive-by shooting. Even from a couple a hundred yards, which is as close as we let them get. This place is like South Central L.A. man, except they don't do no damage or shit. They don't even rile anybody's nerves anymore."

"Why you got this Mother Nature interior?"

The dude laughed. "Government issue. Shit, we asked for *Hustler* or *Playboy* motifs, but the government don't got that. Must be the feminists."

Jorge didn't like that reference to *Hustler* magazine. A guy had come down commissioned by that rag to do a story some years ago and had been blown away, as a matter of fact in the very Sheraton in which they would be bedding down. This town was jaded, he decided. They had become too used to lifting the cover of the garbage can in the morning and finding a stiff squatting at the bottom. "This place is freaky," Jorge said. "Reminds me of *Soylent Green.*"

"What dat?" said the chargé.

"An old movie. The entire earth's filled to the brim with people and towers and there's not a single blade of grass on the planet, except maybe for the emperor's palace or something. It's an old film, but even then I guess they figured some culture like the Japanese would win out. Anyway, old people go to a dying theater. They get this psychedelic experience of grass and mountains and fresh air just like the intent of your wallpaper, and then they're euthanized. What they don't know is that after they're dead they're processed back into the food chain, because with all that overcrowding there's an enormous shortage. They become something that's very suspiciously like that pressed seaweed the Japanese use to form sushi. They call it 'soylent green.' "

The chargé snorted. "Shit, sounds like they must have made that flick in the USSR." He laughed at his own joke. Then he said, "I guess the only people who'd give a shit for the sliced bread y'all are trying to sell in this country would be the Christian Democrats. For sure the right wing would rather see your asses burned than shake your hands. So, for deal making y'all are going to have to deal with the Christian Democrats, there's no way around that. But watch your step, they call them the 'watermelon men.' "

"How so?"

"You know, in El Salvador the peasants can't read. The government sees to that. They figure they don't need readers and writers for the kind of work they do here, harvesting coffee and shit. Everybody over here votes by color. The Christian Democrat party's electoral color is green. Green on the outside, red on the inside, according to the right wing—'the watermelon people.' "

"Great. How about the Company main man?"

"Aw shit, I never cared for spooks anyway, but wait till you see the Company man here, he's a fucking cowboy if ever I've seen one. Reagan holdover. I'm talking Dr. Strangelove, man. But as customary, straight Ivy League."

In a jiffy they were ensconced and taking a briefing in the Company man's office, a clubby affair paneled in faux walnut, just the thing for the Salvadoran volcano- and jungle-rot climate. On the walls were photos of the man shaking hands with his mentor, William F. Buckley, Jr., as well as Old Orange Head himself, and Bush when he was at the helm of the Company. Buckley's spy novels were on the bookshelf.

Jorge had checked the zealot out. He was a personal protégé of Buckley, the guy that some of the AC partners liked to call the "Black Knight." AC people had had a number of altercations with Buckley and his associates, and they had a thick dossier on them all. Sor Juana, the most devout of the senior partners of AC, liked to refer to Good Catholic, Bad Catholic, Not Catholic. She and the Kennedys were good, Buckley bad, and Hidalgo not. "Just teasing, Jorge!" But maybe just barely.

At one level, the jousts between the good knights and the bad knights for the hearts and minds and souls had been going on a long, long time. Jorge Hidalgo's family, before they fled Mexico when the Revolution turned against them, came from a line of campesino and small-town warriors, the dorados of Villa on his mother's side, and on his father's, the carranclanes of Carranza and most especially the great garbanzero, Alvaro Obregón. Junior's father, William F. Buckley, Sr., was ousted from Mexico also, about the same time as Hidalgo's family, but in dramatic counterpoint. Senior, who went by the handle of Will, had become one of the most prominent gringos in Mexico by 1914. He had made a fortune in oil and real estate working first with the advisors of Porfirio Díaz, the científicos, and then with Victoriano Huerta until the Porfirian general was beaten and had to flee the country. Ultimately, Will Buckley lost most of his Mexican fortune to the Revolution, and in 1921 he returned to live in Texas and later Connecticut, but not without revealing himself to be a militant counterrevolutionist whose porfirista zeal led him to attempt to block Woodrow Wilson's 1914 efforts to oust Victoriano Huerta. Will also helped a 1919 aborted coup in Tampico by General Manuel Peláez against Venustiano Carranza, whom he accused of being a Bolshevik when he later testified before the U.S. Senate Foreign Relations Committee. The dossier went on and on. The father came back to the United States with a seething hatred of revolution and a belief that he had personally witnessed in Mexico the first stage of a worldwide Communist revolution against capitalism and Christianity. Bill Buckley, Jr., inherited many of those fatherly beliefs.

In a sense both Hidalgo and Buckley were radicals, and they were similar in that ideas and not lucre were what essentially spurred them on. Add in the capitalism that they both espoused and their Catholic heritage, the former's of the Latin variety, the latter's of Irish immigrant formation in the 1840s. Nevertheless, they were worlds apart ideologically and in their value systems. With the promulgation of the social encyclicals of the 1960s and the radical left turn of the former "Pope's Men," the Jesuits as well as other liberation theologians, it became a real "tractor pull." The one had founded AC on the basis of international venture capitalism conjoined with a consuming sense of honor y vergüenza that manifested itself in chivalric entrepreneurship on behalf of the poor. He took public service and Good Samaritanship to extreme readings. His philosophy was underpinned by the new political era initiated by the Great Depression that began with the discrediting of Republican status quo conservatism. He generally followed the trends or the exempla of Franklin D. Roosevelt, Truman, the Kennedy brothers, Johnson's Great Society, even the Nixon-Kissinger opening to China: the establishment of a new politics of welfare capitalism and internationalism, called "liberalism" in scholarly circles. The Buckleys and their associates also eschewed status quo conservatism. They didn't see themselves at all as defenders of the verities of small-town America in the style of Calvin Coolidge, or later, Robert Taft. They rebelled against those values and viewed themselves as counterrevolutionists dedicated to arresting the global onslaught of the Evil Empire of Soviet communism and the atheistic assault on Christianity. Ronald Reagan had picked up much of his rhetoric from the *National Review.*

Ironically, given the 90s debate on so-called "political correctness," Bill Buckley, Jr., had first made a name for himself in 1950 while still a Yalie with *God and Man at Yale,* damning the Ivy League as a hotbed of atheism and collectivism and calling the idea of academic freedom a hoax. He claimed that Yale and the other universities had never subscribed to the unlimited free competition of ideas, but had always imposed limits. He wanted those limits narrowed so that the primary goal of education would be reaffirmed as the inculcation of students within an already-existing temple of truth of which Christianity and free enterprise were the pillars. Upon graduation from Yale, after a brief stint in Mexico as an agent of the CIA under the supervision of E. Howard Hunt (with whom he became a decades-long friend), he wrote his next book, in collaboration with L. Brent Bozell. They stripped away the mere human fallibilities of "Tailgunner Joe" McCarthy in order to advocate McCarthyism as a "public orthodoxy" that should be imposed through legislation outlawing Communists and the Communist party and through "coercive sanctions," which many critics at the time feared meant an attack on First Amendment guarantees justified by a purported life-and-death struggle with communism.

The Buckley protégé in El Salvador had been installed during the heyday of Ronald Reagan, Ollie North, and Elliott Abrams and was still going strong. Jorge gave him a 10 on survival skills. He was no fool either. Out of the Ivy League like so many of his generation who had gone to work for the Company, he had been steeped in the rhetoric of public service for America and warfare against the Evil Empire. Essentially he was still working for peanuts while his college classmates, having plunged America into the leveraged buyout crisis, were now making money all over again, de-leveraging debt for equity. Armed with books beginning with William F. Buckley, Jr.'s, *God and Man at Yale* and *Up from Liberalism* and the *National Review*'s idiosyncratic spin on José Ortega y Gasset's *The Revolt of the Masses* (poor Ortega had represented himself as a mainline liberal and in fact was a cofounder of the "Intellectuals in the Service of the Spanish Republic"), straight out of college he had sallied forth to make the world safe for democracy. He was, most definitely, in the league of the true believers, the forces of the "Black Knight."

Yet, there is this way that time and expediency soften everything. By 1982 the enfant terrible was of the establishment and defending the Reagan administration's support of Duarte against the New Right's anger at his Social Democrat background. Buckley, despite the outrage of conservatives around the nation—including George Will, who was also an ardent Reagan supporter—even demurred over the administration's token response to the 1982 Soviet and Polish crackdown on Lech Walesa and the trade-union movement. Hidalgo had reason to believe that at least in El Salvador, the CIA would work together with them in alleged common purpose: for agricultural reform, country, and capitalism. Perhaps not necessarily in that order.

"Gentlemen, with your help we are really going to accomplish something in El Salvador. I don't want to sound glib, because it won't be easy to accomplish, and part of the problem here, paradoxically, is that the Salvadorans, despite their flirtation with Marxist historical dialectics, are a curiously ahistorical people. They have these tradiciones arraigadas that go on for all time. Mr. Knight, I admire some of your humanistic writings about Hispanicity. These people are really good subjects for the investigation of Unamunian intrahistoria. What really takes place goes on in the eternal, atemporal sea, beneath the surface waves of history. For this reason, they have this very strange sense of time. It's like only yesterday the Conquistadors were taking over shop. Then they jump to 1823 when the bloody place got its independence from what was then the Captaincy General of Guatemala. At that time they applied to the United States for statehood and got turned down cold. From there the collective memory moves up to the Matanza that started in 1932, Archbishop Romero's assassination in 1980, and maybe, at best, a year ago. Everything's condensed into the present, even what happened in 1500. The long-term perspective is, at best, a year from today, either direction. But now the world has changed, and the fact that Salvadorans reside in the omnipresent is perfect for their interests and ours. We live in the post-Communist world and these people are going to be entrusting themselves to us to help get their economy afloat, including their agriculture. We're the only option around. That's a sacred trust, as I'm sure you agree, and we will honor it, accomplish land reform, Salvadoran style to be sure, and help our own agricultural machinery sector as well."

"Why is there still so much killing going on?"

The zealot responded with well-practiced ease. "Well, that's the obvious question around here and we've given it a lot of thought. Basically, this has always been a very violent place. There have *always* been a lot of clannish acts of violence, you know, like Hatfield and McCoy, except here it's the Gómezes against the Sandinos, or whatever. How much is simply baseline action and how much is genuine delta, I'm not sure, but I can tell you that 1980 was a lot more violent than this. Compared to 1980, I would say that the delta factor is way, way down. And it will actually go below the historic baseline; however, one might be able to compute it, with your help, gentlemen. America is genuinely committed to economic reform here, including land reform, and that we believe will correlate negatively with violence."

"Any thought to reforming the military here?" Jorge asked.

"Of course, in fact we are *constantly* working on upgrading the military, both in skills and sensibilities. But you know, frankly, this is still an extremely macho place in the traditional sense of the word. Surely I don't have to explain that to you, Mr. Knight. My sense is that even the campesino over here looks up to the guy with the huevos. The one who can get something done. I was in the Philippines before here, another somewhat Hispanic-flavored, primarily agricultural economy, and it was much the same way. That's one of the reasons why D'Aubuisson won so handily in 1989, because the people, almost all of them despite their political sympathies, were disgusted with the war and looked to a strong man to stop it. And believe me, both the American government and American policy haven't really quite recovered—we're talking confidentially, understand, I don't want to bad-mouth the inheritors of D'Aubuisson's power base, who I simply am compelled by Salvadoran realities to work with. But we really haven't quite gotten over the 1989 vote. The campesinos along with every other sector voted for ARENA enthusiastically."

Hidalgo appreciated the slickness of the performance; however, although there were dangers in alienating the Company man, he decided to try to get some info out of him with confrontation. "Christ, to listen to you, we're living in the province of Panglossia. As far as we can tell, from our admittedly remote perspective on the mainland, the land reform initiative has been unalloyed shit."

"What do you mean? We see it as a great success!" And he added resentfully, "It ought to be for someone such as you as well, who stands to make millions in commissions."

"Yeah, for us gray ops bandidos I suppose it will do fine. I meant for the people for whom the decrees were allegedly intended. What I hear, the land reform program is simply based on buying time for good old Uncle Sam, giving a little to gain a lot. We hear it's a shadowy minifundismo in support of continued latifundismo. Of course, as an exercise in public relations, it can't be beat as a way for the administration to certify to the U.S. Congress that the Salvadoran government is making the progress required for the appropriation of additional aid."

"Look, Hidalgo, you're simply mouthing *New York Times* horseshit. No way! Land reform may not yet be a total economic success, but up to this point it has been a class A, smashing political success. I'm firm on that. There is a direct correlation between the agrarian reforms and the peasants not having become more radicalized. And it's up to you potential sole-source vendors, I might add, to now help make it more of an economic success."

"Okay, dude, calm down. I'm just doing my Cheech Marín in Lalaland act. How about we meet for frozen margaritas tonight at the Camino Real bar? You and whoever you want from your staff, then we'll have dinner and review parameters and plot a little. I'm with you, big guy, 'land-to-the-tiller,' furrow to the max!"

The Company man turned easy again. "Sure, absolutely, we're all on the same side, the winners." Then he said, "I would like to remind you that we are very much involved in initiatives here to stop giving aid to OTMs. As a major Hispanic player with a presence and stake throughout Central America and elsewhere, I'm asking for Adventure Capitalists' strong support in this regard."

Hidalgo was startled. He searched the Company agent for further signs, but none were offered. Hidalgo interpreted the comment as a not unfriendly warning from a strict Company man who was prepared to do business with Adventure Capitalists but who was telling him in no uncertain terms not to engage in sanctuary movement work. Obviously he knew something, but he almost certainly thought that AC people were merely dabblers, and probably only at the individual rather than corporate level. Naturally, the federal Company couldn't be implicated in any relationship with the sanctuarists. He was doing his job, getting this message across. Hidalgo responded politely as if they were talking about something theoretical with little actual relevance to their collaboration. "Thank you for reminding us, we will meet our obligations as an American corporation. You can count on that."

"I appreciate it."

The acronym OTM referred to "Other Than Mexicans." The government, particularly the U.S. Border Patrol, used it for refugees from places like El Salvador, Guatemala, and Nicaragua. The Quakers had taken leadership in providing sanctuary to Salvadoran refugees. For them the issue and its operational redress was not unlike the underground railroad over a century earlier that they had operated to help slaves escape the South. AC was up to its neck in partnership with the Quakers, a network of like-minded Catholic clerics and laypeople, and others to provide sanctuary for Central American refugees. With the CIA now sufficiently knowledgeable for this agent to warn him of danger, clearly there was a breach in security, despite the fact that AC had carefully kept its support unofficial and under wraps. Jorge decided that he would need to access a secure line in El Salvador, no small feat, or get a confidential message out to AC headquarters pronto. They needed to put the kibosh on this breach and to completely restructure their portfolio and reroute their lines of support. Hidalgo brooded. Someday, and that day might never come, someone might introduce a high profile accusation linking AC and the CIA as partners in sanctuary. That would produce quite a row.

They were unwinding and drinking frozen margaritas on the terrace of the Sheraton Conquistador. A marine noncom much sweeter than the earlier batch had ferried them to their hotel and they invited him to stay for a drink. On the terrace they ran into a friendly print-media man who was staying at the hotel and seemed Salvador-wise. They took to drinking, talking shop, and ogling the toucan that was cracking seeds and pecking peels in a big wrought-iron cage on the terrace. Despite the fact that several gringos had died over the last 12 years at the Sheraton, including a couple of land reform experts and the so-called journalist from *Hustler,* Jorge and Rodrigo felt more relaxed than in the armored car. Jorge explained to the marine that probably they were pretty much home free. If anyone who knew their arrival schedule had wanted to blow them away, the perfect place to have done it would be on the run from the airport, where they would have been without recourse in that van, like spam in a can. The marine looked at him with an ambiguous smile. The print man chimed in that while this was all true, they'd probably be back in the danger zone once they went down around the main post office, as everybody did, to trade dollars on the currency black market for Salvadoran colones.

"Oh, assuredly," said Safos. "But in that case it will be a kinder, gentler danger. They'll only be trying to off us for our dollars, not our politics."

"Land-to-the-Tiller." Jorge intoned. "It does have a good rhetorical ring about it, like most of the horseshit around here. Might as well try to plough the sea."

Safos grinned. "You've heard that slogan before, Jorge, or at least I have. When I got briefed in D.C. for this adventure and the term came up, it rang a bell. 'Land-to-the-Tiller' is the Salvadoran version of a program with exactly the same title that was implemented in Nam. It's American Institute for Free Labor Development stuff; they and U.S. AID take it out, dust it off, and put it everywhere it seems to fit."

"I do believe! God damn, what goes around, comes around."

Safos laughed. "Don't forget, carnal, ahora tú estás con Safos." He turned to the print guy, the cagatintas. "Say, little ink pisser, what do you do for relaxation here? And don't tell me a thing about Salvadoran women. I'm a respectful Latino male who is not interested in being offed."

The ink pisser shrugged. "Not much going on. A little mariachi music, maybe some salsa. Actually, I'd rather be in Belfast. Here, now that the media moguls have up and gone to Tbilisi or Alma-Ata or wherever lenspeople go, there's no movies. With them here they'd put on flicks like *Salvador, Romero, J.F.K.,* or Woody Allen's *Bananas* on their video recorders at midnight. They were amply endowed. Now that they've gone, the kitchen has even closed down the breakfast buffet."

Safos laughed and began to talk like W.C. Fields, "I once went to Belfast. It gave better bed and breakfast."

It was ironic. Safos had turned his back to the street and started complaining to the toucan in his version of Salvadoran toucan-Spanish that his bullet-proof vest was raspy and itchy in this humidity. Jorge brooding over what the Company knew about Sanctuary and lulled by the drink, absently thought that Safos was too relaxed. This was not really like Gorditor, usually he acted like Wyatt Earp in a public place, back to the wall, front to the action. At that moment a Cherokee Chief, the van of preference of the Salvadoran government, including the right-wing paramilitary, stopped on the side street close to the outside entrance to the terrace. Oddly, some very lean adolescents got out, looking very respectful. Jorge didn't register that much, but suddenly Safos, who had his back to the kids, perhaps overcompensating (Jorge spent so much time later going over every second of it, agonizing on the what, the how, the why) or maybe seeing something reflected in the plate glass of the bar, turned around abruptly. The adolescents had entered the terrace already; there were four of them, and they were like those humble peasants in *Viva Zapata!* on their way to an audience with Don Porfirio in the palace, but a lot younger, really kids. The lead kid stopped and his face betrayed panic. Safos ripped out his sidearm and went for a canvas bag he had on a close-by seat that had high-tech accoutrements and a shotgun. The kids revealed their weapons. Rodrigo got off the first shot. The first kid's cephalic mass came off and flew into the air and along an empty table. It's funny, the things you do and out of what instinct: Jorge threw up his hands and spread out his legs, just like a vato loco pinched by the San Diego fuzz. From someplace out of sight a withering barrage of scope-focused bullets shattered the media man and the noncom, who had barely registered surprise. Safos fell too, head up on the table. Jorge's last, sidelong glance at his beloved Gorditor was at a head parted like a wake of water opened by a speed boat. There was raw brain in the margaritas. Quickly, arms outstretched and legs as wide open as practical, Hidalgo walked to meet the three muchachos who remained alive.

*   *   *

In Jorge Luis Borges's "El sur," the little intellectual shnook from cosmopolitan Buenos Aires is dying from a silly septicemia—fresh paint was on the door that he bumped into while walking up the stairs engrossed in the Weil edition of the *Thousand and One Nights* that had just arrived in the post. While the poor, meek, terminally ill daydreamer deludes in his hospital hell, the quixotic wit that he had always lived by takes advantage of his hallucinatory state to prepare a virtual reality that fits his bookish imagination of pampa pundonor like a glove; perhaps more accurately, like a custom-tailored condom. In his mind's eye the little intellectual leaves the hospital sound of body and mind and takes the train south, to a place that seems like a voyage to the vast and elemental yet more intimate past, where life, while violent, is simpler and clearer. There, in the South, rather than taking death in the Buenos Aires intensive-care ward, he chooses to accept the challenge of a few self-serving gauchos and dies pundono-rosamente with an unfamiliar but honorable daga in his hands. Don Jorge dwelt on that tale of the rehabilitation of self-esteem that transcended the decay of the body for all that happened to him with los muchachos. He especially appreciated in the Borges story the opportunity afforded the meek intellectual to pick up a knife that was thrown to him in order to justify his own death.

Don Jorge was taken by his captors, bad-complexioned guerrilla muchachos the age of his own schoolchildren, to the other side of the volcano, the Guazapa. There he stayed for as long, it seemed, as Cervantes had spent in Algiers captive of Barbary pirates, eventually rising in rank to serve ambiguously as comandante of procurement, maintenance, and transportation of military matériel of the Guaza-pan, Christian-based arm of the Farabundo Martí National Libera-tion Front (FMLN). On the other side of the volcano he met and polemicized with a renegade soldier of Christ, Father Ignacio. And there he lost all bearings and moorings to his normal upper midwest-ern life and fell in love . . . again, this time with one guerrillera y aventurera, a lady of mournful countenance, Dulce Tobosa, or "Sweet Dulce" as she was often known to him.

Naturally, these singular conversions were not as Hermelinda del Pimental, the mathematical theoretician of chaos, might term them, a "single product moment," but were accomplished in timely (or perhaps untimely) stages. It is important to point this out because so many of the standard accounts would have our knight-errant (or was it errant knight?) emerge to the status of a Patty Hearst or the Manchurian Candidate, like flashing-eyed, armored Athena fully formed directly from the head of Zeus. That would seem to be missing the point. There are all these lives that one lives, Hidalgo tells us, by word and by deed. And we travel in time and in space across various states of being such as those Jean Paul Sartre defined with those elusive categories of good faith, bad faith, sincerity, cynicism, and authenticity that in concept so tantalized our adventurous Chicano.

The first weeks our knight seemed to be traveling somewhat more mundanely: with a dark sack around his head that effectively limited his sight and other senses. "I regret that I'm such an estorbo," he would say from time to time. "I know I'm interfering with your mobility." But gentilities were rarely reciprocated by los muchachos. Usually they would respond with "Cállate el hocico." Occasionally they varied with "Tápate el pico." Given these guys' propensity for ruralisms, blind Jorge figured they must be the genuine article, authentic guerrillas, puros muchachos although not necessarily muchachos puros.

Not only was it hard for the garrulous Jorge to maintain an imposed silence, the stuff that *he* heard was not precisely to his satisfaction. It seemed that something was rotten in Salvador; some-thing very wrong had happened and very contrary to muchacho expectations. Now, apparently separated from command and con-trol, los muchachos debated their next moves. Some of their sugges-tions regarding his unwanted presence had the physical finality that he feared and was not yet ready in his soul to submit to. Unhappily, the climate was not right for singing one's praises and arguing one's worth to these adolescents. Silence truly seemed to be golden with these boys, as Jorge soon learned. Trying to take advantage of a lull in the conversation among them to assert his point of view was usually met with the now familiar refrain, "cállate el hocico," plus a swift and breathtaking thrust of a rifle butt in his gut.

At first Hidalgo tried to cope with his captivity by transporting himself to some other place. He found that his imagination was in a sorry rut, landing him in all the horrid spots that a man of arms and letters premonishes in his most masochistic moments: Patty Hearst's closet, the place where the Chicano marine who had been guarding the Iranian embassy lived blindfolded, Jacobo Timerman's cell without a number, the hovels of the Beirut captives, screaming and being forced into silence as the soles of their feet were beaten. . . . This is to no avail, he thought. Better to be here, presente, and rise to la altura de las circunstancias. Except that it was so hard to do much rising to the occasion with a dark sack around his head depriving him of senses or station, his hands bound behind him like a fowl waiting to be plucked and his silver-tongued arsenal of wit completely quashed.

This went on for weeks and our knight began to lose all sense of time, of place, even of self. With the sack over his head, forced to be mute, and his hands bound behind his back like a French chevalier waiting for the wrathful justice of the revolutionary paysans, he could not bear silence around him, for it made him fear that at any moment they would put out his life. He feared he would be snuffed as suddenly as the dumbest brute in the stockyard. Not sensing or comprehending a thing, they would simply extinguish him somewhere on the anonymous jungle floor or on the side of some volcano that emitted noxious sulfurs that surely came from the bowels of hell itself. He craved their sounds, especially the sounds of normalcy, of eating, slurping, or jesting. Of passing gas. On the other hand, shivers of fear entered him when they talked about what to do with him in that funky Spanish of theirs that seemed descended only yesterday from the original adventurers who had roamed this land and were later aggrandized as conquistadores.

One night the usually indifferent, occasionally courteous stance of los muchachos was broken and one of them approached his covered head. The smell of spirits was on him and with ardent rancor he told Hidalgo, "Very soon now, gringo hijo de puta, perhaps today, tomorrow, soon, without even foreseeing a thing, you are going to be slaughtered here in the dirt and you will be left dead and uncovered in the dirt where you fall. Not even covered with a plastic shroud, you will lie in the dirt and the scavengers will come and share you and take you away in parts."

At that moment he had mustered the sufficiency to mutter some inanities about que será, será and the need for the good Christian to always be ready to meet his maker (actually, wasn't this more the venue of the honorable Japanese code of Bushido?), but in the days that followed this encounter haunted him and verily he felt he might take leave of his senses. Grim night of the soul! He believed himself bereft of the family and friends he had once loved, of God who as a youth he had so passionately relied on in his foragings for tin and lead in border dumps, of the sense of his own self that once he had in such abundance.

Then suddenly, without warning, the sack was removed from his head just as the scales from the sinner's eyes, and when after some time he was able to focus again, it was clear to him that he had been given dispensation to return to the earlier, simpler time. He was captive now in a place with motors and engines, and peering like Narcissus, except not into the waters but into a pool of used Quaker State on the earthen floor, he saw the bearded face that stared back blinking, and he blessed his visage and whatever good fortune and breath of life were left to him. How opportune, familiar, and comforting was the smell of worn lubricating oil! He looked around at the vehicles—the vans and jeeps and sedans—and back at himself in the puddle, and uttered his first, saving joke in many weeks, "Return of the low rider!"

Sometime later a man of the word in a grimy, worn, white guayabera appeared before him in his thatch hut close to what apparently was a guerrilla motor pool, where other than being well bound and chained, Hidalgo had been exercising unlimited use of sight, sound, and apportioned opportunities for bodily relief.

He called himself Father Ignacio. "I can't tell you how much I grieve for your misfortune, for the deaths of your friends that it has caused, and for the deaths of many, many of our muchachos and supporters. A great tragedy has occurred. There are really no words that I can convey to express my sorrow for the current condition you find yourself in, removed from all those who love you and who are totally in the dark about your status, and who must be desperate or despairing. This was never to have happened."

Then the priest hugged his captive tightly and tears came to Hidalgo's eyes. "Will you free me?"

"I cannot. I will explain in greater detail later, but I don't have the authority and the secular arm considers your captive status to be necessary for *razones de estado*." Later, Hidalgo was to learn that Father Ignacio identified with one whom he liked to call his *tocayo*, Saint Ignatius of Loyola, the soldier of Christ who had prescribed in his *Spiritual Exercises* that aspirant novices, in order to fully attain the grace that they sought, participate *physically* in the agony of Christ.

"Let me explain that we have both been betrayed. Our autonomous army of Christian-based muchachos received word that your company called Adventure Capitalists was highly unusual and not the sort of enterprise that we might have expected from the United States. We were told that you wanted to visit with us on-site. We were told that you genuinely wanted to help in the implementation of agricultural reform and that in order to learn more about the need for agricultural equipment and vehicles from the revolutionary perspective you wanted to inspect muchacho-controlled territories and talk with us directly. Of course, we were very suspicious of anyone working with Cristiani and the rest of Salvadoran officialdom, despite the fact that on the face of it you were here to help implement the progressive second phase of the *ley agrícola*. Nevertheless, we decided that we would meet with you, but of course we took what in our mind were suitable precautions. We received word through intermediaries that you were waiting to be picked up by our people at an agreed-upon hour at your hotel and that we would escort you to a safe haven. I regret terribly what happened. From our perspective, at the moment of the tragic encounter, your bodyguard committed an unexpected, inexplicable act of aggression and we responded in kind."

Hidalgo sighed. "There was a rat. We were just sitting on the veranda having a drink and ogling the toucan. We had received no word of any meeting or any contact with your group."

"It is clear now that we were both set up. Some third party wanted this tragedy to occur and staged it, although we are not entirely sure why. Most probably, to create international tensions and thus to forestall agricultural reform, which is exactly what has happened. We also have no idea who arranged for this—that is, which faction or group. There are so many." The priest looked down at the ground.

"Can I go outside?"

"Surely." The priest arranged for him to be unchained from his rock. Hidalgo gathered up his chain and walked out of the hut. The sun was setting on the guerrilla camp that was nestled in a ravine on the side of the volcano.

"What is this place?"

"It is called the Guazapa. It is the lee side of the Guazapa volcano, which naturally shelters us from Salvadoran officialdom. I call it the place of the 'Ultra-Montanes.' This is a Jesuit's joke, although I myself am a member of the Missionaries of the Sacred Heart. In the olden days when they were the 'Pope's men' and not their own, the Jesuits were called that by the 'Cis-Montanes' on the other side of the Alps who hated them for backing the papacy." The priest went on, "We have been independent here for over a decade, although as you well know, most days they bomb us from the air. Since the bombing of Tenancingo, the air war has become so bad here, due to the increase of U.S. military aid to the Salvadoran Air Force, that most of the civilian population have taken whatever they could and evacuated. We'll stay here though, until Kingdom Come. You are in a military camp of one of the Christian armies of the FMLN.

Hidalgo looked up toward the Guazapa. The sun was setting over the volcano. It was a cathedral sunset; majestic beams of light bathed the barren peak that tossed its volcanic sulfurs into the air like the glowburn that his children liked to throw on the log in their fireplace at home on a wintry night. With all of that sulfur in the air causing diffraction, perhaps it was the most magnificent sunset he had ever seen.

Hidalgo said to the priest, "There's no shortage of possible conspirators. It could have been the right wing creating an international scandal that would undermine or stall progress on the ley agrícola. It could even have been a competitor trying to keep us from closing a deal."

There was an awkward silence. Neither the militant priest nor the adventure capitalist wanted to continue. Jorge relived the last moment with Safos, with the top of his head blown off and the cerebral mass parted as indifferently as a pomegranate. He looked up toward the Guazapa. The pinnacle of the volcano pierced the falling sun like a scabbard in a pie. "Why have you treated me as you have?"

"You mean, kept you like a blind prisoner?"

"Yes."

The priest sighed. "It is so hard to explain the peripeteias of war. Incompetence, or rather, inexperience, misunderstanding, suspicion. When the supposed rendezvous and escort of your party went all wrong there were enormous repercussions. It is a common cycle here in El Salvador. With the dead marine, the dead journalist, and your colleague, the military attacked on all sides. Hundreds of people were killed in the cities, military operations swept the countryside. Priests and religious were killed. The muchachos responded in kind. Hostages were taken, village mayors were killed, sappers entered the capital. I can't estimate how many hundreds of people have died from this affair. It spiraled on and on. Our entourage that had taken you was entirely separated from our command and very often in grave danger. Finally they were able to come back here by going north, almost into Honduras, and backing down south. The last 24 weeks have been a sheer hell—the newest emanation from hell, certainly not the last.

"Twenty-four weeks? Have I been captive that long?"

"I'm afraid so."

"Can word be given to my family that I'm alive?"

"I'm not the secular authority here, Mr. Hidalgo. Puñonrostro decides that."

*   *   *

Integration into the community.

Hidalgo, "gringo" grease monkey for the Revolution, with his blackamoor hands that guerrilla cleansing agents are woefully incapable of bleaching, holds on to Sweet Dulce for dear life. He's like a consoling cat. He embraces her at the waist. Later around her shoulders, down at the knees. He massages the small of her back, her taut neck. Sometimes she subsides. Not tonight.

She fell into deepest sleep just as the whippoorwill began its nightly oration. The bird has repeated its vigorous, deliberate call, accented on the first and third syllables, a full 400 times without stopping. Yet, she still shakes uncontrollably. Most nights there is at least one of these episodes. He often has one of his own version too.

While she dreams of the goriest details, he dreams about nothingness, stretching out forever. Just as he apprehends the defining quality of forever, of infinity, he wakes up in a panic. For some reason his night thrashings keep falling on his shins, which have sprouted scabs.

The lovers know why she suffers. Night Dulce breaks free from the discipline of the ego and returns against her will to relive the holocaust of El Mozote. Not so much the holocaust itself as the shame of having survived it. She is wracked by emotions. Sobbing, piteous groans, the shakes. The worst shakes Hidalgo could ever imagine, as if she were in the throes of the deepest paludismo that the Salvadoran savanna could offer. When she comes out of it she doesn't remember much, and it's a good thing too.

Soon after having received whatever explanations of his status that Father Ignacio could afford him, Hidalgo was offered continued captivity in chains or productive work under revolutionary supervision. The latter appeared to Hidalgo like the blessing offered to Borges's intellectual by the gauchos of the South. He readily chose work with the caveat that his captors should understand that he considered himself a prisoner, and he would exercise his prisoner's options including the obligation to attempt escape.

El Pájaro Loco, who became his general supervisor, laughed rudely. "I wouldn't try that. We guerrillas are a benign bunch in comparison to the other side. They wouldn't want to take a mysterious gringo into the capital, whoever you were. Better that you should disappear into the bush. I would suspect that if they got you they'd make a delectable pebre out of your carcass!" At that allusion, the revolutionary motormen laughed lustily.

Hidalgo was assigned to the shop that had originally serviced the vehicles of the plantation Café de los Dioses. It was there that he made a name for himself for high mechanical ingenuity and skill, which would eventually lead in future years to his appointment as head of procurement, maintenance, and transportation of revolutionary matériel, reporting directly to Pájaro Loco, who appeared to be, in Hidalguian jargon, the chief operating officer of the guerrilla camp. In turn, el Pájaro Loco, who Jorge sometimes called Woody Woodpecker, reported directly to the CEO, Jesús Salvador Puñonrostro. Confidently and in the manner of his namesake, the woodpecker rat-a-tatted staccato waves of directives down to combat, supply, ordnance, and the rest, including the few civies who had survived the 1986 Operation Phoenix in the Guazapa.

The vehicles of the Guazapan Christian-based arm of the Salvadoran revolution mostly dated from 1979 or earlier when the region had achieved autonomous status and the assets of the latifundias had been taken over by the guerrillas. What few spare parts and tools there were, much less new vehicles, had to be captured as a result of guerrilla operations against military or government-controlled facilities. It was a losing battle, but the guerrilla motor jockeys did the best they could. These muchachos displayed the highest esprit de corps, and pretty soon, despite his sorrow, our knight made the effort to kid around with the best of them and it helped his morale greatly.

He even taught them some of his border caló. But they kept calling him gringo, and it pissed him off.

"Hey gringo, are you going to live the rest of your life in that gringo outfit?"

Hidalgo flushed. "You incompetentes are the ones who took me away without even a change of underpants! What do you think I'm going to wear? I'm not flacucho and chaparro like you muertos de hambre. And, me cago en la leche de la chotacabra chillona, stop calling me gringo. I am not now, nor have I ever been a gringo."

"Oh yeah? You look like a gringo to me."

"I look like a gringo? With this brown face and Latino features? Me, with these mustachios?"

"What about that gringo sport jacket and sport shirt you wear every day? Why don't you change it? Have you ever seen a Salvadoran peasant in a seersucker jacket?"

"C'mon, dale una quebrada," one of them said in newly learned Spanglish. "He's already told us a hundred times about his seersucketa jacket. He can't change it. He's got a gringo body. Nothing Salvadoran fits him. He's gonna wear his gringo sport jacket till the end of the Revolution."

The guys laughed. "UUUUUUhhhhhh. Could be a long time."

One of the motor muchachos who had been in the U.S. had gotten deported back to El Salvador, and had made it to the guerrilla lines said, "So, okay, you're not a gringo. You just play a gringo on TV."

Another guy got some of the camouflage paint. "Mira, gringuito. Ven aquí. I'll fix you up real good. You can wear gringo clothes for your gringo body, but I'll paint you up like the field vans. Then you'll be a camouflaged gringo. Nobody will be able to tell!"

It reminded Hidalgo of an incident some twenty years ago. He hadn't thought about it much at the time, but just as he and his carnal Safos liked to say, what goes around, comes around. Hidalgo had arranged for an investment seminar for Chicano workers at a border-run blue jeans factory. He was encouraging them to consider a savings plan for their children's college tuition, even if it were only $10 a week. A Jewish friend of his, Juliet "of the spirits" Rosen, a lifelong investment banker of the border region, agreed to participate, and Hidalgo had managed to get an Irish guy from the New York office of a large mutual fund. The Irishman didn't know anything at all about the Chicano community, and he was publicly getting bent out of shape. He reacted badly to being pigeonholed an "Anglo." Finally, Juliet told him with a sort of definitive relish, "You come down here to the border, you're fair haired and can't speak a word of Spanish, you think that a taco is something made with a deep-fried shell into which is stuffed velveeta cheese and shredded lettuce, you're an Anglo, man." Everybody had applauded and the poor, fair Irishman, who in fact disdained all Brits, changed color. Better then to take the kidding, but he would look for his advantage. Even in the Salvadoran bush, Jorge was the most competitive vato of them all.

Hidalgo found that in certain ways he was not unprepared for the events that befell him. His other college major, existential philosophy, had prepared an armor of letters for him, and first as a student and later an adventure capitalist, perhaps vaguely intimating such eventualities brought about by his line of work, he had often read in the literature of prison solitude. During the days in the motor pool and the nights with his campesino compinches he remembered whole passages from Dostoyevsky's *The House of the Dead.*

> I also recall an ardent desire to be resuscitated, to be reborn into a new life, that gave me the strength to resist, to wait and to hope. . . . I still remember that, surrounded by hundreds of comrades, I was frightfully alone, and that I came to love that solitude. Isolated amid the crowd of prisoners, I reviewed my former life, I analyzed its slightest details, I pondered it and I judged myself pitilessly; sometimes I thanked the destiny which had granted me that solitude, without which I could never have judged myself nor plunged back into my past life. Some hope sprouted in my heart

then! I thought, I decided, I swore to myself never again to commit the mistakes I had made and to avoid the falls that had broken me. I drew up my future program, promising myself to abide by it. I believed blindly that I would accomplish, that I could accomplish anything I wished. I waited, I looked joyously forward to my free-dom. . . . I wanted to try my strength again in a new struggle. . . . I write this because I think everyone will understand me, because everyone will feel as I did, who has the misfortune to be sentenced and imprisoned in the prime of life, in full possession of his strength.

One day Hidalgo inquired about a group of vans that had been accumulating on the side. "¿Qué pasa?"

"Oh, those? We don't know what to do about them. They all need valve jobs. They're too good to cannibalize for spare parts, but we simply can't find or commandeer padding for the rings. We don't think they exist anymore in the region. Maybe we should raid Honduras?"

Hidalgo listened with mock disbelief and with great enthusiasm. Problem solving, even in such odious circumstances, that was his greatest pleasure. "Valve jobs! Valve jobs! I'm the king of valve jobs!"

The muchachos laughed. "Are you the king of the válvula or of the vulva?"

"Of both, actually. If given half a chance. When this is over we can open a shop, Válvulas somos nosotros. We'll make a dólar. Let me at those suckers."

Hidalgo came back two hours later after having inspected the vans. "Certainly, you are right, they are all rehabilitable but we need padding for the rings. I can do this. We Chicanos are always in the same straits. We are the greatest opportunistic mechanics, the greatest low riders in the nation. We make do." Excitedly he asked, "Do you have any cork?"

The head mechanic looked at Hidalgo without comprehension. Then suddenly he jerked forward; his monkey wrench crossed his heart like a divine instrument as a very great presentiment passed his brow. "Cork, yes, cork padding. Of course we have it. The hacienda used it to cover their jars of Café de los Dioses. We've got sheets of it, thousands. That will do it, that will serve?"

"Most definitely, illustrious comrade in wrenches. Compliments of the ingenuity of the Chicano nation, all derechos reservados. It won't give you 20,000 miles per overhaul, but if properly formed by a . . ." he clicked his heels, "master craftsman, it will give you 3,000 serviceable miles, that is 5,000 kilometers, and another 2,000 kilometers leaking 40 grade oil like an insufferable pig. What the hell, we'll just hoist them up every 5,000 kilometers and give them another good corking. We're the best motor shop in the Revolution anyway, aren't we muchachos? I did it myself a half-dozen times on my border-running troca, although the last time was on my seventeenth birthday. But we can do it. A cork, a cork, our kingdom for a corking!"

And so, not unlike Cervantes in Algerian captivity, whose ingenuity came to the fore, Hidalgo became renowned as a minor folk-hero among the Christian Base Community. The man who had combatted the leaking valves with hacienda cork, who had overcome adversity to refashion materials of the Salvadoran oligarchy to revolutionary advantage, who had made the Cherokee vans run beyond their time. It worked so well that in two months' time mechanics from other guerrilla-liberated regions of El Salvador were traveling by night to the Guazapa motor shop for a training session in cork-formed valve rings.

El Pájaro Loco presented Hidalgo with an official commendation of the revolutionary council of the Farabundo Martí Liberation Front, countersigned by Puñonrostro as chief of the Guazapa region. It read in part, to his great satisfaction, "To Jorge Hidalgo, the Chicano whose ingenuity made a major contribution to the Salvadoran Revolution . . ."

"Well," Hidalgo said, "somebody knows what Chicano means around here, finally. I wouldn't want this to get back to the wrong people though, they would get the idea that I'm your muchacho."

Pájaro Loco laughed. "Why not, why not join us? You know we are on the side of the angels."

"I'm not sure angels, except maybe for fallen ones, live on the side of a smelly volcano. Why hasn't Puñonrostro presented this to me personally? I don't think I've seen him except a couple of times in passing. He's not that busy."

Pájaro Loco laughed easily. "I don't think he wants to talk to you directly. You're something of an embarrassment. You might ask him something that he wouldn't be able to answer easily."

"You mean like being let free?"

Pájaro Loco laughed again with comradely good cheer, but would only say, "The Revolution knows how to acknowledge its favorite sons and daughters."

Soon after his brief explosion of notoriety, Hidalgo sensed that a very homely, intense woman about his age was staring at him as he sweated over the rods and valve action of the dangling engine of a bullet-ridden Cherokee Chief he had laughingly told the uncomprehending mechanical muchachos, "had been hoisted up on its own petard." He inquired about the woman with Pájaro Loco.

"¿Ella? She's an exaltada."

"What do you mean?"

"Don't worry about her. She's unable to work. Very troubled. She's got time on her hands. A bad thing in this place."

"She keeps staring at me. What am I supposed to do?"

Pájaro Loco flushed. Clearly he didn't want to talk but felt he had to. He went out and came back with two lukewarm Pilsners expropriated from a local latifundia that he had been saving for months. "Let's drink this and forget our martirio for a minute. She has lost her bearings. Finding herself alive and wanting to have died, she is tormented and angry. Una apasionada. Una exaltada."

"How did she become so?"

"She lost everyone, her husband, her children, the entire village. And she watched in hiding. Then she want wildly into San Salvador to foreign amnesty people, to Tutela Legal, to the American embassy, and told her story. We got her out of the capital without a second to spare and now she's with us. She's marked from the outside by the Salvadoran authorities, marked on the inside by el fuero interno."

A few days later she came up to him. "¿Qué tú eres?"

"What do you mean?"

She looked at him incredulously. "What do I mean? What are you?"

"A prisoner. Like a prisoner of war."

She became exasperated. "You are Mexican? Or are you gringo? Some say you are gringo, some say you're one of us."

"Yes Mexican, but of the United States."

"Oh, Mexican but of the United States. Like Los Angeles?" She smiled timidly. "Alexis Argüello, el Nica. He fights in Los Angeles. Like him, el Nica?"

"Precisamente. And like many salvadoreños who have found refuge in Los Angeles."

"But you are Mexican?"

"Yes, puro mexicano."

Suddenly she looked very determined. "Los tuyos had a revolution, earlier, one hundred years ago. Some of your women were revolutionaries. They were cacicas. They wore crisscrossed cartucheras over each shoulder."

"Yes, they did."

"I will wear crisscrossed cartucheras over each shoulder. You will show me!"

"Why do you want to wear them like that?"

"To mark and set me off correctly."

"They would be heavy. The cartucheras."

"The heavier the better." She looked at him matter of factly. "I have set my course to die." She smiled then, timidly. "Or to go with you and be a salvadoreña in Los Angeles." Then she walked off somewhat haughtily with considerable Hispanic show, and Hidalgo knew that although she was clearly exaltada, the spirit in her still groped for a way out.

A week or two later she came up to him again. "I have chosen you as mine."

"¿Por qué?"

"Porque hay poco tiempo."

Hidalgo felt a shiver of premonition because he thought that she knew something about what the guerrillas were planning for him. But she was talking about her own time frame.

He lived with her then in what was remarkable revolutionary luxury, but one that was deemed necessary by the guerrilla council for the camp's well-being because of the extraordinary exaltada sounds that came out of her night throat. She was considered by the Revolution as extraordinarily ugly. Also, some guerrillas had come to think of her as one of those wounded that the enemy leave alive in order to more effectively burden their opponent. After all, the dead do not require maintenance. For Hidalgo, in whom had always resided something of the neoplatonist, she was extraordinarily radiant. Surely the Renaissance thinkers had been inspired when they formulated the belief that humans became captives of love, an illness that entered through the eyes and could only be cured by ever greater doses of love. She had insufficient formal education to read or write, but she displayed blazing intuitions. He fell deeply in love with her, physically and chivalrically. Un feucho y una feucha, he told himself. No, that was not true, Hidalgo realized. Only he was feucho, a Chicano gringo caught in a volcanic spell worthy of the evil magician Merlín. She, on the other hand, merited his fealty as much as the fairest damsel in a libro de caballería. She is saving my life, he thought, saving me from madness.

They had their own thatch and earthen choza apart from the camp, well-hidden from aircraft in its own small ravine, underneath an immense wild rubber tree where the chotacabra chillona, the Salvadoran whippoorwill, made its raucous home. There the alternately terrorized and enraged Sir Jorge and the in-parts enraged and self-condemning Dulce Tobosa made a category of desperate, consuming love, seasoned by the sense that each night might be their last. On the earthen floor they spread whatever bedding was theirs and spent together whatever time of night was allotted by the Revolution to the satisfactions of the body or its desperate forebodings or its regurgitated shame. Erich Fromm once termed "love" to be the product of "art." These two—Hidalgo and Dulce—construed a category of love that by dint of will submerged the self into the vast oceanic unconsciousness, the carnal seas.

One night under the rubber tree he suggested that she tell him her angustia so that it might be opened to discourse and perhaps even lightened.

"All right," she said matter of factly. She had done this before. It was no big thing, to retell it. It retold itself constantly. And she launched into it, but Hidalgo immediately noted that this was not the woman who had once wildly gone to Amnesty International and to the Tutela Legal. She had stepped behind armor, and in that ravine fastness she told her story with this dreadful dispassion and displacement that made all the more stirring the nightly counterpoint of uncontrolled and even unrealized delirium tremens. She told him, stripped of all emotion, how the Atlacatl Batallion had come to the department of Morazán, had entered the hamlet of El Mozote, and had completely wiped it out together with nine other hamlets in the same department.

When the soldiers had come the villagers had initially not thought much of it. It was the fourth time that year the armed forces had operated in Morazán. The villagers, including Dulce's husband, had been warned of the impending military operation by the FMLN. Some did leave. Those who chose to stay—among them the evangelical Protestants, who were trained by the American missionaries to judge the Catholics to be children of Satan, and the local stand vendors and service people—considered themselves neutral in the conflict and friendly with the army. As for Dulce and her husband, they felt safe. Her husband, who was one of the few in El Mozote who could read and write and who hired himself out with an ancient Underwood to type whatever business or personal correspondence might be required, was on good terms with the local military and even had a military safe-conduct. But the soldiers came at about five in the morning, and making no communications or representations of any kind, they began taking people from their homes.

All of the villagers were rounded up and separated into men, women, and children. She was placed with the other women in a one-room building. She knew there was a hole at the bottom of the mud wall that was covered over with cardboard, and she scurried through it into some trees near the building and climbed high into one of the trees. None of the other women dared to follow for fear of disobeying the soldiers. Later it was too late. From the trees she was forced to view the massacre. At noon, the men were blindfolded and killed in the town square. Among them was Dulce's husband. In the early afternoon the young women were taken to the hills nearby, where they were raped, then killed and burned. The old women were taken next and shot. From her hiding place, Dulce heard soldiers discuss choking the children to death. Subsequently she heard the children calling for help, but no shots. Among the children murdered were the three of Dulce's, all under ten years of age. Then the soldiers went away and left her in the tree. She went to San Salvador. She and some survivors of the other nine hamlets in which the killings took place gave depositions and were questioned by the press. Almost immediately afterward she was spirited out of San Salvador by the puñonrostristas in order to save her life since, as they say in Salvador, she was quemada, marked for death. That was all there was to say.

"Why did they do this?" her lover asked.

"For the terror of it. I believe they wanted to terrorize the people. For that reason only. Simply for the terror."

Hidalgo went to the priest. "She told me what happened to her."

"In that removed, frightening way of hers?"

Hidalgo sighed. "Yes."

"Everything she says is true. It's all been written down in the July 20th supplement to the "Report on Human Rights in El Salvador," prepared scrupulously by the Americas Watch Committee and the

American Civil Liberties Union. I have a copy in the Casa Comunal. I'm sure you'll want to see it."

Hidalgo began to weep with rage, with self-pity. He wanted to kill. But who?

"Come now, get hold of yourself. You are overwrought. You'll be okay."

"I've fallen in love with her, out of my own distraction, need, and rage."

"That would be good, a project of love. We are all creatures of God, made in the Lord's image, and we must account for and comfort each other. Hold her tight at night, Don Jorge, hold her and give her succor and help her put herself together once again. Es que hay tan poco tiempo."

"Why is there so little time?"

Ignacio smiled shyly. "Don't be alarmed for your safety by us. You are so valuable to us! And besides, you're not really gringo the way we had thought. Thou art puro mexicano, ¿eh?, even with Zapata's bigotes. But there is little time. The world is changing so rapidly in the former Soviet Union, in Eastern Europe, in Nicaragua, and in Cuba. Can it be any different here? Circumstances are taking on the trappings of a new problemática and I don't think there will be much time. Maybe soon they'll come out for us and then we'll need to make our stand, with—and I think you'll like this—both arms and letters, guns and manifestos."

The so-elusive Puñonrostro appeared at that moment, deus ex machina, seeking advice from Father Ignacio and unexpectedly finding the gringo, so the priest moved to close the conversation with a quip. "So, make love in that hospitable, edenic chozuela that the Revolution has agreeably billeted to you, and help to make her well. Love is so therapeutic!"

Puñonrostro looked at Father Ignacio with something like disbelief. Unable to control himself any longer, he turned to Hidalgo and said with great sarcasm, "Now our gringo has fulfilled all of the touristic conditions of his kind, living off the Revolution in his own native shack and placing his green chile into a Salvadoran woman."

Ignacio became cross with Puñonrostro. "Listen, machito. You need to be fair. Especially you, as leader. You know it's not like that at all. We have messed up with this fellow and so to the extent that we can, we try to make amends. Also, he did not pick this Salvadoran woman, machito. This is a new age where women pick men also, and she has done so with all deliberation. After all, these two are the most marked, the most extreme each in his or her own way, in this entire camp. Let them come together and serve each other like that American movie, the odd copula." Ignacio laughed at his own joke, which the campesino comandante couldn't have possibly fathomed. "And besides, el chile verde is so therapeutic."

Puñonrostro was not reconciled. "What of his own family? He has his own family in his own country which he betrays here by consorting with a Salvadoran woman."

At that point Hidalgo interrupted. "Let me get a message to them. Any kind of discreet message that will tell them I'm still alive, and I swear to you I'll be as chaste and distant as you wish."

Puñonrostro looked at him with unease. He turned to the priest for a cue, but found only impassivity. He turned back to the Chicano. "What you wish for is correct and understandable. If I felt we could comply in good faith, I would do so immediately. But I must postpone your wish for now. You deserve what you ask for, certainly, but I must postpone it for now, por razón de estado. At this moment it would not be wise for us to publicly admit our mistakes."

And so they abandoned further discourse, all aware that Hidalgo continued to occupy the status of desaparecido and that if conditions required it, the Revolution could dispatch him and simply exercise its option to back date his death to the day that he had been taken captive.

The scandalized Jesús Salvador Puñonrostro was not finished, though, with Hidalgo's lovemaking under the rubber tree. He let a few days go by and then he called for the knight peremptorily. It was the first time that Hidalgo was in his headquarters. Puñonrostro said to him, "Oye, la negrita salvadoreña que tú estás fucking, don't bestow upon the Revolution one of those mixed-blood gringo bastard babies. We're not making revolution for that."

Holding in his anger, Hidalgo said, "I'll do my best."

"That might not be enough." He took the bayonet blade out of its scabbard that was attached to his belt. "Heed me, ¿que no? O se los quito." Then, remembering an old saying, and perhaps thinking back to the priest's joke which he couldn't understand and which in all probability was at his expense, he laughed. "Porque hay una gran diferencia entre una cinta negra y una negra encinta." Puñonrostro dismissed him as peremptorily as he had summoned him.

Hidalgo had only the priest upon whom to discharge his fury. He stalked off to find him and once having had his say, he looked at his grease-blackened hand, which was trembling around a large monkey wrench. "The Revolution doesn't provide quality detergent."

"Calm down, Jorge. It's actually a positive. It's his way of trying to get used to a gringo or even a Chicano fuereño consorting with one of his people. In fact, he's actually asserted his authority to authorize it, in his own peculiar way."

"Well, in that case I think I'll walk down to Aguilares to the Revco and stock up on Trojans." He added sarcastically, "Can I get you anything? Some chocolate-covered raisins? Some gummy bears?"

The priest, sensing that his masculinity had been lampooned, was mildly offended. "Aguilares doesn't have an American chain store yet. Perhaps after the Revolution. Better to follow the traditional prescription on this matter. It's conservative but proven effective: coitus interruptus."

Some days later la Dulce walked by the motor pool and waved. Hidalgo had just been appointed head of the motor shop, a position he wasn't sure at first he could accept, given his condition of captive and political adversary. Finally, wanting the responsibilities so badly and the opportunity that came with it to reorganize the motor shop on a more efficient basis, he rationalized that the work was purely technocratic, not involved in ideologies or political allegiances. Two of his grease monkeys who didn't know of his sworn fealty to sweet Dulce waved back, thinking that her affectionate gesture was directed to them. When she had gone, one said to the other, "Why is it that hechizada was the only one in the village of El Mozote to survive the massacre?"

"I don't know," the other said casually. "Será que está más feucha que la chingada."

As with so many other incidents, Hidalgo kept his hurt to himself, understanding that it was in the nature of revolution to reshuffle lifestyles, often producing painful or incongruous behavioral results. Nevertheless, the incident only made him vow that in this topsy-turvy mundo he must redouble his constancy to the fair Dulce Tobosa. Saint Irenaeus was right: *gloria dei vivens homo,* or in this case, *femina.* God's glory is the living human being.

*   *   *

We who transcribe need reflect on how efficiently the chronicler of deeds can dispatch years, a mere matter of a few hundred or thousand heroic quatrains. Living days and years is somewhat more involved and arduous.

Hidalgo's stay in the Guazapa turned into years. Long before he had been captured, beginning in the early 1980s, the guerrilla warfare had ground down into a ritualized stalemate. Each day the American-donated airplanes of the Salvadoran air force carpeted the Guazapa with bombs. The Salvadoran military periodically attempted to move out from its fortified enclaves to control more of the region. This was a singularly desultory effort. Occasionally they cruelly killed some of the few civilians who had not fled the Guazapa. Sometimes they ran into guerrilla mine fields and had their legs blown away. These attempts were punctuated by a major coordinated effort every six months or so, usually during the dry season. Nothing came of it, except for additional casualties on both sides. The muchachos controlled the night. Once in a while they would raid a bridge, a power substation, or a military facility to confirm their prowess. The Salvadoran government would respond with a propaganda barrage to the effect that they were cowards. "Son valientes con los puentes."

After six years of the customary artillery barrages, aerial bombardments, and infantry sweeps, the government had not seriously weakened the muchachos' control of the countryside. At dawn on January 10, 1986, the army launched "Operation Phoenix." It was followed by others such as "Operation Chávez" in March 1987. At the time, Operation Phoenix was proclaimed by the army as its greatest success of the entire war. It was successful because its actual target was not the guerrillas but the civilian population; it was so successful that at the end of the operation there were hardly any civilians left in Guazapa. The army barely engaged the guerrillas, who quickly abandoned the area, regrouped, and executed their own counteroperations. Despite more than 20 major military operations in the years since Operation Phoenix and almost daily bombing, the army had been unable to dislodge Puñonrostro, Ignacio, and their Christian soldiers from their mountain fortresses in Guazapa.

Hidalgo's presence did lead to one change in the combat ritual. Each day the airplanes were gone by sunset, and Father Ignacio and Hidalgo set up a tertulia by the side of the volcano. They drank what was among the finest coffees in the world and for an hour, the heure bleue, discoursed on whatever caught their fancy.

One mountain sunset was particularly magnificent after an especially virulent bombing, and Father Ignacio remarked, "Napalm makes pretty."

Hidalgo remarked sarcastically, "Meaningful work. High recognition by my superiors. Love and companionship. Orgasms that through their ingenious mimesis of the violent death my Sweet Lady and I both consciously dread and obsessively enthrall successfully efface the *hic et nunc* beyond all recognition. A witty and artful companion in philosophic disputation. Above all, a Salvadoran coffee that would make el exigente himself swoon, taken in a sunset that would send the most demanding samurai into verse. Who could ask for anything more?"

"Truly, then, this is heaven on earth."

"Yes, the heaven of the fallen angels. Of course, a little calvados to go with this coffee . . . that would be heaven. Calvados and freedom. As we Americans put it, freedom now."

Jorge was astonished that Father Ignacio called Saint Ignatius of Loyola, the founder of the Jesuits and bastion of the Counter-Reformation, his tocayo. Here stood surely either the most soberbio of them all or a model of a man who had taken full and accurate measure of his self-identity. However, Hidalgo wondered if the Saint were the priest's antipode rather than his exemplum. After all, Ignatius had been converted from a knight to an ascetic. Ignacio appeared to have gone in the opposite direction. Apparently, what moved Ignacio to identification with his namesake was Loyola's conception, even after his conversion to religious life, of the service of God as holy chivalry. That and Saint Ignatius's genius as an educator and as an organizer in the effort to win the hearts and souls of many and diverse peoples.

Over the years, Hidalgo came to learn Father Ignacio's life story and to love him for it. The son of an Asturian miner, as a child Ignacio had been attracted to the Missionaries of the Sacred Heart, an order committed, long before Vatican II, to the struggle to help the downtrodden in Spain and in exotic places that the boy could only imagine. Ignacio saw his calling as part of the titanic engagement against evil for the souls and physical well-being of the marginalized children of God, and, applying himself with all of his intellectual, spiritual, and bodily energies, he eventually became a member of the congregation.

Hidalgo was sure that from the beginning the young priest was possessed by a sort of divine rage. Nothing filled him with more anger or bullheaded resolve than bureaucratic obstacles and the defeatism of the poor. In Spain he spent several years as a *sacerdote obrero*, helping to build housing cooperatives and spending more time in the carpenter's shop than in church. Among certain clerics he had begun to gain a reputation as a "snob" slumming among the poor, a superficial priest most interested in showy social action and forgetful of his links with God. Ignacio did not seem to care what they said; his conscience was clear.

Ignacio's order had a call to conscience by the Second Vatican Council of 1964 and the conference of Latin American bishops at Medellín in 1968. The Church reassessed its traditional role and adopted what became known as its "preferential option for the poor." In 1968 students took to the streets both in Europe and the Americas. Men and women examined their consciences and underwent social, moral, and political transformations; the Medellín Conference issued a call for priests to combat social oppression; and the progressive wing of the Catholic church grew every day more militant. The Missionaries of the Sacred Heart launched a call for volunteers. Central America was desperately in need of priests. Father Ignacio arrived in the Guazapa region of El Salvador just in time for the soccer war with Honduras.

As soon as Ignacio arrived in the department he threw himself into social improvements. He had seen poverty in Asturias but that was softer, European; the contrasts here between *ricos* and *pelados* were profoundly shocking. There was only one doctor in the entire region, but his fees were prohibitive and his clientele was limited to the rich. There were only a few schools and they were too costly for the average family. Very few people knew how to read. Children began to work at the age of five or six.

The *oligarquía* held all of the productive soil and the *campesinos* worked on their *latifundias* for subsistence-level wages or were allotted small plots for sharecropping under infamous financial terms. Changes in land tenure and the subdivision or overexploitation of tiny family units had combined to force the peasants off the land. More and more families were required to rent rather than own their land and to pay the landlord his rent in cash rather than in kind—rent often demanded in advance. The landless population grew from 12% in 1960 to 40% in 1975, and by 1980 it reached an estimated 60%. Life in the countryside became so very hard. The peasants had to rely increasingly on seasonal labor to earn money and pay rent.

The diet of almost all of Father Ignacio's parishioners consisted of scant rations of corn for Salvadoran tortillas, which when complemented with some meager filling were called pupusas. Maybe there was a plantain now and then, and rice and beans; when mixed together, the latter was the national staple, a dish the priest was used to calling moros y cristianos but which the natives called gallo pinto. Occasionally a lucky campesino with a good dog was able to scare up a few garrobos, an iguanalike lizard that was the basis for the excellent cornmeal-thickened stew, pebre de garrobo. But for the most part Ignacio found his campesinos to be malnourished, chronically sick, illiterate, exploited, yet stubbornly fixed in their ways. He raged against their unwillingness to entertain even the possibility of change, of communal action, of breaking out of their fatalism.

Upon his arrival in the Guazapa, he was given the parsonage that went with the parish. It was large and elegant, with high ceilings and a lovely walled garden, grander than any house he had ever inhabited in all of his life. Mortified by the expectation that he would join the privileged class, he turned this "Casa Cural" into a "Casa Comunal." Campesinos from the countryside of the North where they lived in their own ravines but who came to town to do marketing, receive religious instruction, or transact other business and who couldn't return to their homesteads by nightfall were encouraged to use the Casa Comunal free of charge as overnight guests. Affronted by the level of drunkenness in his parish—the oligarquía had seen to it that rum was extraordinarily plentiful and cheap—in the afternoon and early evening, the prime drinking times, the Casa served as a club where adults of drinking age could engage in dominó, naipes, and similar activities. Copious amounts of nonalcoholic fruit juices were served as well. Soon the place was the haunt of a core of shouting, laughing, and hostile regulars who had routed the others. Clearly, rum was being poured under the table, and it got so bad that Ignacio had to close down what had become a poorly disguised drinking establishment.

Later on Ignacio attempted to organize into a cooperative the muleteers who free-lanced in the region to haul coffee, pineapple, tobacco, and other crops from the latifundias to paved highways or even to San Salvador. At the mercy of the landed gentry, they competed with each other so savagely that the latifundias found them to be cheaper than establishing their own crews of haulers. No sooner had Ignacio begun his course of instruction on trade-unionism than an "expert" from the capital appeared to help him, filled with case histories to show the people how dangerous unions could be for the happiness and security of such as muleteers. He offered the priest all the "help" he needed, including money. Suddenly, attendance among the muleteers plummeted, and word began to go around the Guazapa that Ignacio was a "Communist priest." An investigation that the priest made back in the capital pointed to the expert as an operative possibly under contract to an organization funded by the CIA.

Ignacio turned to yet another campaign. Somehow he scraped up funds for a dozen sewing machines and a teacher to train the Guazapan women how to use them. Problems arose almost instantly. Which women would get to keep the machines in their homes? Who would use them first? Why should others have to wait? Gradually the bickering overwhelmed them and the sewing workshop evaporated.

Within the Church, Ignacio was more successful. He began a Bible reading and study group. At the Casa, the people learned a new way of reading the Bible and understanding their faith by relating it to what was happening around them. The fatalism of the people began to wane and new possibilities opened up. Jesus' statement "The poor you have always with you" no longer legitimized an exploitive economic system. Instead, Jesus' whole message took on liberating force. He was seen to take a stand with the poor. Soon, in collaboration with the feligreses, the priest stopped sending parish funds to the diocese, which ordinarily would have paid his salary and provided funds for specific parish expenses. Instead he created a commission of parishioners who would decide how parish funds were to be spent. For most of the guazapeños it was their first experience in democracy and communal responsibility. For himself, Ignacio only accepted the equivalent of the monthly salary of a poor sharecropper, and even most of that income he distributed to more desperate people in the parish. He achieved the reputation of the Penniless Priest. He had also begun the first grass-roots Christian community in the department.

The 1970s were good to Father Ignacio and to his version of liberation theology, although he would not have appreciated it at the time. The Republic of El Salvador was becoming increasingly violent and polarized, and this led to the loosening of control over the Guazapa by the central authorities as well as its physical abandonment by the landowners and other wealthies of the region, leaving administration of their holdings to surrogates who were necessarily less zealous in their practices. Although the department was only a few hours by car from the capital, it had always been on the "other side" of the natural boundary of the imposing Guazapa volcano. The government, the army, the right-wing death squads were making a more concerted stand in the regions closer to San Salvador and other major population centers. Accordingly, great streams of refugees moved into what at that time was the relative shelter of the Guazapa. Even as the abject string of personal crises of hunger, illness, violence, and drunkenness drove the priest close to despair, the seeds of autonomy were being planted. Squatters were rife all over the latifundias. There was simply no place to put the people and energy waned in the effort to remove them from the land. Petty theft and pillage had become pandemic, weakening public security and structures of transportation and distribution. Fewer foodstuffs were making their way out of the region for the export market. The local constabularies felt things getting out of control and called on the Guardia Nacional (GN) for help in order to "avoid anarchy." The response from San Salvador was muted. The GN was needed closer to home.

Father Ignacio was hardly alone in his liberation theology efforts. The Medellín Conference had called upon the Church "to defend the rights of the oppressed"; to promote grass-roots organizations; "to denounce the unjust action of world powers that works against the self-determination of weaker nations"; and to make a "preferential option for the poor." The primary means of accomplishing these ends became the development of Christian Base Communities. Ignacio felt, along with colleagues like Father Rutilio Grande in Aguilares, Father Rafael Barahona in San Vicente, and many other clerics, that these communities could be the most revolutionary development in the Latin American church because for the first time in history the masses of the people would begin to participate in and take responsibility for the major elements of their own lives and each other's.

"The people are no longer mere observers to a ritual conducted for their benefit by a priest," Ignacio explained to his captive Knight. "The people, the poor people of this Guazapa and thousands of impoverished regions around the world, are now irrupting into the Church as active subjects, doers, makers of Christianity. Under Western colonial Christendom it was very difficult to participate except passively even for the middle and upper classes, impossible for the poor. Now it's entirely different—the political, the spiritual, even the reading and interpretation of the Bible. I refuse to serve as heaven's go-between, a salaried alcahuete put in place to baptize, hear confession, say mass, marry people, and do all of the conventional things to prepare them for heaven. Now we work together to make complete human beings, so that then we can make good Christians. The material life of the poor is inseparable from their spiritual life. The poor must be taught to understand the nature of their existence and to not think of all parts of it as unchangeable. God may love the poor, but He does not love poverty. We are engaged in a process of conscientización that emphasizes communal social action, challenges entrenched power structures, even challenges these structures militarily. And together we read and interpret the Bible and apply it to our daily lives."

The message of Jesus' "preferential option for the poor" was having effects. El Salvador was joining a movement that was mushrooming over Latin America and many other parts of the world and was in the process of gaining the allegiance of several million Christians around the globe. Eight months after the arrival of Father Rutilio Grande and his Jesuit colleagues in Aguilares, on May 24, 1973, 1,600 workers in the La Babaña sugar mill struck on payday for six hours because they did not receive an orally promised salary increase. The strike was peaceful and ended when management granted a raise, although less than what was originally promised.

By mid-1975 the priests were being called "subversives." That Christmas, then Salvadoran President Molina made public statements against "liberationist clerics." Father Ignacio received the first really serious warning that he was in mortal danger. Father Rafael Barahona had been taken into custody in San Vicente and transported to GN headquarters in San Salvador, where he was beaten severely by assailants who struck him in tandem to the chant, "I am excommunicated, I am excommunicated." Barahona's bishop, Monseñor Aparicio, obliged the torturers. "The torturer who clamored for excommunication now has it." In return, 5 more priests were arrested and 18 others expelled. Fliers circulated around the capital urging Salvadorans to "Be a Patriot! Kill a Priest!"

The ambush and death of Father Rutilio Grande with two of his followers, 72-year-old Manuel Solórzano and Nelson Rutilio Lemus, 16, on March 12, 1977, was one of Father Ignacio's greatest personal tragedies. The Jesuit had been one of Ignacio's closest colleagues and collaborators. Just a month earlier the priest had delivered a sermon at an open-air gathering to protest the expulsion from El Salvador of Father Mario Bernal. At the gathering, Father Rutilio spoke on the danger of being a Christian. "Dear brothers and friends, I am fully aware that very soon the Bible and the Gospels will not be allowed to cross the border. All that will reach us will be the covers, since all the pages are subversive—against sin, it is said. So that if Jesus crosses the border at Chalatenango, they will not allow him to enter. They would accuse him, the Man-God, the prototype of man, of being an agitator." One month later Father Rutilio was driving past sugarcane plantations on his way to celebrate mass in El Paisnal, where he had lived as a child. The assassins riddled his body with more than 10 bullets.

Father Ignacio told the adventure capitalist that even as he had grieved, tormented and confused, this shedding of clerical blood only accelerated the process of what Ignacio and subsequently Puñonrostro were to call the "emancipation of the Guazapa." A revolutionary state was being built in the volcanic region "on a staircase of Catholic martyrs."

On March 24, 1980, El Salvador's Archbishop Oscar Romero delivered what was to be his last sermon.

> Let no one be offended because we use the divine words read at our mass to shed light on the social, political and economic situation of our people. Not to do so would be un-Christian. Christ desires to unite himself with humanity, so that the light he brings from God might become life for nations and individuals. I know many are shocked by this preaching and want to accuse us of foresaking the gospel for politics. But I reject this accusation. . . . Each week I go about the country listening to the cries of the people, their pain from so much crime, and the ignominy of so much violence. Each week I ask the Lord to give me the right words to console, to denounce, to call for repentance. And even though I may be a voice crying in the desert, I know that the church is making the effort to fulfill its mission. . . .

The martyrdom of Archbishop Romero, at least as it was explained to Hidalgo by Father Ignacio, confirmed in the Chicano's mind a major rift in the Church and the emergence of a new force not only in El Salvador but in Latin America and elsewhere that might represent a renewed Christian philosophy, an innovative social structure, and a compact of human relationships suitable for many peoples and societies. Shortly after Romero's death the popular wing formed the National Coordination of the Popular Church (CONIP). The majority of parishes in which CONIP was present were located in the "zones of control," areas of the country from which government forces had been driven by the guerrillas and replaced by local civilian administration. Many villages that had a strong Base Community movement in the 1970s were now in these zones. The highest body of the Catholic church in El Salvador, the Episcopal Conference (CEDES), was located in the capital and active in those areas of the nation under army control. While CONIP specifically denied that it was a "parallel church" and asserted that it was "not a church that grew out of the people in opposition to the church of the hierarchy," it became clear after Archbishop Romero's death that the Church, from the point of view of decision making, pastoral activities, constituent support, and geographic tradition, had split into a "popular church" and a traditionally defined Catholic church. In a certain sense, Pope John Paul II's trip to El Salvador confirmed this. Although his primary objectives were to emphasize the need for reconciliation as a means of bringing an end to violence in the region and to stress the need for unity within the Church, his visits to El Salvador and Nicaragua more sharply highlighted the split in the Church. The popular church was disappointed with his visit and said so. Father Rutilio Sánchez observed that the "Pope spoke as if he were in a different country: he never mentioned our war, as if El Salvador were at peace. We felt very disappointed."

For its part, the Salvadoran popular church referred to one of Jesuit Juan Luis Segundo's main observations in *Evolution and Guilt,* that "the revolutionary dialectic has to overcome the sin of conservatism of the Church." Liberation theologians pointed out that Christianity was born in Galilee and Palestine, which had been the Third World of the Roman empire. Later it grew among the poorest and most marginalized peoples. But from the sixteenth century onward, it spread to Latin America, Africa, and Asia as part of the expansion of Western colonialism. It was now necessary to remove the stamp of this Western colonialist period, to decolonialize the Church, to return it to its origins and recover its identity in Third World terms. Simple human justice and the integrity of the Church and its values required this. Among the orders, perhaps the Jesuit high command took the most militant action, making a complete volte-face from its original establishment as the "Pope's men." In 1983, the Father General of the Society of Jesus issued a promise from Rome that integral to his job was to ensure that continued Jesuit quests for justice not be distracted by the "groaning complaints of popes."

By the time that the three American nuns and American lay churchworker were raped and murdered on the night of December 2, 1981, the Guazapa had become for most purposes a semiautonomous region. The Salvadoran army controlled a few strongholds, which they supplied or serviced only by day, usually by reinforced convoy given the dangers. Otherwise it was the revolutionary army of the night: the countryside was in the control of the Puñonrostro wing of what was called, beginning in November 1980, the Farabundo Martí Liberation Front, the political-military arm of the Democratic Revolutionary Front, which earlier had been a separate faction, the People's Revolutionary Army (ERP), in turn developed from a split in the left wing of the Christian Democratic party. In principle the puñonrostristas were a unit of FMLN; in practice Puñonrostro, ably advised by his associates such as Pájaro Loco and Father Ignacio, functioned as a separate command that was not even asked, much less obliged, to operate under revolutionary discipline except in the most critical guerrilla razones de estado.

The emergence and rise of Puñonrostro within the calculus of revolutionary Guazapa would seem to obey the traditional trajectory of the emergent Hispanic peasant leader. So much so that Hidalgo, with sufficient hostility toward the campesino comandante to pursue mental fancies of this sort, craved the company of Hermelinda del Pimental with her Mandelbrot equations and her fractals. Together they could analyze guerrilla comandantes and make "scientific history." Perhaps they could bring in a Braudelian long-wave specialist and seek longitudinal trends. Start with Spartacus. Why not?

Or maybe Puñonrostro's aurora at the precise revolutionary moment mimicked the astral bodies? Among the recent sightings of peasant "Mars" along the long axis of siervo versus señor, El Empecinado had appeared at just the right moment to give Pepe Botella and the Napoleonic army a series of thrashings on the Iberian peninsula. In El Salvador itself in 1831 the indio Anastasio Aquino had risen up against the Spaniards and the Hispanicized ladinos. Later, transplanted to the caciquismo of mestizaje, in 1910 the southern star of Emiliano Zapata had emerged from behind the Popocatepetl volcano

at Amecameca, opportunely advancing ¡tierra y libertad! in the twilight of the porfiriato. Hidalgo judged that, given the concatenation of
the usual astropolitical conditions, one could derive and predict with
complete confidence from some yet undiscovered grand unified
theory the sudden rise and zenith in the heavenly firmament of the
requisite revolutionary leader. He couldn't wait to tell the good priest
about his theories at the evening's volcanic disputandum.

Curiously, the priest had his own perspective. Like a good psy-
choanalyst he pounced on the element of high rage in Don Jorge and
his not unwarranted thirsting for revenge as well as his jealousy of the
priest's affection for the peasant comandante. The priest concluded
with a plea that the knight honor the emerging charism of the rude,
unlettered peasant.

"All that you say, I wouldn't deny, whether couched in directional
whatnot or in ordinary vocabulary. When we needed a leader around
here there were several who suddenly emerged and more or less
butted heads like elks.

"What happened is that ORDEN, a nationwide paramilitary
organization that had been set up in the 1960s with advice and funds
from U.S. Army Special Forces, the 'Green Berets,' became very
active in our region. It was the government's last major effort.
ORDEN established a network of agents and informants in our
hamlets by drawing on ex-army conscripts and offering them certain
privileges in exchange for denunciations and strong-arm tactics. In
practice, they were dirty-warfare gangs along the lines of the European fascist movements of the 1930s. As a result, the death squads
took so many people from their houses at night and dumped the
bodies in the street that the road from Aguilares to Suchitoto was
turned into a cemetery. Even today we sometimes find the bones of
the dumped corpses. The ORDEN death squads were formed from
the same peasant population as their victims. That violence did not
crush our peasant movement; instead it further radicalized the peasants, strengthened our resolve to fight.

"Puñonrostro rose from that milieu. He had the determination
and the stomach to do what was necessary. He is capable of the
greatest violence, do not think otherwise. He fought ORDEN in the
only way possible, ripping its members out like the cancer that they
were in our communities. So, add to your astral comandante theories components of Darwinian natural selection. What matters is that
natural man has the innate good sense to lead us successfully in

revolution, with all the required complexities of tactics and organization. The people follow him. Ultimately, I follow him, even as I give him the best advice that I can. He is the man of action, the Zapata, and I, the man of word, his Soto y Gama. I am staking not only my life on him, but my credo as well."

Hidalgo was mildly scandalized into silence by this outburst. He had been disarmed not only by the priest's unmasking of his hostility toward "Fist in your Face," as Hidalgo liked to call him under his breath, but the cleric's allegiance to this rude, uneducated "natural man."

The following eventide under the sulfurous setting sun, the knight persisted in his enterprise. Hidalgo in his desperate captivity and the priest in his frantic euphoria wrangled over the issue of Puñonrostro's charism and his other qualities of leadership as if their very lives depended on it, which was in fact close to reality.

The key difference between Puñonrostro and all the peasant leaders manqué whom Hidalgo delighted in throwing at the priest was precisely that this "natural man" had Father Ignacio as his mentor. The latter, although he might deny the extent of his influence, swam with the leader as close as the pilot fish to the shark. Yet, hadn't such peasant leaders always had their intellectuals, and hadn't they invariably reneged on those of prudent counsel and relied, usually disastrously, on their own gut instincts? Even Zapata, the great Chicano icon, had spurned the advice of clearer heads and rode out to contrive arms deals with allegedly renegade federales. And from the captive's own point of view, wasn't it probably true that if Father Ignacio were in control he would free him and let him return home? Hidalgo judged that Ignacio's engagement in the priestly education of the peasant prince appeared to have the side effect of sacrificing his freedom to Puñonrostro's learning curve.

The disputation over Puñonrostro helps us to better understand the mysterious, counterintuitive actions of Hidalgo in the final set of this adventure, which have caused so many cronistas to claim the "brainwashing" of Hidalgo or his succumbing to the "Patty Hearst effect," where the captive ultimately adheres to the values of the captors. Quite in contrast to the accounts of the conventional cronistas, who explain everything as a consequence of Hidalgo's captivity, thus leaving his final actions so superficially examined, in our verdadera historia de la conversión we highlight the complex Hidalgo-Puñonrostro-Ignacio relationship as key, finding in it the elucidation of our Chicano's ultimate behavior in a manner that binds the focused moral tale of an individual's mixed motives with the general philosophic account of national revolution.

Our knight, departing from his contempt of Puñonrostro, artfully parried by the priest, began to analyze other dimensions of the Guazapan revolutionary compact, and finally his own relationship to them.

Hidalgo conceded that the tow of current world affairs had fostered the emergence of charismatic men and women. In fact, the force of events had created them even when the individuals didn't seem to have the right stuff. Gorbachev would seem to fit the conventionally viewed leader, but the prima facie buffoon Yeltsin now seemed to be the most prominent leader of them all. Violeta Barrios de Chamorro had been propelled by events to lead Nicaragua in the most uncertain of times. The "great figures" posture toward history had seemed to reduce the logic of historical determinism into so many messy little puddles. Hidalgo needed to consider that Father Ignacio might be a wiser mentor than any of those who had counseled guerrilla leaders in the centuries and millenia before him. Had not Hermelinda del Pimental called for the addition of delta to the calculation of long-wave chaos? Hadn't Father Ignacio himself pointed to "natural selection"? Didn't the finest Jesuit evolutionist of them all, Teilhard de Chardin, surmise the development of human consciousness to a noosphere that might culminate at the omega point? One had to consider evolution in its broadest sense, including the developed accumulation of intellectual and perhaps even spiritual assets over time. Didn't every war between siervos and señores have its own unique elements that were unlike any that had come before it? Those who claimed that each new conflagration was "the war to end all wars" had proven to be spectacularly foolish. However, who could deny that each new war was a step into the unknown, not only technologically but philosophically unlike any of those that had preceded it?

This analysis in turn led Hidalgo to review his affections. He came to realize the intensity of his love for the priest and his love for his lady, Sweet Dulce, neither of whom spurned old "Fist in Your Face." If importuned, who would he follow? He could see himself dying for his Father or for his Lady given, as he put it to himself with wry irony, "the right circumstances."

And this line of thought led to liberation theology. Was it the product of the "best and brightest" or merely the newest, fashionable node on the philosophic *stambaum?* In their own time, the medieval and renaissance princes had been educated by the best teachers and informed with the best—or at least most current—philosophies available to them. Had the leading edge of carnal and spiritual truth emerged here among the Latin American Christian Base Communities of the "people's church"? The key term of these liberation theologians was conscientización, giving the oppressed the gift of awareness, a higher understanding of their lives and what need be done to improve them. The *quaestiones disputatae* between priest and capitalist took a new turn. The priest was more than a mere theoretician. He was building his cyclotron or cyclone, it was hard to tell which. Puñonrostro was being developed into a demonstrable concientizado model of the priest's theology for this profoundly unjust world. The campesino comandante provided an empirical test case of the model's effectiveness.

Clearly, Father Ignacio was applying his conscientización not only to the enhancement of Puñonrostro's leadership but to Jorge Hidalgo's head. He was deploying his spiritual assets in an effort to convert the adventure capitalist to his liberation-based ethic and ideology of revolution. Ultimately, love does conquer all, and in the end the venture capitalist was captivated by the venture and decided to invest his own human capital in its outcome.

Father Ignacio told Hidalgo that he had not genuinely understood the extent of the government's insufficiency until he began to actually live outside the system. For as the Guazapa began to achieve its increasingly separate and self-sufficient status it became apparent to him that the institutions of government were lies, a smoke screen, a trap.

"The system itself was the enemy. Nothing was to be accomplished by serving the system with reformist activities that did not change the larger structure. Why become an advocate for campesinos instead of teaching them how to advocate for, organize, and become government themselves? The problem was and is systemic. Those parts still under government control cannot be improved with schools to combat ignorance or medical clinics or any combination of palliatives. The system is organized to ensure that there will always be a large supply of poor people and consequently a large supply of labor available, but dirt cheap. And making sure that there will always be poverty and ignorance are a handful of families who are able to live not simply the lives of the rich, but of the fabulously wealthy. They reach outside of the Salvadoran sphere of semifeudal limitation and live internationally, importing whatever they like and using their wealth to make trips to Miami to purchase clothes and other amenities, to get world-class medical treatment in Houston, and to pay for university educations for their progeny at Yale, Heidelberg, the Sorbonne, and 'fine schools everywhere' eager to accept their wealth.

"To maintain the system it is quite necessary that the overwhelming majority of Salvadorans live in the most abject poverty. The rich become ever more rich at the expense of the poor becoming poorer. This was not necessary, natural, nor an inevitable product of economic, social, and political factors. The oligarchy established a level of poverty that, as was stated at Medellín and at Puebla, 'cries out to heaven' and is 'contrary to the plan of the Creator.' The conscious construction of this poverty by the oligarchy is a sin, absolutely in opposition to God. It cannot be condoned or tempered.

"And more than that: this Salvadoran system fully coincides with the capitalist system of North American imperialism, which requires a base of many very poor, dependent, and servile countries to maintain one country in great riches."

Now the padre had trod the capitalist's turf, and Hidalgo plunged in. "Wait, Father. You paint a vivid and desperate picture of Salvadoran society. I don't dispute your conclusion about the oligarchy and the way it has impoverished the common Salvadoran. I concede to you its effects elsewhere on human nature; a number, perhaps even a large number of American individuals and organizations have either colluded with the oligarchs or unthinkingly made deals with them with little or no concern about morality. Or they deluded themselves that they should support these evildoers in order to combat the deeper evil of communism, or they have simply accepted their money in the open marketplace to give them goods or services. All those evil, petty, or callous behaviors, I think we both agree, are contemptible. But we must put those behaviors in an accurate context. That last conclusion, that the sorry state of El Salvador and particularly of its agriculture is integral to a North American imperialistic and capitalistic system, I don't agree with a word of that, Father. Not a word of it. In the first place, when you use the word capitalism, you don't mean what we Americans mean. Your institutions remind me of what Adam Smith railed against in Britain in 1776, a social order dominated by the landowners and the mercantile elite who were committed neither to entrepreneurial economic activity nor to markets open to every class of citizenry. In El Salvador, institutions maintain the continuity of the viceregal period. Friends and family are favored, and in fact here and elsewhere in Latin America you actively discriminate against capitalist activities, certainly among the poor, and you even discourage internal investment and invention among the affluent. That the United States requires maintaining you in economic dependency in order to enrich itself? How in these times can you even utter such a thing? Don't you see that the Soviet Union passed into the dustbin of history partly because it sapped all initiative from the peasants and workers? They emasculated themselves so well by the system of Communist paternalism with ever-diminishing economic fruits that, ironically, now many of the former Soviets support a right-wing restoration of the 'halcyon' days when they pretended to work and the system pretended to recompense them. You yourself have spent half your life railing against peasant defeatism. That system had the best lock on that quality of impoverished initiative I am aware of!"

"Don't preach to me from the Book of Soviet Fatalism! We are not arguing the merits of that system over capitalism. I know they were a historical perversion, no better in fact than American imperialism. They had their own oligarquía and merely paid lip service to the equitable distribution of wealth. The only things that really energized them were building military might and proselytizing atheism, depriving the people even of any spiritual solace. They were governed by fascists. Hitler and Stalin, fascists. I see a difference only in degree between the two."

"All right, padre, I won't debate the nature of the Soviet system with you, although I suspect I view it far more as a flawed and failed experiment than an evil, atheistic empire. Tell me, why do you think that the majority in El Salvador voted for ARENA, essentially for D'Aubuisson, in 1989?"

"The people had begun to lose hope. We've been at this for 15, 20 years, or more. The U.S. is too strong and too helpful to the other side. The people had gotten to the point that they wanted peace at any price."

"Well, I'm sure that is true. But how did the FMLN fare with the industrial worker?"

"Poorly. We need to improve our support with them. It is very difficult because they are in the government-controlled sector. They're brainwashed by propaganda, by all the powerful methods of coercion."

"The economy here has a great many so-called 'informals,' doesn't it? Artisans, street vendors, small manufacturers who essentially work outside the system?"

"Oh, yes. We know all about the informals. We have them here as in other parts of Latin America."

"What is your level of support with them?"

"Probably very poor. They all want to be capitalists, successful ones just like you."

"Is that a terrible thing? You are telling me that you don't represent all of the poor, and certainly not all of the lower middle and middle classes. Perhaps it's because the Salvadoran government is doing such a great job in propagandizing them. Perhaps it's because your ideas are not sufficiently powerful or inclusive of the urban workers and entrepreneurials. Perhaps even the peasants, who I'm sure are devoted to the Christian Base Communities, might prefer to combine the best elements in those ideals with private property ownership rather than with Christian communitarianism. Where are the incentives for commerce, invention, discovery, entrepreneurship, enterprise, and investment? Could it be that your economic program continues the long-standing Latin American tradition that is hostile to commerce and economic dynamism, which it considers vulgar, of little esteem, more than a little tainted with evil?"

"Possibly. You need to understand that we work to create a new human being, not encourage greedy peasants to supplant greedy hacendados. Miguel d'Escoto, the Maryknoll priest who is the former foreign minister of Nicaragua, said that the basic problem with capitalism is that it is intrinsically wrong at its base. The basic notion is that humankind is selfish and we should be realistic and accept and cater to it rather than change it."

"It is hard, perhaps excruciatingly difficult, to design and foster a humane capitalism. As a Chicano in the U.S., how well I know that. Certainly, eternal vigilance is the price, even in the U.S. However, I'm not sure that any other system is easier. An option for the poor is entirely admirable. The U.S. Statue of Liberty expresses it, too. There are many conflicting social philosophies that claim to lift up the 'huddled masses, yearning to breathe free.' You should not be blind to the aim of democratic capitalism as the liberal societies of the

Northern hemisphere conceive it. Do not misinterpret or underestimate the metaphysic of liberalism nor the positive social role of markets. Your liberation theological accounts of capitalism are almost unrecognizable to me; they reflect the pre-capitalist, mercantilistic, and patrimonial institutions that prevail in Latin America. Like the socialism of Latin American liberation theologians, we too seek to lift up the poor. We believe as you do that today there is no excuse for the suffocation of the spirit inflicted on the poor by material destitution. However, our goals, our analogs to liberation theology, are saturated in our institutions, practices, and habits. North American 'liberation theology' exists much more powerfully in society than in books. It has hardly yet begun to achieve self-consciousness. By contrast, Latin American liberation theology presently exists much more powerfully in books than in society. In reality, it has entered the lives of only a few million of Latin America's 400 million inhabitants. The radical question is a practical one. Which sorts of economic institutions do in fact lift up the poor? The issue as to which does the better job can only be settled by actual achievements."

"Verily, you do love your country, don't you, m'hijo?"

"Yes, I do. Sometimes in my country people accuse me of disloyalty, more often they suspect it silently. They fear my Chicano biculture. That grieves me greatly. I am a loyal American and I will go to almost any length to safeguard my country. But also to improve it. I am not insensitive to the warts and I will not turn away from injustice, and we have done grave injustices here in El Salvador and in many other places. I don't think that a capitalist conspiracy to keep you economically dependent happens to be one of them." Hidalgo went on. "I also love the informals. That is, I love the entrepreneurs. The gray marketers are my people. The citizens of Hong Kong, Malaysia, the renegade PRC province of Guangdong. In Peru some two and one half million street vendors, artisans, and manufacturers work without legal protection because they are impeded by the government. Let's liberate them! Ninety-five percent of Lima's buses and taxis are run by the illegal informal sector. Forty-three percent of all Peruvian housing built during the past 30 years has been built informally. Sixty percent of Lima's food is distributed informally. To build homes formally requires 7 to 14 years to receive government authorization. In bribes, government fees, and forgone income, it is estimated that it costs an average worker's annual earnings to form a legal corporation. In Latin America our cofradía has set up an organization called "Acción Latina" to help the informals and the entre-preneurs get small loans to make and sell until they drop. Creating and selling, that's such a high. And I don't feel at all a selfish person although I began quite poor and now happen to be a fabulously wealthy capitalist. My conscience is clear, at least on that score."

"Ah, but you are not the normal carpetbagger, are you, who comes down to scam the locals? Your small cofradía is the excep-tion, caballeros andantes."

"Maybe, but that is what laws, religions, moral systems, civic action groups, charities, foundations, commissions, and professional organizations are for, the whole fabric of participatory democracy. On the one hand, we limit the authority of persons and groups to manageable scale, and on the other, we work toward a common purpose without consideration of such factors as class interest. What really turns me on here in the Guazapa are your experiments with grassroots Christian communities, because this nation and this region have so few of the institutions that make my nation strong. Liberation theology says that Latin America is capitalist and needs a socialist revolution. Latin America does need a fundamental change, in fact the whole structure needs to be shaken at its foundation and rebuilt upon new pediments. But its present system is mercantilist and quasi-feudal, not capitalist, and the revolution it needs is both liberal and Catholic. The present order is not free but statist, privilege-centered, not open to the poor but protective of the rich. In contrast to places like Hong Kong where you can legally open a business for 30 dollars, here the poor are prevented by law from founding and incorporating their own enterprises. They are denied access to credit. They are held back by a legal structure designed to protect the ancient privileges of a precapitalist elite. This elite invents nothing, risks nothing, takes no new initiatives. It is parasitic upon and distributes the goods and services of foreign enterprises, whose inventiveness and dynamism it does not emulate. Thus do the Latin American elites sit behind a thick wall of law, corruption, and tradi-tional ways of thinking and operating, whose purpose is to prevent capitalism from arising. These elites fear economic competition. Their greatest preoccupation is the protection of ancient privilege. They are willing to buy and sell, but only behind protective walls. They are not creators. Too few were born among the poor. The elite needs to yield place to the talented millions among the poor who show greater imagination, initiative, inventiveness, and creativity.

The economic skills of the poor—presently unrecognized in law— need to be legitimated, promoted, and given full scope. The 'informals,' now outsiders, need to be brought inside the law. When law is aimed at liberating the poor for economic activism, only then has a capitalist revolution begun against entrenched, noncapitalist privilege and old hereditary elites. Until then, government officials continue to act as did viceroys of the colonial period, restricting legal economic activities to their family and friends."

"Well, we do plan to get rid of them. That's what our Revolution is for. However, we find the United States partly culpable if not in the creation ab initio of these elites, at least in their maintenance. Could it be that the United States is something like classical Athens? A democracy for its own elite, a wonderful place for a select circle of citizens, but not for women, slaves, or barbarians outside the pale?"

Hidalgo laughed uproariously. "You're a hard case, Father. It's a strong analogy, but it gets the Latin American swine off the hook too easily. We've been talking about what in economic parlance is called 'dependency theory.' One of the most influential liberation theologians, the Quechua-Hispanic mestizo Gustavo Gutiérrez, writes in *The Power of the Poor in History* that Latin America was born dependent. This may be true, but it also suits the Latin American mind-set of looking elsewhere for economic, political, and cultural leadership. With the notable exception of liberation theology itself, post-1492 Latin American thought has never led. On the contrary, it has followed the paths of others, often with less success than those who it imitated. Nor is it easy to think of other areas of life until recently where Latin America has taken the lead. Until recently, Latin America has been a continent with a dependent frame of mind."

"I find it ironic that you bring up Gustavo Gutiérrez, since he more than anyone has shown us how the notion of development was promoted by non-Latin Americans and is clearly bankrupt in Latin America. He helped us understand that development and underdevelopment are connected and complementary parts of the capitalist system. Underdeveloped countries will always remain dependent on the developed countries that exercise the mechanisms of control through, among others, multinational corporations and the international banking community, including both public interests such as the International Monetary Fund and private ones like Citibank and Bank of America. American interests made fabulous profits from so-called development money. However, Gutiérrez showed us how development for us meant dependent development that would help a few rich Latin Americans get richer and make the poor get poorer. It was Gustavo Gutiérrez who slew the dragon of development and replaced it with the goal of liberation."

"Father Ignacio, it may have seemed that American interests made money at the time, but in fact, ultimately, Latin America helped the American money centers sucker themselves to the point of bankruptcy. And now there is no turning around. The money-center banks—Citi, Chase, Manny Hanny, Bank of America—went into partnership with Latin America up to their necks, and generally in good faith. The losses that were incurred have led to the demise of the American banks as the collective center of international financial strength and the passing on of the mantle to the Pacific Rim, primarily Japan. The claim, beginning 15 or 20 years ago, strongly supported by the Latin American left, was that in order to break the dependency on multinational corporations, Latin Americans would borrow funds to become masters of their own development. My dirty little secret is that I functioned as the knowledgeable bicultural amphibian who acted on Latin American ways of doing business, with all the attendant ceremonies and palm-greasings, and on North American capitalist assumptions and methods to produce the deals. The money went to Latin American governments and to large, state-controlled entities. But ultimately, only the broker, Adventure Capitalists, made money. The Latin Americans suckered your so-called "American interests" to the point that the debt that was engendered brought the money-center banks to the verge of bankruptcy. Possibly to an extent never seen anywhere before, borrowed money was squandered, stolen, used for self-aggrandizement, or secretly taken out of the target country. Even when it stayed in the country it was used poorly, not for development, but to subvent the cost of consumer products. Hundreds of billions of dollars of borrowed money were spent without visibly creating new wealth in Latin America."

"Pobrecitos. Forgive me if I display some skepticism about the good faith of the American banks. First they helped create a rapacious, uncharitable, idolatrous mentality among the Latin American elite who amass wealth in this country. Then they come to Latin America to lend their billions in petrodollars and are taken advantage of by that very elite. It seems to me that they have reaped what they have sown."

"I don't think that American banks had much to do with the attitude that prevails in this region about wealth. In fact, the debacle was more a product of divergent views about lending and borrowing than convergent ones. The prevailing view of wealth in this region, including among liberation theologians and traditional business leaders, is dead wrong. You seem to think of it as finite and fixed like a candy bar. Something that can only be sliced up so many ways. Not at all, the creation of wealth obeys a cycle. Basically, there is an upward bias. Wealth, capital formation, is in a general state of expansion, although at any one time in certain regions it will be contracting, and occasionally, as in the Great Depression, it will be in contraction worldwide. Usually it is expanding because we are constantly increasing the productivity of societies as we create ever more efficient ways of producing things or serving needs. What this country needs to do is revolutionize itself in order to concentrate on productivity. Money does not create wealth, only the creative use of money does. And that depends upon institutions and habits that reward, rather than punish, creativity. In Latin America, everything is top down, nothing is bottom up. State control, not free private decision making, dominates the major portion of most Latin American economies."

"And so, my son, you represent the American interests that are willing to come to our country and help us in this productivity effort, is that so? For the mutual profit of everyone, I assume?"

"Father, I appreciate your irony and I realize my own ambiguous and precarious status. However, more generally, while Latin American theologians often seem to assume that North American corporations are not only inherently rapacious but clamoring to enter Latin American markets, during recent decades the trend has been exactly the opposite. Even regional giants like the United Fruit Company have been discouraged in Latin American markets and have retrenched and diversified elsewhere. The days of brigand-style North American colonial imperialism in this region are fast fading. My beloved Mexico provides the best example of what I mean both with respect to the problem and its solution. When Salinas de Gortari assumed the presidency of Mexico, he quickly realized that capital would not go to his nation but rather to the newly liberated Eastern bloc unless he competed for it with utmost vigor and skill.

Salinas de Gortari, who—modesty aside—has all of the professional training and characteristics of a perfect Adventure Capitalist, provides a model that can be emulated here. He has acted to create free trade between Mexico, the U.S., and Canada. He has taken the necessary and initially painful actions of reducing debt, inflation, and overreliance on the government. Fugitive money is returning, corruption is down, democracy is expanding. Even the ejido system, that grand experiment in agrarian communalism that achieved scale during the presidency of Lázaro Cárdenas but which has proved to have outlived its usefulness, is going private. In the U.S. only two percent of the population is engaged in farming, and yet it produces food in unimaginable abundance. It's not that we have better land, it's the system that matters. In Brazil, whose population is only half that of the United States and which boasts of immense tracts of uninhabited land, it is extraordinarily painful to hear the liberationist Hugo Assman speak of the country as 'a land where cows never see people and people never eat meat.' Follow the model of Mexico, which is going to successfully change all of that, actively, competitively, and democratically. My theory is that Mexico is likely to become one of the next economic 'miracles' of the 1990s, just like the Four Dragons were the developing world's story of the 1980s."

Hidalgo continued, "A moderate view of dependency theory could easily conclude that Latin America would achieve greater economic and cultural independence through democratic capitalism. It could pursue its own distinctive experiment in free and democratically driven economic development from the bottom up. It could encourage greater self-reliance on locally generated capital. Latin America is held back much more by authoritarian regimes, by statism and the corruption that statism encourages, by the lack of democracy, by feudal-style agriculture, by the discouragement of civic virtues, grassroots Christian communities excepted, than by so-called dependency on Western capitalism."

Father Ignacio smiled wanly. Hidalgo felt uneasy. He knew the priest well enough to judge that his polemicist sensed advantage. "I find it instructive, my son, that you rely so heavily on the model of Gortari and so-called Mexican democratic capitalism, since among the obvious challenges or defects of the model, including extraordinary economic dependence on the U.S. and overwhelming narcotraffic problems—again arguably a by-product of the spirit-deadening, U.S. capitalistic system—we must count the apparent theft of the election by the party, the PRI, which this adventure capitalist heads. Mexico is not a pretty example of democracy, at least at the electoral level. In any event, apparently you came to El Salvador with the best of intentions to help us make our agricultural reform, hand in hand, of course, with the American military-industrial complex, including the CIA, and with the most enlightened Salvadoran heirs of José Napoleón Duarte. If you were genuinely interested in doing more than selling American equipment, didn't you realize how cosmetic your enterprise was and how dubious your partners with respect to the reform goals? And even then, rather than promoting the veneer of agricultural reform, rather than applying the lipstick and the eyeliner, they seem to have preferred to set you up. Forgive me my quip, but you seem to have landed here like the Avon lady who fell out of grace with the jungle."

Hidalgo had little to argue against the reality of miscalculations and blunders. "What can I say, padre? Obviously we messed up. But the interests I represented were American manufacturers of agricultural and construction equipment, and only within the context of agricultural reform. I never represented and I have never supported the aid given to the Salvadoran military by any American entities, including our government or private interests."

"I accept that, my friend. All right, then, if you feel I have inaccurately evaluated the role of America within international economic development, let us prune that issue away just as we have the Soviet Union. Let's cut out Cuba too, and Nicaragua and its special problems and status. Most of all, let us eliminate the alleged concern that we Salvadorans might spawn an evil, international communism bent on subverting our lovely Central American neighbors, garden spots like Honduras and Guatemala. Simply put, controlling for all of those external issues that distract from our sorry circumstances, our fundamental problem is that a small minority owns and enjoys all the wealth of the land, while an overwhelming majority lives in conditions of absolute misery. To the rich in this country the people are no more than beasts of burden, to be worked until the last drop of sweat is extracted—they are not human beings who deserve a decent life. This is why huge sums of money are spent to maintain the armed forces, the police forces, the security forces, the paramilitary forces, the intelligence forces, and the death squads, while the budget for health is totally insufficient to meet the needs of the people.

"For example, illiteracy in El Salvador exists precisely because of this injustice. Here we grow agricultural produce for export abroad—coffee, sugar, and cotton. The raw material is produced cheaply and sent for processing in the industrial world, and for this the plants must be cultivated and harvested. Well, it is the peasant who does this work. So those who own the means of production and the wealth must keep the peasant—and all his generations to follow—permanently a peasant, to maintain the system that gives them their wealth. The only way to guarantee this is to keep them illiterate, and that is why 84% of the peasants in El Salvador are illiterate. Nationwide, 65% of the whole population is illiterate.

"The Salvadoran oligarchy is utterly, grotesquely intransigent. And from their perspective it makes a perverse sort of sense because, just like what occurred with the Soviet *nomenclatura,* once they relinquish a centimeter, their whole apparatus will collapse, possibly in a week or a novena. Their privileges have been so great that they are unwilling to give up any part of them, however small. But sooner or later things are going to change here. In fact, I think that by your own logic you should join us, particularly since it is in your personal interest to do so now that you find yourself here in our splendid company creating a new Eden. If international capitalism is as you suggest, and since the Communist threat is 'nonesuch,' as you have eloquently elucidated during various Guazapan sunsets, then, presuming that you agree with me that what we have here is an atavism, a fascistic semifeudalism imposed with military high technology, let us combine resources to slay the perverse dragon. Then your system, which I might describe as 'trickle-down' capitalism—certainly my words, not yours—and my system, which you might describe as 'ethereal and fantastical Christian communitarianism,' can duke it out in your so sacred 'open marketplace' or on your equally vaunted 'level playing field.' "

"Splendid discourse, padre. How I wish I could bring it up to the Sunday morning group. Did I ever tell you that every Sunday morning, surely while you were saying mass, I would be drinking Jerez de la Frontera and giving my partners a neuropsychic review of the marketplace?"

Ignacio seemed amused. "No."

"God knows, I may die in this vile war. But I suspect I'll die a contrarian. It's my nature. I have a friend and fellow traveler who in the financial world carries the placa of Oso Polar. He has pointed out that the marketplace stances of the investment world, so seemingly secular, in fact are uncannily analogical to the great religions. What are the popular images of the investor? The modern brigand looking for a profit, the bigger the better, but always with some shady angle or crooked ploy; the hard-nosed analyst who does his or her homework, exercises split-second market timing, in sum, a financial wizard . . . maybe two or three other cartoons. That's poppycock. The investment world is primarily moved by congregations or herds: Growth, Value, Income, even Contrary Opinion dominate the marketplace much as Christianity, Judaism, Islam, Hinduism, Buddhism, and Taoism dominate the spiritplace. The practitioners of these 'investment styles' appear to be guided by a matrix of beliefs and routines similar to those of religions. Part of my job for Adventure Capitalists was to analyze those styles, which in fact seemed just as amenable to analysis as rituals guided by dogmas."

"And why, my son, did you make such analyses?"

"For profit, Father. Ultimately, for profit, the intervening variable being prediction."

"So then, m'hijo, you function as a prophet of profits?"

"You're getting the hang of it, padre. Predicting investment styles means predicting the future of the market, and that, predicted successfully, is at the heart of profit. A curious element of these investment styles, not without its analog in this Salvadoran milieu, is that each stylist is customarily intolerant of the others. Each investment style has its true believers, its high priests, its proselytizers and practitioners, its sacred writings.

"Take Growth. Rather like Buddhism. The Growth investors look for a state of grace in which they will be liberated from the laws of reincarnation. For them perpetual growth is nirvana, a state of complete investment redemption. On the other hand, we Contrarians are the Hindus, believing in birth and reincarnation. We buy stocks when they are so down they've become 'untouchable' and sell them when they are reborn into a higher caste. We have our bible, *It Pays to be Contrary,* and our first gospel: When everyone thinks alike, everyone is likely to be wrong. Income investors are the Taoists. Taoism holds that by nonaction and the avoidance of human striving it is possible for one to live in harmony with the principles that govern the universe. Perhaps that explains the vast sums that lie fallow, remaining in instruments like money funds even when short-term rates fall and the stock market goes up. The Taoist seeks virtue before profit. And the value investors are the Jews of the investment world, placing great weight on commandments, laws, and tradition. Thou shalt not pay more than book value."

"I get the picture, my son, but not its implication. What conclusion do you derive from this analogy?"

Don Jorge sighed. "The marketplace, it is so open, so free and variegated. I love it so. I want to live, Father, in this new world that has become so exciting, volatile, and redolent of new and intriguing variables. I don't want to die here, Father, even though your cause has much merit. I want to live and to continue to grow, to learn, perhaps even to measure and predict."

"I'm so sorry, Don Jorge, for what has befallen you. Even as I have so greatly appreciated our learning from you. I empathize with what you say. We too, who have committed ourselves to the people's church and Christian Base Communities, feel ourselves living in a nuevo mundo. God grant us all the prayer that we may live in order to learn and mature!"

* * *

It started out so awkwardly, this thing of peasant leaders who speak non sequitor and without warning of their deepest motives. It was pitch dark and Hidalgo was inspecting an engine under a Coleman lantern, giving assignments to other mechanics, harried in every possible way, exhausted, and, just like atop his Renaissance Tower in an earlier life, profoundly alarmed about making his deadlines. Puñonrostro appeared from nowhere and tapped him on the shoulder. Hidalgo turned to face his carcelero.

Puñonrostro looked Hidalgo firmly in the eye. He talked slowly, measuring and tasting each word in that classic peasant-leader way, probably, Hidalgo thought, because this business of making weighty decisions was so utterly novel. Even the Zapata of the movies, Hidalgo recalled wryly, especially the Zapata who was a disguised Marlon Brando, talked like that. "Father Ignacio has explained to me about poverty and I hold his words in my deepest place, my fuero interno. In our Guazapa, in El Salvador, in all of our mundo latino-americano, poverty is the compadre of death. Poverty does not mean simply that we do not have something that is available to los ricos. Poverty overwhelms our bodies and our spirits like burdens that are too heavy, and yet we are forced to carry both in the day and at nighttime. It leaves us unable to control our lives even at the most basic level. Poverty is close to death, and the poor are destined to die before their time. This is why poverty is a grito for life, a grito for survival. Before he was murdered in 1973, I heard Father Rutilio Grande say that the God who has given us this wide world wants a shared table for all of humanity. Today God sees that his creation is threatened and destroyed. We believe now that the creation of God has not arrived in El Salvador because life is not the basic reality of poor people. Instead, in this society a serious sin exists because the socioeconomic system—the first idol, as our martyred archbishop Romero called it—is organized to produce a slow death for the poor."

That was Puñonrostro's set piece, a tap on the shoulder and launching right in without the slightest warm up. Even though Hidalgo was not disposed toward the peasant leader, he felt tears well in his eyes. That priest has done a good job, he thought to himself. He embraced the peasant student-prince. "You speak well."

"I want to tell you one more thing. And this I have thought myself," he said, with great pleasure in the thinking and the phrasing. "The day that we make our next salida, we will kill a lot of them, and those who we kill will be the sons and daughters of the poor. We fight them and we are poor and they are poor. The rich do not recruit the sons of the oligarchy or the middle class but only the poor. And we are the poor who are going to kill them to free ourselves from poverty, and they are the poor who are going to kill us to defend the system simply because they get a mere extra handful of pupusas from their masters. It's a very great evil."

Shortly after that encounter Hidalgo was made aware that things were going badly for the Guazapan guerrillas. Ironically, the situation was supposed to be improving, but Hidalgo, the master of the counterintuitive, was not surprised. At their sunset colloquy, Ignacio was very disturbed. He had Puñonrostro with him and he produced two recent stories side by side in the *New York Times*. The first described a rebel-decreed, unilateral truce to which President Cristiani responded with praise for what he called the rebels' "good will" and a promise that the government would take "corresponding unilateral measures." Those unilateral measures turned out to be large troop movements specifically in the Guazapa, trying to take undue advantage of the truce. Hidalgo was confused. "What's happening?"

"It's another rat. The FMLN has done the right thing. We are trying to negotiate a genuine peace now that so many of the external factors like the Cold War and Nicaraguan and Cuban support for certain elements of the FMLN are nonexistent or greatly reduced. Nevertheless, under the cover of our unilateral ceasefire, the government, while mouthing positives, is secretly mobilizing specifically against us in the Guazapa."

"Will the FMLN support you? Will they denounce this?"

"Probably, but not necessarily, and not necessarily in time. We have realized for a long time that we have a separate and somewhat controversial status within the FMLN. The FMLN has numerous factions; some of them, as you know, are not receptive to Christian soldiers who are so militantly Christian. This complicated politic is part of the reason that Puñonrostro has resisted announcing that you are alive and safe with us."

"What is the other article?"

"It's front page news. A panel of United States House Democrats has concluded that there is compelling circumstantial evidence to suggest that the 1989 killings of the six Jesuit priests was plotted by senior Salvadoran army officers, including General René Emilio Ponce, currently Defense Minister and then army chief of staff. It was suggested that General Juan Rafael Bustillo, then commander of the air force, was the mastermind behind the plot to kill the Jesuits. Other senior military personnel were named who have already been known to have figured among the active plotters, including Colonel Guillermo Alfredo Benavides, then head of the military academy. It was confirmed that the elite Atlacatl batallion, trained by the United States, did the killing. It was suggested that the CIA was not interested in getting to the bottom of the case because General Bustillo had permitted a supply operation out of the Ilopango airport near San Salvador for the United States-backed Contras in Nicaragua. A spokesman for the CIA says there is no basis for these allegations by the House investigators."

"Nobody's going to do anything to bring those murderers to justice, are they?" asked Hidalgo. "Certainly no element of the executive branch of the U.S. government."

"It would seem so. But they and those worms who aided them will have to appear before the tribunal of the Lord. My dear Knight, I believe that our position in the Guazapa is gravely compromised. We could be sacrificial lambs in what you have called 'political endgame' from time to time in our engaging discussions."

"Is there any chance you can free me? I haven't aided and abetted any worms that I am aware of, at least in the Salvadoran theater. I've comported myself productively on behalf of your cause, despite the most difficult circumstances. But I'm serving as a motor man, not a warrior, in this theater. Now that you are entering endgame, let me go with my godsent lady Dulce Tobosa, who I'd like to take to Los Angeles and for whom I would arrange refugee status and psychiatric care."

Father Ignacio spoke up. "I have no problems with that. I think it would be wise, actually. But I give to the secular arm that which is the purview of the secular arm."

They both turned to Puñonrostro. He had that way of pulling on his peasant's beard when he thought about something that was right out of Dostoyevsky, Hidalgo thought. This time he pondered for a long time and Hidalgo accepted with stoicism the emerging statesman's dictum. "We will be going soon into la boca del lobo. I can't let you go now. To once again give you gratuitous privileges that Americans have come to expect as their due would go against the ideals that we are fighting for. But, if we survive our encounters intact, as I am confident we will, I will surely release you from your obligations to the revolutionary army and possibly present you as well with a medal for your valor."

The priest turned to the peasant. "Let me implore you, my beloved compañero Puñonrostro, to take this matter under continued consideration, particularly before the revolutionary council. Let us try to do whatever we can for our friend and model prisoner."

Puñonrostro gave a little gasp. Even Hidalgo could see that the cares of state were weighing on him. "That certainly. Let us say that nothing is resolved on this matter with any finality until the council reviews it and makes a decision."

It was only two days later that Ignacio and Puñonrostro came to Hidalgo with an air of resolution. Clearly they had a plan.

Father Ignacio said, "Now the moment of truth has come, my friend!"

"I've heard that before," Hidalgo said, "except last time it was 'the big whiffer.' "

Puñonrostro talked solemnly. "The revolutionary council has made the decision to take an action of irrevocable, international consequences. It is one that affects every member of our group. We beseech you, compañero Jorge, to give us all the help you can. In fact, our plan can't work effectively without your participation. If things work as we envision, you will be able to walk out of San Salvador a free man."

Hidalgo was moved. It was the first time that the guerrilla coman-dante had called him by the most intimate of muchacho epithets, compañero. The adventurer turned to the priest and smiled timidly. "The three amigos, is that it? The ones who succumbed to a lethal elixir of Quixotitis. It all sounds suspiciously familiar, like what in my parlance we call the 'best and final offer.' "

"Before compañero Puñonrostro explains, I would like us all to pray. Would you indulge me? For whatever the reasons and cares of revolution, we have not all prayed together. Let us do that, and then we will explain." At this the man of cloth firmly took with one hand the man of popular formation and with the other the man of capital formation, and in good faith they kneeled on the earth before them. Amidst the purring motors and the jesting and cursing of motor jockeys and the used lubricants that had seeped into this place, with the guidance of padre Ignacio together they prayed for godspeed to Jesus Christ, King, Son of God, and above all to Nuestra Señora, the fair mother of Christ and protector of all who are hispanos, that this venture be graced and executed with success. And at that Hidalgo was inducted into the fold of the guerrilla enterados and was no longer an alien to all who knew him nor to his own visage that looked back at him in pools of Quaker State. If not precisely in a state of grace, he did indeed judge himself enlightened.

The plan was to take over the National Palace of Justice in the capital. There they would capture and hold hostage all who were unfortunate enough to be inside. Simultaneously, sappers would infiltrate the city, pick up preselected "enemies of the people," and bring them to the Palace. Then they would hook up with CNN, the BBC, and the rest of the media and hold press conferences. Hidalgo would be allowed to surface and would attain prominent media status as one of a number of Christian guerrilla spokespersons that would also include Puñonrostro and Father Ignacio. The muchachos would state their position, explain the perfidy of the Salvadoran military and the government, and offer honest and just terms for resolving the situation in the immediate theater of action. This would include the guerrillas freeing the hostages and the Salvadoran mil-itary minimally returning the Guazapa to the lines of demarcation prior to its most recent incursions. In that way the Guazapa would be genuinely incorporated, with its interests intact, in the cease-fire and the forthcoming peace negotiations. If the Salvadoran government wanted to improve that minimum, all the better, but all the rebels would ask for was a simple return to the status quo ante at both the Palace of Justice and the Guazapa: a suspension of Salvadoran military encroachment and a return to the lines of control that had been prevailing in the region for 10 years. As for Hidalgo, he would transit to the outside with the other hostages, hopefully with positive and possibly even celebrity status, at least in some quarters such as Christian militants, progressive politicians, some Latinos, and the people of the sanctuary movement. In any event, while he would return to his own status quo ante (with Sweet Dulce at his arm, the personal complications were his own problem), on his own initiative he would function as an unofficial ambassador for the Guazapan cause. "We may not be able to get the coverage that you would like in *Forbes*, Don Jorge, but I can almost guarantee your picture on the cover of *America*, the Jesuit magazine."

Hidalgo enthusiastically approved the plan. All of the senior Guazapan revolutionaries were confident that they had a realistic chance of making it work, particularly if they could take the Palace of Justice without so much bloodshed that neither the Salvadoran nor the United States authorities would deal with them. That would be the key, the willingness of the Salvadoran and United States governments to negotiate with them in good faith. Moreover, Hidalgo's emergence alive and well as a powerful speaker for los muchachos would be brilliant coup de théâtre with the press.

The capitalist warrior was promoted to the rank of comandante as camp chief of procurement, maintenance, and transportation of military matériel and was given the responsibility to have ready the necessary military vehicles to sneak into San Salvador. The venture's demands on matériel and on his person were the intensest of his almost three years of revolutionary service. But he could not claim that he was unhappy. He worked all day and had no time to worry or brood, falling at night into the arms of his Fair Lady, who in turn spent as much time as she could practicing her weaponry and combat skills. She had determined, with the reluctant acquiescence of the revolutionary council given her improved but still unstable condition, that she would participate in the capacity of sapper in what was by now popularly known as Operation *Mater et Magistra*.

The leaders of los muchachos estimated that they had only three weeks left to pull off *Mater et Magistra* before their position would become so constricted by the Salvadoran military that they would have no reasonable chance to conduct a secret convoy through enemy lines and infiltrate the capital. Thus, the motor muchachos consumed themselves with work. The convoy vans needed to be decorated with all the right ornamentation so that they would pass through the multiple roadblocks and checkpoints as bona fide. Captured uniforms were resewn and cleaned so that bullet holes and other telltale hearts would not give them away. The captured M-16s that they would be using were put into correct working order. Among the myriad of details, the workaholic Hidalgo felt so alive—a superreal, volcanic-mountain high, working in a frenzied position of authority with his compañeros de revolución for the forthcoming operation.

They made their deadlines. Vans to conduct guerrilleros y guerrilleras, six hundred strong. As they came down the line, perfectly dirty in the natural ways, the motor muchachos christened each of them in a secret place.

"And this one will be called Babieca!" said Hidalgo.

"¡Qué chingao! What the hell is that?"

"A classic. El Cid's horse!"

"Always the cryptic one, this comandante. Just for that, this one we will baptize la pupusa de oro."

"All right then, this one we will call Bucephalus!"

"And this one we will call, in your honor, tápate el hocico."

"And this one, Rocinante."

"And this one, pebre de garrobo."

"And this one, Knight of the Mournful Countenance."

"And this one, Farabundo Martí."

"And this one, Rodrigo con Safos."

"And this one, Anastasio Aquino."

"And this one, Pierre Teilhard de Chardin."

"Who?"

"A leader, he takes us to the Omega point."

"Está bien. Then we will call this one Cristo Rey, who takes us past all the points to where the stars merge with the Sacred Heart."

"No, nonesuch," said a pious muchacho. "That is lack of respect and of understanding, for Christ goes with us in our souls, but He is divine and would not incarnate an instrument of war."

Hidalgo had become increasingly agitated. Finally he broke down and wept.

The muchachos couldn't understand. "Why are you weeping?"

"I'm not sure, carnales. Because you are so good and so real. Lloro de pura rabia, de emoción, del amor que os tengo."

* * *

Yes, friends and carnales, there was a party in the barranca. How could it not be, despite what shallow, uninformed outsiders have made of the Hispanic fiesta? In order that it might not interfere with their abilities, the Christian guerrillas chose to have their celebration three days in advance of the salida, culminating it with a special midnight service of the misa popular salvadoreña.

At a New York dinner party, hadn't Teilhard de Chardin once praised "a foie gras directly imported from Perigord and good enough to make one weep"? Hidalgo found himself saying the same thing, almost by magical, Buñuelian déjà vu, courtesy of the commemorating revolutionary release of the hoarded stocks that they had confiscated from the haciendas: the finest, choicest, and most rarified luxuries that the Salvadoran squires had brought from all over the world and stocked in their pantries and cellars.

So let us eat, my compañeros, pupusas topped with goose liver and cleanse our palates with Dom Perignon in order that we may partake of suckling pig and dip our tortillas into thick pebres and unwrap festive nacatamales and make cuba libres with Ron Barrilito and two liter Diet Cokes (no deposit, no return).

And dance and sing in revolutionary camaraderie. Epa la marimba, for we sing "La guerra,"

> Una guerra que nunca quisimos
> Una guerra que ya acabaremos
> Para que junto a nuestros niños
> Recorramos alegres las calles
> de El Salvador liberado.

And this one we dedicate to our spiritual leader, padre Ignacio.

> Vamos ganando la paz
> Abrazados en la lucha
> Cada hermano una trinchera

> Porque amamos la paz
> Vamos ganando la paz.

And this one, "El machete encachimbado," which sounds so Mexican, for our fuereño friend who has come from allá en el rancho grande to help the muchachos compañeros,

> Mi patrón me ha despedido
> Me ha rompido el corazón
> . . .
> Que se apliquen los machetes
> para la revolución.

And for our máximo comandante, who will lead us in glorious actions in the effort to liberate El Salvador, we sing "No a la intervención,"

> Con un verso y otro verso
> Haremos una canción
> Con un plomo y otro plomo
> Liberaremos a El Salvador.
> No, no, no a la intervención
> El pueblo quiere revolución,
> No, no, no a la intervención
> El pueblo quiere revolución,
> Si no se van, si no se van
> Si no se van, si no se van
> Les va a pasar como en Vietnam.

And then they sang songs from all over. They sang the songs from the Cuban nueva trova and they sang José Martí's versos adapted to music by Pablo Milanés. They sang old Salvadoran ballads and laments, Silvio Rodríguez, cha-cha-cha ("los marcianos llegaron ya, y llegaron bailando cha-cha-cha"), Rubén Blades, sandinista war songs ("es Sandino que vive"), and songs of the Mexican Revolution. They also sang the songs of the Mexican movies and of Lola Beltrán, Lucha Villa, Jorge Negrete, and Pedro Infante like "Cucurrucucu paloma," "El sauce y la palma," "Ojos tapatíos," "No volveré," and "Pénjamo." Hidalgo was moved to sing "México lindo."

> Yo te canto a tus volcanes
> a tus praderas y flores

> que son como talismanes
> del amor de mis amores.
>
> México lindo y querido
> si muero lejos de ti,
> que digan que estoy dormido
> y que me traigan aquí,
> que digan que estoy dormido
> y que me traigan aquí,
> Mexico lindo y querido
> si muero lejos de ti.

When he was done, Dulce laughed and observed with soft mockery about his delivery, was that cantando or was it rebuznando? The revelers warmed up for a good old-fashioned song joust. Dulce parodied Hidalgo, who by now was drunk and sloppy, by singing "Llegó borracho, el borracho." During the last weeks she seemed to have gathered strength in her commitments. One way or another it would be over. She was pleased with the rifle in her hand. Tonight she seemed so alegre and spontaneous that Hidalgo was enthralled.

> ¡Ajúa!
> Llegó borracho, el borracho
> Pidiendo cinco tequilas
>
> . . .
> Gritó de pronto el borracho
> La vida no vale nada
> Y le dijo el cantinero
> Mi vida está asegurada
> Si vienes echando habladas
> Yo te contesto con balas
>
> . . .
> De pronto los dos cayeron
> Haciendo cruz con sus brazos.

Hidalgo returned the favor, evoking the dubious peasant leader from his favorite Hemingway novel. "I refuse to be provoked." He sang the most macho or most drunken songs he knew, stuff like "El papalote," "Las tres botellas," "Copa tras copa," and "Con un polvo y otro polvo."

Con un polvo y otro polvo
se formó una polvareda
una copa y otra copa
se hacen una borrachera . . .

And this one, remember it?

Siempre que me emborracho
palabra que algo me pasa
voy derechito a verte
y me equivoco de casa.

Siempre que me emborracho
yo no más pienso en ella
y no me tranquilizo
hasta acabar la botella.

In revanche, Dulce sang "María la bandida."

Este es el corrido de una hembra preciosa
que todos conocen como la bandida
María, María, María la bandida
no sabe ni entiende
de cosas de amores
sus ojos grandotes no expresan cariño
quién sabe si tuvo muchas decepciones
quién sabe lo negro que
fue su destino
María, María, María la bandida
. . .
con ella se gana o se pierde la vida
por algo le llaman María bandida.

It was Hidalgo's turn. Feigning remorse for his drunken indiscretions, he sang "Por el amor a mi madre."

Por el amor a mi madre
voy a dejar la parranda,
y aunque me digan cobarde,
a mí no me importa nada.

Mi madrecita llorando,
me dice que ya no tome,

> la vida se está acabando,
> y temo que me abandone.
>
> Adiós botellas de vino,
> adiós mujeres alegres,
> adiós todos mis amigos,
> adiós los falsos quereres.

Dulce hiked up her overalls, which were weighted down by her crisscrossing cartucheras. She had insisted on appearing in formal cacica attire. She belted out "La bala perdida," and Hidalgo wondered if perhaps this was the reason that she insisted on arriving at the fiesta in full armor.

> Las balas perdidas pegaron siempre en mi pecho,
> Las balas perdidas pegaron siempre en mi pecho,
> pero tus besos me inyectaron
> nueva vida
> bala perdida, bala perdida
> viene ya el máuser
> que te ha tronado, que te ha tronado
> para acabar, para acabar
> para acabar con mi vida.

Puñonrostro called for a moment of silence. He presented Hidalgo with a dusty, heavily tinted bottle. "I understand that you know and value this essence?"

Don Jorge inspected it curiously. "¡Válgame Dios! The finest calvados!"

"Expropriated from the foulest hacendado in all of the Guazapa, who of course maintained the finest cellar."

Eagerly Hidalgo decanted, but even as he prepared to imbibe, to his mind came a sick and surely capitalist thought, for the life of growth spirals would seem to be perfectly Hobbesian in nature. "The grappa," he muttered under his breath, "but where's the grappa?" Then, reminded at that moment of his last lunch with Gary Gnu, he exclaimed, first to the mystification, then to the jubilation of all, "It is claimed that the highest desire of the honorable Japanese when they go into battle is merely to ensure that they be bathed and in clean undergarments. For us capitalists, it is this fiery calvados that is worth dying for. I propose then a toast of the finest apple juice in the world, to the finest compañeros in this revolution."

"¡Viva la revolución!"

"And to our máximo comandante to whose generosity of spirit we owe this essence that fortifies our militant ardor!"

"¡Viva Jesús Salvador Puñonrostro!"

"And then to one Gary Gnu, master of juvenile TV, to whom primary credit should go for my presence among such exalted company."

"¡Viva el egnu!"

"And finally, to the fairest revolutionary of our lot, the most exalted of us all, la Dulce Tobosa, whose privilege will be mine, if need be, to die in her open arms—arm and arm in combat for the just cause."

"¡Viva la Dulce Tobosa de El Mozote!"

Hidalgo went on, looking at Ignacio. "Clearly in this land, so aptly named for the Savior who let his side be opened so that the blood might spill from His divine body onto the earth to redeem us from our sins, clearly in this conundrum of El Salvador lies the deepest, most profound configuration of our unending quest for the Holy Grail!"

With this, our Sweet Dulce ordinarily so apartada y enajenada, stepped forward tipsily, sporting her doublet cartucheras that formed an X in the middle of her chest and the knot of her back, and taking the calvados, she first took a prodigious draught of its fire and then raised it with la siniestra while at the same time raising high her polished, immaculate M-16 with la diestra.

The Spanish priest, so imbued with the mythos of Republican Spain and of his tocayo, the Christian soldier of God, cried out, "¡Que viva la Pasionaria! ¡Que viva!", and Hidalgo, who fancied that some of his relatives had traveled with the Mexican cristeros, cried out their war cry, ¡Que viva Cristo Rey!" The jubilants echoed these gritos with bacchanalian abandon, despite their subcontextual confusion: "¡Que viva! ¡Que viva!"

Sweet Dulce fired into the night sky, and such an intemperate action quelled everyone. "And now I shall speak. Yes, I am the most exaltada of this illustrious company, and for this simple honor of being with you in this just and necessary mission I willingly and of sound and clear mind lay down my life for you, gentle muchachas y muchachos. God died three years ago in El Mozote."

There were murmurs of confusion at such heterodoxy.

"Did he not die? Verily, it is true. I witnessed the many ways of death of nuestro salvador. He was shot, he was raped, he was torn to shreds in the plaza, and he was suffocated to death in the manger. And so I, too, died in my spirit, hung high in a tree and forced to look down at God's death in my people, my husband, mis hijos. But now I have risen, and only because in the cold place donde estaba mi alma I have seen you rise. You have risen from your misery and come together and nurtured and succored each other; you have conceived and planned this holy project in which all of us can find work, our place, and satisfaction. So now, knowing finally that God is dead and that ¡Nosotras somos Dios!, that we are all accountable to each other and that all of us count, I consider myself miraculously fortunate to andar con vos.

"Finally, let divine providence grant me one little thing, that if I die with my beloved chicano, mi viejo"—then she hiccuped with grand guignol effect, "let it be like the old song, 'Llegó borracho, el borracho,' so that in our fallen militancy our arms and legs should light upon each other in the form of a crucifix. God grant me this one last miracle!"

With that Father Ignacio came to Dulce and embraced her as if to comfort her.

"I'm not that drunk, Father. Just enough to make the words come out. It's what I want."

"We understand, corazón dulce. We understand and we respect your wishes." He turned to his Christian army and told them that it was close to midnight and that he would cap their fiesta with the misa popular salvadoreña.

The marimba, woodwinds, and percussion took their place at one side, the men and women of the choir at the other, and they sang the mass. They sang to the glory of God and of those who would thwart His message of life ever after in Kingdom Come, and they sang of freedom in this world.

> Ahora Señor podrás ser Tú glorificado
> al como antes allá en el monte Tabor
> cuando Tú veas a tu pueblo transformado
> y haya vida y libertad en El Salvador
> Gloria al Señor, Gloria al Señor
> Gloria al patrón de nuestra tierra,
> El Salvador
> No hay redención de otro señor
> sólo un patrón, nuestro divino Salvador.

> Pero los dioses del poder y del dinero
> Se oponen a que haya transfiguración
> Por eso ahora vos Señor sos el primero
> En levantar tu brazo contra la opresión.
>
> Gloria al Señor, Gloria al Señor
> Gloria al patrón de nuestra tierra,
> El Salvador
> No hay redención de otro señor
> sólo un patrón, nuestro divino Salvador.

And they sang to the Holy Spirit that accompanied them in their struggle.

> Santo santo santo santo
> Santo santo es nuestro Dios
> Señor de toda la tierra
> Santo santo es nuestro Dios
> santo santo santo santo
> santo santo es nuestro Dios
> Señor de toda la historia
> santo santo es nuestro Dios.
>
> Que acompaña a nuestro pueblo,
> que vive en nuestras luchas,
> en el universo entero
> el único Señor.
> Bendito los que en su nombre
> el evangelio anuncian,
> la buena y gran noticia
> de la liberación.

And all of these devout songs and alabados were seasoned by the sorts of exuberant shouts and urgings that Hidalgo, until he had entered this Salvadoran milieu, had always associated with the most secular of his momentos mexicanos y chicanos.

Even as they sang of the most blessed sacrament, the transubstantiation of the body and blood of Christ, it was peppered with the most enthusiastic cries:

"¡Entrale compadre!"

"Ya vamos llegando."

"¡Upale!"

"Y mira la gente, mira cuánta gente, compadre."

"Ay compadre, ¡qué bella está la misa!"

Surely, Hidalgo thought, this was a splendid way to breach the distance between the padre and his pueblo and to establish genuine, active participation in the service. Hidalgo promised himself that if he made it back to la chicanada and to Mexico, he would speak about this among his own people.

Finally, Father Ignacio evoked some of the most memorable words of the martyred Archbishop Romero, and many in the army of Christ wept as the familiar words swept over them.

> Queremos que el gobierno tome en serio que de nada sirven las reformas si van teñidas con tanta sangre. En nombre de Dios pues, y en nombre de este sufrido pueblo, cuyos lamentos suben hasta al cielo cada día más tumultuosos, les suplico, les ruego, les ordeno en nombre de Dios, ¡Cesen la represión!

And now it was the "Canto de despedida."

> Cuando el pobre
> cree en el pobre
> ya podremos cantar libertad
> cuando el pobre
> cree en el pobre
> construiremos la fraternidad.

With this the muchachas y muchachos embraced each other and their spiritual and secular leaders, then dispersed to their abodes to turn to final matters of ordering their life affairs and making last-minute preparations. In three days, Operation *Mater et Magistra* would begin.

As for Sweet Dulce, that night she slept in a state close to grace, a state that sometimes comes to those who assert themselves after a long period of quiescence. Her arms and legs embraced her "beloved Chicano," who for his part played the role of Pascal's frail but thinking reed. The French in their infinite wisdom distributed the *Pensées* to every conscript in the first great war to end all wars; the giant network of trenches and barriers on the battlefield was to become strewn with mud- and blood-soiled *pensées*.

Dizzily, it all passed before him. Sartre's nausea, Pascal's bet on the existence of God, the missing grappa of which, in his great malestar, he felt he needed a final sip "more than life itself." Finally his fleeting attention came to focus egotistically on the image that he might convey to the press. He imagined what the media would make of him, especially with a gentle nudge from the Salvadoran government spinmeisters, even the federal Company itself.

KNIGHT SURFACES AS SALVADORAN GUERRILLA; WAS IT ALL STAGED?

Today a group of wildly erratic guerrilla zealots who represented themselves as all things to all people—Communists, Christians, venture capitalists, and everything else—took the most important and eminent jurists of the Republic of Salvador hostage and captured the Palace of Justice. With the Salvadoran war effectively over it was the most extreme act of senseless defiance since the Japanese kamikazes made their last stand in World War II. Except that made more sense. This was more on the order of the Kool-Aid massacre in Georgetown, Guyana. Among the entourage were identified a Communist Catholic priest; a landless, illiterate, but charismatic peasant leader whose name in Spanish translates literally as "Fist in Your Face"; a guerrillera cacica with two cartucheras crisscrossing her body like the Mexican revolutionaries of 1910; and a Chicano adventure capitalist with the bilingual name George Knight/Jorge Hidalgo, the most prominent example since Patty Hearst of the brainwashing of a captive American.

Perhaps it wouldn't be that bad. Maybe after a few months some investigative reporter of the *New York Times* or *Mother Jones* would take an interest. Maybe a writer, God knows, even a film-maker. Besides, he was exaggerating. The press wouldn't give it that much attention anyway. In the first place, they didn't know enough Spanish to give it the appropriate flavor. But the clincher was that this would be happening in Central America, no comprendo land of mañana Margaritaville. Front page coverage, but without inspiration.

In the morning Dulce was struck with apprehensions about a new eventuality: grave disability on the battlefield that would prevent her from returning to the Guazapa. "Don't worry," he said. "It's only the hangover that makes you melancholy."

She made love to him, assuring him that this would be their last opportunity before entering battle. It was a deliberate, torrid affair, the first time they had made love by daylight. Un feucho y una feucha, he thought, transmogrified into mythic titans, sparks shooting from their sweating bodies under the sun, the rubber tree, and the hushed whippoorwill, while far away the rest of the camp went about its business allocating the last goat or cat or worldly possession to those who weren't entering battle. Then, when they had recuperated, she dictated a note the way one of her customers might have done through the instrumentality of her dead husband. Hidalgo faithfully recorded the letter, and she pinned it prominently to her blouse so that it might be found if she fell in combat.

To the Authorities of the Salvadoran Government:

My name is Dulce Tobosa. Check your records; my husband always paid the tax even though it was unjust. I am the only survivor of the little hamlet of El Mozote. Check the records of Tutela Legal. I bore witness there to your evil acts. You killed everyone, ensuring that you did it the most cruel way possible to the men and to the women and even to the children and the smallest baby, and then I had to make la guinda because you would have killed me to hush me up. But if you find this letter on me you will know I did my duty to God, and for Jesús Salvador Puñonrostro, God bless his coming to lead us, and for our little Spanish priest, the most revered Ignacio, a holy man, and for all the muchachos y muchachas. We are God because we are doing God's work here in El Salvador. And that means ridding the earth of such people; it's almost impossible to imagine they are of the same human race. So, if I am sin conciencia in this battle, for the sake of my humanity and in God's name do not revive me only to keep me in your hell. Stab me or shoot me. Let me die in the place I have made my just stand. Or if you are to revive me, allow me to go to América with Jorge Hidalgo (also American name, George Knight), a good Chicano American who has become famous in El Salvador because we kidnapped him, and who I am in love with in my most profound being and who has sworn to me faithfully that he will take me to his country. I know he is married and with a fine family and we have talked about this many times. We are both in extremis and he would take me to his country only so I would make a new life. This is the most profound request of a citizen who has suffered beyond endurance.

Signed, Dulce Tobosa, ciudadana de El Nuevo Salvador

P.S. If you have any doubts about what to do with me, any doubts at all, kill me. I'd rather be safe than sorry. I'd rather not wake up in hell. Please God, make them obey you!

"Are you sure you want this long explanation pinned to your body?"

"I probably won't need it. I'll probably live or die. Or in doubt, I'll go straight forward and fire my rifle into them and make sure I die. But I want it. I've never killed anyone. I've never fired this at anything that moved, only at fixed targets. I should wear it. It would resolve an uncertainty."

"Dear Dulce, I swear you are a mathematician. When we go to America, you'll talk with Hermelinda about analyzing outcomes."

"Yes, when we go to America."

"Too bad I don't have one of the little machines that we sell in my country."

"A little machine?"

"Yes, you can wear it and if you're hurt or whatever you call into the machine: 'I've fallen and I can't get up,' and the authorities come quickly."

"Well, your country is very efficient. Here we have no little machines. Here we hire a scribe like my husband and pin notes to our clothes." Then she said, "Will you write one for yourself?"

"Me, what would I write?"

She laughed. "Tú que eres tan leído y escribido. You know what to write. Do this for me, to resolve the little doubt."

"Of course I will. Do you know you're reinventing something called set theory?"

"¿Qué es eso? ¿Será queso?"

"Well, it's sort of like analyzing all of the eventualities—the yes, the no, the maybes—and covering them all." Then Hidalgo considered the matter at hand with all due gravity since the request came from his Fair Lady, and he redacted his message. He read it to her.

To my dearest carnales and carnalas and to all interested parties:

My name is bilingual and bicultural, Jorge and George Hidalgo and Knight. I am an American and a Chicano who disappeared from San Salvador almost three years ago, who was taken captive by Christian guerrillas of the Guazapa, and who has learned to love them, especially my compañera, Dulce Tobosa, and my priest and confessor, Father Ignacio. Check your records; it was my distinct pleasure not only to always pay taxes but to amass great amounts of profit in order to do so prodigiously. I believe in capitalism but also in the maximum allocation of capital to the economically needy so that they in turn can be more productive. My most basic sense of morality tells me that since we are all human with hearts and bellies and souls, and since resources count, we should obey a moral imperative to provide adequately for the belly, the heart, and the soul, all of these organs or entities without exception.

There is so much I could say about what I have learned and I will, if I have an opportunity. But if I am found dead with this note pinned on me, I simply want to observe two things. Ultimately, I chose my fate. In the beginning, I was coerced, of course, and I do not agree with some of their actions nor their disposition to keep me secretly captive, but ultimately I exercised my free will, and persuaded on balance by the worthy behavior of the Christian guerrillas, I embraced both their love and their cause.

The other thing I must say is that I am both a patriotic American and a proper Chicano, and I am profoundly offended and embarrassed by my country's behavior in El Salvador, to which it has contributed great misery. There is so much I could say, but having thought about this every day that our Guazapa was bombed from the air, what follows is at the heart of it.

U.S. policymakers have this absurd belief that we can build and train armies in Latin America that will guarantee democratic development rather than subvert it. This is folly. As fast as we have professionalized armies, they have been converted to political ends. And the most sadly instructive examples have been in Nicaragua and El Salvador. In Nicaragua, beginning in the 1920s we attempted to depoliticize the armed forces and we built a new force, the Guardia Nacional, from the ground up. It gave us the Somoza family dictatorship that lasted for more than 43 years. Here in El Salvador we commit the same mistake. We have created the Frankenstein and the monster doesn't even understand our language. When members of the Salvadoran military say they are not involved and do not want to be involved with political parties, this does not mean that they are removing themselves from the political arena; they are simply placing themselves squarely above it. Ever since the October 1979 military coup, Salvadoran civilian politicos have said they were in the process of gaining control over the army and the other security forces. In fact, the reverse has been true. Please, now that the world has changed and the potential for East-West war by proxy in El Salvador and the rest of Latin America has practically vanished, remove your support from the military and place it in productive institutions. You will be so much more successful.

Signed, su seguro servidor, Jorge/George Hidalgo/Knight

P.S. I'd like to be buried in the United States of America. If this is not possible, please bury me in Guamuchil, Sinaloa, where two of my cousins have built a motel for the tourist trade and named it in my honor.

On the day before the operation, Puñonrostro and El Pájaro Loco presented themselves to Hidalgo. "These artifacts are of your ownership."

Hidalgo took the canvas sack and looked into it with mild curiosity. "It having been a few years, I forget. Ah yes, smaller-than-your-hand camcorder with advanced 'fuzzy logic' circuitry. Where did you get all of this?"

"While you were occupied that moment with your sorrow, one of our muchachos took everything that was in the area of the deceased."

"Shit, that camcorder might come in handy over at Justice. Let's see, what else? Nishika depth-capturing, three-dimension camera with fixed-focus quadra lens system. Yoda hologram wristwatch that captures the likeness of the wizened old master of 'The Force.' Did you know George Lucas gave George Bush one of these? Fax-sending minicomputer. Hammacher Schlemmer swore to me that it would be five years before this got to the ordinary market. I may be in a position to check the accuracy of their claim. State-of-the-art, voice-changing, digital-signal cellular telephone. Hey, we should definitely be able to use this sucker where we are going. It comes with a telephone tap detector as well, employing four separate systems to detect low and high impedance taps, wireless bugs, off-hook extensions, and automatic tape recorders. Of course, batteries not included. Maybe we can stop at the local Radio Shack on the way."

*   *   *

TWELVE DAYS THAT SHOOK EL SALVADOR!

December 11, various — Hope is fading in Washington, Rome, and San Salvador for a nonviolent resolution of the Palace of Justice stalemate as the deadline imposed by the Salvadoran government expires tomorrow, December 12, on the feast of Our Lady of Guadalupe, the day that the Church celebrates Mary as patron saint of the Americas. A shoot-out at the Palace of Justice seems almost inevitable, although the Pope is calling for one last effort and for delay. The Salvadoran government insists that the 12-day crisis has endangered the entire country and already caused hundreds of deaths, and it adamantly refuses to prolong the stalemate and the crisis. Government officials say the guerrillas must surrender peacefully. A senior White House aide, insisting on anonymity, observed that the El Salvador crisis will have lasting foreign policy effects in the U.S. as well as "enormous geopolitical repercussions." Riots have appeared to abate at National City, where the San Diego naval base is located, as both Chicanos and their supporters as well as right-wing extremists turn to television sets for the announced "final resolution" of the Salvadoran crisis. In Detroit, the Ku Klux Klan has denied having anything to do with the torching of Adventure Capitalists' headquarters. However, the Grand Dragon observed, "While I have no idea who did it, they certainly had it coming. They're the most racist, un-American group in America." In Washington, D.C., a spokesperson for the National Association of Chicano and Hispanic Organizations in Solidarity (NACHOS), Rey de los Magallanes, strongly denounced the claim that the organization was a front for Adventure Capitalists or any other organization, "right-wing, left-wing, or broken-wing." He went on to state: "This is dirty, political mudslinging, and to take callous advantage of this crisis which is causing so much hurt and pain to all Americans, including Latinos, is outrageous and reprehensible."

—Detroit Free Press

On the first day of "Twelve Days That Shook El Salvador," Gary Gnu was rudely awakened at 3:32 a.m.

"Gnu here," he answered groggily. Only a call on the sanctum sanctorum, the celestial blue line, could have penetrated his privacy at this hour. He tried to clear his head, but he wasn't prepared for the torrent of invective from Henry. "You dufus of dumbfuck! Do you know what you've done?"

"Henry! What is it? What are you talking about?"

"He's alive. He's turned traitor. He's on CNN this very second mouthing shit from the Little Catholic Commie's Red Book."

"Oh my God, you mean Knight? He's alive?!"

"Alive! Alive, you Commie Christian and slimy spic sympathizer! Did you set me up, is that it? You've decided to ruin Motors and ruin America?"

"Henry, please, calm down. I had no idea. I thought he was dead."

"You gave him the gig. You gave him lots of gigs, dumbfuck. You've been working toward this day, haven't you, just like a deep mole, you Christian Commie?"

"Henry, please, he and his people made us lots of money for decades, billions."

"Turn on the TV. Turn it on, dufus, and see what he's saying now to a billion people around the globe. I'm telling you right now, I'm washing my hands of Gnu shit. It's your skin. You better make it well or it's your skin. You'll be as loved as Salman Rushdie in Tehran. Christ. When it's through, when it's through . . . I'll make sure they never let you back in the Chop House."

"Are you a Communist, Father Ignacio?"

"His head, for Chrissakes, his head's not in. Please, do it over again, but with his head!"

"Calm down, Mack, this is not exactly your typical studio situation."

"Calm down? Fine, I'll calm down. There'll be a billion people around the globe looking at the headless horseman."

"Okay, okay, Father, please, just a little more to the . . . right, yeah, to the . . . left. Good. God, okay. Now, take number six. And a one, and a two, and a . . . Are you a Communist, Father Ignacio?"

"Most certainly not, although I obey a tradition of community values that comes directly from Christ and his earliest disciples."

"So then, what do you call yourself, padre, rightist or leftist?"

"If by left you mean the struggle for social justice, the battle for the social and economic redemption of our people, the incorporation of peasants and workers into the mainstream of society, culture, and civilization, then undeniably we are leftist. If, however, by left you mean historical materialism, Communist totalitarianism, and the suppression of personal liberty, then in no way are we leftist. If by right is understood the conservation of the spiritual values of civilization, the historical legacy of humanity, and the dignity and spiritual life of humankind, then there can be no doubt that we are rightists. But if by right you suggest the conservation of an economic order based on the exploitation of the poor by the rich, on social injustice, we militantly refuse the name of rightists."

"That's fine, Father. Believe me, we can work with this. I know you want to get your message across and we . . . well, we are totally dedicated to accuracy. But, national, international news. You could help if you just shaved it down a bit, give us your best punch, you know what I mean? Look, here's my chin, give me a good one-line shot. Blast me! Demolish me! You know? KO! Christ, we can edit it down, but you know I once had to bring a Fidel Castro speech—heck he talked virtually non-stop for six hours, and in the blazing sun too, my God—I had to get it down to a minute and fifteen."

"Okay, we're rolling, take seven. A one and a two and . . . Well, Father, I see that you adamantly refuse to be represented as a Communist. Do you consider yourself a Christian, sir?"

"Yes, not only a Christian but a sincere Catholic priest, whose measures might be somewhat—actually, considerably—extreme, but not for that reason heterodox."

"Just somewhat extreme, sir? You do realize that you've captured the Salvadoran Palace of Justice and taken hostage not only many eminent jurists but specific members of the government and business communities as well as landowners?"

"We sincerely wish not to harm anyone who we have taken inside with us. They are here as an index of the crisis in the Guazapa that the Salvadoran government has caused. We will let everyone out of here completely unharmed once we resolve this in accordance with our requirements, which are basically to acknowledge the autonomy of the Guazapa that we won over 10 years ago and to return to the lines of political and military demarcation that prevailed before the government took military advantage of the ceasefire."

"And you countenance this behavior?"

"Yes, actually I'm optimistic from the point of view of Christian hope. This is the hope I try to communicate to the people, because I am certain there is a God who is close to our problems and He will not let us down."

But Father, surely, as a Catholic priest . . . you are not only supporting but actively fomenting warfare among the peasants. What about turning the other cheek? Surely . . ."

"There is a season for everything. We are in an extreme crisis, and I cannot let my people down. I am convinced that in such crises Christianity permits—in fact, solicits—active, militant resistance. In my home country, just where I lived on the way to Santiago de Compostela, almost every church had its Saint James treading on the infidels. And then there were the Crusades. I wish there were another way, I pray that out of this operation we will find common ground for our Christian soldiers and the regular soldiers of the Salvadoran army, also Christians of course. We don't do this except out of extreme self-defense and because we see no other way at this moment."

"Well, Father, a prominent Salvadoran intellectual claims that your Christian revolution is strictly a sham. He claims that you preface 'Christian' before revolution, just as the Communists talk about people's army or people's revolution, simply to deceive the masses. He's also furious that you call your action Operation *Mater et Magistra*. He considers that an offense to the Church, Pope John XXIII, and the Holy Mother. In fact, you might be able to hear protesters this instant outside the Palace of Justice screaming *Mater sí, Magistra no*."

Ignacio laughed. "We chose the name of Pope John's 1961 encyclical because it is the first to reiterate the Church's commitment to the world's poor and oppressed, to devote much attention to the problems of developing countries, and to call for an end to colonialism. As for the claim that we are duping the people, nothing of the sort; we help develop the revolutionaries here, we don't control or order them. Let your friend come out to the Guazapa and say this . . ." He stopped and tugged the sleeve of a beaming Puñonrostro, "to the new, improved version of the secular arm!"

Some of the press howled with laughter, others responded with catcalls.

"Mr. Jesús Salvador Puñonrostro, is that it? Is that a pseudonym or something? You know, like Stalin which means steel?"

"That's my given name."

"It's sort of different, isn't it? I mean, Jesus 'Fist in your Face' plus the country's name? Are you for real?"

"¡Viva Puñonrostro! ¡Viva nuestro comandante! Stop making fun of us!"

"Mr. Jesús Puñonrostro. It's been said by a sympathetic observer in the U.S. that you remind him of Frank Sinatra in that film *The Pride and the Passion,* you know, the one where he and Sofia Loren carry this cannon around Spain and blow up the walls of Avila and vanquish the French? I wonder what your reaction to that analogy might be?"

"In our country they don't let in movies of that sort. We've seen what American kitchens look like from Doris Day and Rock Hudson. As for me, I believe that I represent a militant Christian movement that is sympathetic to all freedom-loving peoples, including both the Spanish and the French."

"Mr. Puñonrostro, let me be perfectly frank with you. The media around the world are baffled by your timing. It was our impression that the post-Communist world had come to El Salvador and that the right and the left had accepted a ceasefire and agreed on the general outlines of a negotiated peace plan. Why is this happening now? Wasn't the fighting supposed to be *over?*"

"The Christian army of the Guazapa would love for it to be over. However, we have been betrayed by the two-faced Salvadoran government, which is trying not only to improve its military position under the cover of the ceasefire but is actually attempting to exterminate us in the Guazapa. We never would have attempted such a radical and dangerous operation as this one were it not for the fact that we had become mortally endangered and needed to defend our very existence."

"But why the Palace of Justice, Mr. Puñonrostro? Why not some barracks or a bridge or an electrical substation?"

"You don't blow up a bridge when they are trying to tear out your heart. Besides, justice should not be housed in a palace. This is not the proper site for justice. We want open justice for the people."

For the first time in almost three years, Hidalgo officially existed. He was clean shaven and they had found clothes that fit him, courtesy of a hostage judge who had been stripped down. His heart was palpitating. All that had happened to him over the years of his captivity seemed too soul-wrenching and contrary for ordering in his mind, much less explaining to ravenous media hounds.

"We've gotten reports that you have actually been working for los muchachos. On the other hand, the Salvadoran government says it's all lies, that in fact they've treated you much like the Beirut hostages. Kept you blindfolded, chained and beaten you. Can you tell us what's true?"

"I don't mean to confound you, sir, and I realize you'll only have maybe a minute fifteen on the air, so a lot of this will be for print media. I don't think I can tell you what's true. I mean, I'm not sure I know. And I'm of clear and sound mind, God knows. But the facts—well, they did keep me blindfolded for a number of weeks. But wait, that was because they thought I meant them harm. They never really intended to capture me. They had anticipated meeting with me and my dear friend and colleague Rodrigo Safos, but it was a setup. A third party, still unknown, betrayed both Adventure Capitalists and the Christian army of the Guazapa. We didn't know of their intentions and thought they were aggressive. After some weeks in captivity, I decided that all things considered—and this is so very complex I would have to refer you to Sartre's *Being and Nothingness*—I'd rather work for the revolutionary cause than exist as a passive captive or hostage. I gave oath to the effect that I would work for them for the sake of the work and yet would also consider myself their captive. Still later, years later, I came to believe in the essential justice of the Guazapan cause, although certainly I have never been in agreement with the way they handled my case in certain aspects, particularly keeping me totally under wraps. I have risen in the ranks from a basic mechanic-captive to become an active member as chief of procurement, maintenance, and transportation of military matériel of the Jesús Salvador Puñonrostro wing of the Farabundo Martí National Liberation Front."

"Jesus," the media man said, "you must be pretty good; even with los muchachos you rose fast in the ranks."

Hidalgo responded, "I've been a live desaparecido, as it were, for almost three years. Given my plight, to paraphrase an old Gershwin song, it's pretty good work if you can get it. I don't want you to think I'm a traitor. That would be so very, very wrong. Let me state for the record that I have not changed my fundamental, capitalist outlook on economic life. If I had the opportunity to leave this place, I believe I would return to the U.S. or wherever to continue to work for the distribution of the tractors and other capital equipment to the people here who need it in pursuit of the land reform that was promoted by Duarte and betrayed by the oligarchy. These were precisely the reasons that I came here in the first place, although I had a shallow and naive understanding of the problems here and placed far too much trust in the good will of both the Salvadoran and American governments. If I survive this confrontation with sufficient energy and presence of mind, I will return to that same effort, but with a better understanding. And, I might add, not entirely unselfishly. I intend to present a bill to my employers that adequately covers the hazards of this mission, which were grossly misrepresented to me."

Again there was both laughter and catcalls among the press.

"On the other hand, my spiritual, psychological, and physical life have been tangibly changed. Although I do not totally agree with their solutions, I believe that the grievances of the Farabundo Martí Liberation Front are legitimate and that their struggle is a just one. I must express my deep shame as a patriotic American at the role our government has played in aiding elements that have oppressed the Salvadoran people and that have committed heinous atrocities throughout the countryside, among others to peasants and workers, to priests, even to Americans."

There was a confused buzz. "Mr. Knight, Mr. Knight!"

"Call me Hidalgo. It may be the last time you call me at all, better call me Hidalgo."

"All right, Hidalgo. Ryan here from the *Detroit Free Press*."

"I've always appreciated your column, Ryan."

"Thank you, Mr. Hidalgo, I take it then that you are in the Palace of Justice out of your own free will?"

"Not exactly." Hidalgo laughed. "I'd represent myself as a considerably more clear-headed Patty Hearst. If my captors and now fellow coreligionists were to permit me to leave Justice at this point, and to take out with me a dear friend I have made who has been egregiously abused by the Salvadoran military, I would strongly consider scurrying to save my hide. However, that is not in the stars, and I understand and in fact partially sympathize with their point of view. The American government should take cognizance of my plight, which is essentially the result of circumstances beyond my control. Fellow Americans, if you want to see me safely removed from this place, please negotiate in good faith with the Christian army. They are rational and ultimately fair, and what they are asking for is eminently reasonable. But, if I must stay, I prefer to make my stand not as a hostage but as a firm compañero of Father Ignacio, Jesús Salvador Puñonrostro, Sweet Dulce Tobosa, and the people

I've come to love. I realize that I may die, possibly even within the hour." Hidalgo laughed again. "It's probably a safer bet than trying to prognosticate where the long bond will stand in 18 months. But standing up for what is essentially just here in El Salvador has its attractions. If I must die, I want to die a patriotic American on behalf of a just cause, and I want to expiate my guilt as an American for what we have done in this country over many decades and especially since 1980. I am a loyal American citizen, but I represent the loyal opposition. I've come to the end of the *Quijote*. If I'm to die, then I will die, desengañado of my patriotic myopias, as Alonso Quijano, the Good."

Suddenly Father Ignacio began grinning, and he whispered to Hidalgo to the dismay of the cameraman, "Even when Don Quijote was plain Alonso Quijano, el Bueno, just as when he was Don Quixote de la Mancha, he was of such estimable nature that he was much beloved, not only by those of his own family, but by all who came to know him."

"Frankly, Mr. Hidalgo, your statement is so muddled, so illogical, wouldn't you have to agree that many, perhaps most Americans will judge that you have become profoundly undone psychologically by your ordeal?"

Hidalgo laughed with apparent good humor. "I didn't refer you to Patty Hearst's case, Sartre's book, and the Quixote's multiexemplary behavior for nuttin'."

SEX AND THE SALVADORAN GUERRILLAS!

The amazing story of the adventure capitalist who was taken away by the most brutal cult of guerrillas in all of El Salvador and who was presumed murdered. Now we find out that George Knight lives! And what was Sir George *really* doing for almost 3 years in the Central American bush? Find out tonight, December 3rd, at 9:00 p.m. (8:00 central), live from the no-holds-barred camera of Jerry Rivers/Geraldo Rivera, the unfolding story of George Knight and the undercover Christian communitarians of El Salvador. This week's "Geraldo" is a torrid exclusive about the new revolutionary Christian sexuality and communitarianism in El Salvador and Latin America. Gunshots and orgasms: these people are living out the visionary utopia of Tommaso Campanella's 17th century *City of the Sun*, which called for a world without private property, poverty, or undue wealth and where, just like matins and vespers, the bell rang for sexual intercourse!

SALVADORAN NEGOTIATIONS IN PALACE OF JUSTICE TAKE OMINOUS TURN

December 4, San Salvador — The negotiations between the Christian guerrillas of the Guazapa and the Salvadoran government seem to have stalled. The Salvadoran government has imposed a "nonnegotiable" deadline of December 12, which is one week from today, to resolve the crisis, or they "will take all necessary actions" to resolve it on their own. A senior officer of the military close to the negotiations, in an exclusive interview with this reporter and on condition of anonymity, could barely contain his anger and frustration. "I can't tell you how impossible it is to deal with these people. They are fanatical zealots. They are living a crusade of the 12th century. They will stop at nothing. First they kidnapped and brainwashed the American and in so doing killed his friends and associates. Now they have created havoc around the capital, kidnapping and holding hostage important government and public figures. Do they honestly expect that we will permit them to leave the premises fully armed, with their hostages and all their booty? Is that what the American army, the Green Berets who have trained our army, would have us do?"

—Washington Post

SALVADOR GOES GA GA! KNIGHT'S PARAMOUR UP IN FLAMES!

December 5, El Salvador — In one of the most bloody days of the entire civil war, the capital city of San Salvador was consumed by violence. Apparently, in the wake of the collapse of negotiations between the FMLN and the government, right-wing death squads and other paramilitary units began to roam the city of San Salvador, picking up and "disappearing" people, allegedly "at random." Fighting, kidnapping, and other violent actions have spread to Chalatenango, Morazán, and Usulután departments. Later that night, a unit of the Christian army of the Guazapa, which a Salvadoran government spokesperson described as "a drugged-up, hopped-up group of about 100 death-seeking fanatics in the best tradition of psychedelic kamikazes," was surprised and fired on in the process of moving their force from a sewer that connects the streets with the Palace of Justice. A full-scale battle ensued and at least 17 guerrillas are reported dead, as well as 3 Salvadoran soldiers. The army at this moment is conducting house-to-house searches for the remaining 80 highly armed and desperate guerrillas who escaped the battle outside the Palace of Justice but who are now cut off from the main force and are at large and roaming the streets of the capital. The military spokesman attempted to document his characterization of the guerrillas as "hopped-up kamikazes" by reading from a letter by one "Sweet" Dulce Tobosa, who was killed in action. In her letter she both claims to be the lover of the controversial captive-turned-revolutionary George Knight and to be seeking revenge and martyrdom in return for atrocities committed by the Salvadoran government against her people.

Other news in the war-torn nation was almost as stunning. In an unconfirmed report, 95 human ears were found nailed to the door of the Metropolitan Cathedral of San Salvador, one of the holiest shrines in the nation since it is the place where the national hero, Archbishop Romero, was assassinated. FMLN spokespeople called the act a great atrocity by the right-wing death squads, who have been known to cut off the ears of their victims in order to "prove" death counts. In yet another development in Sabanetas, close to the Honduran border, a rebel leader associated with the left that is unaffiliated with liberation theology seemed to withdraw support from the Guazapan movement, observing that its extremist zeal might ruin the working arrangement that the FMLN had established with the Salvadoran government. "Ultimately, we must note that our Guazapan partners acted on their own initiative, certainly as a result of great provocation by the Salvadoran government, but independently of and without the countenance of the FMLN high command."

Meanwhile, the American government has issued its highest alert in El Salvador. All civilian and most government personnel are being urged to report to the American embassy. It is also reported that military facilities in Panama and in the U.S., including the San Diego naval base, have been put on alert.

—*New York Post*

PALACE REBELS GRIEF–STRICKEN OVER LOSS
OF THEIR "CHRISTIAN WARRIORS"

December 6, San Salvador — In a new development in the ongoing Salvadoran crisis that has captured attention around the world, a CNN camera crew was able to penetrate the Palace of Justice, probably through the sewage system which the guerrillas have occasionally tried to use, despite the ban on such televised activity recently imposed by the Salvadoran government. The mood appears to have become very somber in the Palace as expectations for the nonviolent success of the rebels have been totally crushed by the events of the last two days. Despite the setback, the rebels, led by their grim-faced leaders, Jesús Salvador Puñonrostro and Father Ignacio, seem to be adamant in their resolution, even if it means violently resisting a projected assault on the Palace by the Salvadoran military.

During the interview, captive-turned-revolutionary Jorge Hidalgo (George Knight) confirmed that one of the women killed in a shoot-out with the Salvadoran military, "Sweet" Dulce Tobosa, was his intimate companion during his years in the guerrilla-controlled Guazapa. In Hidalgo's statement he said, "The love of my life has gone to meet her maker. Although she relished even the truncated life the Salvadoran tyranny permitted her, I know she died spiritually fulfilled. I reaffirm the fealty that I have sworn to Fair Dulce and the cause for which she died and to which all of us in the Palace of Justice have committed our lives and our souls. There is no turning back now. We stand firm here, ¡victoria o muerte! What Dulce suffered on this earth is almost beyond the conception of ordinary mortals. It included personally witnessing the murder of her husband and her three small children and the massacre of her entire village of El Mozote. In the time I spent with her, she never could escape that anguish, not in daylight, nor in her sleep. Yet her life was far from tragic, it was extraordinary. At her side I had the rare privilege of experiencing how a courageous woman, neither trained nor naturally equipped for the terror and grief imposed upon her by vicious people, ultimately, despite the enormous difficulty of the project, was able to carry her sorrow and transport it to a new, uncharted region of humanity. Hers was a revolution of the spirit."

—Los Angeles Times

PANDEMONIUM BREAKS OUT
AT DETROIT NEWS CONFERENCE

December 7, Detroit — What had been billed as a "humanitarian" statement and press conference by Henry, who is not particularly known for his sensitivity or tact, was aborted amidst mass confusion and anger at Renaissance Tower Plaza today when tensions between the auto magnate and one of his most senior and trusted associates, the so-called "Gary Gnu," broke out spontaneously into the open. Gnu is under intense scrutiny and has been subpoenaed by a hastily formed, ad hoc House Subcommittee on Anti-American Christian Communist Activities, which has been stacked with conservative legislators. He has also been under severe attack by conservative figures including *National Review* editor and celebrity interviewer William F. Buckley, Jr. He appeared to crack under the strain when Henry made a number of innuendo-laden remarks in his direction. The "Gnu" virtually broke down and emotionally defended his patriotism and his American credentials. He also claimed to have been a classmate of Buckley's at Yale, whose behavior he characterized as "unworthy of a true Eli." Gnu also accused Henry of having the "worst racist antecedents in American industry." Upon that remark, he was pulled off the podium by private security men. The incident left the crowd in utter confusion.

Shortly after the aborted press conference, disturbances were reported at the Hamtramck Motor Works, one of the nation's oldest automobile assembly lines, where workers, many of them Latinos who have felt under great pressure recently, were reportedly "mad as hell and not going to take it anymore." They appeared to be throwing monkey wrenches into assembly-line machinery, shouting slogans like "Take this, Henry." There is an unconfirmed report that a group of affronted workers and clergy in the Latino neighborhood of Detroit is planning a march tomorrow morning during rush hour from La Tolteca, a local tortilla factory and distributor, to Renaissance Tower, and that they plan to tie up traffic on Woodward Avenue and other main arteries.

—Detroit Free Press

EXTREMISTS "BLOCKADE" SAN DIEGO NAVAL BASE

December 8, San Diego — In the midst of the bloody Salvadoran crisis and speculation that the American military may be mobilized,

Chicano, Salvadoran, and other Latino extremists together with members of the sanctuary movement and other radicals in the San Diego and border areas took actions today not seen since the heyday of the Vietnam War. Working out of the California headquarters of Adventure Capitalists, Ltd., in National City, the Latino coalition "blockaded" the San Diego naval base by chaining themselves to all entrances. Reacting in part to the endangered status of the controversial Jorge Hidalgo, first a captive and now a comandante of the Salvadoran guerrillas, and responding to what appears to be an imminent strike against the Palace of Justice, the Latinos vowed that they would maintain their blockade for the duration of this crisis. Similarly, the Tijuana border was disrupted by waves of protestors who lay on the highways and approach roads, snarling traffic 15 miles in each direction from the U.S.-Mexico crossings. A binational coalition of enraged Mexican citizens and United States Latinos of Mexican and Central American origin converged on the border stations and held rallies protesting Washington's policies and its support of the Salvadoran government in the current crisis. The rallies themselves were described as "highly volatile" by on-site observers. For example, shouting and pushing matches erupted between, on the one hand, conservative members of the Catholic church and various Protestant evangelical denominations operating in El Salvador and elsewhere in Latin America and, on the other side, a large entourage from the California- and Arizona-based sanctuary movements, radical liberation theologians, and representatives of Christian Base Communities and literacy campaigns in Latin America.

In National City, Hermelinda del Pimental, spokesperson for the extremists, claimed, "If the Salvadoran fascist military maintains its insane blockade of the Salvadoran Christian freedom fighters and peremptorily prepares to slaughter them, our conscience requires that we maintain this blockade here at the San Diego naval base and not let American servicemen aid this lunacy in any manner. The American government has the power to stop this madness and must exercise it."

—*San Diego Union*

PITCHED BATTLE BETWEEN
MILITANT LEFT AND RIGHT WINGS

December 9, San Diego, Los Angeles, San Francisco — One of the most violent race riots in recent memory has broken out in the San Diego area at the National City (birthplace of founder and Salvadoran captive-turned-revolutionary Jorge Hidalgo) headquarters of Adventure Capitalists, Ltd., and to a lesser extent in other cities in California. Sailors from the naval base joined with skinheads and other right-wing extremists to "liberate" the naval base from enraged Chicanos, Salvadorans, and other left-wing extremists who had been attempting a "blockade" of the facility for a second day. In central San Diego at "Barrio Logan" there was a second race riot as the Chicano community fought with young white hoodlums intent on destroying murals in the park. Professor Darío Barrera, a political scientist and filmmaker who several years ago produced a film on community action in Barrio Logan, stated that he "had never seen such chaos. This must be just like the original Zoot Suit Riots against Chicanos 50 years ago!"

In Los Angeles there were several minor disturbances reflecting the various viewpoints and divided loyalties that the Salvadoran crisis has engendered in the Central American and other communities. In the San Francisco bay area, local poets and teachers were preparing readings and teach-ins in the Mission District and at the University of California, Berkeley.

—San Diego Union

EX-GOVERNOR OF ARIZONA DENOUNCES
"COMMUNIST CABAL" IN CIA

December 10, Phoenix — Claiming that he had in his pocket the names of 69 Communist-sympathizing moles in the CIA, the former, very short-term governor of Arizona (elected in 1986, impeached in 1988) announced that he has located a "Communist cabal" that operates at various high levels around the country, including Arizona University, the American automobile industry centered in Detroit, and the "inner circle of the CIA." He claims that Adventure Capitalists, Ltd., the firm led by the controversial and charismatic Jorge Hidalgo, former guerrilla captive but now allegedly a leader of the Guazapan Christian-based arm of the Farabundo Martí National

Liberation Front, is a subversive operation, at the same time both a CIA front and an instrument of Communist plots. "It's the essence of simplicity," the former governor alleged. "Adventure Capitalists has been doing business for years in the gray market with the motor industry and the CIA, who for whatever disgusting and anti-American reasons have been knowingly paying that company millions in largesse that has gone to ferment [sic] unrest among minority groups in the U.S., particularly Latinos. They have been artfully receiving and laundering money from the automobile industry and the CIA for decades and redistributing it to subversive activities. This is an operation that makes the Iran Contra scandal positively benign by comparison."

The ex-governor went on to claim that, "using the crisis in El Salvador, which clearly is a total fraud manufactured by their Communist leader, George Knight, who arranged to have himself 'kidnapped' by people who are actually his allies, Adventure Capitalists has manipulated and distorted events and through seditious underground channels has caused race riots and other major disturbances in San Diego, Detroit, and a dozen other cities around the nation." For example, the ex-governor claims that at Arizona University in Yuma and at several university strongholds in Michigan the Adventure Capitalists have planted a front, the so-called Hispanic Academic and Career Service (HACS), to broadcast propaganda, seditious messages, and detailed instructions for subverting government installations such as the San Diego Naval Station on a non-stop basis, 24 hours a day, over telephone lines, computer networks, electronic bulletin boards, and automated fax machines. "Over the years, and with the unwitting help of either dupes or deep moles in the CIA, Adventure Capitalists has established a network of over 20,000 supporters. They are using the El Salvador crisis which they themselves manufactured to call in their cards and test their support. This is just the first stage!"

In response to the allegations, Ulíses Garzas, a senior representative of HACS, conceded that they are on retainer to Adventure Capitalists, but also to "GM, IBM, Oxy Pete, Freddie Mac, Manny Hanny, Sallie Mae, DOE, DOT, DOD, and over 500 other corporations and units of government around the United States and the world who look to hire Hispanic experts or retain them as consultants or even make them corporate board members. We provide good prospects for employment by the corporations of the world."

Mr. Garzas scoffed at the charge that the service was broadcasting sedition, pointing out that the operation had been transmitting information in hard copy and electronically for over 20 years and had never once been called into question. "It is true that we are reporting news from and about the El Salvador crisis to our subscription network. Obviously it is an important Latino issue, and we proudly point to Jorge Hidalgo as one of the original backers of the service. But the information that we are transmitting is simply breaking news, no different from what is being released by the *New York Times,* Associated Press, or Reuters. In fact, it is in many cases identical to Associated Press, with which we have a licensing arrangement just like any other media operation!"

Garzas went on to call into question the motives of the accuser. "All I can say is that the guy who made these allegations is a known quantity. He's a bartender's nightmare, pardon my Russian allusion, a Molotov cocktail, one part megalomania, one part paranoia, and one part hypocritical, self-righteous, right-wing moralisms. He's the one with the utterly impeachable credentials, and in fact he *has* been impeached. Ask him how he lost the governorship. Ask him how come the automobile industry purged him from his dealership. I'll tell you why, he's a rogue! But not to worry, of one thing we can be certain: he's been running for governor almost since the state was born, and you can be sure he'll be running now on this bogus issue!"

—*Arizona Republic*

SANCTUARY MOVEMENT CALLS FOR CONSCIOUSNESS-RAISING

December 11, Chicago — In response to recent attacks against it stemming from the current crisis in El Salvador, the sanctuary movement has called for a day of prayer, vigil, and demonstrations around the country. One of the largest prayer meetings this Sunday, jointly organized by the Chicago Religious Task Force on Central America (CRTFCA) and the American Friends Service Committee, a Quaker organization, took place at the University of Notre Dame. At the service, a young Salvadoran woman, simply called Alicia to protect her family in El Salvador, told the congregation about her life as a catechist in San Salvador. The security forces had shot her priest and tortured one of her fellow church workers. "Such things were not unusual," she told them, "the vultures in El Salvador were well fed. People have gotten used to seeing dogs running down the street with human feet and hands in their mouths."

Carmen Valenzuela, recently convicted of smuggling illegal aliens across the U.S.-Mexican border, and her lawyer, Daniel Sheehan, a former Jesuit priest and one of the attorneys in the Karen Silkwood case, also offered their views. Valenzuela said, "We've lost sight of the fact that when our sister or brother anywhere hurts, we hurt. I see that and I have to respond. If we participate in a demonstration here it's not likely we'll be shot. In El Salvador, it *is* likely. If we teach people to read, we aren't called subversive and Communist and then disappear. In El Salvador, it is likely. For there is no justice. We've already seen tens of thousands of deaths there, mostly civilians killed by government forces. The U.S. government continues to support that government whose most significant achievement has been to create the refugees. I'm no celebrity. I'm not a martyr. And I'm no felon. I am a woman with a heart and a mind. My faith and commitment connects me to people and to justice."

The American Friends Service Committee provided documentation of the murders shortly after their return to El Salvador of yet another five Salvadoran refugees who had been deported from the United States. In addition, Notre Dame research professor Malachi J. Sullivan described the terrible trials of refugees attempting to come to the United States through Guatemala. "The fighting has forced an estimated 500,000 Salvadorans from their homes in rural areas to either refugee camps, city slums, or adjacent foreign countries. A chain of terror and corruption has been created from El Salvador through Guatemala and Mexico into the United States. Guatemalan and Mexican police are now specializing in extortion, rape, beatings, and other contemptible acts against Salvadoran and other Central American refugees. Those attempting to cross the border face all sorts of mortal perils. We estimate that in order to raise money, several thousand refugee women have been forced to work in brothels on the 'camino a la USA' all the way from Tapachula, Mexico, to Tijuana and Ciudad Juárez. Those few who survive the Guatemalan and Mexican police, the "coyotes," and the vampires who infest the border and manage to make it into the United States then become subject to the activities of the INS and other federal agents, and face possible deportation. Only three percent of Salvadoran deportation cases result in a favorable decision on behalf of the refugee. In contrast, the INS grants political asylum in about 30 percent of the cases it decides. Iranian applicants fleeing the Ayatollah Khomeini got favorable decisions 71 percent of the time, and 62 percent of those running from the Soviet puppet regime in Afghanistan were successful. Polish and Ethiopian applicants, also fleeing Communist governments, were successful a little over 25 percent of the time."

—Chicago Tribune

HOPE FADES IN EL SALVADOR; POPE PROSTRATES HIMSELF BEFORE PIETA

IN DETROIT, PIZZA MAGNATE TOMMASO MONAGHAN OFFERS TO DONATE 10 MILLION DOLLARS TO ALLEVIATE SALVADORAN CRISIS

WORLD PRAYS AND WATCHES EVENTS ON TELEVISION

December 11, Milan — *Corriere Della Sera*

LESSONS OF EL SALVADOR: MADNESS WITHIN, MADNESS WITHOUT

December 11, Washington, D.C. — Even as the world has changed so enormously and positively in the larger dimension over the last three years, we have become beset with what in its original meaning in Spanish are called *guerrillas,* "little wars" or conflagrations at the local level. Yugoslavia, the Republic of Georgia, and various other republics of the former Soviet Union, Ireland, Lebanon, Sri Lanka and the Kashmir, Nicaragua, El Salvador . . . the list appears to grow weekly. Two factors operate here and we must deal with both. One is that while the axial tensions between the former East and West monolithic blocs have been so greatly reduced, the conflict between North and South, between the enormously wealthy and the desperately poor, has become premier. Starvation besets some areas around the world; in other spots, the effect of ruthless, unvarnished capitalism now gets the attention that it always deserved but which was crowded out by East-West conflicts. The new conflagrations that have emerged are either nonideological in nature or of a vastly different philosophy from the one that Washington is used to dealing with, such as the governing principles and political practices of liberation theology or the legitimate concerns of minority racial and ethnic groups within larger states.

This brings us to the second point. The current Salvadoran crisis highlights Washington's abject lack of preparation and policy for these sorts of conflicts. As has been the norm in Washington for the last decade, the intelligence community was caught off guard by the guerrillas' reactions to the Salvadoran military incursion into the areas they had under their control, in some cases for a decade or more. Consequently, some policymakers have been complaining that these events subvert what has proven to be their unfounded optimism that peace was genuinely in the offing in El Salvador. They deny the legitimacy of what is happening because there was sup- posed to be a truce and the initiation of a long-term solution to the Salvadoran civil war. Other officials have been dusting off obsoles- cent rhetoric about a last-gasp Communist insurgency, flavored by liberationist, militant clergy, so-called "Communist clerics." Neither view is accurate. The current Salvadoran crisis continues to reflect the basic, implacable contradiction of the Salvadoran economy and the government that supports it. El Salvador (and many other places around the world) is hardly capitalist in the sense that the industrial- ized world understands that concept, since the countryside, on the basis of an essentially feudal economy, produces a population that is 1 percent squire and 99 percent serf. Clearly, the current administra- tion needs to establish with utmost urgency policies and specific plans to address heretofore mostly submerged problems around the world—vast inequities in material wealth, nutrition and health, gain- ful employment, and political, cultural, and language rights between the privileged elite and the underclass—that had been artificially repressed by centralized, authoritarian governments, but which now have emerged with a vengeance.

In our own nation, the tensions, demonstrations, and even race riots that have emerged as a result of this crisis, further inflamed by the artful but cynical use of the brainwashed hostage, Jorge Hidalgo, once again point to what is basically a nonideologized empathy on the part of many Americans for the poor and their desperate call for plain and simple social justice. We cannot help but concede that Latinos all over the world, including those in the United States, sense the inherent social and economic injustice in El Salvador, and they march to redress that injustice. They are working to reform the system from within, not to topple it from without. In that sense,

Hidalgo's self-identification as a patriotic American of the "loyal opposition" has had a vast resonance among U.S. Latinos, both impoverished and prosperous. With the collapse of the East-West wars, we need to be more sensitive rather than less to our contradictions, to our North-South tensions, to our homegrown Georgias.

El Salvador may be a test case for the future of such American policies. We plead with each of the warring parties to cease this madness, to take one step backward from the brink. Washington must spare no effort in convincing the Salvadoran government not to storm the Palace of Justice. Similarly, the Guazapan guerrillas must agree to return to the lines of political and military jurisdiction that prevailed before their attack on the capital of San Salvador. They must also agree to immediately release all the hostages that they have taken and hand over to the United States government for medical treatment the deranged Chicano chevalier, Jorge Hidalgo, whom they have shamelessly brainwashed and have been using as a propaganda pawn. . . .

—*Christian Science Monitor,* editorial page

Associated Press flash news service, December 12, 8:37 a.m.
Central Standard Time, breaking news, El Salvador Crisis.

Eerie dawn at the Palace of Justice, San Salvador, recalls Attica, N.Y. massacre as Atlacatl division makes ready for attack; tanks and armored vans surround the area, all media barred from environs . . . in Detroit, on commemorative day of Our Lady of Guadalupe, patron saint of the Americas, Marta Hidalgo, her children, and officials of Adventure Capitalists are attending mass at the parish church of Nuestra Señora de Guadalupe, as are tens of thousands of members of the alliance that has formed among Latinos, Christian Base Communitarians, liberation theologians, sanctuary movement supporters, migrant workers, and even the undocumented workers around the nation. But they're bringing portable TVs with them to church to continuously monitor events . . . in New York a report was leaked early this morning in order to influence today's so-called "junk bond" market, indicating that whatever financial difficulties Ted Turner's media empire might be experiencing, they should be tangibly softened by the impact of increased CNN viewership as a result of the Salvador crisis. An analyst for Bear Stearns indicated that "this guy has a charmed life; once again world events play into the hands of TBS at the eleventh hour" . . . in Washington a representative of the National Association of Manufacturers (NAM) complained: "It seems like every Christmas selling season it's one thing or another to divert the attention of the consumer. One year it's the fall of the Berlin Wall, next it's Operation Desert Storm or the collapse of the Soviet Union. Now this, right at the high point of the season. No one is going to the malls! They're glued to their televisions, and ultimately it's really going to hurt us all. Chrissakes, why couldn't they wait till Easter?"

At the very end the portable generators that the muchachos had carried into the Palace began to fail. They conserved the energy for the telephone and fax system that they had patched together. Hidalgo had a horn back in his hands. It felt good. Hermelinda del Pimental on the line.

"I'm so sorry, Don Jorge. I wish there was something I could do."

"Let's not be awkward, dear kindred soul. This is endgame and a knight spends his life preparing to play it well. Tell me, did the KKK really torch our headquarters?"

"You got the CNN version? Yellow journalism and coup de théâtre. There's a few charred places here and there, especially in the reception area, but basically the condition-C security system stopped them in their tracks. Some of those guys must still have the mother of all headaches."

"I figured as much."

"The only problem is that the front office smells like a high school teacher's biology lab. You know, frogs in formaldehyde. Back room's fine, though."

"How are the Mandelbrot equations? The fractals? Still looking for the singular structure that spirals out symmetrically from the infinitesimal to the noosphere?"

"Not much time for the noosphere these days, boss. I'm over with the homeboys doing the woman storming the Bastille thing with one breast hanging free. That or peacemaker. Strictly into asymmetry. Did you hear about the special 'Geraldo'?"

"I got minor wind of it. I'd rather not comment in deference to the memory of my Fair Lady. Some things hurt. A lot. But maybe this Christian sociopolitical compact is the newer, kinder, gentler opposition. For sure the world won't remain a one-way street for very long.

There's always got to be a countervailing force. Vector analysis would confirm that, wouldn't it, doctor?"

"Good math, Don Jorge. As for the politics, I don't do crystal balls."

"I guess not. Any possibility you could get me Hesburgh?"

"You mean the old guy, former prez of Our Lady?"

"Don't be an ageist or I'll sic the thought police on you. I don't really know the new administration at Notre Dame that well, but Hesburgh and I go back almost to the beginning. I really wouldn't mind filling his dance card for one more cha-cha. But from what I can tell from surrounding commotions around here, I would need to talk to him within the next 15 minutes."

"God knows where he is. After all, where do ex-presidents from Nuestra Dama go? For all I know he's with the Trappists up to his ankles in grape mash or raspberry jam."

"Cute, Ms. Pepper Patch. You're making me feel a lot better already. He should be somewhere in the ecosystem. After all, Duarte was his baby. Well, never mind. Give him this message instead, ¿tú sabes? Tell him my last thoughts at Armageddon were of the Golden Dome and that I think that since Julián Samora retired they've done diddly-squat for Latinos. He should fix that. Y para colmo de males, Michigan State went and established a Julián Samora Research Center, which is great for State but only compounds Our Lady's accountability. And tell him I've got Notre Dame cold on the numbers. Since Samora retired they've been zip in the graduation of Latino Ph.D.'s. I mean, yesteryear it was *being* and today it's *nothingness*. Samora was their entire commitment and now he's gone. Tell him, if Our Lady is willing, that the homeboys who'll be coming out of the woodwork can donate to a new Latino center instead of flowers for the . . . you know. And if they want to give me a tiny slice of credit, maybe a plaque on a building, I won't be shy. After what the press has done to my ass, I could use the coverage."

"We'll tell him. God, Jorge, you're always thinking! That's great leverage."

"Well, it's okay as a lump sum death benefit. I've got other chestnuts for the long axis, la acequia madre. Believe me, I've got a couple of high-tech tricks or two up my sleeves. Holographs will be emanating from my persona long after my carcass is a worm hole. I'm planning on being the Chicano Nostradamus, a prophet for our vexed times. And please, if the spooks haven't heard my bragging by now in quintuplicate, make sure they do. I assume you did right by my compadre?"

"Oh yeah, boss. His family, we took care of them real good. They're gonna be in their own Golden Dome, three generations minimum. And we've established a 'Con Safos' Institute right at that brand new Cal State campus in the valley. San Marcos, you know, his hometown. He was such a scholarly pachuco, we thought he'd love it, his own 'Con Safos' center. As a matter of fact, Chuy Negrete and the Menudo Brothers are gonna do the inauguration."

"That's good. I'm glad we've done the right thing. Just like for Frankie Five Angels, right?"

"Don't make bad cosa nuestra jokes, boss, people will take 'em the wrong way, even inside the company, except maybe for insiders like 'Doc' Olivas and his Houston operation."

"You're probably right, dear heart. The press, the politics, this has all been a revelation to me. Yes, Hermelinda, just as they say, when you die all of your life, all of your cultural reality passes in a flash before your eyes. This is especially true when it takes three years for you to die. But all the better, for in my case it has been a whole lot of biculturalism. All of Hispania, all of Anglosaxonia has passed before my eyes. If by some chance I don't get to tell you later, have a feliz navidad y próspero año nuevo. God, I love you, I love you all. They should be putting on *It's a Wonderful Life* soon for Christmas, if I know a thing or two about Americana. Think of me when you see Jimmy Stewart blubbering at the end with the Madonna and Child in a newly rendered, colorized version."

"Don Jorge, Gary Gnu's on my line. He's in Motown and begging to talk to you. What do you want to do?"

"Is this déjà vu all over again, or what? Put him on."

Gnu was blubbering and rambling, calling him all four names—Hidalgo, George, Jorge, Knight—being incapable of any consistency whatsoever.

Hidalgo interrupted. "How now, true-blue Gnu? Is it fact or fiction that Henry pulled you off the podium?"

"Oh, worse than that, George. I'm out, barred, and nonentitied more effectively than even the KGB could have done in their heyday. They won't even let me in the Chop House."

"Yikes. Maybe you should come down here and dine on Perigord goose-liver pupusas with the finest calvados. You could do worse. It's pretty good fare, courtesy of the oligarchy. So what's happening,

Gnu? I don't think I'm ready for another salida quite yet. I'm even stiffer of wing, and I find I'm living in real time, which for a high-tech guy is weird and disorienting. Also real money. Apparently my corporate AT&T calling card has been cancelled for nonperformance."

"From their sick point of view they claim you've Patty Hearsted us by our own petard."

"Interesting that you mention her. Apparently, the pundits are giving me no quarter, despite all of the extenuating circumstances. But hey, I can understand that. After all, my family were mere border banditos when hers were magnates hobnobbing with the Black Knight's daddy and making out fabulously with Don Porfirio."

The Gnu blurted it out. "Hidalgo, I thank God I've gotten you. I just have to tell you that I had nothing to do with what you've called a setup, nothing at all. I don't have the faintest idea."

The Gnu obsessed with getting him 15 minutes before ground zero? Hidalgo had that same tingling feeling from three years ago. You could never tell with that guy. It smelled like rancid Wasp guilt. Under his breath Hidalgo muttered his oldest son's favorite passage from *Macbeth*.

> By the pricking of my thumbs
> Something wicked this way comes
> Open locks whoever knocks.

Then the bad vibes moved off and Hidalgo felt himself again. Far endgame. Sure, he would comfort the Gnu. "Gee, Gnu, calling to reassure me? That's very white of you, guy. Please don't worry, I didn't blame you for a second. Just atone for all your other sins. Give and give till it hurts to all the Latino projects you can think of. And while we're at it, let me fess up that I've felt bad for three years myself. I wish I hadn't gone so far. Mentioning Iacocca at the Chop House. That was really uncalled for."

The Gnu began to laugh uproariously. "You actually remembered that after all these years? You're a prince, George. There's never been one like you. You're the best amphibian we've ever had. Thou art much Chicano operative."

"Don't slobber goobers on me, Gnu. Even Hemingway and those other Wasp icons wouldn't like that. You were always too enamored of Hemingway, you know? He was such a romantic gringo, the son of privilege, a doctor's scion. Better you see about scholarship money for the League of United Latin American Citizens."

"Affirmative, Don Jorge. I'll see to it. Henry himself will see to it. Tú eres mucho chicano."

"Henry? Where the fuck are you calling from?"

"Oh, I'm at Motors headquarters. Henry's around but he wouldn't talk to me or to you. But he's paid a fortune for the Salvadoran point captain to fix a miniature camcorder to his helmet. The entire industry's here, watching it on the big screen. Like a sports bar! You know Henry, he wants a world-class view."

That was just like Gnu, holding himself up against Henry and positioning himself as the kinder, gentler Wasp, a signal improvement over Henry and his sort. "A world-class view to a kill, is that it? Tell Henry he's a model-A people fucker. Between you and me we made him billions."

"You'll tell him yourself, George. You'll get out and tell him yourself."

"Think so? Suddenly I'd really like to live, if only to pull Henry off the podium. Either that or to peer into the future. We live in such haunting times."

"Don't get apocalyptic, George. You've got a reasonable prognosis. As a matter of fact, we're looking at them set up right now. The Atlacatl is in fixed positions, they've moved up some armored cars, a few tanks."

"Is that all? Hey, all in buena fe."

"Stick with me, George, and I'll guide you over the phone. You've got to play the percentages. Keep your head down, my friend. It'll be quick like those rolls of the dice that you love so. It'll be one wave, and chances are most of you will come out of it with your nuts still on. Like at Attica. Remember, after all, not that many actually died."

"Attica, I appreciate the classical allusion, guy. You always had a flair for comparison. Remember what John Donne said about no being is an island. I've got to scoot, the bell is tolling for me and the máximo comandante needs to talk."

"I'll hold on the line. Get back to me, Jorge, and I'll guide you in. God bless. I love you. I can't tell you how bad I've felt. I love your people. ¡Viva la raza!"

"10-4." Hidalgo gave the phone to the máximo líder.

Puñonrostro pushed a button and began talking to some Salvadoran high pooh-bah. They wrangled over the phone. "Is that your best and final offer?"

Hidalgo turned to the priest and smirked. "Tell me about end-game and the marketplace. It's the call of the blood."

Father Ignacio had gone over to the lee side, the "Ultra-Montane." Since the slaughter at the San Salvador sewer, his moral authority and his zeal for earthly revolution caído de menos, his eyes were on the other world. "This is all chatter," he said somberly, "filled with sound and fury, signifying nothing. We go now to the *via crucis,* my dear friend."

After a while, incoming came around to Hidalgo again. It was Marta Hidalgo and the children. The more conventional homiletics affirm that Hidalgo pleaded for the understanding of his family and counseled his progeny that the only way to mature adulthood is through the road of self-examination and adherence to the ideals of love. That seems a set piece. For our part, let us exercise discretion out of simple respect toward the most intimate adiós of a man who experienced as much as our adventure capitalist, confining our-selves merely to the observation, so obvious que cae de maduro, that our hero, despite his travails, had much in the way of explanations to make to his family, and precious little time to make them.

The frontline muchachos were crouching now and placing their rifles in slits. No one had to be told. Jorge thought it instructive how ultimate forms of knowledge are pandemic. Strange people from other time zones had accumulated in the Palace over the 12 days. Some of them seemed familiar, as if they had wandered in from Managua or from a life of border folklore or from Borges's stories. One had the halo of Teresita Urrea, "la santa de Cabora," who had inspired the town of Tomochic to hold off 1,500 federales. One was a ringer for Ramón del Valle Inclán, barbas de chivo, who had stood on line the first day the Spanish Republic legalized divorce in order to "try it." Another was Miguel de Unamuno, holding out for nothing less than an afterlife of personal carne y hueso. Rubén Darío was present, composing *Cantos de vida y esperanza* with blue ink. La Pasionaria, José Martí, Che Guevara, Emma Tenayuca, César Chávez—they were all backing them up in the Palace of Justice, some with antennaed telephones. A living wax museum of solidarity.

A Franciscan brother who until just yesterday had been dressed in a business suit had now donned a friar's robe and carved the traditional bald spot out of the center of his fine head of hair. He took out his guitar and began to play.

Adiós muchachos, compañeros de la vida . . .

Puñonrostro and El Pájaro Loco passed by Jorge with bayonets, prodding a dozen men handcuffed and beaded at their necks with chains. Father Ignacio trod behind the two revolutionary peasants, cast into última duda, so somber, so afflicted by the catastrophic killings that he never wanted to have occurred. Hidalgo was pained for the priest, for the beaded men who looked like Cervantine galley slaves, by this demoralizing scene. He made a last plea for the hostages. He appealed to Puñonrostro's sense of honor y vergüenza. Why not release them into the milieu of general disorder to fend for themselves, just like any of the muchachos and clerics? After all, they had made their point. It served no purpose to actually kill these hostages in cold blood, did it? That should appeal to the muchacho army, to their sense of chaotic democracy and randomized fate. Let them all, siervos y señores, be shuffled into the great deck.

Puñonrostro looked at the chained men with disgust. He spat on the floor. "Father Ignacio thought it a good idea to save the rehabilitable ones, and for maximum effect we have put them in the sewer tunnels. When we're all dead or captured, they will be able to come out, proving that we are moral. As for these specimens, they're not even human." He prodded one with his bayonet. "Why are you here?"

The prisoner was almost in a swoon. "For what you say, comandante."

"Because it was your specialty to terrorize the campesinos by catching a few and spreading them naked on the ground and applying animal fat to their genitals. Was it not? And then you would set famished dogs on your victims."

The prisoner's eyes bulged. "Just as you say, comandante."

Puñonrostro turned to Hidalgo, "We selected correctly the sin-vergüenzas we took hostage. The snuffing out of these deformities will be my last service to God and to the Revolution."

Hidalgo looked questioningly to Father Ignacio and then to El Pájaro Loco, who had on his comic mask and dancing eyes that had served him for the entire Revolution and for all the years before that as well.

Father Ignacio swept away the tears in his eyes. *"Homo homini lupus.* To his fellow man, man is a wolf. We go forward now to Dies Irae. All of us shall be judged soon for our actions."

"All right then, Father. We make our stand on what has been given to us. And building upon our successes and our errors, from which we have learned so much, tomorrow we create excelsior."

The priest's last words to the Chicano evoked the *Quixote.* "Dear Hidalgo, for me alone was Puñonrostro born, and I for him. His was the power of deeds, mine of words, and we two are one."

Puñonrostro gave Hidalgo an embrace, and the priest gave the knight his blessing. Puñonrostro said to the Chicano, "Try to hide behind one of those imposing classical pillars of the palace. They won't collapse. Salud a tu cuerpo. As for me, I will go down as I came up, with the liberated fist. ¡Victoria o muerte!"

El Pájaro Loco embraced Jorge and said with that easy smile that reminded the Chicano of the bravest dead man of the Mexican Revolution, David Berlanga, "Como dice tu gente, carnal, ay te huacho . . . en el otro mundo."

"I love you, Woody Woodpecker. Como un hermano."

The Palace of Justice stopped shaking and became eerie, like the playing field that becomes vast and hushed in homage to a deceased notable. The quiet was punctuated only by the urgent buzzings of personages on cellular telephones, antennae stretched taut, lurking in the nooks of the Palace's fine Corinthian pillars. Then a grave voice on an amplifier from the outer world began to speak the most lovely, formal, and final Spanish that Jorge had ever heard in his life. Awash in his own category of morbid dread, Hidalgo knew that he had never before heard such splendid discourse, had never even known before this moment of what pinnacles rhetoric was capable. One could surrender oneself into its bosom.

Now the hypnotic voice entered the venerable domain of the future subjunctive, which no citizen of *Hispania Nostra* had actually spoken for at least one hundred years. But Jorge had read snippets of this sonorous style from time to time in the leather-bound *Amadis of Gaul* that he had kept ready and at arm's reach all these decades with *Standard and Poor's* on the teak bookshelf directly behind his power desk. Fuere lo que fuere, if he had to dream or choose a death in the deep South, Don Jorge Hidalgo knew then that he would choose one that observed the word.

Zapata Rose in 1992

They came forth, these things and creatures of spring,
   glowing with desire and with assertion. They came
like crests of foam, out of the blue flood of strength,
   and they came coloured and tangible, evanescent,
yet deathless in their coming. The man who had died
looked on the great swing into existence of things that
   had not died, but he saw no longer their tremulous
      desire to exist and to be. He heard instead their
ringing, defiant challenge to all other things existing.
   —D. H. Lawrence, *The Man Who Died*

El culto de Zapata . . . debe buscarse
donde realmente existe, en las humildes rancherías surianas
alejadas de las ciudades, en los caminos olvidados por donde
transitan medio desnudos y descalzos los hijos de aquellos
campesinos que hicieron la revolución en buena parte, y,
más aún, en los hogares indígenas, donde se levanta un afecto
constante desde el abuelo hasta el niño harapiento, a su recuerdo
maravilloso y único, limpio en la gran limpieza de quienes
oyeron su palabra y creyeron algún día, fielmente, que él,
sólo él, lograría la justicia social.
   —Baltasar Dromundo, *Vida de Emiliano Zapata*

Lightning out of Amecameca! The fearsome bolt broke the More-
lian night like an immense, electric river that split at the end into a
luscious white delta. The Amerindian line was lit with halos from
Milpa Alta and Ajusco in the North through the center at Huitzilac,
Tepoztlán, Cuautla, and Anenecuilco, culminating in Tlaquiltenango
and Jojutla in the South. Silver frenzy backlit the lover volcanoes,
Popo and Ixta, prefiguring dawn on the altiplano.

   At that very prefiguration a man who had been betrayed woke
from the long sleep. He awoke numb and cold inside a sacred

sepulchre carved from the living rock 1000 years ago by Toltecs and kept from the white man in grave confidence for five centuries by generations of indios of the South.

The body of this warrior was full of original hurt. He did not open his eyes. He lay numb and rigid. The wounds had not healed; they were open the same as the day they were made. He knew he was awake and that he could open his eyes, but he had no want. Who would come back from that? From the dead, with the original betrayal still buried in leaden clusters in his body? A deep nausea stirred in him. It was the premonition of movement and movement itself. He had not wished this. He wanted to stay in the marrow of the living rock, where even memory is stone dead.

But now something returned to Miliano; the trace of an ideal or grievance, and in that return he lay spent with nausea. Yet suddenly his cold and sore hands lifted up to push away the lid of the sepulchre: a mammoth Toltec stone cover carved with plumed serpents and sacred corn wending its scalloped way from the bosom of the earth toward the sun. An emperor had been interred in this tomb before and had given way a thousand years later to this man. But the limbs of the man who had been unspeakably ambushed fell back again, sick from having moved so much, unwilling to move further.

The warrior settled back into the cold, comforting bowels of death, resting in it like a bleached skull in its niche. It was most desirable. And once again he completed the null union with cold stone. Yet when he was most nearly gone, suddenly driven by the cold ache of his limbs, his feet stirred, even while his heart, pierced with corroded lead, lay cold and still.

And at last the eyes opened. The same dark, inside out! Yet perhaps there was a pale of tenuous light prizing the pure dark. He did not move his head. It was still richly pierced by old lead, the gift provided by traitors that infamous, recorded day at the Hacienda de Chinameca. His eyes closed. Again it was finished.

Then suddenly he sat up. The narrow walls of rock that had been carved out by the Amerindian ancestors closed upon him and gave him the new anguish of imprisonment. There were rays of light. The old grievance, the old anger returned. With strength that came from revulsion, Miliano was born anew, rose up, and faced the vengeful onrush of light.

Slowly, with the caution of the bitterly wounded, he crawled out of his carved sepulchre. ¡El 30-30! They had left his carbine leaning against the stone coffin and next to it a box of cartridges and one inscribed, golden bullet. These were the articles his followers had left for him. What they deemed necessary to cross from the outpost of the living to the kingdom of the dead and to cross back again to make revolution among the living. The cartridges were still dry. With his wounded hands he emptied the box and stuffed the cartridges into the pockets of his bone white peasant's pants and shirt. The indios of the southern revolution had stripped him of all superfluous finery and entrusted him to the living rock in solemn peasant's white.

Emiliano Zapata was alone and, having died, was beyond loneliness.

The town of Anenecuilco boasts a genuine pulquería, the type found in the places that progress has completely passed by, but for which the tradeoff is authenticity. The walls of the pulquería were painted alfresco. Here the devil tempts a careburdened campesino with a flagon of tequila, there an enamored, magnificently dressed charro with silver spurs and a silver-embroidered hat accompanied by a fine group of mariachis serenades his sweetheart who peeks decorously from the balcony window. On the same wall is an impassioned rendition of a stunning Virgin of Guadalupe revealing herself to the ardent indio, Juan Diego.

In counterpoint to the divine, the secular and the profane. The long wall of the pulquería was devoted to the lost heroes of Mexican history. It was rather like the Salle de Batailles at Versailles, where each great military victory won by the French is set in place. In the Anenecuilco pulquería, however, quite understandably, attention was placed on the frustrations and failures as well as the victories. Hidalgo, the father of the Revolution of 1810, was seen in a diptych, first leading the tumulto of peasants against the Spanish and criollo masters, subsequently being executed in Chihuahua City. José María Morelos, Franciso and Gustavo Madero, Domingo Arenas, Emiliano Zapata, Venustiano Carranza, and Francisco Villa all made their presence known, dying in one violent form or another.

The villagers of Anenecuilco considered the son of one of the most famous zapatistas to be a chismoso. The father of Soto y Gama, hijo, had acted. The son had been content to live off income generated by a few properties that had accrued to him from his anarchist and revolutionary paterfamilias. This pleasant vivir de las rentas had permitted him to indulge a passive but curious nature and to busy himself with collecting and writing the lore of zapatismo in small newspapers and periodicals in Morelos, Puebla, and Michoacán. Soto y Gama, hijo, was comfortable with his identity, and no one did more than grumble about the chismes that the nostalgic codger mined from the past. In fact, Soto y Gama was so comfortable that he even cultivated a file on the chismes about his own person. This file indicated, at least in Soto y Gama's mind, that what bothered the pueblo was how he kept them straight on zapatismo. Sure, in all things they preferred the myth, la invención, and the stirring moment, but he gave them genuine reality. A necessary price to pay in order to maintain the credo of the honest historian. And his mind, Soto y Gama thought with great satisfaction, in comparison to the doddering body, was still as sharp as an obsidian dagger that pierces the chest and exposes truth like a living heart.

So, they grumbled, but this was Anenecuilco, and they were still respectful and indulgent of a codger's foibles. Anenecuilco, still almost puro indio even now, was a place where people, especially if they became passionate, would revert to speaking what they called mexicano and which was actually their own variant of Nahuatl. It didn't matter what they thought of him, Soto y Gama thought. Everyone associated with the Zapata movement had fallen into decline, why not him? Communal agrarianism was out of favor. Salinas de Gortari and his economic wizards were busy privatizing many of the ejidos. Revolutions now had a bad name, particularly those that were said to prefigure the great Bolshevik fiasco. Not good years for zapatismo, although it still was quite necessary for los políticos—¡siempre los políticos!—to come down from Mexico City to commemorate Miliano's birthday on August 8th. They gave their speeches at the Anenecuilco pavilion that had been built for little else than an anniversary. The politicians were gone each year before the early afternoon summer rain, leaving the village hot and melancholy, the quiet punctured only by respectful, well-behaved Indian children playing serpientes y escaleras en la plaza.

Soto y Gama had noticed the young fedreño early that morning in the cemetery. Not surprising, a Sunday afternoon occasionally found a writer from Mexico City, searching for a story and finding the tombstones as interesting as the local conversation. Fidencio Espejo, Zapata's father-in-law, 1909. Miliano's two sisters, María de Jesús Zapata, 1940, and María de la Luz Zapata, 1944. The stalwart village continuer of the dead revolutionary's work, Francisco Franco, murdered with his two sons in 1947 by national troops, the effect of the evil of Nicolás Zapata. What distinguished this young stranger was that he didn't dress like a chilango, an inhabitant of Mexico City. In fact, he appeared to be in costume, a Mexican campesino from the period of the revolution. It wasn't very genuine, Soto y Gama thought, miffed that an outsider would come to his pueblo looking like he had dressed according to a photograph of the period.

The young man who gazed so intently at the tombstones earlier that morning, just as he gazed at him now in the familiar pulquería, must be searching for Emiliano Zapata's grave. The genuinely naive or misinformed invariably did.

"It's not here," Soto y Gama had called earlier from the other side of the camposanto.

The intent stranger hadn't bothered to face the elderly folk historian. "What's not?"

"The grave of the most famous man born in this region."

"I know."

Soto y Gama had taken the response of the fuereño as odd. Given the costume of the young man, at first he thought he was an actor. A few young actors had diligently attempted to capture Miliano's essence. But this young man had a certain aggrieved, sinister air about him. He seemed respectful enough and Soto y Gama felt no fear of him, but there was this quality of honor and ceremony that one found more commonly in campesinos of genuinely agrarian formation from the hinterlands. For that reason, Soto y Gama determined that the young outsider came from Central America. The visitors from Nicaragua, El Salvador, and Guatemala (or as he liked to jest with them, Guatepeor) also were known in Anenecuilco. Most were exiles from their home country. Earlier the sandinistas had come, seeking inspiration in their fight against Somoza. But that was the 70s. The sandinistas had won their revolution but then had lost control of the government. A familiar story to a Mexican. What need did they have now of zapatista inspiration? Most probably this young fellow was one of the salvadoreños. The Salvadoran exiles who occasionally came to Anenecuilco were a particularly respectful lot. They tended to be peasant revolutionaries organized around the ideals of Christian Base Communities. A Salvadoran provenance would also explain this young man's dress. Those traditional campesinos of the Central American latifundias lived a good 50 years behind even rural Mexico, Soto y Gama thought wryly.

"So, if you know Miliano's not here, why do you look so intensely?"

At that the stranger turned to face the elderly man. "There's something to learn from the dead. Did the sisters fare well?"

"Pretty well, but things got bad here in the 40s about when they died."

"And Nicolás?" the young man said softly.

Once again the old man was disconcerted. "You know about him too?"

"Is he still alive? Or gone?"

Soto y Gama became irritated. "If you know that much you should know that we don't like to talk about the bad Zapata, may he rot in hell for the great evil that he has done to Anenecuilco and to the campesinos!"

A decade ago, Soto y Gama wouldn't have considered taking pulque any way but straight. Now he liked it flavored. This time he ordered strawberry, tomorrow, perhaps, chocolate or melón. The fuereño took it flavored too, most likely because only a nahua would be used to the bitter taste of raw pulque. Or perhaps it was his health. At one time he must have been a dashing fellow, with his florid mustaches from an earlier era, but now the stranger looked very bad. He had pasty scabs on his temple. His complexion was sallow, gray, cadaverous. When he had shaken Soto y Gama's hand, it felt so cold that the elderly man started and drew back. Most likely this youngster was a Salvadoran rebel who had been wounded, had come within a hair of losing his life, and had been sent to Mexico to convalesce.

"Did you know I'm the son of the most famous man in these parts? My father founded the Liberal party. He was a great and passionate anarchist before anyone had even heard of Emiliano Zapata. He was Zapata's personal secretary after Palafox fell out of favor. He and his brother Conrado wrote the manifestos that Zapata signed. After they murdered Zapata he carried on the cause. He was effective."

"Your father was a great man."

"So, why have you come to Anenecuilco?"

"To learn."

"To learn? So then, which are you, writer, actor, or warrior?"

The man seemed to consider the question seriously. "Warrior."

Soto y Gama was satisfied then que había acertado. No need to inquire further nor disturb the cover of this exiled, wounded fighter from Central America who spoke Spanish with a lilt from an earlier, simpler time. "México and Anenecuilco welcome you as a comrade in arms. Está usted en su casa. May you find inspiration in our great revolution."

The man didn't respond. His deeply set eyes emerged from those furrowed brows and gazed at him with haunting effect. He even looked vaguely like Zapata, although clearly, despite his disastrous physical condition, he was a younger man than Zapata when Casasola had photographed him with Pancho Villa sitting in the presidential chair in Mexico City in 1914. Even the genuine Zapata at his revolutionary zenith with all of his military and political woes hadn't appeared like such a young man. Doubts emerged again. Perhaps this alleged revolutionary was an imposter after all. Merely an actor, seeking to impersonate the Zapata persona. Soto y Gama grunted. He stirred his flavored pulque. He looked over his shoulder at the bola who were discutiendo garrulously about who knew what, the crops, the latest politiquería, news from the capital. He rolled his eyes as if to express his irritation with the noisy group, but in fact the folk historian found the bola to be deeply comforting. They all came to this splendid pulquería whenever they could and certainly on Sunday afternoon. Soto y Gama would be discoursing with the bola at this very moment, if it weren't for the welcome distraction of this stranger.

"You want to know about Nicolás, the bad Zapata?"

"Yes."

"And about Emiliano, the good Zapata?"

"Him, too."

"How about my father, the non-Zapata? Ask me something. Get me started, because I know just about everything there is to know."

"Why is he called the bad Zapata?"

Soto y Gama looked at the stranger with feigned disgust; in fact, he was delighted. No one ever asked about the Zapata son, the Zapata of his own generation. Maybe Soto y Gama, hijo, was a mere shadow of his father, but he was a good shadow, an example when compared to el maldito Nicolás. Displaying country ways, he scolded the frail young man. "Why do you want to know about that little rat, Nicolás, anyway?"

Soto y Gama noted that the young man seemed visibly affected. He made a decision that he would act to destroy the myths that this foreigner appeared to have swallowed about Zapata and his progeny. Besides, Nicolás *was* a little rat. That was beyond dispute. Soto y Gama spat on the sawdust floor. "To begin with evil lineage, that's a bad augury. You know how they say, the bad drives out the good." He drank pulque, pulled up phlegm, spat again on sawdust. Finally, after prolonging matters as tantalizingly as he could, the old man, who fancied himself a masterful pueblerino storyteller, proceeded.

"I knew Nicolás from the beginning. We were both mozuelos, eight years old, present at that first encounter between Miliano and Pancho Villa. Nicolás, even then you could tell he was a disinterested snot, he slept through it all. Pero yo era muy vivo. I still remember every moment. The Centaur of the South sitting down for the first time with the Attila of the North, and if truth be told, the hero of us all, Emiliano Zapata, was very uncomfortable, very nervous. I remember how Villa and Zapata sat there, right in lover's Xochimilco like two country sweethearts in an embarrassed silence, occasionally broken by some insignificant remark. And Zapata studying Villa all the time. Finally Villa mentioned how 'high and mighty' Carranza was and Zapata said, 'I always told them so, I always said he was hideputa,' and they warmed up to each other a bit. And then Zapata called for cognac. Villa didn't drink, ever. His abstinence made him seem even more cold-blooded and calculating. But on this occasion, he took a cognac dutifully for a toast to the fraternal reunion of the South and the North, and upon sipping the fire, he almost choked. With tears in his eyes like a cartoon guy he called for water—almost like a gringo eating hot chile peppers. And we kids who were present, we just howled with laughter at poor, cruel, funny Villa. But not the esquintle mocoso, Nicolás, who was sound asleep and might just as well have been sucking at his mother's breast although he was years too old for that. It's funny, isn't it, how from the beginning, bad blood, or in my case, good blood, makes its nature known?"

The outsider looked impassively; he was very dark, muy indio, but with Hispanic features too, surely that notable mustache. Perhaps a touch of black blood as well? Was there this hint of ire behind the ceremony? The old man began to feel good. He was being effective, destroying those stupid myths that foreigners harbored about Zapata and his family. Now 1992 was surely time to set the record straight. "Zapata, you know, he was such a young man when the village elders turned over the post of calpuleque to him. Times were so very bad and in 1910 the elders did what they invariably did in hard times. They turned command over to a warrior. ¡Zapata! The family was among the best of Anenecuilco's line. Earlier, during the Reforma, Zapatas had fought courageously under young general Porfirio Díaz, who had been Juárez's most effective warrior.

"So by 1914 we zapatistas had been at it for five long years. Things were going very well. We were about to enter the capital. But in the good going one could detect the formation of dark clouds. No, that's not right at all. Speaking as a historian, it was precisely because of the successes that one could predict the failures, if only one were attentive to them. The failures were embedded in the successes, just like the coin cannot come up águila unless there is sol on the flip side.

"In truth, I don't think my father, who I hope you might know went on to become the most prominent zapatista of them all, ever really recovered from those glorious and simultaneously dismal days of 1914. You could just tell that victory would not be won, if only you had the presence of mind to read the signs. Late in the evening of November 24, the last of the carrancistas evacuated the capital, and the Centaur's troops entered the city. But not at all like águilas, more like cuatro gatitos muy quietitos. Out of their mundo, they were lost. Did they plunder or sack? Or even administer the city efficiently? Quite the contrary, they wandered about like lost children in the heart of Cem-Anáhuatl and knocked on the doors of the patroncitos of the capital, asking for food like seekers of alms. My father told me one night how the vaunted zapatistas spied a fiery red machine speeding down the lane and making a terrifying clangor. The inocentes conceived it to be some mythic and fearful modality of armor, and they put a stop to the infernal machine with their rifles, at the cost of the lives of 12 innocent firemen! And Zapata was no better. When the carranclanes took over Mexico City, their chingones billeted themselves in the fine residences in the center that had belonged to the científicos who had fled for their lives. But not Miliano! He moved into a grimy hotel next to the railroad station that met the trains from Cuautla. What do you think of that?"

The curious young man considered the question at length. "I think that Miliano was a man of the people, always one of the people, and a man of that sort does not go and live in the home of patrones or terratenientes. A man like that stays close to the railroad that provides his army sustenance."

"Well, you're right there! But that was precisely the problem. His strength became his maximum weakness. He now strutted on the national stage, even the international theater, and he was still wedded to the venerable little town of Anenecuilco and its local agravios, to the land that falls under the shadow of the twin lover volcanoes, Popo and Ixta. He didn't grow. His best part was also his most limiting feature."

"I take it that your father did grow?"

Soto y Gama, hijo, looked at him with a sort of amazement or perhaps feigned amazement. "Well, if you know a thing at all about zapatismo then you know that. If you know things about the evil Zapata or the obsure Zapata sisters, then my God, you must know that my father became the greatest zapatista of them all!"

The convalescent youngster then seemed to Soto y Gama to be on the brink of some action, probably to terminate their discussion, and Soto y Gama felt a certain panic. He needed badly to tell this man the true story of post-Zapata zapatismo. So to preserve the spell, he tantalized the youngster with a precious tidbit.

"Did you know, incredible irony, that Zapata's most trusted man in this village of Anenecuilco had exactly the same name as the Spanish fascist?"

The young man seemed confused.

"Yes, history is strange, isn't it? Francisco Franco, poor peasant who never spent a day of his tragic, malogrado life but in white campesino clothes, who had shown himself to be a true son of Anenecuilco and worthy heir of Zapata's legacy. He died, you know that, faithfully keeping his word to Miliano to save those land titles that so obsessed our leader!"

The young convalescent suddenly became very agitated. "Where are those titles?" he demanded.

The old man smiled slyly. Clearly he had this convalescent revolutionary back on the hook. "They're lost to this postrevolutionary mundo, surely buried where only the Indian sages know! But I'll tell you the sad story of Francisco Franco, their last sacred trustee. Miliano believed devoutly in the value of the land titles that were passed on to him as calpuleque. These were more than mere legal claims; they were the accumulated trust of all past generations of the pueblo, dating back to the viceroys and before that, to the Aztecs, the Toltecs themselves. Miliano went to the parish priest of Tetel-cingo, an expert on the ancients, and had him verify the authenticity of the oldest and most venerable of the Anenecuilcan land titles replete with pictographs and Nahuatl place names, drawn on sacred Aztec amátl bark paper. When Miliano decided to commit Anene-cuilco to revolution in 1910, he buried the land titles in a strongbox under the floor of the church. In the course of revolution, federal troops came and ravaged the district of Cuautla, and Miliano feared they might uncover the village's sacred patrimony which he held in trust. He sent his secretary on the village council, Francisco Franco, to dig up the strongbox and bring it to him. This Francisco did, and in the midst of deadly revolution, Zapata decided to take extra precau-tions. He entrusted the documents to Franco, instructing him that henceforth his life's sole duty was to preserve these titles. He was to stay out of all danger zones and to avoid all of life's possible com-promises like the plague. And so while Miliano often referred to the titles, he was comforted by the fact that they would not be lost with him. 'I'm bound to die some day,' Miliano would say, 'but my pueblo's papers stand to get guaranteed.' In 1914, emissaries came from the revolutionaries in Michoacán and they asked proof of Zapata's sincerity. They asked him why he fought. Miliano had the documents displayed. 'Por esto peleo,' that is what the Centaur said to them!"

Soto y Gama felt a sudden wellspring of distrust. He was straining so hard for the pinnacles of juglaría. Was it wasted on this fuereño? He decided to test him. "¡Ay, fuereño! What do you suppose that Miliano meant? Did he really make revolution for those mere pieces of paper, centuries of titles and futile claims to titles?"

One of the bola, the man who administered the tiny government-owned Pemex station for the village and who had closed the pumps down at 1:00 p.m., as always on Sundays, tottered to the victrola and inserted a token. Out came one of those baleful Mexican ballads that recount an incident of honor y vergüenza, ending, naturally, in more than one violent death. Dead and reborn Miliano fixed his eyes on the elder. "Yes! Miliano believed in those sacred writings. Because those documents were the record of the just cause of generations of indios of Anenecuilco! They were the sacred written identity of Anene-cuilco on this earth from the beginning of recorded Amerindian history through the colonial period and the establishment of the Republic of Mexico."

Soto y Gama felt a shiver as if the angel of death had brushed his shoulder. But he was old and was not unacquainted with the angel of death. What counted was this man who had proved to be a worthy listener, and he forged on with renewed intensity.

"Zapata was betrayed and murdered, and Francisco Franco returned to Anenecuilco and hid the strongbox. The villagers elected Franco their new calpuleque. After the rebellion of the obregonistas and the murder of Venustiano Carranza in 1920, Franco presented claim to the federales for the definitive and rightful restitution of the Anenecuilco fields. The lands were given back to the villagers, and a sort of justice and recompense for martyred Emiliano was realized. Yet that is where the monumentally evil Nicolás Zapata enters, for he was responsible for the loss of our lands once more!"

Zapata looked at the wizened elf of folk history with a high authority that had a shivering familiarity to it, that stirred the twilight bones of he who until this moment had been the scolder. Even the revelers in the pulquería, la bola, sensed some halo or electricity in the air, and they became quiet and attentive. "Now you will proceed to tell me about my son, Nicolás. You will tell me everything that I need to know!"

Without further ado or indirection he launched into it, basking in the attention of this strange, authoritative man and becoming ever more agitated as the intensity of his anger, so long submerged, began to unfold itself in the retelling of Nicolás's malevolence. Soto y Gama told the man how Emiliano Zapata's son, Nicolás, had come to learn too well the rudiments of politics, which in turn had rotted his sense of obligation. He told him how in 1937 at the age of 30, Nicolás had taken advantage of his name to entrench and promote himself. How the son, oh great mother of ironies! had used his name identity to become a prominent landowner by stealing the land that had been given to the Indians of Anenecuilco by President Lázaro Cárdenas. "Nicolás took advantage of his position in the official club, the Zapatista Front, to become a deputy in the Morelos legislature, and he used his position to acquire over a hundred acres of the Anenecuilco communal lands. When the villagers resisted, he forced them off their plots!"

Much later, after due and intense reflection, Soto y Gama, hijo, would recognize the mysterious skills of this impostor, a histrion from another mundo who had played upon his emotions and drawn him into his clever skit, causing him great embarrassment for having lost his sense of reality and propriety. The old man concluded that the effective little actor's quirk had been decisive. A con man's trick, but not without results. Emiliano Zapata—the real Zapata—had been known for his determination. A quiet man, he drank less than most of the others in the village, and he got quieter when he did. Although no one ever dared to fool with him, at those quiet times he might brood, and when people looked at him, he would seem very close to tears. That was the little trick, Soto y Gama concluded in hindsight, that had fooled the old man and had swept him from his objective perch into the impostor's morality play. For at the time, this outsider had looked exactly as Zapata was reputed to look, with that smouldering anger, the pinched face, eyes and mouth swollen, almost ready to explode in wrath or sorrow. And the impostor had said with such apparent amazement, such determination and touching effect: "My son never could have done such things. Never!"

And the old man, forgetting himself in a haze of strawberry pulque, had responded with genuine empathy and sorrow to this impostor, taking his theater for reality. "¡Ay, Emiliano! What do you know? You left him to grow on his own. Even when you lived you went to revolution and he stayed at home and grew not straight with the instilled respect of Anenecuilcan children, but in the soil of otherworldliness. And when you were gone and nothing more than mythos, he feasted on you like the bloodsucking vampire, growing to selfish maturity in your perfect mirror image. The one, pure, incarnate evil Zapata!"

The pulquería had become deathly quiet. The young impostor seemed to barely contain his emotions, and the old man was moved to touch him, to ease pseudo-Zapata's pain. Then from the far end of the bar one of the garrulous borrachos let out an ¡ajua! and shouted for everyone to hear, "¡Mira! Old Soto y Gama, ¡imbécil chismoso! Se ha vuelto lunático and now he talks to the ghost of Emiliano Zapata!"

How they laughed at this poor, learned but duped folk gossip.

*   *   *

Closer to the ethers than earth in a somewhere the apocalyptic poets strive to define, a man and a woman discoursed with Zapata.

"What did Jesus Christ know and when did he know it?" Miguel said with satisfaction. Finally, he was mastering the cant of current times. "Why not subject Jesus to post-Watergate morality? As we will in good time to freshly reborn Emiliano here. What did Miliano know ¿y cuando lo supo?" Miguel had come to appreciate 1992 for its fresh nuances, but it was a momentous struggle to stay put and not to slacken and drift dreamily out into the ethers. God knows why he remained in this hic et nunc. Worst of all was the dryness of his mouth. He had died of complications from diabetes in 1616 and was wont to claim that not all of the water of the Guadalquivir could slake his thirst. This place between ethers and the earth was still the spot of dryest throat, a convergence point that the enthusiasts of 1992 might call a worm hole in the universe, but which he preferred to see as the slim waist of the hourglass, transecting the two fat halves of life and death or life and otherlife. A centipede's soul easily passes with the precious grains through the prim waist of the glass, in and out, or down and up and down again as the hourglass is turned over and the grains of sand trickle anew.

Teresa considered Miguel's question seriously, which caused him droll amusement. On matters of Christ, who after all was her spouse, she became grave. Finally Teresa spoke with deliberation. "Miguel, I believe that what He knew depends on what Christ you are conjuring, the Man-God, or the God-Man."

Miguel smiled sarcastically; truly he was realizing himself as the postmodern intellectual. "Mellow out, Tere. For Christ's sake, literally. When you get solemn you remind me of Old Spain where a guy, especially like me, who wrote for the theater, could be swiftly Torquemadatized for one false start. Of course you know I was referring to the Man-God for I accept the God-Man's omniscience as theologically correct. But we stray afield for you know I was merely tailoring a polemical suit out of the current cant for little Miliano here, whose ánima comes to us dressed in white campesino jammies from 1919. Perfect opposites of the Vietnamese black jammies from the same acequia madre, ¿que no? Isn't he the sweetest Christ? My God, he looks fluffy and chulo, one of those Day of the Dead skulls of pure cane sugar! And what does he know in our 1992 of the effect he has had on el mundo since 1919? It's an interesting question! As for Christ, if only we could touch him, or he us! What might He tell us of how they've botched up His teachings? Zounds!"

As soon as Miguel uttered that once saucy euphemism for "His Wounds" he knew he was off, and no doubt by hundreds of years. No matter, invoke poetic license and press on. "Forget Christ. My God, we do it all the time. What about Peter, Paul, and that engaging doubting Thomas? What did they know and when did they know it? Wait a second, let's get back to Christ. What might BeJesus say about Peter the Rock? Paul is now generally considered misogynistic and gender incorrect. So keep to Christus and Petrus and their work during the early years! What did Christ know, and when did he know it? That's Miliano's dilemma as well, dulce campesino Christ. Isn't it, Miliano? I'm so sorry about Nicolás. An undutiful son. Well, not exactly sorry for Nicolás himself, who can't be helped. After all, that's the point of free will, ¿que no? I'm sorry for you on account of Nicolás, because, as that folk rogue of Anenecuilco, Soto y Gama expressed to you in Zapata's Revelations, Chapter One, in this otherlife one assumes that the sins of the children are visited upon their makers. Here we stand time and sin and grace on their pointed heads. ¿Que no? Isn't that the point of lingering in the future, to find out how things *turn out?* You are the cause, you are responsible for your effects. We'll have no uncaused causer, unmoved mover sleight of hand here, tan lejos de Dios y tan cerca de los Estados Unidos. Surely you're here to take a little responsibility for it all, for Christ's sake! You never were a shirker, were you, Miliano? That's why you find yourself in the company of zanies like us!"

"Pobrecito, enamorado," Teresa said in her best madonnic form. "Is Miguel giving you a migraine? He's true to his 17th century essence, you know. When they took him he was doing the final touches on the *Persiles y Segismunda*. These 17th century masculinists, they go for baroque!"

Miliano rubbed his eyes. He felt like chunks of tripitas were swirling in the menudo of his mind. The babble that tumbled out of the bearded man's mouth seemed familiar, almost pertinent, but ultimately an indecipherable irritant. The man was going on again. "Hear me, my dear revolutionary Zapata, we are dealing with what in 1992 they call the problem of real time. You come out of your 73-year stupor and a Toltec crypt, and they sock it to you, baby! Life, death, all of time's cycles and action's consequences. Welcome to our little gameboard, where the past and the future merge into one pastiche. It's a matter of fast forward and reverse. You'll appreciate it here soon enough, for this place was made for you. Miliano, truly, you are an alltimer!" Miguel knew that he was merely confusing simple Miliano, but wasn't that his stock in trade? As a self-taught he still needed to pull the legs of a simpleminded peón, with deleite e instrucción. And upon Miguel was growing an enormous apprehension that was of the essence. In all probability this country bumpkin had never read the *Quijote,* and if Miliano turned out as big a loser on trivial pursuit as Miguel was beginning to surmise, it was going to be the equivalent of the writer losing his appeal to the parole board of his fuero interno, tantamount to yet another term in limbo.

Miliano was coming out of his swirling, soupy confusion. The man who was called Miguel looked confusingly familiar, like a person he genuinely knew, except as an archaic figure in a daguerreotype. "I know you, don't I? Were you . . . you were a boarder at that hotel by the railroad station when we took over the capital?"

Miguel shaped his Golden Age beard to a nice sharp point. "My dear revolutionary, you don't know me *that* well. After all, I'm 300 years your senior. But certainly, through my get. Through el prole everyone knows me." He put on a mournful countenance. It was meant for parody, but given his relationship to his children, it was apt.

"How are you called?"

"Call me Cerbantes or Servantes or Çervantes or Çerbantes, just don't call me late to literary dispute. In this age of systematization and uniformity, Cervantes will do nicely. Miguel would even be simpler."

Miliano became more confused, troubled actually. The name, well, it felt like he should know it, but he didn't quite place it. Miliano wracked his memory and came up with warriors, people of the revolution, but this man, he couldn't be of 1910. As Miliano searched his memory, he could tell he was producing pain in the soul of this so-called Cervantes. That made him feel bad too, because of the deficiencies of his education. Revolutionary life had been exceedingly hard that way. Every day a raft of decisions, some with immediate effects, others with repercussions almost unimaginable, unforeseeable, and for all time. And he was quite aware that he hadn't been all that good. Most of the time he had to rely on those rural school teachers like Palafox, or wild-eyed anarchists like Soto y Gama. Had they been that good? Hadn't he always felt dependent on the treacherous little intellectuals—the leídos y escribidos—to articulate the revolution that he and his campesinos made with their iron fists, but couldn't fix for all time and space without their preciosity?

The woman was very close but somewhere out of Miliano's sight. Her direction was illuminated. She spoke and seemed to smooth over the trouble spot. "All those variations on your name are nothing, Miguel, compared to my polyphonic spelling. I may be increasingly irrelevant to simple people who would seek God, but I am known by more than mere hagiographers. If I become stale with the people, the morphologists and phoneticians will always find value in my *Vida* for the lovely, natural way I spelled words!"

Miguel returned to humor, that is, to his natural authority. "Oh, Tere, the folk language of your diaries is a sight to behold! You are natural speech incarnate! Those spellings, my god, seven different variations on the same page! But of course, another self-taught, right? How else did women learn in the 16th?"

Then Cervantes turned to Miliano and sighed. "I will tell you from where I get my sustenance. Do you recall an old man on a sorry, gallant nag tilting at windmills and a fat, lazy campesino who is surely the archtype for the Mexican peón sleeping under his hat against a prickly cactus?"

"El Quijote? Sancho Panza?"

"None other."

"And what are you to them?"

"I to them?" The man blushed with indignation. "They live purely by the grace of my quill!"

Miliano reacted with consternation to the vehemence of this strange man. But without comprehension.

With the predictable finality of classical theater, the crash of hubris against the uncaring volcano's side, Cervantes perceived in Zapata the typical response of the unlettered. Clearly Miliano didn't even know about the existence of his book, or if he did, he perceived it merely as a remote and irrelevant artifact. The characters themselves this indio of popular formation knew well enough, but only as they had existed in puppet theater, papier-mâché carnivalia, the juglaría of wandering bards. There had been a time when every tall, skinny man was liable to be called Quijote, just as fat, dumpy ones were greeted by lettered and unlettered alike as Sancho, and every raquítico nag was automatically a Rocinante. Once again Miguel faced the epistemology of Quijote and Sancho, totally stripped of literary moorings and authorial authority. They lived vividly and outsized in the mind of this Emiliano Zapata and countless other inocentes, strictly through the medium of popular culture. It was a familiar story, his own children out of reach of his artistic artifice, and in Cervantes's mind, the presumptive reason he remained plantado in this mundo rather than divinely transported into the ethers. Of course, Cervantes told himself with self-mocking irony, this was sheer speculation on his exile from heaven, his best shot at self-knowledge and its effects on the surrounding physical or metaphysical world. After all, he was hardly the ultimate omniscience who presumably knew all things all ways always and for whom words like "what" and "when" were simply communicative crosswalks to His or Her mortal creatures. Miguel spoke again to Emiliano. "So why are you here in '92? What's coming down, bro? Give me your best rap!"

"Stop that, Miguel!" the voice of the woman said. "He doesn't even know that 92 stands for a year!"

"He will soon enough! Then he'll have to figure out if he's here for apocalypse now, judgment day, or merely Armageddon in evolutionary notches. I hope you don't hit him soon with your speculations, Tere. Your theory of the evolutionary accrual of spiritual assets in the cosmos sounds to me suspiciously like the buildup of plaque in the arteries!" He turned to Emiliano. "Why do you think you are here, turned out of death's cradle?" Without giving blinking Zapata a chance to answer, he went on blithely. "Surely, it is because of the will of your people, of los indios, who said all along that the body Carranza's malhechores riddled was that of an impostor. The art of the people is so powerful that reality can only obey it! Of course, Teresa has her own theory and she's gonna perform it on your bones! She believes that your rebirth has something to do with the evolution of spirit on the planet."

"Don't vulgarize my theories! You impertinent wag!"

"Beloved Tere, you know I have no such motive, I merely examine them in the crucible of Golden Age mockery. If they withstand the corrosive agents, then they may have some value. As for vulgarization, making poor Zapata an incarnation of the second coming! Indeed! Although I'll concede that you are at least true to your creed. You mystics all want betrothal in the here and now. You all want God, red meat, and garlic soup on the same plato mundanal."

Now the environment changed and became pageantlike. To Miliano the place seemed bathed in noble kinesis. Miguel said, "Uh oh, get ready for act two of *Who's Afraid of Virginia Woolf?*," but revolutionary Zapata listened to the saint who said, "Come to me, beloved."

Zapata rubbed his eyes and tried to fix time and space. He turned to and fro, searching for a source. He got up (had he been down?) and turned in what seemed to be the proper direction.

Saint Teresa was before him in all her naturalness and the great revolutionary was smitten. Purest awe engulfed him, the power of noblest love entered through his eyes, his nostrils, his mouth, and the aural orifices and penetrated his interior.

From afar Miguel de Cervantes called out, "¡Ponte chango, vato!"

Emiliano Zapata, out of pure, instinctive mexicanidad, fell enraptured to his knees as might have the indio, Juan Diego, on December 12, 1531, before the divine presence of the Virgin of Guadalupe.

The saint caressed him with her ardent visage and tears welled in his eyes, beads of sweat formed above his brow, his heart butted against the cage of his ribs like a magnificent gallo that would be free, and from his loins stirred the great serpent. "Thou art still with the mark of death on thy body, beloved. And the stigma of betrayal by petty souls burdens thy soul. Fly now, into my arms and thou shall live anew!"

"It's all done with smoke and mirrors, Emiliano!" called Miguel de Cervantes. "Beware the spectacle of the speculum. It's holographic! You haven't a clue about the sort of stuff they're capable of these days! Virtual reality. If truth be told, she's a very lonely woman. Her dead body's been ripped and portioned into tiny pieces like Osiris himself, for Christian thrill seekers. A piece of her lies in every church in Christendom!"

Zapata now felt a proprietary rage. He was a staunch-hearted elk, ready to butt heads and destroy his rival for the possession of this woman. He moved to protect his own, but the saint stopped the calpuleque in his tracks with her outstretched arms. "Pay no heed to that amusing schmuck. In good time we will readmit him into our covenant. Come, Miliano, into my arms, and together we will make ourselves whole!"

In the arms of his beloved, Miliano felt the poisons of venal life drained from him. The open wounds that ranged over his body, the base lead that had entered him deeply and profusely and lodged against his bones or in his organs was cleansed and the great elixir of caring love covered him like a balm or an aphrodisiac or a psychedelic.

Zapata swooned in the arms of his beloved. From his fleet limbs to the uncoiled serpent in his loins to his great heart to his canny, unerring eagle-warrior's eye, he tingled with the fiery raptures of the santa's caring love. La santa held him by the chin and lifted him effortlessly by his jaw. He was putty in her arms, but enraptured putty, his limbs rising high above the ground just as his manly sex that had curled in on itself for eight limp decades rose and displayed its prowess, and his eyes regained the focus of the indio guerrero. "Verily, I am risen anew!"

Then Zapata received from the saint the thrust of a cleansing arrow that traveled into his entrails and pierced his heart and his manhood. La santa's arrow emerged from his body, and Zapata saw the bright flame at its fiery tip. She beckoned again with the arrow and willingly dead Zapata opened himself to receive, and with an all-loving diligence, la santa plunged the shaft into him again, and Zapata knew the saint by a pain so delicious and a torment so exquisite that no pleasure in life could give more delight.

And so dead and reborn Zapata knew Teresa in her natural womanness and he knew the sanctity that la santa had developed on this earth to save her sisters and her brothers. He knew her and was one with her unearthly body, and he knew her as her grateful charge, a recipient of her good works and intercessions on behalf of her earthly children.

Miguel gazed at Zapata with macho smugness. "I see you got the full treatment. Golden Flower of the Other, what? That woman, she's a piece of work!"

The tears welled in Zapata's eyes, that pinched look, that grave stare of total commitment. He said menacingly, "Do not mock—no te mofes de mi dama."

Cervantes laughed with an easy literary disdain he might reserve for Lope de Vega, and also with kindness. "You sound like a knight I once lived with intimately as did a father with his son. I'll be sure not to mock. When that woman reams a guy, well, that's no ordinary affection. All the pipes are cleaned, ¿que no? And didn't Jung say, but, of course, you wouldn't know about Jung, would you, ¡mi general! Yet truly he said the cocksure macho's syzygy is the hensure hembra."

Again Zapata was baffled by the web of startling, impertinent images and obscure locutions that came at him from around the corner. He said with deep Hispanic ceremony, "I would give my life for her."

"Now, now, chaval. You've given your life once already and for a mighty revolution. Don't be so free with your life. But that holy woman, surely she gives good resurrection, ¿que no? She started out sedately enough founding one new house, the Discalced Carmelites. But in 1567 when her Superior General granted her authority to start as many branches of her new order 'as she had hairs on her head,' well, she ended up traveling many thousands of kilometers, mostly by oxcart and by mule. She's an inveterate performer, I wish I had her in my troupe. For the love of Christ and her human flock, she suffered from extreme heat and cold, from fever and angina. She's slept in almost every dubious inn in Spain, bothered, as she put it, by 'fleas, poltergeists and all the inconveniences of travel.' The only thing that rivals her show is the treatment that the torturers give. They have it down pat all over Latin America and lots of other places. The torturers! But they are hell, and this is heaven, ¿que no?"

Infuriated with the bard, Zapata reared toward him like an elk, but Miguel blew him off with a sneer of superiority, and the revolutionary suddenly had a sense of place and realized that he had to compete in a different arena. Presently Teresa came. "I heard that, Miguel. And what you said earlier, which is essentially true. I am a lonely woman. Like Osiris, my dead body rent asunder, scattered and cast into reliquary containers across the world. My body is a medium, a common currency of Christian voyeurs who trade in nail clippings and hair fibers."

Awkward Zapata would go to his knees and swear fealty, but she would not have it. "So, will you respect me in the morning?" she quipped. She took Miliano by the hand and hugged him affectionately like a brother, and the calpuleque felt the fire of God's seraph in her body pressed against his. Zapata vowed with the same solemnity that he had offered to the *Plan de Ayala*. "I will help you. I will help you gather your body together and make it whole, as you have made me one again."

She looked at him with great melancholy. "You are sweet and committed, Miliano. Would that such a mission were realizable." She sighed. "Once I feared poltergeists. I would see the tails of demons sticking out jauntily from under the robes of nuns. Now I believe an active saint, she's just another, special sort of ghost that haunts the world."

Miguel smiled indulgently. "Tere, surely you're a saint for this season. The feminist saint, and in 1515 clearly avant la lettre, before the word feminist was even coined. Surely, your time has genuinely come. This era needs the feminist saint, which probably is why you are plantado here, and not divinely in ethers."

"Nonsense, Miguel. You know all three of us are stuck here for personal reasons. Why else would we hang back from heaven? You know, this quincentenary of 1492 is germane to my family. I had nine brothers and seven of them went to the Indies with bought captaincies permitted to the *hidalguía*. And how we had to fight for that *hidalguía*! My grandfather was a most prominent Toledan Jew, you know? Part of our family had been Jew, Christian, Jew, and shortly before 1492, about to become Christian again." Her eyes danced with merry irony as she looked into the eyes of naive, awestruck Miliano, syncretized Nahua and Christian, who found totalmente fuera de quicio these inklings of apostasy. "One of my Jewish cousins in fact chose a nice Christian name that I always appreciated, Fernando de Santa Catalina. The symbol of St. Catherine, you know, is the wheel."

"So Tere, are you then prepared to preside over the infamous 1492?" Miguel asked.

"To preside? Hardly! To recognize the expulsion of the Jews with sorrow and perhaps a glimmer of understanding, of course, among other 1492s! We need to open ourselves to these historical truths; isn't that the deeper purpose of these commemorations? In 1492 Christopher Columbus sailed the ocean blue and discovered Watling Island on October 12, Cuba on the 18th, and wrecked the Santa María off Haiti on Christmas Day. Leonardo da Vinci drew a flying machine. The profession of book publisher emerged consisting of three parts, type founder, printer, and bookseller. Nebrija wrote the first Latin-Spanish dictionary, a milestone in my own career as a linguist's primary source! The last Moorish kingdom, Granada, was extinguished and inquisitor-general Torquemada gave the Jews three months to accept Christianity or leave the country. That last datum was what mattered most for my family. My grandfather, Juan Sánchez, had been a nominal Christian and a secret Jew for some time, but the noose of the Inquisition tightened around Toledo, the tolerant city of the three faiths, and on June 22, 1485, he was placed on the docket together with my father and my uncle Alvaro, who was 12 years old. They confessed to 'grave crimes of apostasy and heresy against our Holy Catholic Faith' and were condemned to go in penitential procession on successive Fridays to all the churches in Toledo, wearing the *sambenitillo con sus cruces*. The *sambenito*, a full-length garment painted with flames and devils, was worn to the stake. The *sambenitillo* was merely knee-length, yellow, and marked with black crosses, shoulder to hem, front and back. Toledanos knew that religiously correct behavior required a proper rain of stones and spittle upon sighting someone in a *sambenitillo* lest one be exposed as weak in their faith, and in Toledo, correctness had become rampant. Dearest Daddy never forgot the faces of those who cursed, spat upon him, and stoned him for the greater glory of Christ."

"Did so many of your brothers leave for América because the family had been spat upon?" questioned Miliano.

"There's something to that. In 1486 our family had to pay lots of money to the Inquisition in fines, but we still retained considerable resources, and especially after 1492 when the Jews were expelled, those families that had been officially 'reconciled' to the Christian faith took over Spanish finances, taxes, and the like, which had become chaotic. My family was more into financial administration than ever. One was the bishop of Palencia and had the title of Commissar of the Crusade, that is, he was chief fund-raiser for Spain's holy wars. As for my father, he moved to Avila, changed his Sánchez name to Don Alonso de Cepeda and met my mother, Beatriz de Ahumada, dear sad little Doña Quijote she, and knocked her up. The Ahumadas didn't want her to marry a converso, but when they found their 13-year-old daughter to be pregnant, what was to be done? Besides, my father paid all along the line. To the Church, to the family, even a carta de dote to the province of Aragón for 1,000 gold florins in honor of his bride's virginity. On the day of the wedding, my mother signed her X on the document and within 15 months she had given birth to two healthy sons. But all of this officiousness and legajería was one thing, tongue wagging quite another. There was cruelty and mockery. My brother Hernando was a tough customer and took things in stride. He ended up a governor in the Indies. Poor Juan could not bear to live in Avila as a perceived half-Jew. He ran away and joined the infantry. There was a great need for cannon fodder, and this 14-year-old boy easily met the need. He was shipped off to North Africa and killed by the Moors in his first engagement; he was dead before my ninth birthday. Gone to heaven, a one-way trip on the short line."

Zapata looked at her reverentially. "He died in battle. He is in your heaven?"

Cervantes looked kindly at Zapata. "I'll let you down gently. We know nothing more than you about final issues, only that the ethers beckon and although we're dead, we live on much as we did before. There is no heaven and there is no hell in our limbo."

Teresa added, "And no personally known God. Just the God that we take on faith. But at the turn of the 15th century it was a routine comfort to families of the victims of Spain's holy wars that they died 'martyrs.' At eight, I believed it. And a few years later my brother and I ran away from home to seek out the Moors, begging our way for the love of God, so that they would cut our heads off there, and ensure our pain and our glory forever. How my young brother Rodrigo and I savored the word and said it over and over, pa' siempre, pa' siempre. We returned home though, before we strayed more than a few days down the line, for the sake of our mother, who had taken the death of her son poorly. She had become a recluse, wearing the shabby black of an old woman and chain-reading novels about knights. She died, in childbirth, naturally, before I was 14. I read those novels about gallant knights too. For my mother, they weren't as injurious, for she did not lose her purity over them."

"Novelas de caballería. We have that in common too, my dear Catholic saint. Too bad your blessed mother didn't have the opportunity to see you grow into your vocation!" Cervantes mocked Teresa.

Teresa smiled seductively. "I was a daughter of the double standard. It wasn't until much later that I became very, very good and effective. As a young woman I was good only at getting my way."

Cervantes looked at Zapata. "Do you read? I will teach you excruciatingly well if you like." He pointed to Teresa. "Your lady, you know, her books are absolutely dynamite! Torrid stuff by the standards of the times. Let me see. I remember one passage about emerging out of puberty into womanhood: 'Then outgrowing childhood, I began to understand the bodily charms the Lord had given me—they were very great, according to what people say—and when I should have given thanks for them, I began to use them to sin against Him, as I will tell you now.' Those bodily charms, eh, my mezcal-drinking compañero, they're worth living life over again and not throwing it away this time, ¿que no?"

Teresa took Zapata's hand. "You fight with your heart and your limbs and Cervantes with his quill and his tongue. We'll choose our battle stations, won't we, beloved? You must know that Miguel and I lived in a bawdy age. When I had my visions, they were not to the tastes of the time. My artistry was not Christ bound to the pillar or lashed and crowned with thorns or on His way to Golgotha bowed by the weight of His Cross. I saw him with the golden crown of His victory over death, royal and radiant, a King! My then confessor, Baltasar—Bless his soul!—sought to cure me of my visions. He and the holy committee saw so clearly that they were Satan in disguise. They figured out an ingenious tactic."

Zapata mustered the courage to ask the saint directly, "What was it?"

"To give figs to Satan. I was to tuck my thumb between the first two fingers and give the finger to the devil! Giving figs would hardly have been a problem for me, but I could give them only to the devil, and my visions were of Christ. To finger Christ, that would be unbearable! And so I continued to have my visions. Later, my sanest adviser, Domingo Báñez,—Bless his soul!—laughed at this. If those visions came from Satan, he said, they were still beautiful. Does one refuse to be moved by a fine religious picture until one is sure that the painter's private life is up to snuff? A clever one was he, Domingo, who knew that many painterly madonnas were the mistresses of the artist! You might have guessed that with anxieties such as these, the talk was rife about my multiple affairs with my confessors and other members religious." Then Teresa sniffed properly. "All lies, I might add, properly put to rest with my canonization. By that time I was so very, very good. Except that each good Christian wanted to keep a little piece of me for her or his personal salvation. And when I was dead and supposedly past protest, they carved me up into parts like pieces o' eight and took me into their homes like a talisman."

Miguel looked at her with knowing irony, and she made a shrill, embarrassed laugh. "I got my way in a man's world! I was effective. I did what it took. My raptures were not a comfort but a delirium. Sometimes they would go on for days, even in mixed company. I would hug myself with my pain, and it caused me the greatest suffering when they began to be gossiped about. But they were my raptures. And the order of Discalced Carmelites that I created was my conception too! The chapters grew over Spain like a divine fungus!"

With some allotment of time, Miliano grew in familiarity of Miguel and Teresa. Cervantes, honed wit formed out of the rhetorical wars of the Siglo de Oro, was both his comrade and a wag, mocking him mercilessly. Teresa succored him from the spate of malintentioned barbs that came from Cervantes's artifice. Her image became genuinely recognizable to him. He remembered that one of his sisters had manifested devotion for the Discalced Carmelites during his youth. Hadn't the image of the venerable saint stood on the home altar, beside the Virgin of Guadalupe, Cristo Rey, and Benito Juárez, to whom so many Zapatas se habían encomendado las vidas?

Zapata had recovered from the trauma to his body, but he had not reconciled himself to the postrevolutionary course of his son, Nicolás. The first comment that Cervantes had made about the sins of the children visited on their parents transformed itself into an idée fixe, namely that his reawakening had some element of expiation in it.

When he asked again why they thought he awoke here and now in 1992, Cervantes, who Zapata eventually came to learn detested direct inquiry, took yet another tack, this time to tease not only him, but his lady. "Because God is a pícaro just like you and me. Hidebound masculinist!" He gave a sidelong glance at Teresa and plunged in, "He even made that one there, the sainted lady, a pícara. That's why you are here, to indulge our fancy, and us yours. Do you like to gamble? I haven't played a good game of whist since 1616!" He wiggled his withered arm at Zapata. "I'll play you first with this one. If you prove not to be a patzer, then I'll play you with the good one. How about you, Tere, are you in with the men? I tell you what, whist is awful with less than four. Let's play that amusing new game, strip poker. No tears, no fears. This is definitely a game for dismembered saints! Are you in with the boys? Or as usual for creatures of your persuasion, out?"

Teresa smiled at the artist with indulgence and total authority. Zapata swelled with reverence. Her bearing, her station and control! Truly, this was beyond the human pale. But surprisingly she became vindictive. "Ah yes, the manco de Lepanto proffers his withered arm to the wheel of fortune. Or is it the manqué de Lepanto, the one whose literary creations got the better of him exercising a sullen artifice?"

Cervantes stared crossly at her and all was left hanging. But Zapata could not avoid the question of the timing of his rebirth and his ultimate destiny for long, and soon he broached it again, a shade more discreetly. Now Miguel pursued a different conceit. "We three are here for our own sins and no others. There's this guy in Cuba I've been following, Fidel." He tried a joke in his lame, self-taught Latin. "Semper Fidel." Miguel was so sensitive about his status of autodidact and opismath that he took advantage of any opportunity to show off classical knowledge. "There's one who achieved a genuine revolution, at least for 30 years. He called those who couldn't keep up with his revolution the plantados, and that is precisely what we are. Except we are the metaphysical plantados. Me, with my inferiority complex. After all, it's hard to adjust to the fact that one's fictions are at a higher plane of being than their creator of flesh and blood. And this has been going on and getting ever worse since my death in 1616! They are gaining spiritual assets at a much higher rate. It's the being gap! Christ, they seem to be continually performing on the great white way, and I suppose there's nothing to be done about it." Miguel glanced at Teresa. "And Tere here, she may deny it, but verily she spends her time trying to somehow get her act or, rather, her body together. It's all desparramado in church reliquaries from Santiago de Compostela to Santiago de Chile to Santiago de Cuba. ¡Pobrecita! And now there's you, Emiliano Zapata, revolutionary manqué, come to life to preside over the quincentenary I would suspect. Or is it to finish unfinished business? You speak for the struggle to regain the pre-Columbian Quinto Sol, ¿que no? I do say, dear boy, I envy you, fixed in time and space, alfresco, as it were, on the walls of public buildings in Mexico, in finer poster shops world over. On your white horse, with your 30-30, mustaches to the wind, that serious, melancholy look. No one forgets your radical face, no one has even genuinely seen mine! Zapata, you are the genuine article, a true alltimer." Cervantes paused a moment and mused. "Of course, you're more like the Quijote than like poor carne y hueso me. An icon yourself. Wind that swept Mexico, what? In Chicanolandia you wouldn't even recognize yourself, you've become such a big fucking deal. And in Mexico, the artists that have served you . . . Diego Rivera, David Alfaro Siqueiros, José Clemente Orozco. Sheer genius!"

Zapata could not be consoled by mere artifice. Miguel, Renaissance man of arms and letters, understood that well. Tere stated that while there was certainly some obsession that kept them plantados to the world, each of them also had a divine project. "Emiliano, yours is to achieve justice and well-being for your people; Miguel, to 'instruct us deleitando' in our humanity; and mine, to serve God as best I can." Zapata found it all very pat and mundane given the enormity of his regestation and rebirth, and most of all the inculcation of caring love in what had previously been the mere mobile vessel of his body.

"I believe Miliano is becoming dissatisfied, even bored in this overly intellectual place," said Miguel. "At least I'm becoming bored. We best be showing freshborn Miliano here this world that he is to rectify and justify before the date on his package expires and he goes stale, like yogurt at the market! We ought be errabundus mundus. How about a movie, Miliano? You should barely know such things from 1919. Ah, the silent period! While silence may have been golden, movies are better now! And they're in surround sound and living color!"

"Well, what did you think of the movie?"

Zapata looked at him incredulously. "¡Mierda!"

Cervantes feigned surprise. "Now, Miliano, just because the *Plan de Ayala* didn't get much attention doesn't mean there's no art to it! It's canonical. It's on the boob tube at least once a year. At any number of campuses, Chicano student organizations put it on nicely for Cinco de Mayo."

"That little gringuita runt, my wife? My wife! My own wife a gringuita!"

"Poor boy, that's the way the spearmint chews. That runtolette made stardom on the film vehicle of your vida."

"And me, standing on the balcony in pijama bottoms, speaking to the peasant army of the South? I read, don't you know that? I read, I give speeches! I'm not an ignorant fool that doesn't read. I give speeches in Spanish, in Nahuatl."

"Well, I'm sorry, dear boy. Of course you read, in a manner of speaking, or speak in a manner of . . . well, I thought Marlon Brando was simply fantabulous! Would that he performed my *Liberal Lover* or my *Jealous Extremaduran*. He could turn my poor machito into a King Lear himself! What we could have done with our theater in the 16th with some real method acting. Although I must say, Anthony Quinn, ¡eso sí es raza! he stole the show as your pícaro brother, Eufemio!"

"I didn't die that way either, don't you understand? Not like that, for a stupid white horse. And what was that meeting with Villa, ¿eh?

Was that supposed to be the meeting at Xochimilco? That mockery?"

"My God! Art critiqued by the standard of its fidelity to quotidian reality. What a bloody bore! Tere, when I was alive I never could deal with this sort of naiveté, and I still can't. Tell your beloved ingenue that those who 'know best' . . . " Cervantes laughed testily and with wry self-mockery, "the critics and scholars, the serious historians and catedráticos, they all claim that the film does justice to him in the essential ways. Zapata is forbidden to complain! He should see the films that were made about my children. One by Russians that justified their own revolution. Actually, it was an interesting ensayo. Another, well there were so many, another, a musical, a zarzueloid thing, a gringo absurdity. 'The impossible dream.' But that was for the stage actually, an interesting ensayo. As God is my witness, I can say nothing against these adaptations. Having written theater for the vulgo myself, I don't complain. It is the way of art, not to mention making money. And you shouldn't complain either. That movie alone, *¡Viva Zapata!*, has made you famous all over the world, ¡hasta en Tibet!"

Zapata twisted his mustache. Then he stopped, slightly embarrassed. It was becoming a nervous habit, due to his frustration. Miguel said, "Well, if the film doesn't turn you on to your fame, maybe the poster shop will." They stopped by the shop where the college youths who had come out of the movie house pressed the attendants for Zapata posters. "My god," said Cervantes, "you're outselling Pancho Villa ten to one!"

Teresa said, "See these youths, grim, determined, excited, euphoric, headlong, who are buying up your likeness? You have something vital to offer them. You mean something great to them. Even though they relate to you as dead over 70 years ago and through a silly American movie, you speak to them. Your project thrills them. It is as vital and fresh as the day you mounted your mythical white horse!"

"God, how I love Teresa!" said Cervantes. He ribbed Zapata, knowingly, just to fan the Mexican revolutionary's jealousy. "I hope to be with la Tere forever, which in all probability . . . Isn't this death or afterlife or whatever it is like the richest moments of life itself? The openness, the dilemmas, all the same issues, but heightened and intense. This death, it is like life, but rendered into art. It is just like theater, that is, like life, but with all the waiting and the boring parts cut out!"

Tere responded, "You are right, Miguel. We have evolved into another style of life. A denser, more unitary one, but still life."

Zapata twisted his mustache again. They were giving him vertigo, and he wanted to return to more familiar ground. "That other thing. What was it called?"

"Oh, the other Brando on the double bill. Just a dumb gringada. They call it *The Wild One.*"

Zapata's fierce look set the novelist ashiver, and for the first time Miguel de Cervantes had a presentiment of the revolutionary indio. "That was a revelation! The mechanized rebirth of caballería! Give me 600 of those infernal motocicletas, and I would lay siege to the inner circle of hell itself!"

"Well you're right there!" Miguel said. The author was warming up to the idea. "Six hundred of those cycles with Quijotes or Zapatas or Hell's Angels on them, and one could take over a good chunk of central Los Angeles!"

On the bridge across the Guadalquivir, equidistant between the World's Fair and the old city, Cervantes shouted with enthusiasm, "Forget that plastic futuristic 1992 crap! This is my Seville! I know its great cathedral and its infamous prison, its court of thieves and school of thieves where Rinconete and Cortadillo were instructed, and its Giralda which was already an ancient Moorish minaret when I roamed it as a boy, then being coiffed with a new Renaissance cupola.

"This was the international city of its time. By legend, Hercules built it and Caesar girdled it with strong walls. We called it the Athens of Spain for the number of its schools. When I lived here eight rivers flowed into the city: water, wine, oil, milk, honey, sugar, gold, and silver. It sat round and fat, its kilometers of walls studded with 160 towers, the flower of the Spanish empire, a place where sometimes even the beggars went on horseback.

"And sailing day! The most moving sight in the West! Every spring and fall, scores of ships massed before us in the Guadalquivir to load supplies for the colonists of the New World; every fall, scores more would arrive, pressed deep in the water by their loads of precious metals, hides, pearls, ambergris, timber, medicinal plants, spices, and sugar. As many as a hundred ships—most of them under one hundred tons displacement, with an occasional thousand-ton monster hulking over them like a fat boy in a street gang—would be moored in the port in a labyrinth of sails, masts, and cables. The streets swarmed with Portuguese, Bretons, Flemings, Ragusans, Moriscos, and blacks. And everywhere the toughs, smoothing their mustaches and glaring out of their cowls at the crowds, looking for a purse to cut, a silk kerchief to filch, perhaps a commission to dispatch a rival in love, business, or honor. From where they stood, they could also see the six prison galleys in the harbor, and like my Rinconete y Cortadillo, the sight would make them 'sigh and dread the day when they might make a mistake that would cause them to spend the rest of their lives in them.' Disaster to the fleet would spread financial panic as far away as Riga. But a safe return touched off an explosion of joy. Suddenly Seville was full of money. The stalls of the Alcaicería, the old Moorish souk, were gorged with gold and silver objects, pearls, crystal, jewels, and silks. Much of it realized off the backs of the autochthonous peoples of America, Africa, the Far East, and the South Seas. In the fine houses lining the 900 paces from the Alcaicería to the Jerez gate, the celebrations went on night and day. The flea market outside the Arsenal gate bulged with contraband bargains. Most spectacular of all were the convoys of bullion, files of hundreds of bullock carts creaking under loads of metal and precious stones.

"At the end of the Calle de las Sierpes, the discovery of América brought with it the enlargement of the royal prison to accommodate its rapidly expanding clientele. For no just reason I spent a stay there and conceived parts of the *Quijote* in one of its many dungeons. The prison of Seville was almost like a fiendish hotel. Everything was for sale, even a day pass to freedom if you had the money. You came and went through the 'gold gate' if you had the big money and the power. If you were ordinary, you entered through the 'silver gate.' If you were like me, an elderly man, almost a pauper, you entered through the 'copper gate.'

"But if you had the money for a view, even from the prison there was much to watch: pastry cooks making frog pies or the ruinously elaborate Corpus Christi festivals when players' companies in carts moved from plaza to plaza declaiming the eucharistic dramas, las autosacramentales and the scabrous farces, the scandalous zarabanda that was danced in the holy processions and even, it was said, by the nuns in the convents. In October there was the wine fair, two weeks of autumnal madness which I evoked in my portrait of the whore in *The Dogs' Colloquy*. And then the autos-da-fé, odious and frightful spectacles, but staged with crushing dignity and unsurpassed dramatic skill: the essence of exquisite evil. From the moment the procession began moving across this very bridge on the Guadalquivir to the sound of trumpets blaring the Call to Justice, until the climax in fire wrought before the huge wooden cross in the Plaza de San Francisco, a Sevillan auto was a perfect lesson in neo-Aristotelian theatrics. The holiday crowds came away from it consumed and renewed with righteous horror. I hated that so-called 'theater' and vowed, following the master of the entremeses, Lope de Rueda, to find a more smiling form of stagecraft."

At the entrance to the great cathedral of Seville, a gypsy mother ran up to Miliano and put a blood red rose into his hands. "For you!" A gypsy child of no more than eight looked mournfully at the campesino and tugged at his sleeve.

"I forgot to tell you," Cervantes said, "this city was also known for its abundance of pícaros, putas, pleytos, polvos, piedras, puercos, perros, piojos, and pulgas. But above all, gypsies. Beware all gypsies!"

Miliano wasn't sure how one confronted a gypsy whelp. "Thank you," he muttered pleasantly and moved forward toward the cathedral. Seeing her prospect simply disregarding her, the gypsy became enraged. She ran forward and confronted Miliano angrily and plucked the rose from his hands. "You thief!" she screamed. Suddenly, with Herculean energy the child all but ripped the traveling bag that debilitated Miliano had slung over his shoulder. Who knows what accoutrements are carried by the living dead!

Miliano made a move as if to discipline the disrespectful whelp and once again it was the gypsy mother's turn. She spat with practiced accomplishment on Miliano, missing his face but landing on his broad, revolutionary, peasant straw hat. This seemed to infuriate her only more. "Thief!" she screamed. A Spanish policeman who had been through this too many times looked nonchalantly from the other side of the wrought iron gate that circled the cathedral and sheltered him from the gypsies. "Calma, por favor. Let's have a little calm."

Miguel patted Miliano on the back soothingly. "Ah, the gypsies! Some things in Spain are eternal. I recall about 400 years ago close to this spot how two cheerful ones picked the sacristan's pocket." And then, admonishing the gypsy mother with his forefinger, he said, "¡Quien no vio Sevilla, no vio maravilla!" Cervantes came back to Miliano and gave him a vigorous poke in the ribs. "What do gypsies do during otherworldly apparitions?" When he saw he would get no response from the confused revolutionary, he answered himself. "They go on being gypsies, naturally!"

The three travelers queued for entrance tickets to the Sevillan cathedral, the gypsy mother cursing them all the while. Some of it was in gypsy language of which poor, mortified Miliano was blissfully ignorant. There was enough Spanish though for him to follow all too well. "Shitty foreign tourists who try and rip off a poor humble mother. Look at that one dressed in white! ¡Parece payaso! And the other one with a goatee, he looks like he came out of a museum. Who do you think you are, the great Lope de Vega? And that pendeja in the robe with them, clearly a bawd, she ought not be permitted into a holy place."

Miguel rolled his eyes in the direction of the guardia. That projection onto his person of the great Satan, Lope de Vega, was too ironic for coincidence, he thought. Maybe they were being tracked and set up by some pranksters from the ethers. The guardia of socialist Spain refused to come close, limiting himself to calling from the other side of the comforting rejas, "Now, mamá grande, stop your fuss. Remember you're pura gitana." A touring bus with Dusseldorfer marked on its side rolled up and fair-skinned people with Leicas streamed out of it. The gypsy quickly forgot her earlier targets and with an arsenal of roses in each hand moved with her son toward the newer, brighter prospects, along with lottery vendors, hawkers of nougat, hand-painted ceramics, Spanish lace made in the People's Republic of China, and Christopher Columbus quincentennial key chains.

As the three travelers moved toward the cathedral entrance, the Spanish policeman in a fine, three-cornered hat approached them. With a kind of national pride he said, "I'm sorry, Spanish gypsies, they are the worst in Europe, simply incorrigible."

Cervantes cast a sidelong glance at Emiliano Zapata. "Francisco Franco, the bad Franco, would never have tolerated them."

The guard nodded in resigned assent. "Yes, let's say that our tolerance of gypsies is a new mark of our civilized country."

Cervantes smiled. "Which is why you guard from inside the fence!"

The policeman laughed indulgently.

At the cathedral's entrance one of the informales approached them. "I'm your guide!"

Teresa looked down at him. "We don't need a guide! We are Spanish!"

"You're Spanish? You look like you came from Mars, either that or a costume party! You need a guide for sure or you'll miss everything. Did you know that this is the largest Gothic structure in the world, even though it incorporates the minaret and the outer court of the great mosque built by Yusuf II in 1172? It's also the world's third-largest church, after St. Peter's in Rome and St. Paul's in London."

With a sort of nonchalance that masked her anxiety, Teresa asked, "Do you have a relic of Santa Teresa?"

"Por supuesto we have a Santa Teresa. Doesn't everyone? Here we have the left eye of San Martín de Porres himself, St. John the XXIII's fingernail from the index finger he always pointed with, charred wood from the stake of Joan of Arc, and above all, the very bones of the greatest man who ever lived." He pointed proudly to a magnificent sepulchre just inside the cathedral entrance, borne aloft by knights representing the four medieval kingdoms of Spain, Castilla, León, Aragón, and Navarra. "Here's where Christopher Columbus, the gran almirante lies."

Miguel poked Miliano in the ribs. "Don't believe a word of it. He's also buried in the great cathedral of Santo Domingo in the Dominican Republic and a few other places." Miguel would have said a few other things, but he became concerned about Teresa. She looked grave, like she was suffering from indigestion, and he whispered to her, "Maybe this is a bad idea. We should have tried the prison instead."

Miliano gazed at the tomb of Columbus or perhaps pseudo-Columbus. Maybe he was unused to this business of apparitions, but it almost seemed that the body inside was preparing to emerge from the sepulchre, appear before them, and make a formal account of its identity. Zapata prepared for an indio challenge to the European.

They moved to a dark place. The guide said, "Quick, give me dos duros." Dutifully Cervantes looked into his money bag and produced the coins. The guide inserted them into a box and suddenly the chapel was bathed in light. The guide beamed, "See, Saint Christopher!" Cervantes poked Miliano in the ribs. "Apocryphal. Not too many decades ago, a commission of the Holy See pronounced the good saint and protector of all travelers to be toast, a mere figment of popular lore, a being that never was! You know, like Quijote and Sancho!"

"Now," the guide said, "for another five pesetas, we can light up five of the electric candles. You see, one peseta, one electric candle. They stay lit for a good ten minutes. And for twenty-five pesetas, you can light up the entire set of votive candles."

Miguel laughed. "What the capitalists call an efficiency of scale!"

Teresa gasped. "I've seen a few things in my life and a few more in my death, but this is gross!"

"Not at all, dear Tere. Merely the fine tuning of Christian worship, calibrated to the technology of our times."

The saint looked at Cervantes with irritation, then she turned to the great organ, the same that 19th century Gustavo Adolfo Bécquer had conjured in his story of ghosts. Suddenly the organ thundered forth the tune of "Old Time Religion." Was that the ghost of Gustavo himself at the immense stops?

Tourists and habitués alike came forward and the saint led them in song. Everyone, even Emiliano and Miguel, seemed to know the lyrics perfectly.

> Oh give me that old time religion
> Give me that old time religion
> Give me that old time religion It's
> good enough for me Let us pray

> with Aphrodite
> Let us pray with Aphrodite
> She wears that see-through nightie
> And it's good enough for me

> We will pray with those Egyptians
> Build pyramids to put our crypts in
> Cover subways with inscriptions
> And it's good enough for me

> We will pray with those old Druids
> They drink fermented fluids
> Waltzing naked through the woo-ods
> And it's good enough for me

> I will rise at early morning
> When the Lord gives me a warning
> That the solar age is dawning
> And that's good enough for me.

The guide was so flabbergasted that he forgot to ask for his tip. He made the sign of the cross, shouting, "This is the work of Satanás!" and fled behind the possible tomb of crypto-Columbus.

May Day had been renamed "The Day of Spring and Labor," and some of the onlookers on Red Square felt it was another of capitalism's fiascos. Diehard communists looked up at the top of the Lenin mausoleum from where the politburo used to review the parade, but it was empty. A demonstrator in traditional Cossack costume, medals plastered over his chest, exclaimed, "The government failed again! It couldn't even sell Red Square to advertisers!" He pointed to the GUM department store where a billboard advertised the lure of the Canary Islands. "Warm Nature and 328 Days of Sun!" "That's the only sign that was commissioned. They tried to sell Red Square advertisement rights for a million, and the Canaries were all they got!"

"Give them a break! They started late. It was a last minute effort."

The crowd guffawed. "That's the history of this government. Always a useless, last-minute effort!"

Another demonstrator called out, "The people cried for bread! And they were given the Canaries!"

Father Pichugin, dressed in a red cassock and known to his followers as the "red priest," warned the people. "God does not forgive those who have humiliated Mother Russia. America will be punished by a great earthquake. America will be rent apart by riots and fires." His supporters raised placards and signs. One showed Uncle Sam with the Soviet Union in the shape of a can in his grocery bag, reaching to take Cuba off the same supermarket shelf. Another said, "The Yeltsin criminals are the puppets of the U.S.A." A third warned that "The American-Israeli bourgeoisie conspired to take over Mother Russia."

Countervailed against Father Pichugin was Dr. Pirogen, who railed against the Pichuginiks and vented against the "totalitarian skygods." "Beware the skygods. Zealots read from an inferior book of the Bronze Age and gave us Judaism, Christianity, and Mohammedanism. The skygods stand for denial. They say no to equality for women, to making love to the same sex, to tolerance for others. Reject the totalitarian skygods. Take your stand with the humanists!"

A supporter of the skygods stuck his placard in the face of one of Pirogen's people. It read, "Christ, the Creator of Communism!"

Three hundred elderly men with medals and Lenin pins and red ribbons in their lapels marched in front of Lenin's tomb.

The supporters of Pichugin moved to stop them. "Death to the cult of Lenin! Hail Christ, the Creator of Communism!" The followers of Pirogen surged forward as well. "Death to the Leninites and the followers of Christian communism as well! Give us secular humanism!"

Cervantes tugged at Zapata's sleeve. "This is madness! An immense hodgepodge. Let's wait a decade for things to make some sense and return in 2002. By that time the old time communists will probably have entered the nostalgic phase." He sighed theatrically, "¡Ay, cómo echo de menos los tiempos de Don Porfirio!"

Zapata was becoming increasingly irritated with Cervantes who seemed to treat him like a naïf. Besides, this tumulto and factionalism felt familiar, like Mexico in 1914. "We should stay," he said. "Something important is coming out of this ferment. And if you tug at me or rib me again, you will be sorry for it!"

Now Miguel was upset, and so he displayed high Castilian ceremony.

A rumor ran through the crowd like a plague of locusts. Gorbachev was running away to America with the body of Lenin which he had just sold to *Forbes* magazine. See that limousine, it's Gorby and the body of Lenin, headed for the private *Forbes* airplane, "The Capitalist Tool." Infuriated, hundreds ran to block the limo. Teresa exclaimed, "Esto es una basura. We'll not find truth, nor God, nor even the Antichrist in this confused place. ¡Vámonos!"

In a kind, fatherly guise, Miguel turned to Miliano. "Looking for a tumulto? For ferment? A young man, Eddie Zapata, and his family are in big trouble in the City of Angels."

Shortly they found themselves in south-central Los Angeles. The fires were dying down. For those who had families, panic was setting in.

"You dudes! You with the beard, you güerita valentina. You

dressed all in white like a hindu at a funeral. What are you, unemployed, rampaging actors?"

"Make way," said Cervantes. "We're looking for Eddie Zapata!"

Wolfie Lobo piped up. "I don't know whether to off them or laugh at them! Man. They're nothing. They're jafos. Out to get a story."

Miguel responded in what he believed to be the local germanía. "No way, homes. We're no jafos. We've seen the shit come down. We see how the pigs pull you off your wheels all the time, for no fucking reason at all, treat you like garbage."

"That's right, the pigs! This time they gonna pay. They beat up on Rodney King and they beat up on us all the time. We gonna mess them up."

"But not this way," Zapata said. "You've got to fix your targets. This messing up just anybody who gets in your way, all the inocentes, that's not right. Eso es el caos. You've got to have a strategy."

"You a funny dude. Who do you think you are, a general or something? These are days of rage."

"Why you burning all this down? Where are you going to sleep tomorrow?"

A rap man spoke up. "Fuck tomorrow. I tell you how it is. I was born in America. Does this seem like America? We be mad, we be bad. The outsiders come in and take our money and move out. It be payback time."

A cholo brandished his fila. "¡Que chinga la mañana! Tomorrow we, or you, may be dead. Let tomorrow take care of its own, we control today!"

"Aw come on," Wolfie Lobo said. "¡No te exaltes!"

"They're bad, man. They gonna hurt us!"

A man who looked like a true Zapata to Miliano came forward. "Let him be, that's Loco. He's got that placa 'cause he's as loco as a coco and just out of the psycho ward. Let him be and he'll calm down."

The cholo only became more infuriated. "Cállate el hocico, pinche Eddie. Aquí viene mi movida. I'm gonna cut these fucking bolillos open. This indio is the coco, brown on the outside and all white inside. And that white woman ought to be a statue in church! Alabaster bitch, I'll cut you too!"

Teresa rushed forward and hugged Loco hard. He let out air like a flat tire, and she thrust her sainted tongue down his mouth. The cholo's legs crumpled, and she let him down gently. He sat in a lotus position, fila in hand, his head tilted beatifically to heaven.

"Hey, lady, what the hell you do to him?"

"I just loved him up!"

"Jesus," Wolfie Lobo circled the cholo who seemed to be in a deep rapture. "What you kiss him with, a cattle prod?"

Teresa smiled authoritatively. "You need the power of positive thinking!"

Miliano went up to the man called Eddie and identified himself as an authentic Zapata from Morelos.

"And you say you're the real Zapata?"

"I am."

"I mean you're the real one, from the real family?"

"That's right."

"What's your name? Your whole name."

"Emiliano. Emiliano Zapata."

"Isn't that . . . Wasn't that the name of the original chingón?"

"Sure."

"So what are you, his nephew or something?"

"Yeah, maybe grandson."

"Well, I'm Eddie Zapata. It's funny that I hadn't met you in el barrio before. I guess it took these riots to make it happen!"

Miliano tried out his newly acquired caló. "¡Qué desmadre that it took a riot against the cuicos for the batos around Los to really cotorear."

"¡Orale, raza! Now we've got these cuicos marranos totally futi futi! Did you see how those 12 black and whites that moved on Florence and Vermont se rajaron?"

"Seguro que sí, ¡viva la revolución!"

Eddie looked at his pariente incredulously. "You really into that Zapata shit, aren't you, carnal? Forget the revolución, man. At this point I need a roof over my head and some diapers and milk for la nenita. You know they burned me out? Los mismos carnales. I don't blame them; they didn't know it was me. We got burned out on Wednesday, and we've been camping out in the basement of the First African Methodist Episcopal ever since. They're the only people who've helped me. Can you help a carnal, Emiliano?"

Miliano looked at him very solemnly. "I don't live anywhere."

"Hey man, I can relate. You living out of your car? What wheels you drive?"

Miliano wasn't sure what to answer. He thought of Marlon Brando in *The Wild One*. "Harley Davidson."

"¡Ah, un bato juilador! You run with the Angels?"

"You could say that."

"Runs with the Angels. All right. You not really a homeboy, are you, carnal? 'Cause if you were then I would know you. Eso lo explica todo, runs with the Angels. Anyway, carnal, your machine ever tap out, come see me. I'm the best freelance mechanic, el mejor informal off of Crenshaw. I'll fix your machine real good, I work right out of the middle of the street. Mira carnal, I've got two kids, six years old and two months old. There's no milk or diapers left in this barrio. Can you help me out? A little advance on work to be performed? After all, we've got the same placa."

Suddenly, Teresa disappeared and soon she reappeared with a gallon of milk and the largest box Eddie had ever seen filled with Huggies.

Eddie turned from the groceries to Loco the cholo who seemed as happy as a toddler in a sandbox on the smouldering ground of the City of Angels. Eddie scratched his head. He looked into the cholo's face. The fila was in Loco's hand tight as a rattle. "Ga Ga, Goo Goo."

Teresa came up to him, and Eddie turned pale and backed off. Quickly he picked up the groceries. "This is like a miracle! See you, carnales." And he was off.

*   *   *

Lefty Womack felt they were a motley crew. He had come from the Boston airport to meet the rest of the entourage at Miami and Miguel León-Portilla with whom he had a difficult relationship had come up from Mexico City for the same purpose. The Phoenix group consisted of César Chávez, who had just received a doctorate, honoris causa, from Arizona State University, and an assortment of other Phoenicians that included the young migrant worker turned experimental psychologist, José Náñez, the distinguished left-wing historian, Estevan Galarza, and a weirdo who called himself Huichli-pichli, or Huitzilopochtli. No, his name was El Huitlacoche, although Lefty didn't understand why anybody would call himself that since he knew it to be Aztec fungus that grew on corn and was considered gourmet fare in Mesoamérica. This guy represented himself as a "street poet" who had written verse about Zapata for the American

1976 bicentennial, replete with old Posada images of calaveras, that he claimed Chicanos still read with enthusiasm.

The Phoenix group was going to participate in a ceremony featuring César Chávez on October 12, Columbus Day, at the American pavilion of Expo '92 in Seville. Womack and León-Portilla were headed together, rather ironically the Harvard professor judged, for the Mexican pavilion on the same day. Some 15 years ago, León-Portilla had taken Lefty to task in his book, *Los manifiestos en náhuatl de Emiliano Zapata,* written on the occasion of the centenary of the revolutionary's birth. He had criticized Womack's own book, *Zapata and the Mexican Revolution,* for its downplaying of Zapata's knowledge of Nahuatl and Womack's claim that the revolutionary did not show much initiative in bringing indios into the Mexican Revolution. Womack had decided that 15 years of tension was enough and that 1992 was the time to clear the air; he was determined to approach the Mexican scholar in order to resolve the lingering disgustos.

Lefty admired César Chávez. When he had the opportunity, he asked the Chicano leader something that he had wanted to verify for a long time. "César, is it true that as a youth you actually lived in a barrio in San Jose called 'Sal Si Puedes'?"

César smiled so gently, so winningly, it was his trademark. "Yes, but if you think that is very novel, you shouldn't. The term 'Sal Si Puedes' has a venerable past. Even in Cervantes's time, the then new capital of Madrid had its one back alley called Sal Si Puedes."

The entourage arrived in Seville the following morning, checked in at their hotel, and immediately went to bed, having been in flight all night. They agreed to go out together later. Lefty woke up earlier, about six, and went on his own to a local bar where he had arranged to meet his former graduate student, Alfonso Caso y Casas. Alfonso was waiting for him on a bar stool. The physiognomy of his head was unmistakable; he looked like a pure-blooded Maya, a living model for a frieze out of a Palenque temple. Lefty had great affection for Alfonso, who had overcome poverty to earn a degree with highest honors at the Universidad Nacional Autónoma de México and then had gone to Harvard for his graduate work. Lefty hadn't seen him since he had been made head of national security of the Republic of Mexico.

Over sherry and tapas, gambas al ajillo and octopus salad, Lefty reminisced with his student. "I never would have predicted that you would end up the chief spook of the Republic of Mexico!"

"Me neither, but then again, I never would have predicted that Salinas de Gortari would become President of Mexico!"

"Will you come out with us tonight, Alfonso? César Chávez is everything I hoped for. Humble, authoritative, charismatic; there is almost a halo around his head!"

"Profe, you always veered toward romanticism despite your hardheaded, left-leaning calculus! I would love to, but I simply can't!"

"Why don't you just cancel out whatever you're doing and go with us? There's even a street poet with a Nahuatl name. Together, we may just be able to lance his ego. By myself, I'm sure I'll fail."

"I'd love to, but the security issues are too complicated. I'm here strictly on business. You wouldn't want to read that César died of food poisoning, would you? Especially since he fasts so much nobody is sure he eats at all!"

"Alfonso, is there something I should know about?"

"No, Profe, other than the normal 1992 expectations. Is there anything that I should know about?"

Lefty paused. "Maybe, as you put it, it's the normal 1992 ballyhoo, but I've been feeling, well, funny. It's been going on for months."

Alfonso looked at him quizzically. "Funny you should mention it."

"You too?"

"Yeah, but of course, I don't know if it's because of my job. After all, I'm *paid* to feel funny. On the other hand, at nights when I look up, it's like a different sky. The heavens feel like they're about to give birth. And then, there's been these recurring dreams. And forebodings."

"What kind of dreams?"

"I don't know. Dreams of change, or renewal. If I had only one word, I'd use birthing."

"Alfonso, in this age of feminism, pregnancy's not just for women anymore!"

"You've been feeling funny too then?"

"Yeah, especially about my work. Especially about Emiliano Zapata. I read his *Manifesto to the Mexican People* the other day and I began to cry. Suddenly the words had a freshness and a relevance that I hadn't experienced since the days I did my own doctoral dissertation on the revolution of the South."

"You could have picked a worse hero."

"What the heck. I hadn't thought I would start off my Columbus Day presentation with Zapata. When I was first invited to Seville as a guest of your government, I thought I'd start out with something more ninety-twoish. Perhaps something from Columbus's letters to the Reyes Católicos, or Bernal Díaz del Castillo. Perhaps Fray Bartolomé de las Casas on the decimation of the Indians. The ghost of Zapata got the best of me. Either that or my overweening ego, and so you'll hear the *Manifesto* from me first off day after tomorrow. You're coming to that, aren't you?"

"Wouldn't miss it for the world. Of course, I might be packing a rod and scanning the crowd for soreheads! Kidding aside, I can't wait to hear what you have to say, although it might have the possible side effect of increasing my pregnant condition!"

Lefty laughed heartily. "What the heck! We're all waiting for Zapata! Alfonso, I breathe easier with you as Mexico's chief spook. With your historical knowledge and both your Western and traditional upbringing, if anybody can decode the heavens satisfactorily, it's you. You're perfect for both national security and for soothsaying. Clearly Salinas or the gods know something!"

Later that evening Lefty and the rest of the entourage that would represent either Mexico or the United States on Columbus Day found themselves in one of the local bistros, El Rincón del Gitano. Right away Huichlipichli or whatever had to prove his street authenticity. He went for Lefty. "Hey, Harvard boy! Sport me a bota of red and I'll show you how I pour it from afar into my mouth."

"That's a lot to sport, street dude, for something I've seen done many times."

"Is that so, gringo dude? Then sport me a bota and I'll let wine land on the middle of my forehead and trickle down between the socket of my left eye and the side of my nose onto my esthete's tongue and down my Chicano barriga. I'll do it the mero gitano Andalucian way. Have you seen that, Cambridge dude?"

"No, and maybe I'll sport your street-writing self to some fine red wine if first you kiss my Cambridge ass and apologize to me in your huichlipichli style."

Estevan Galarza, so noble and diplomatic, smoothed things over. "It would be an honor to subvent our dear Chicano poet laureate his first bota of fine Sevillan wine." He called for the waiter.

Looking with disdain at both Womack and León-Portilla, Huichli turned to Estevan. "Esto se lo brindo al mejor y más honorable scholar at the table." He poured the wine with a firm hand. It hit his forehead, splashed all over his clothes, and spotted some others as well. The entire table howled with laughter. A Spanish waiter hustled forward with a napkin. "Shit," Huitla said. "At least I tried! What have you querulous miedosos ever ventured? Excepting of course Don César, who is a secular saint." With that, the street poet took the leather bota and put it in his mouth like a bottle of soda pop and consumed it in one very long draught. Soon he was drunk and demanding another flagon of red in order to recite his bilingual artifices which he called "real poetría."

Lefty said, "I'll pay you not to recite. What'll it be, street poet, the wine or the words?"

José Náñez, who by now was a bit tipsy, chimed in as well. "Tú que eres poeta, y en el aire los compones. Hazme una chaqueta sin bajarme los calzones."

With the arrogance that only a spurned artist can summon, Huitla refused Bacchus and recited from his 1976 bicentennial poem, "The Urban(e) Chicano's 76." It was one of his fondest creations. In 1976, he had traveled the Southwest reciting it at fairs, colleges, prisons, and an occasional shopping mall, and wherever he recited it, committed Chicanas wanted to meet him.

> Pues, I'm just a vato loco man
> but if I had my way again
> I'd ask for 'Miliano Zapata's rise
> Steinbeck claims he never died
> I crave that dude at my side
> I'd deal him aces at Circus-Circus
> under the glazed gaze of the pit boss
> Man, I'd drag him to the Catskills
> learn him all my washing dish skills
> We'd sing Mex war songs like 30-30
> drink a little and talk some dirty,
> Oh yeah, we'd besport like meros machos
> make it with couple of blondas gabachas
> I'd take you see a double flick
> *¡Viva Zapata!* and *Wild One!*—what you think?
> Maybe we'd take dead John's advice
> learn ourselves to read and write.

Lefty was incensed with the farcical impertinence of this logrón and payaso. "This is without a doubt the worst piece of doggerel I've ever heard! Who's your muse, Cheech? Or is it Chong?"

The next day the party visited Expo '92. They had the Sunday free to tour. Tomorrow, Columbus Day, they were on the program. They took the cable car from Seville proper across the eastern branch of the Guadalquivir, and it left them on the island of Cartuja just next to the Moroccan replica of a Moorish palace, fit for, well, King Hassan. José Náñez said that César Chávez was particularly interested in visiting the Basque pavilion.

"Why is that?"

César explained that he had been invited to las vascongadas earlier in 1992 to visit the famous cooperatives of Mondragón, which the Catholic church had established during the franquista period. They were a notable example of unifying agricultural workers even in a fascist, authoritarian state. Francisco Franco had not wanted to confront the Church.

León-Portilla smiled ironically. "Oh, the bad Francisco Franco. We zapatistas . . ." He looked with coldness at Lefty Womack even as he included him in the set, "have a good Francisco Franco, Zapata's trusted friend and the last calpuleque of the original village of Anenecuilco!"

The party headed toward the pavilions of Spain's 17 regions ringing the artificial Lago España. Lefty soon ducked off by himself though. He felt too tense with León-Portilla there since he had not gotten a moment to talk to him privately. And that street clown Huichlipichli didn't make him feel any more at ease. He determined to experience Expo '92 as if he were a metal filing obeying the magnetized flow of crowds. He had no fixed expectations and only time for a very quick fix. To be abroad in October was inappropriate, and essentially he had only this one free day to visit the great Sevillan fair. Classes were in full swing, and he had to return to Harvard as soon as practical. The throng sped him to the Japanese exhibit which the locals, in their goal to establish an international hierarchy of pavilions, had awarded status as the jewel of the fair. The Japanese had eschewed the brayings of high tech video that abounded most everywhere else in Expo '92 and had created what was billed as the largest wooden building in the world. Lefty thought he had already seen the record holder in medieval, Buddhist-dominant Nara. The structure evoked a temple but with an escalator leading to its heights. The crowd admired the human face of Japan: the full-size colored photographs of ordinary Japanese, the images of Nippon's countryside done in the traditional origami style, the reproduction of an entire section of the 16th-century Azuchi castle in perfect detail.

The people and Lefty decided that architectural awards went to Britain with its water cascade down a huge fashionable glass front, to Germany for its front patio shaded by an enormous painter's palette, to France with its stunning mirrored courtyard, to Canada for its walkways suspended from thick wire, and to Switzerland for its enormous paper tower. Mexico's pavilion had the quality of an insider's joke to Lefty. It had a long arm that ended in two imposing Xs and the scholar was reminded of the wildly idiosyncratic author of the Spanish generation of 1898, bearded Ramón del Valle Inclán, who had decided to visit Mexico allegedly because of the mysteriousness of the middle X in the country's name and who subsequently wrote a haunting and painful novel of Mexican rural manners and caciquismo, *Tirano Banderas*.

In front of the Mexican pavilion the famed Voladores de Papantla were preparing to do their flying spectacle, a headfirst ballet on ropes attached to a high pole. The Voladores had survived Spanish repression because the Conquistadors had thought of it as a sport rather than a pagan rite. Also, Hernán Cortés had taken kindly to the Totonacas of Veracruz, the practioners of the spectacle, who were the first Amerindians to ally themselves with the Spaniards. In fact, the dance, although it was performed Sunday afternoons after mass, was a pre-Columbian Nahua ritual of time, space, and fertility. It involved five men, a leader who provided music on flute and drum and four performers. They represented the five earthly directions— the four cardinal points and the center, from earth to heaven. The five climbed to a small platform atop the pole. The leader played and directed prayers for the fertility of the land in every direction while the four dancers tied ropes, coiled tightly around the top of the pole, to their waists and flung themselves headfirst into space. The onlookers gasped at this bold and dangerous move. As the indios voladores spiralled down in ever-increasing circles, they made 13 revolutions, each symbolizing the 52-year cycle of the Nahua calendar. At the last moment they righted themselves up as they touched ground. The onlookers cheered.

Lefty knew the Voladores very well, having seen them perform for Corpus Christi and on Sunday afternoons in front of he Papantla church, and even more impressively at the Pyramid of the Niches in the magnificent archaeological site of El Tajín in the state of Veracruz.

It was time to have lunch. Restaurant food seemed outrageously expensive, so he opted with the pueblo for fast food, what seemed like acceptable enough calamar a la romana, unfortunately fried to rubbery imperfection, downed with a wonderfully icy bottle of beer, and finally helado from one of the veritable army of itinerant vendors.

With the pueblo, Lefty climbed over the reproduction of the Niña, the Pinta, and the Santa María, amazed at their miniscule scale. It was like returning to the setting of his Norman, Oklahoma, childhood and finding that what once had seemed grand structures and open spaces were now almost comically small. Lefty and everyone else stopped to stare at a piece of Antarctic iceberg that Chile had lugged over the seven seas, to gaze at the denizens in Monaco's walk-through aquarium, to admire a Bedouin desert tent, to experience the recreated tropical jungles of Costa Rica, Honduras, and Panamá, and to admire a Hungarian tree with roots displayed under a glass floor. He touched a section of the Berlin wall and tears welled in the professional historian's eyes at the memory of that November morning in 1989 when he had awoken, turned on CNN, and to his utter amazement found the German people atop the wall, partying and pickaxing. Along with the crowd, he utterly ignored the endless models of spacecraft in front of the Russian pavilion (it had originally been designed for the USSR), opting instead to witness a bell-ringing performance in front of a model Russian Orthodox church.

Great art was everywhere. The Holy See had weighed in with a celebration of the quincentenary of the evangelization of the Americas with works by Spanish and Italian Old Masters and religious art from Europe and America and a collection of pre-Columbian pieces from Amerindia. Italy had brought flying machines by da Vinci, the Netherlands displayed Rembrandt, Mondrian, and Van Gogh. Even the Spanish regions like Aragón had their own art displays with 10 additional Goyas. Lefty turned from the crowd at this point, which was more interested in experiencing Panamanian salsa, Brazilian samba, and Argentine tango. Instead he lingered in the treasures section of the Spanish pavilion. The array of works! El Greco, Rivera, Murillo, Zurbarán, Velázquez, Goya, Picasso, Miró, and Dalí.

And then there was the United States pavilion, scraped together with insufficient funds. The main U.S. exhibit was dedicated to the Bill of Rights, with Connecticut's version of the original placed on a stage surrounded by pillars and flowers as if waiting to be worshiped.

Lefty returned to his hotel room worn out. He was too tired even to go to dinner with the rest of the entourage. He stayed in his room and ate food he had brought up from the bar, an order of fresh anchovies, a wedge of tortilla española, and green olives stuffed with blanched almonds. He washed the food down with a bottle of lovely vinho verde. He decided to go over his speech one last time and hit the sack.

The year 1992. It hadn't meant all that much to him. Now, with what had happened and what was transpiring around the globe, it meant quite a lot. He thought wryly, the year 1992 and the year 2010; he would need to compare them, if he made it to the later date. That would be his year, 2010. Still, these premonitions. The feeling of presence, a beckoning. Sometimes Lefty woke up short of breath. It was as if his conscience bothered him, as if there were almas en pena depending on him, whom he shouldn't let down.

Lefty reviewed the translation that he had done of Zapata's 1918 manifesto. It was the last important manifesto that the revolutionary had signed. He felt slightly embarrassed because he was so closely associated with Zapata in the academic world. But Lefty decided that he'd start with Zapata, the great calpuleque of Anenecuilco because, after all, the Mexican warrior truly reflected an Indian viewpoint in the 20th century. Zapata and zapatismo, with all their attendant glories and limitations, they were genuinely indio. And they went back. Their logic, which achieved so little reception, went back to the Council of the Indies and the virreinatos and to much before that, to the pre-Columbian division of property and administration of rights. One might argue that, for 20th-century Native Americans over the entire continent from Baffin Island to Tierra del Fuego, Emiliano Zapata was the greatest American Indian revolutionary model of them all. There would be few other serious contenders for that distinction. So, to bind this quincentenary business, to go back to 1492 and centuries before that, and to touch upon the 20th century, one not formed primarily by Western philosophies such as Marxism, anarchism, socialism, capitalism, one still discernably Indian at its core, to project into the future, and the surely forthcoming struggles of native peoples to empower themselves, who better than the caudillo of tierra y libertad?

Lefty began to turn the pages of the *Manifesto to the Mexican People* of 1918 and to rehearse his reading. It was a remarkable document that Zapata had signed, authored primarily by Conrado Díaz Soto y Gama, and its emphasis on the rights of the Indian and on land reform seemed remarkably relevant to today's issues, even among revolutionaries and liberation theologists in Latin America. Lefty sighed. He was so very tired. He had fought so many battles in the academic halls and elsewhere. He fell asleep, in situ, as it were, on top of the hotel bed with manuscripts on his chest. An hour before dawn on October 12, 1992, he was awakened by a fierce electric storm outside. A delta of lightning from the heavens came into his room but attenuated and softened by the blinds. It diffused the room with radiant pale green and blue light and gently touched his translation and haloed it for a moment, as if to give it life and send it on its way. He turned to the translation. Not enough sleep and obsessed by noble, tragic ghosts of the past. He would be shot by the end of this day too, surely, but he supposed the adrenaline would get him through. Like always. One final read of the manifesto and then prepare for dawn and the morrow.

MANIFESTO TO THE MEXICAN PEOPLE

We believe that our first and highest duty is to fulfill the trust that the Mexican people have deposited in us and in our armed defense of and ultimate revindication of our people's liberty. Thus the time has come to formulate before the Mexican people a clear and precise profession of our faith, and to make a frank statement of our goals and objectives.

Where goes the Revolution? What propose we children of the people who have risen in arms?

The Revolution proposes: to redeem the Indian race, returning its lands and, therefore, restoring its freedom to it; to permit those who work the fields and who are now slaves of the haciendas to become free persons and shapers of their own destinies by means of ownership of small properties; to improve the economic, intellectual, and moral status of urban workers, protecting them against capitalist oppression; to abolish dictatorship and to wrest broad and effective political freedoms for the Mexican people.

This is the essential program of the Revolution; but to develop it, to establish each element in detail, to obtain an adequate solution to each problem and in order not to forget the special circumstances of certain regions or the particular needs of specific populations, it is necessary to count on the support of all of the revolutionaries in the country and to understand the positions of each of them.

In each region of the country special needs make their presence known and for each there are and there should be solutions that accommodate themselves to specific circumstances. This is why we do not attempt the absurdity of imposing one fixed, uniform position; rather, in the attempt to improve the condition of the Indian and of the proletariat—the supreme goal of the Revolution—we wish that the leaders who represent diverse states or jurisdictions of the Republic offer themselves as interpreters of the wishes, needs, and aspirations of their respective groups, and, in this fashion, by means of a mutual and fraternal intercommunication of ideas, the program of the Revolution will be elaborated, accounting for and satisfying local needs, incorporating the goals of everyone, and establishing the foundations for the reconstruction of our national identity.

And in order to avoid the exercise of undue influence over the Revolution by any exclusivist faction or personage, we have agreed to adopt the following simple procedure: as soon as the revolutionary forces occupy the capital of the Republic, a meeting will be set where all of the revolutionary leaders from around the nation will gather, without exclusion of any faction or banner. At this meeting viewpoints will be interchanged and each group will air its opinion, and each will state the special goals and the needs of the region in which it operates.

At this meeting, therefore, the national voice will be heard. The voice of the people represented ably by its children who have risen in arms, through a Congress of the Union as the authentic and genuine organ of the common purpose, will diligently move to resolve our national problems as soon as a provisional revolutionary government is established.

The leaders who will attend this meeting will express their viewpoints or the principles that each desires to see converted into laws or elevated to the status of constitutional precepts, once the government that has emanated from the Revolution is formed. At that meeting also, by general agreement (and not by the willful imposition of one man or one single group as the carrancistas operate), a provisional government will be established, composed of conscientious and honorable representatives who will satisfy the revolutionary aspirations and who will be led by a civilian Chief of State, designated by and sincerely supported by all of the military elements.

Agrarian reform, revindication of the workers, purification and improvement of the administration of justice, constitutional establishment of municipal prerogatives, establishment of parlamentarianism as the saving system of government, abolition of local bossism in all of its forms, enhancement of the various branches of the legislature so that it responds to the need of our times and to the demands of the urban and rural proletariat, all of this, seriously considered and discussed extensively and openly by all, will form the marrow and the soul of the revolutionary program, the base and the launching point for national reconstruction.

Against such a patriotic, inclusive, fraternal, and progressive project only the personally ambitious would refrain from joining; only those who presume to impose their will against that of everyone else; or those who would pretend to use the Revolution in order to realize personal gain, lucre, or revenge would deny.

But those of us who rise above our passions for the good of the cause, who set aside any personal ambition for the supreme interests of the Republic, understand very well that it is now time to unite and come to a common understanding. The hour has arrived for peace to emerge from victory, the peace that follows triumph; it is now necessary that we return to the tranquility of our homes, that we open the doors of our shops, that we permit the rebirth of credit around the nation, and frankly, that we permit the channeling of the national effort in the direction of progress.

Self-serving Carranza impedes all of this and he must be toppled. Old rancors, bothersome suspicions, vulgar passions also intrude and they must be removed, we must expunge them.

We base the triumph of our ideals and the reconstruction of the Mexican homeland on the union of all honorable revolutionaries, military and civilian, on the cordial rapprochement of all partisans, and on a mutual and freely established consensus of all parties.

And so that there be a document that manifests our solemn obligation to fulfill these promises made now and those made earlier, we commit to paper our signatures on the above, with which we pledge our dignity as men and our honor as revolutionaries.

Reform, Freedom, Justice, and Law.

Signed in Tlaltizapán, Morelos, April 25, 1918

The Commanding General of the Liberating Army
EMILIANO ZAPATA

* * *

What a fine development, thought Miliano, that he who since 1919 had become such a masculine icon in the phenomenal world should assume the mystic guise of woman to meet and share rapture with his beloved. In this Emiliano Zapata obeyed the orthodoxies of the Spanish mystic tradition. Teresa had told him of her beloved St. John of the Cross, her disciple and assistant, and how together they had midwifed a marvelous new spiritual order of Discalced Carmelites in the phenomenal world. She had taught him St. John's mystic poetry. Emiliano had bypassed the allegory of the purgation of the soul in its darkest night and had responded directly to the imagery of the furtive lover sneaking from her home by the secret stairway to meet her beloved. He took his imagery straight; Teresa was not troubled, for was not this the whole point of the vía iluminativa?

> En una noche oscura,
> con ansias en amores inflamada,
> ¡Oh dichosa ventura!,
> salí sin ser notada,
> estando ya mi casa sosegada.
>   A escuras y segura,
> por la secreta escala disfrazada,
> ¡oh dichosa ventura!,
> a escuras y en celada,
> estando ya mi casa sosegada.

Now he, Zapata, was the disciple and the assistant and would be her secular arm in any and all of the marvelous things that she would wish wrought. The poetry of amorous rapture coursed euphorically in his veins as he prepared to become one with his beloved. St. John's "Dark Night of the Soul" seemed to Miliano almost directly written for him, who had died and been reborn through the power of love. He found himself singing the lines of the poem to an old revolutionary melody as he made ready.

¡Oh noche que guiaste!
¡oh noche amable más que el alborada!
¡oh noche que juntaste
Amado con amada,
amada en el Amado transformada!

When it was time, Zapata flew into the arms of his Beloved and in her amorous embrace his cares were drained, and he was filled with her love and boundless confidence.

Quedéme y olvidéme,
el rostro recliné sobre el amado,
cesó todo, y dejéme,
dejando mi cuidado
entre las azucenas olvidado.

Après mystic rapture, for everyone comes down eventually from the slopes, Miliano spoke solemnly. "Dearest Teresa, I traveled with you in the phenomenal world and now I must know what only you can tell me."

She smiled mischievously. It was the same old thing and how could it not be so? Why, wherefore, and whither! "Why ask me and not Miguel de Cervantes who also traveled with you long and hard? Or some other ánima in pena of this mundo? Mine is not the power of the word! I think we had better call on Miguel!"

"God save me from that razor-tongued devil!"

"Come now, what's become of the compact of the three manqués?"

But Zapata had grown in experience and confidence, and he was firm in his resolve. "I've fallen hard for you, Tere! Just like Juan Diego for his Lupe!"

Teresa blushed and her long, divine, unorthodox hair swung and emitted a shimmering halo. "¡Qué piropo! But Mexican men are always falling hard for their Spanish saints. Especially Juan Diego and his virgin. Look what together they wrought!"

"Then help me! Tell me!"

Teresa sniffed. "As for me, María Magdalena was the saint of my deepest devotion. I could relate to her circumstances, and after all, except for Mother herself, she was the closest to God." Then la santa said, "I see then that you are about ready for solo flight."

"Yes," said Miliano. "Give me my orders!"

"I have none."

"Tell me my purpose in this phenomenal world!"

"Dear heart, if only I could. But I am ignorant!"

Zapata sighed. His cares had returned. "I knew this, Teresa. Then, only I can fathom my purpose for being reborn in this here and now? And must I decipher my responsibilities even as I go errabundo and tuerto in the world?"

"In essence, nothing has changed, Miliano."

"You have given me your love, and it has made me. If there are no certainties, at least tell me your faith! What do you believe after 410 years of reviewing this phenomenal world?"

"I will not tease or tantalize you, dear heart. Verily, I knew that when you were ready to solo, you would come to me seeking ultimate knowledge. I cannot offer you ultimate knowledge for ultimately I am a poor dismembered woman, plantada in this phenomenal world. But I do believe that you have purpose in 1992 and that your awakening is not entirely of your own doing, much less of chance, but rather of some authorial artifice beyond you, beyond us all. What I believe is that you and I are re-membering. The physical members, so dismembered, are re-membering, the soul and the heart recollect themselves. And the intellect re-members itself into the future. And the future is potentially glorious!"

"I'm sure that I did not awaken for nothing! But I'm in this here and now of 1992, not 1919! And everything has changed, the sands have shifted, what was a valley is now a peak. What can I do in 1992 when I failed in 1919? Do I need to do anything at all?"

"Well, we re-member into the future anyway, whether we wish to or not. If you were living in 1919 the psychological phenomenon would be the same! Memories of crimes past like your betrayal or the suppression of the aboriginal peoples do not hang dead in the air. On the contrary, the dynamics that shaped attitudes and the forces that caused travesties to be committed still function and need to be re-membered." Teresa became very solemn. "But I will tell you why I believe at least I still commit to this phenomenal world." She smiled playfully, "And it's not only re-membering physically with an ardent lover such as yourself, splendid conceit though that may be! It is that I sense the essence of Him in this phenomenal world. And of course, it is Him I seek, for I am Teresa de Jesús. Some divine or another, probably St. Augustine, once said, 'God did not create the world and then quit.' "

"God help me, Teresa. Need I be a Christian to love you? I've had a bittersweet attitude toward the Church, at least the Mexican church. I don't know if I'm a Christian. The gods course through me, your Christ on one side, on the other Quetzalcoatl and his peers. And then, well, good Soto y Gama instructed me in the anarchists and anarcho-syndicalists, and we valued them too and what was to become their great atheistic enterprise for social justice and the desengaño del pueblo. What I believe in is you and you alone, ¡De Teresa soy, Tereso soy!"

"Very flattering, duckie. But remember, Christian, Nahua, or atheist, you go now on a solo flight. All I can tell you is my limited faith. You know there was this French priest, what a piece of work was he who died on Easter Sunday 1955!"

She saw how he stiffened at the mention of what he considered another rival. And worse, that she would apply words from a rival's mouth to clarify his own Zapatesque dilemma! The euphoric, willing boy who would be taught to fly by Mother Teresa, but on a boy's terms. The same old story, these masculine routines. But she resolved that to the extent she could, she would focus on what was novel and important. "This man believed so devoutly in Him. But what was genuinely important was his science. This priest was a scientist, and he found the presence of God in the application of his science. He was an evolutionist, and he found that man and the cosmos were evolving, mentally, socially, physically toward a final unity. Isn't that a providential stroke? The unreconstructed materialists claimed that it was enough to teach the scientific conception of humankind and the cosmos for the outdated myth of religion to disappear forever. And that which they used to destroy faith, this scientist, expert in the evolutionary origins of humankind, used to confirm it! He did not deny any part of the phenomenal world. No more, but also no less. He would say to me, 'nothing but the phenomenon, yet the whole phenomenon.' And so he helped the technologically and scientifically advanced people of this age rediscover faith without their having to alter their scientific conception of this world, simply by coming to a better understanding of its true significance. And he helped the millions of people who have no technological prowess to separate the scientific from the magical or the supernatural and to find the spiritual presence in scientific phenomena themselves."

She paused and was filled with great compassion for poor Miliano who looked at her with some comprehension of what she said, but with the same fear and uncertainty she had seen in him all the while. A dead and reborn revolutionary, wanting and willing to do the right thing, almost obliged to justify his rebirth and taxed almost daily by new facts and strange, brain-stretching hypotheses. How he wanted to be given marching orders so he could sally forth and uncritically accomplish justice for his pueblo and vindication for the trust placed in him by his very rebirth. She asked him, "When I put my tongue down the throat of that poor exaltado in Los Angeles, it bothered you?"

He nodded. "I thought he'd do you harm."

"That's not at all what you thought!"

"No, I wanted to kill him! And not with love!"

"But you died in the fire of rage and now you are reborn in the phenomenal world and not the ethers. Could it be that the world in its evolution is accruing love? In the phenomenal world, scientists have discovered or predicted basic particles, entities that are hypothesized to be the basic constituents of matter or mediators of all physical forces. These entities discovered or predicted include the leptons and the quarks, the basic constituents of the atom, the gluons that govern the strong nuclear force, the weakons that control the weak nuclear force, the gravitons that intermediate the force of gravity, and the photons that define the electromagnetic force. My 410 years of review of the phenomenal world, as you put it earlier, and my intercourse with scientists who investigate humankind and the cosmos lead me to similar hypotheses on the evolution of caring love. Is it possible that there is a physical quality to love, that it is an asset, or say a particle like the gluons? Could it be that when these assets, this accrual of caringly configured loveons or love-ins or buen amor or whatever, reaches a critical mass, then all sorts of marvelous phenomena are triggered? Caring people return to life, the heavens are filled with rare occurrences, the earth takes another quantum leap toward its evolved destiny to a spiritual unity that we can barely fathom now, but that, nevertheless, vislumbra, reveals itself as a glimmer tantalizing us with possibilities?"

"If the world moves forward to a more spiritual, caring purpose, and I can do my tiny little thing to advance that purpose, so I will. I can't help but do so. I have come to adore you, even not as a manly warrior but in my mystical guise of woman, opening myself to your ardent, caring shaft. But that is nothing—mere role reversal."

"Mere role reversal! My, we advance quickly in the afterlife!"

"I don't know about the world and its evolutionary flight, but I know that I still love you, want you for my own, want to declare my fealty to you, take your commands or your words to any quarter of the earth. I want to be your man, your caballero, your staunch arm on this earth!"

"Pobrecito Miliano. And pobrecito Miguel. We are the three mancos. The three manqués. He is the most genial, endearing masculinist who has brought words to life, and you are the most ardent, endearing masculinist who has moved forward the agenda for social justice. Please rest assured that if I should wish to be possessed by a glorious and just revolutionary, you will be the one!"

Zapata looked at her with a great sadness that bordered on resignation. She knew that he was what he was and that neither time, death and rebirth, nor the great authorial artifice could alter that. She said, "But surely a poor woman who lived the double standard her entire phenomenal life will not ask you to be more than true to your own human condition. Accept my love in your own fashion. I don't ask more of you, at least today. For while the new ordering might come tomorrow, I take your love as you give it, with all of your jealousy and desires for ownership. Yours, Zapata, surely must be glorious revolution! Why else would you revive? Go out and do it in 1992! And by the way, since you've been given a second chance, do it right!" Then she added as an afterthought, "And lest I be misconstrued, remember that 'blessed are the gentle, for they shall inherit the earth.' "

*   *   *

Zapata went into the hinterlands of Morelos where there were no genuine roads, electricity, or telephones and where only the mere trappings of Hispania had penetrated and the spirit of Quetzalcoatl still thrived. But portable radio had arrived and even battery-operated VCRs with miniature cassettes. He talked with Pedro, an old indio of the Martínez family, staunch zapatistas who were both traditional and forward-looking. Pedro and his people had been interviewed for 20 years beginning in 1943 by the cultural anthropologist Oscar Lewis, who had written a book about them in 1964. Little had changed since then.

In life Zapata's Nahuatl, what the locals called mexicano, had been strained, like the Spanish an Americanized Chicano speaks with great effort to his abuelos. Among death's privileges was fluency.

The old man was not surprised to see Miliano. He greeted him with respeto. They talked bilingually, mixing with ease Spanish and mexicano. "Hello, Miliano!"

"How do you know me?"

"I've almost been expecting you. We know your likeness very well. Also, your espectro. In these back regions your ghost has been travelling for a long time. We've composed a corrido to honor it, 'El espectro de Zapata.' "

"Please sing it for me!"

The old man recited from the end of the corrido.

> Su cuerpo al fin sepultaron
> llenos de júbilo y gozo
> y muchos, muchos lloraron
> por sus culpas y reposo.
>
> Pero su alma persevera
> en su ideal "Libertador"
> y su horrenda calavera
> anda en penas . . . ¡oh terror!
>
> Tal constancia a todos pasma;
> de la noche en las negruras,
> se ve vagar su fantasma
> por los montes y llanuras.
>
> Se oyen sonar sus espuelas,
> sus horribles maldiciones,
> y, rechinando las muelas,
> cree llevar grandes legiones.
>
> Extiende yerta mano
> y su vista se dilata . . .
> recorre el campo suriano
> el espectro de Zapata.

Zapata smiled. "I feel I almost know those words and almost experienced those nocturnal travels. I thought I had been sleeping all this time rather than frightening you. ¡Pobrecitos! Who is our calpuleque now? I would that you take me to him."

"That's no more, Miliano. Your beloved Francisco Franco was

the last calpuleque of Anenecuilco. It's the same all over the South."

"The one who died as the result of my son's infamies?"

"Ese es, mi general Emiliano. The very one."

"No more calpuleque. Then that son of Soto y Gama told the truth! But there are still hacendados, aren't there?"

"Oh, assuredly, ¡mi general! The tlalpialoanime-quixtianos still abound and prosper as did their fathers and fathers' fathers for generations up and down time. They still occupy the center of Cem-Anáhuatl they took over in 1521."

Emiliano acknowledged with pleasure the original word for hacendados that had been coined at first contact between indios y cristianos, "tlalpialoanime-quixtianos," literally meaning "los poseedores de tierras cristianos." Zapata turned to the concern of his former life. "What about our treasure, our land grants?"

"Oh, those are safe, don Emiliano. You can talk with the soul of Francisco Franco about that. He was loyal and trustworthy to you to the end. Con mucho respeto."

Then Zapata was impelled to ask his question. "Why do you think I've come back?"

The moreliano was not surprised by the question, but he hesitated, considering the issue. He looked above at those Mexican clouds which sometimes by their very haunting patterns seem to offer ciphers of life's mysteries. "That is two questions, mi general. We knew you would return because we never let you leave us. Con mucho respeto, we practice a culto de devoción to your persona. We knew you would return to us because todavía hay mucho que hacer, and you have never failed us."

"A good answer to one question! What is the other?"

"Con mucho respeto, it is why you have come to us now rather than earlier or later."

"That's a good question! What's the answer?"

"Is not this year of 1992 a big year for tlalticpac-nantzi, Mexico, nuestra madrecita la tierra, México, and for los indios who love her so?" the indio questioned.

Miliano smiled broadly. "That's the best answer I've heard! I heard the same claim made by a famous saint and a celebrated humorist, but not as movingly or convincingly made."

"Well, that's it. Por tlalticpac-nantzi, por la tierra y por los indios."

Zapata accepted the response in its oracular form. He meditated on it. He was not satisfied. He wanted to question, indagar, almost as if this respectful indio were one of his intellectuals, a Palafox, a Soto y Gama. But that he could not bring himself to do; a concerted inquiry was totally fuera de contexto, the white man's way, not the indio way. He limited himself to asking the moreliano, "Are you still puro indio?"

The moreliano smiled broadly and with great pleasure, exposing a mouthful of highland gold where some of the teeth had fallen out.

"Oh yes, puro indio, mi calpuleque, y con mucho respeto a vuestra merced."

"¿Y los hijos?"

"Pues sí, también."

"Pero un poco menos. Indios, pero no puros."

"We've seen a lot of change, Miliano. Some of it has come from the outside, because as you well know, we indios don't control much except here in our faraway tierras. You've noticed the radios, the films on the little screens, popular music, wines and beers and machinery and equipment. Many other forms of foreignness have been introduced and we have made them our own. And we indios have changed ourselves, from the inside, since you moved us in 1910, dear and only surviving calpuleque. We have changed in our own fuero interno, but still remain sincere to ourselves. Mi calpuleque, you yourself started this change, more than anybody else, when you took our agravios about las tierras and made from them a magnificent revolution! You took our anger and our passion and with it you captured the capital of our nation. And for the first time in 400 years an army of indios retook what was ours, el viejo Tenochtitlán. ¡Sí, mi máximo general del sur, es cierto! In 1914 we moved into the ancient center, Cem-Anáhautl, and into the past and into the future, and you helped us to become indios, pero del nuevo mundo. So maybe you're here again, mi general, to help us to be indios of the next century!"

"Indios of the 21st century! It has a catchy ring to it. Maybe un lema. Would you still follow me?"

"To the very end of this Aztlán, ¡mi general!"

"And we would make revolution?"

"If revolution is to be made, ¡mi general!"

"Who would make revolution today? Who are your assets?"

"As you know, there are always men who would lanzar." The old, wise indio of the South smiled. "We have the usual suspects. The usual social bandits who would be interested in moving up. There are also the cristeros, our family among them. Begging your forgiveness, in the 1920s we fought the same revolution, but only from the other side, calling not upon the anarchists but upon Jesus Christ, King, as our patron."

Zapata smiled. "There is no shame. It's the same struggle no matter who the figure on the pennant be. So then, there is no one clear living leader?"

The old indio hesitated. "There is one man, good and honest, who holds back, but looks for entry. With you he would be strong. His name is Cuauhtémoc."

"Well, that's a fine indio name! He is indio?"

"Not really. Mestizo."

"Well, yours truly is one of those too and originally a man who favored fine horses over social justice until his conscience was wrung by the infamias he saw with his own eyes!"

"True enough, mi general. This man is the son of Lázaro, who fought in your revolution when he was 12 years old. He is Cuauhtémoc Cárdenas."

"Well, I don't know. I have no easy answers for you. This thing of death or otherlife, it presents the same old problems but from a different dimension." Zapata smiled sadly. He thought of his mission and how he tried to make beautiful revolution and the old nausea came back to him afresh, and the idea of revolution and leading humankind in any mission filled him with repulsion. "I tried to compel you to live, so you compelled me to die. The recoil killed the advance. Perhaps now is my time to be alone."

And the old indio citó a Zapata con el mismo náhuatl con el cual lanzó su manifiesto a los pueblos indios. "Tehuanti tlen tic icxi-chia tlatlani ipehualoni netehuliztle huan nezetiliztle de to nochtin, ti mo-tehuianime itlampa se bandera huan ihcon mo-hueichihuaz non neylolo-cetiliztle. Itech inin yahui to mahuiztica-tláhtol, de cuali-oquichtin ihuan de cuali netechhuiloanime. We yearn that through your struggle you shall realize your principles and achieve unity among us all; those of us who hold this revolutionary banner tightly, we shall achieve ultimate unity in the hearts of our people."

"¡O, indio sabio! You turn my own words on to me!"

"Nochtin nonque altepeme, nochtin nonques tlaltequipanóhque, ti quin yolehua, man mocetilica to nahuac, ihuan tic yolihuitizque zan se netehuiliztle, man ti néhnemica ica nepalehuiliztle de namehuanti, ihuan téhuanti, ixpan necate tecamocayahque ihuan qui máhca yo, qua palehuía tlen in huaxca tlaltequihua-quixtianos ihuan motocayotía netehuiloanime, iquac amitla in chihca. We invite all our peoples, those of us who work the land, we invite you to join together with us in one single struggle so that with your help together we will face the betrayers of our people who, while they call themselves revolutionaries, are nothing of the kind, for they help the hacendados keep our lands."

Zapata smiled warmly and embraced the old indio. Into the ear of the old warrior the young, reborn revolutionary whispered the completed manifesto that had come back to him vividly. He had composed it on April 17, 1918, to recruit the soldiers and officers of the Arenas Division to the zapatista cause after their general, the full-blood Indian Domingo Arenas, had been killed. "Itech inin yahui to mahuiztic-tláhtol, de cuali-oquichtin ihuan de uali netehhuiloanime. To this we pledge our honor as good men and good revolutionaries."

"We remain firmly under your command, ¡general en Jefe del Ejército Libertador! We are not under the constraints of white man's time; we obey the calendar of Quinto Sol!"

Stoic Zapata, who had died and been reborn in the ardent, Christian embrace of his protectress and who had traveled the axis mundi and reviewed a few of its wonders, now, finally, was released of his último tope. Young Zapata embraced the humble milpero in a flood of bittersweet, Nahua tears. "How I love you, tlalticpac-nantzi, Mexico, nuestra madrecita la tierra, México. I irrigated your soil with my young blood, and if need be, I shall do it again."

"Young Zapata, I implore you! Tell us what to do! Give us a command and it shall be fulfilled!"

"Brave guerrillero of the South. I have died and been reborn in a state of openmindedness to the world. I have no clear answer. I have traveled the world in this the 1992, and I have seen extraordinary events in Mexico, in the United States, in Spain and other places in Europe, in old Russia, in Asia, in Africa, and in South America. I have seen social evils as bad or worse than those we fought against in 1910. I have also seen the crumbling of old ways and the possible emergence of the new. My patron saint believes in the natural growth of the spirit!"

With this, Zapata pledged his constancy to the old indio. "Keep on the lookout for me. But you must make your own plans and execute them. Why not act now, wise indio of the South? You answered the second question well. Take it to its conclusion and act in 1992, the year of tlalticpac-nantzi. Of one thing I am becoming convinced. It is necessary for you to come down from the mountain hidings where the tlalpialoanime-quixtianos are happy to have you hidden away. Reveal yourselves in all of your revolutionary power and make your needs known with firmness and with reasonableness. And since you have developed and evolved since 1910, act accordingly. Do not be afraid to move forward or to change, even as your changes remain true to your nature. Examine your assets, calculate your strengths, and marshall yourselves productively on behalf of our revolution. Above all, meet the needs of your children, the newly evolved indios, help them to be indios of the 21st century!"

The old indio of the South nodded in assent, but in his heart he was almost in despair. He saw that Zapata would leave him now and leave him in a confusión humanal and with enormous burdens of responsibility. And he was so weary and close to death.

Young Zapata saw the old indio in all of his confusion, and he felt the ardent, caring love of his patron saint help fill him with the most gentle compassion. "I know, m'hijo," he said to the old indio. "Even as you are so old and care-ridden, yet you are m'hijo, for as young as I am, I'm as old as your father. Know this, m'hijo. To fail is not significant if you are on the right road. Failure on the right road is just another ensayo en la evolución a lo que vamos a ser. For now I will stay plantado in this mundo, although the great ethers, the great ethereal heavens beckon me with ever increasing urgency. I will review this mundo, and if I am needed, I will return again to intervene, and if necessary, ¡con el 30-30! I pledge this to you, and in your moments of despair may it give you some consolation!" With this Zapata gave the old indio of the South a relic that had been buried with him in 1919 and asked that he return this relic to the family to which it had been entrusted earlier. "This will make amends for a certain incident that I regret." Young Zapata smiled with a form of irony that had not been in his original nature. "These relics! They are reputed to do wonders!" From the monte a splendid white steed trotted to them, its noble nostrils flaring. Zapata patted the flanks of his steed, took the silver bridle, and mounted. He saluted the old indio sabio del sur.

"A sus órdenes, ¡mi general!" The old indio put down his machete and returned a sharp salute as Zapata disappeared into el monte.

When Zapata was alone again, he felt a great relief. Never had the ethers beckoned him more greatly than when he had pledged his constancy to the old, wise indio. Zapata realized that he was still indio, mexicano, revolucionario, Lazarus, even icon and relic, but he was no longer any of these things nor all of them combined. He belonged to a new order of spirit. Nothing could be truer in the phenomenal world than that the recoil killed the advance, and Zapata knew that his intervention in the world of the living could be only minimal. Young Zapata resolved then that while he would remain constant to the old indio of the South and those who the indio represented, he would also wander the earth saying nothing and learn of this magnificent earth and how it seemed to be moving in strange and unpredictable ways. For nothing is so marvelous as to be alone in the phenomenal world, which is raging, and yet apart. And I have not seen it, Zapata thought. I was too much blinded by my confusion within it. Now I will wander among the stirrings of the phenomenal world and absorb them.

Zapata examined his commemorative options. In 2002 he would meet Miguel de Cervantes on Red Square, as they had agreed upon earlier, to see what had evolved. He resolved not to see Miguel hasta entonces, 10 years would be quite soon enough. 1993 was the quincentenary of *Intera cetera divina*, the bull published by Roderigo Borgia who had gone by the name of Pope Alexander VI, dividing the New World between Spain and Portugal, as if it were his to divide. Also in 1493, his daughter, Lucrezia Borgia, effective woman who manipulated the double standard, had married Giovanni Sforza. In the same year Colón wandered upon Puerto Rico, Dominica, and Jamaica. In 1495 the Jews were expelled from Portugal, da Vinci began *The Last Supper*, and the great syphilis epidemic spread out from Naples all over Europe. There ought to be quincentennial commemorations of all of those events! 1500 was a very good year. Lucrezia's second husband, Alfonso of Naples, was murdered; the first pawnshop was already two years in operation at a place later to become very famous called Nuremberg; the inquisitor-general, Francisco Jiménez de Cisneros, caused the great Moorish revolt of Granada by forcing mass conversions of Moors in 1499; future Emperor Charles V was born; Aldus of Venice invented *italics*; De Ojeda and Vespucci discovered the mouth of the Amazon; Columbus was arrested and returned to Spain in irons; and the first recorded Caesarean operation on a living woman was performed by a Swiss pig gelder, Jakob Nufer. In 1501, Ahuítzotl the Great died in the disastrous flood that he caused in Tenochtitlán by unleashing the waters of Coyoacán, and in 1502 Motecuzóma II was elected the

Great Speaker of the Aztecs. The last renewal of the New Fire on the Huixachtécatl mountaintop at the end of the 52-year cycle took place in 1507. Then there was 2010, the must-do year, centenary of the Mexican Revolution.

*   *   *

It was Sunday afternoon in the Anenecuilco pulquería and Soto y Gama was enjoying himself drinking chocolate-flavored pulque and telling chismes and having them told to him by the rest of the bola suriana when the oldest, purest indio of the deepest South came in and walked up to their table.

Soto y Gama looked at the old indio with nostalgic approval. He wore the whitest campesino linen and a perfect, museum-quality Saltillo blanket that might have been woven 200 years ago. Around his neck hung three magnificent necklaces. One was of large turquoise and gold nuggets with a central turquoise naja in the form of Omega. The other, an immense bishop's crucifix, with turquoise set in the finest, forged Indian silver. It was the kind that the bishop of Cuautla might wear on Easter Sunday. The third necklace was fiery coral and at its end hung a pendant of the plumed serpent, Quetzal-coatl, made of inlaid jet, mother of pearl, lapis lazuli, serpentine, turquoise, and conch. The Indian's leather sandals were the finest and most formal Soto y Gama had seen in all his life, hand-fashioned leather, again in the plumed serpent motif. Soto y Gama remembered seeing indios like that come down del monte with nuggets of gold to play the peleas de gallos on días feriados. That had been decades ago.

The old folkmaster smiled affectionately at the indio. "Thou art magnífico! But you should know that this Sunday no hay pelea."

The old Indian of the South faced Soto y Gama. He opened his mouth and smiled ambiguously, and the gold in his mouth flashed. "Yo le disparo."

This was a very ambiguous phrase and Soto y Gama felt a trepidation that was shared by the rest of the bola. Their eyes strayed to the little pouch slung over the indio's shoulder. It could contain anything. A weapon to disparar, a bunch of gold nuggets, even a fighting cock wouldn't be untoward.

The indio just stood there smiling his ambiguous smile, not coming forward.

Soto y Gama inquired, "¿Tú me disparas?"

"Sí señor, el pulque, las tequilitas, el mezcal con todos los gusanitos que quisieras. Se los disparo, a todos."

With that the bola brightened up. "¡Orale! Cantinero, trae pulque pa'l benefactor, y tequila y mezcal."

"¡Siéntate compadrito!"

The indio moved forward, always smiling a sort of servile smile of the alien other. "Gracias, compadritos. Were you discussing Zapata?"

One of the bola said, "Him too. Who could fail to discuss Zapata on Sunday afternoon in Anenecuilco? But we were chismografiando about everything."

"Seguro que sí," said the indio. "I saw Zapata yesterday."

The bola smirked, all but Soto y Gama who felt a flush of embarrassment. Was he being set up by la bola? Had they hired this indio to make Sunday burla of him, recreating for their own amusement a farce like the one some months ago when the clever actor had impersonated Zapata at his expense? Soto y Gama felt that same trepidation. The gasoline attendant who had closed Pemex early as he did every Sunday said to the indio, "Menos mal that it was yesterday and not today. Why do they call this the land of mañana? Mejor que they should call it the land of ayer."

The old indio of the South said, "Ya les disparé. Now you'll sing with me."

"Sing with you? Why should we do that, viejo mandón?"

The old indio smiled his servile smile. "Algo pasa." Then he frowned in memory and said, "You remember 'De la muerte de Emiliano Zapata'?" They all shook their heads, except for old Soto y Gama who nodded with great pleasure.

"I haven't heard that mentioned in 50 years! Viejo indio sabio, we must be the same generation. Con gusto I'll sing it with you!"

The indio nodded with approval. "You are a good mestizo, just like Miliano, que bien sabía lo nahua." And they sang.

El buen Emiliano, que amaba a los pobres,
quiso darles la libertad,
por eso los indios de todos los pueblos
con él fueron a luchar.
De Cuauhtla hasta Amecameca, Matamoros y el Ajusco,
con los pelones del viejo don Porfirio se dio gusto.

Trinitaria de los campos, de las vegas de Morelos
¡si preguntan por Zapata, di que ya se fue a los cielos!
Le dijo Zapata a don Pancho Madero,
cuando era ya gobernante:
—Si no nos das las tierras, verás a los indios
de nuevo entrar al combate . . .

The oldest indio of the deepest South unslung his pouch and opened it ceremoniously. From his pouch he took the largest nugget that Soto y Gama had ever seen in his entire life and put it before the folk philosopher.

"Pa' que veas. This is the gold that the Spaniards came seeking like crazy men 500 years ago and which we never gave them. Except the few we captured. For them we meticulously melted the gold and poured it molten down their throats. This is gold from the hidden monte 'onde gente cristiana desconoce."

The bola was deathly quiet. Soto y Gama who of course knew a little bit about everything, including gold, inspected it. "This is the pure article," he announced solemnly.

One of the bola summoned the cantinero and showed him the nugget. "With materia prima like this, forget about the pulque, the mezcal, and the tequila. You could sell him all Anenecuilco and still make a profit!"

Soto y Gama recovered his aplomb. "Viejo sabio del sur, why have you come down del monte?"

"Because I have seen Zapata and he gave me something for you!"

The indio went to his pouch and Soto y Gama gasped. The indio had something in his hand but he wouldn't open it. "You mestizos, are you really de confiar?"

The Pemex man said, "Zapata was as mestizo as us!"

The indio suddenly spoke with great authority, "Cállense el hocico. Zapata spoke our language. He spoke mexicano!" Then the oldest, wisest Indian of the South said very solemnly, "¡Soto y Gama!"

"How do you know my name?"

The old indio spoke slowly and very clearly as if he had been rehearsing. "Soto y Gama. Zapata está 'onde los santos. In my hand is his relic. It is for you para que te animes. You know what to do about it. You are the living intellectual link to the Mexican Revolution. Para que te animes." The indio opened his hand and set a golden bullet on the table.

Soto y Gama shuddered. "¡La bala de oro!" He took the bullet and adjusted his eyeglasses and read, "Esta bala de oro pa' mis compadres, los máximos intelectuales de la revolución mexicana, Antonio y Conrado Díaz Soto y Gama." It was signed, Emiliano Zapata. "This," Soto y Gama said with all his authority, "is the true article! It was given to my family and my father had it buried in 1919 with Emiliano Zapata. You know his grave!"

The Indian nodded in assent. "His grave is unviolated but it is empty. He has risen and the Revolution is reborn!"

Tears of orgullo and rabia filled the eyes of la bola de Anenecuilco and when the indio emptied his pouch and the nuggets of gold came tumbling onto the old wooden table making an ear-shattering noise like so many onyx eggs, imagine their added amazement! When they recovered from their shock the old indio had them procure their guitars and led them in revolutionary song, "El 30-30."

¡Qué pobres estamos todos
Sin un pan para comer,
Porque nuestro pan lo gasta
El patrón en su placer!

Mientras él tiene vestidos
Y palacios y dinero,
Nosotros vamos desnudos
Y vivimos en chiquero.

Nosotros sembramos todo
Y todo lo cosechamos
Pero toda la cosecha
Es para bien de los amos.

Nosotros sufrimos toda
La explotación de la guerra,
Y así nos llaman ladrones
Cuando pedimos la tierra.

Y luego los padrecitos
Nos echan excomuniones,

¡A poco piensan que Cristo
Era para los patrones!

Compañeros del arado
Y los de toda herramienta,
No más nos queda un camino:
¡Agarrar el treinta-treinta!

Now the old indio of the South led old Soto y Gama, hijo, and the rest of the bola out of the dark pulquería and into daylight. Congregated in the plaza and on the sides of the hills were hundreds, perhaps thousands, of solemn Indian adults and children, and old Soto y Gama, hijo, felt a great burden fall from him, and he was filled with una vergüenza limpia and resolve. He embraced el indio who also cried and their tears intermixed. The bola felt such enthusiasm that spontaneously they shouted the old cry, "¡Tierra y libertad!"

El indio spoke. "Miliano said we should review and develop our assets. They're all here." He made a sign to his determined flock. Robust men lifted whole carts filled with gold and treasure that the tribe had kept hidden from the obsessive Spaniards since the times of Hernán Cortés. Sacred glyphs on cloth and on amátl, the Nahua bark paper, elaborate feather garments and headdresses, the finest Indian weavings, weapons ranging from ancient Amerindian spears to rifles of the Mexican Revolution to M-16s and Uzi machine guns. Others lifted their machetes, their scythes, and all tools of the land, or their livestock, their personal jewelry, textiles, sculptures, relics, and icons. Younger indios had brought their Sony Discmen and Walkmen. Soto y Gama thought about what he saw before him, the excitement of his compadritos y compadritas, and then naturally assuming the role of adviser for which he had understudied his entire life, he said solemnly to Pedro Martínez, the zapatista indio patriarch of the South, and to all close enough to listen, "With our treasure and all our material and spiritual assets and the new fire in the bellies of our compadritos indios and reborn Zapata at our side guiding us, we shall now rebuild our home Anenecuilco y recrear un nuevo mundo que no nos fallará."

The indio said to Soto y Gama and all who were close by, "We should go back to Tenochtitlán where all this started and get back on the right road. We need to meet as soon as possible with the federales and start over again on the right footing."

"That's the right strategy!" Soto y Gama confirmed. "Mi comandante nahua, patriarca del sur, I recommend we march to the
Cuautla-Mexico City freeway and commandeer all vehicles on that
road and enter Tenochtitlán . . ." he said with emphasis, "from the
south! If we move now with determination and dispatch, we can have
our people congregated by Monday morning at the original Banco de
México at the corner of the Zócalo and Avenida 16 de Septiembre.
We'll open the bank tomorrow morning on a new sun and count and
develop our assets!"

The word passed down the line and great excitement grew
among the indios, many of whom had hidden themselves away en los
montes and had never been to the capital in their entire lives. Four
fierce Nahua warriors came forward. One held the original strongbox that Zapata had entrusted to the good and revered Francisco
Franco. The Indians who were nearby made reverence to the
strongbox as if it were their patron saint. Pedro Martínez took the
heavy strongbox and with one hand effortlessly lifted it and with the
other took Soto y Gama's hand and lifted it. "We have brought down
from el monte the sacred recordings of our propertied identity. From
this day forward we no longer hide it from sight, but we protect it with
our very lives, for it is the manifestation of our sacred line and that
part of the earth which belongs to us! We will take to Anáhuac these
recordings of our propertied identity from the beginning of time and
make our claim with the current government, los federales! For now,
we have a new calpuleque. I have succeeded our great leader,
Francisco Franco, and for the first time in 50 years we move forward,
organized and in solidarity!"

The pueblo exclaimed with great joy and a sense of deliverance
and now marched forward to the freeway with their carts of gold,
silver, and treasure, their weapons and relics and icons and posters
of Zapata, Cristo Rey, la Virgen de Guadalupe, Pancho Villa, the
great full-blood Indian general, Domingo Arenas, Sor Juana, the
original Cuauhtémoc and Cuauhtémoc Cárdenas, the emperor
Motecuzóma's brother, military leader Cuitláhuac, la Malintzín, the
poet ruler of the Texcocans, Nezahualcóyotl, even César Chávez
and John F. Kennedy.

Circled by the entourage of attack Nahuas, the indio patriarca del
sur, calpuleque by acclamation, moved forward, one hand around
the strongbox and the other clenched in that of the mestizo, Soto y
Gama, son of a great zapatista revolutionary. The calpuleque strode

briskly, and his elderly peer, Soto y Gama, hijo, kept up with him out of pure euphoria. He was thinking of his immense good luck. An old man, child of a revolutionary father, who had cornered himself into the role of passive recorder! And suddenly, at his ripe age to be given a second lease on life! What an opportunity! He would act! He would be effective. His heart was thumping; he did not know if it was because of his condition or out of pure joy. He took the blood thinner that the doctor had prescribed and cast it away. Who needed thin blood in 1992 marching with his compadritos and his compadritas? Instead Soto y Gama took out the golden bullet of reliquary revolution and kissed it as if it were a crucifix or a medallion, or his father himself or the hallowed image of Zapata. He kissed his compadrito calpuleque's hand too, which was clenched in his, and they marched forward in a splendid, festive, exalted mood. "Surely, this is the right road. The road that heads back!"

At the edge of the freeway, thousands of Indian adults and children congregated. As always the great trucks slowly struggled up the grade, filled with goods for the capital. Pedro Martínez, patriarca del sur and calpuleque, counseled his lieutenants to pass the word. "We will take this road and with great respect commandeer the trucks and vehicles and have the drivers take us to the Banco de México where we will congregate for the new dawn, Monday morning, banking hours. We will behave con gran resolución y respeto, without violence but without shirking our solemn duty to reenter Cem-Anáhuac Yoyótili, the Heart of the One World, and reenter the economic life of this world and rebuild our homes and remake our homelands. ¡Entramos al siglo veintiuno!" And Pedro quoted from the Nahua manifesto of 1918 of his máximo comandante: "Itech inin yahui to mahuiztic-tláhtol, de cuali-oquichtin ihuan de uali netehhui-loanime. To this we pledge our honor as good men and good revolutionaries."

Alfonso Caso y Casas was not surprised at being awakened from his tantalizing but ineluctable dream. It taunted him—something about love and grace and a mustachioed man and a stunning woman, or a strange configuration of the heavens, or of indios coming down from the mountain strongholds. It faded back into the unconscious, a great serpent in a circle, head and tail united, the uroboros. A call had awakened him from the oficial de turno at the Centro de Seguridad Militar y Civil de la Républica de los Estados Unidos de México.

Unusual situation on the Cuautla-México D. F. freeway. A few other strange if minor circumstances. Did he want a briefing on the phone or did he want to review incoming firsthand? Caso y Casas sighed. He'd better come down. He'd rest in 1993, which after all was merely the quincentenary of the discovery of Puerto Rico!

He had had numerous emergency calls all year; 1992 had been exceptionally difficult. In addition to the usual matters of national security, the year had presented extraordinary problems, prominent among them the tensions caused by the proposed North American Free Trade Act that was moving forward and the catastrophic explosions in Guadalajara in the spring, where whole blocks had been blown up into rubble because of the egregious neglect of Pemex officials. Now 1992 was winding down into fall, but he was filled with foreboding. For one, the skies were abnormal.

Alfonso Caso y Casas did not identify himself as a government administrator much less a spook, in fact chief spook in service of national security. He had anticipated a comfortable post as a professor of history and the role of reasoned gadfly of the current administration, not the status of the president's chief aide in the quest for both national economic progress and public order. Of course, the key to his status, apart from the fact that he was one of few pure-blooded Indians with a doctorate, lay in networking, primarily the Harvard connection. Caso y Casas had been a student at Harvard with Salinas de Gortari, who was destined to become president of the Republic. At the time, Salinas was earning his degree in economics and Caso y Casas was earning his in history, working under the direction of Lefty Womack on the dissertation topic of the evolution of the concept of property in Mexico among the various social classes that emerged from the Spanish conquest: peninsulares, criollos, mestizos, and indios. The friendship established between the two Mexicans in graduate school had been the beginning. One thing led to another.

No, as he had told Lefty some days ago in Seville, the heavens were not normal. There was something perpetually cryptic about Mexican clouds. Even under normal conditions, they were almost a provocation to soothsayers, but in 1992 he would look up at the sky and see such resolute, almost militant movement in the opaque, moisture-laden clouds as he had never before witnessed. And that was in the daylight! Many nights during the summer he had gone out on the ramada and gazed upon the Mexican night. It felt like an astrophysical carnival! Shooting stars, lightning bolts, and kinesis of unfathomable import. Even the fixed stars made strange constellations in his mind, impassioned figures in flight, jesters and gesticulants, divines with flashy halos around their crowns. One night he remarked to his wife that he felt like one of the magi beckoned by the birth of the infant in the manger. Either that, or the obsessive potato masher and mountain sculptor of *Close Encounters of the Third Kind.* Attempting to soothe him, she had remarked that it was merely his job that filled him with apprehensions, that and the year 1992 so laden with symbolism. But that was the whole point. It didn't seem coincidental but rather overdetermined that the chief spook of the Republic of Mexico would be getting a message.

Caso y Casas entered the situation room of the Centro de Seguridad. It was 100 meters beneath the Zócalo itself which stood at ground zero, Mexico City. When they had carved it out of Aztec foundations 30 years ago during the nuclear race between the U.S. and the USSR, the civil engineers had worked with a team of archaeologists in order to minimize damage to the Aztec temple that was buried there. Essentially they had carved the security stronghold out of the ruins of the core structures of the Aztec empire. In a sense little had changed in Anáhuac. One could take an extremely swift elevator from the Centro de Seguridad in the bowels of old, buried Tenochtitlán to the aboveground private office of Salinas de Gortari, current president of Mexico, who in turn governed from the National Palace that had been built by the Spanish conquistador, Hernán Cortés, on the foundation of Motecuzóma II's palace.

The oficial de turno looked confused. Caso y Casas asked him, "¿Qué pasa?"

"I don't know, licenciado. Nothing earthshaking. But it feels like a pattern."

"What kind of pattern?"

"I don't know." The oficial hesitated. "Historical?"

Caso y Casas knew the oficial de turno to be almost totally disinterested in history and thus his interest piqued. "Historical? How so? You're not getting quincentennialitis?"

The oficial smiled shyly. "Forgive me. You're the historian. Does 'Nenecuilco mean anything to you?"

Caso y Casas reacted sharply. "That's just indio lilt for Anenecuilco, the birthplace of the great revolution of the South, of ¡tierra y libertad! and of Miliano Zapata himself."

"No wonder we've got such detailed reports."

"For sure! I keep a lot of assets in Anenecuilco. I've got the whole place wired." Caso y Casas laughed testily and with heavy irony. "You know how they say that lightning always strikes the same place twice!"

"Licenciado, my first reaction to the reports would have been that our assets had had too much afternoon pulque in Anenecuilco. But there are other occurrences."

"First things first. What news of Anenecuilco?"

"The indios have gone on some binge or mass hysteria, although they're not behaving too unreasonably. First they marched out of the mountains and box canyons of Morelos. Then they massed at the Cuautla-México freeway two kilometers out of Cuautla, cut the road and piled as many people as they could into every vehicle heading north. They've done nothing violent, but they are requiring the drivers, mostly truckers, to take them here."

"Here? You mean the capital?"

"Not exactly, licenciado. Here, the Zócalo. Our assets report they are going to open the Banco de México tomorrow morning, which they claim stands on the exact spot of the original temple to Tonatiuh, the red Tezcatlipoca."

"My God! Why?"

"It's just a complete confusion. But organized. Some say they are going to buy the Banco de México. Others say they are going to buy or otherwise retake the sacred core of Tenochtitlán. You know, like Tiananmen Square! Others say they are simply going to make a deposit of 60 thousand million pesos."

"My God, that's 20 billion dollars!" Caso y Casas immediately regretted his comment; it displayed his American bias. Unfortunately he could not fathom large amounts of pesos except by converting them into dollars.

"I don't know what's going on, licenciado, but all of our assets cannot be under the influence of pulque. They all agree that the indios of the South are bringing in cartloads of treasure, precious stones, gold ingots, nuggets, Aztec wealth, everything. The claim is they've been hiding this from the greedy gachupines and mestizos for 500 years. The claim, and this is pretty consistent, is that they've come down from los montes and they are cashing in and joining the 21st century. But everything else is confusion. They're rallying under the pennants or posters of every possible movement, from Cuauhtémoc Cárdenas to the original Cuauhtémoc, and everybody in between, the old cristeros, the old icons of 1910 like Emiliano Zapata and Domingo Arenas, la Virgen de Guadalupe, everybody."

"So this is what you mean by historical?"

"Not entirely." Again the oficial de turno hesitated. "I've been looking at incoming for the last several hours. Strange."

"Like what?"

"Like disturbances in weird places. Several hours ago a group of Totonaca Indians were reported to be moving to Mexico City from Papantla on trucks, carrying with them their long poles to do the Voladores dance. The claim is that they will get to the Zócalo tonight and set up and start the flying dance tomorrow morning."

"So?"

"Well, not much, except no one in authority has heard about it before, and we cannot confirm that they have gotten permission to do this from anyone in a position of authority. Also, they're talking about doing the dance from a *religious* point of view, not a tourist spectacle. They claim tomorrow marks a 'new dawn, a new sheaf of years.' Then there is the far South. The Indians have closed down Cobá and Tulúm on the Yucatán peninsula to tourists. Nothing violent, but they've brushed aside the entrance attendants and guards. It started with a few dozen indios; now there are more than a thousand Maya-quiché speakers at each site. They seem to be having some kind of, how can I say, be-in, because clearly they are spending the night!"

Caso y Casas went to the screens and processing machines and inspected incoming. He turned to the oficial de turno. "A brand new incident is being reported out on unit six." They inspected the hard copy as the information was being processed. Caso y Casas read, "Two thousand Tlaxcalan Indians are digging a great hole near a dried-out portion of Lake Texcoco. Our operatives on-site say that they claim to be unearthing treasure that they had hidden there in 1521. The same treasure that Hernán Cortés lost in Lake Texcoco on 'La Noche Triste.'" Caso y Casas turned to the oficial de turno. "This is incredible! That battle between Aztecs and Conquistadors and their Indian allies is among the most memorable of the Conquest. The treasure was never found by the Spaniards, who searched for it for decades. They always suspected the indios of having taken it."

"There's more, licenciado. Look at the events that have been mounting up. In San Pedro Tlaquepaque and Tonalá the Indian craftspeople suddenly had a spontaneous demonstration. Apparently they are complaining that their work is being exploited, and they are not receiving enough income."

"Well, that's no big deal, except for this pattern."

"Precisely, licenciado. Apparently a small group of Indians have snuck into the Palenque national park. They'll be spending the night. They're peaceful enough, but they've brought shovels and carts. The attendants don't want to have a ruckus but the army batallion at Villahermosa has been alerted. Here's another one. Maguey workers, almost 100 percent Indian I might add, are planning a demonstration in Tequila, Jalisco. In Tzintzuntzán, Michoacán, it's something similar, except in this case it's the ancient hemp factory."

There was a commotion among the analysts at unit four incoming and the oficial and the licenciado hastened to it. "New disturbance, very similar to what happened on Route 160 out of Cuautla. A group of campesinos, mostly indios, have cut Highway 110 close to Tamazunchale just before it splits into 120 and 105. They are boarding vehicles and coming into the Mexico City region down both highways."

The licenciado pondered, "First from the South, now from the North." Then he said authoritatively, "I want the entire army of the valley of Anáhuac put on alert. But no military discretion is to be exercised in the field. Developments must be reported and requests or recommendations for action must be made to the Centro de Seguridad Militar y Civil." He said to the oficial de turno, "As you know, President Salinas is in Brazil on the follow-up that resulted from the earlier ecology summit. Have communications reconfirm our link. I'm going to call him if things develop further."

The oficial de turno asked, "Tamazunchale . . . does that mean something too?"

"It was the ancient capital of the Huasteca Indians. Even during the Aztec empire it was independent, although a tributary region. It's one of the bastions of Indian culture." Then the licenciado mused. "That Palenque business in Tabasco State and the Quintana Roo incidents at Tulúm and Cobá. What's to make us think it's merely Mexico? It could be going down the line!"

"How are they doing this? Indios, campesinos, workers of ancient industries and crafts like tequila and hemp?" asked the oficial. "It's not like they've got computers or fax machines or other instanta-neous communication. Have they been planning for 1992?"

The licenciado smiled grimly. "It's a mystery to me! Maybe they've been waiting for some sign. Christ, have there been any sightings of Quetzalcoatl or anything like that?"

The workers around the licenciado began to laugh and some of the tension was relieved. The licenciado thought some more, though, and said, "This may be international. Get me national secur-ity in Guatemala City, in Tegucigalpa, and in San Salvador."

Soon enough the report came in from Guatemala. "Everything seems pretty normal except for a few disturbances, but nothing really extraordinary."

"Like what disturbances?"

"Well, for one, the Indian market at Quetzaltenango. It was like a mass hysteria. People kept claiming they were sighting deities and illustrious figures. Someone even saw the Quijote and Sancho Panza."

The licenciado laughed. "I see Sancho Panza every time I see a fat guy selling piloncillo in the marketplace. Is that all?"

"Pretty much, although, frankly, the local gendarmes couldn't control all of the bulla over at the market. It got out of hand and they're worried that tomorrow it might get worse. We just don't have enough information out of Guatemala to do an analysis. The other problem is that there appears to be vast blackouts over certain parts of the country. Wait, wait, we're getting incoming from Teguci, vast electrical blackouts over western Honduras, especially in the inten-sively Indian area and over the ruins such as Copán."

"Blackouts!" the licenciado snorted. "Electrical blackouts is the middle name of Central America." At that moment the lights flick-ered in the Centro de Seguridad as the system went off the grid and on its own generators. The licenciado said ironically: "I forgot, black-outs is our middle name too."

The secure telephone with Washington, D.C., rang. It was Brent Scowcroft, head of national security and the licenciado's analog in the colossus of the North. The licenciado took the call over the large screen so that the two spooks could see each other directly.

"Mr. Scowcroft, it's 6:00 a.m. in D.C. You're up early!"

"I've been up for a couple of hours now. Is President Salinas still down in Brazil for that earth thing?"

"Yes, he's due back tomorrow. How about your president?"

"Same story. Frankly, I'm alarmed. A number of officials, including the President of the United States, are making tours to out of the way, environmentally important places. There have been persistent blackouts."

"Are you out of contact with your president?"

"Oh, no. Nothing like that. As a matter fact I just spoke with him, and he said he's been outside, and they've had this incredible viewing in the heavens of the aurora australis. I would imagine President Salinas is seeing the same thing down there! Right in the middle of the Mato Grosso. While Australian aborigines see the aurora all the time and interpret it to be the dance of the gods, nobody remembers seeing anything like it in the middle of the Brazilian savannah!"

"Blackouts in the Mato Grosso? Maybe it's not the savannah, but the Indian connection."

"What do you mean?"

"Are you having blackouts in the U.S.? Are you having disturbances among Indians?"

"Yes, that's one of the reasons I called, because I'm detecting blackouts in unusual parts of the U.S. and Mexico, Central America, and all down the line, through Peru, Bolivia, and into Brazil. Our technical experts say that these blackouts don't make any sense, and in fact they are technically impossible."

"How so?"

"They don't obey any technically plausible pattern. For one, they seem to be affecting enormous regions, places where very few people live. The few urban areas that are affected, well they're mostly tourist places like Santa Fe, New Mexico, and Flagstaff, Arizona. From the point of view of the electrical grid they appear to be technically impossible. The blackouts do not obey the logic of the electrical grid. They seem to jump all over the lot, crazily bypassing spots on the grid that ought to be affected and reappearing where they shouldn't. Their pattern is more attributable to . . . I hesitate to say it, tourism."

"I don't think so, Brent. It's the Indian connection."

"Indians?"

"Yes, 1992, it's the year of the Indian, ¿que no? Any Indian disturbances?"

"Well, not really until today, but that's natural. After all, it's 1992."

"Right, entirely natural. After all, it's 1992. What do you have?"

"Well, it seems that the entire Taos pueblo left home and is moving down the road to the capitol building in Santa Fe. We think they're marking or commemorating some historic event, perhaps related to 1992. A large group of Navajo Indians, perhaps hundreds or even thousands, are moving from Canyon de Chelly southeast to I-80, perhaps to Gallup, or even Albuquerque or Santa Fe, we're just not sure. They're displaying early photographs of their historic chiefs, Manuelito, Barboncito, and Delgadito, so they're almost certainly protesting the infamous, tragic Long Walk that Kit Carson forced on them in 1864. Other pueblos—Laguna, Santa Clara, Cochiti, who knows how many others—are on the move too, toward Santa Fe. There have been vague reports or rumors of protest or meetings among the Apaches and Utes. Reports out of Shiprock, Window Rock, Monument Valley, but all very sketchy. Something's abuzz around Chaco canyon, but we don't know what. Some Indians apparently are spending the night at Four Corners. In fact, according to one report about 15 minutes ago, unconfirmed I should add, they've cut all traffic either way on Route 160. Frankly, Alfonso, my assets among American Indians are shockingly limited. They might as well be invisible! I could tell you infinitely more about what's going on in Riga or Havana."

"There's a lot going on here, Brent, and the connection is not tourism, but Indians. Among the main developments, Indians from Zapata's birthplace are entering our main plaza and plan some demonstration at the Bank of Mexico."

"But isn't that just 1992 stuff?"

"Yeah, but what is 1992 stuff? Other Indians from the North will be arriving in the Valley of Mexico within two hours. I'm going to sign off now and get back to you in no more than 45 minutes. It's about two hours before dawn here in the valley of Anáhuac. I want to physically inspect the Zócalo of Mexico City."

Dr. Caso y Casas, the oficial de turno, and a group of elite security guards rose to ground zero. They walked along the corridor that featured Diego Rivera's murals depicting highlights of Mexican history, and they left the security of the Palacio Nacional, the center of Mexican government. They emerged into what seemed like total darkness. The entire valley of Anáhuac seemed to have been hushed. The colonial structures like the Monte de Piedad across the Zócalo and the Catedral Metropolitana on the right corner were like ominous shrouds. But the sky! The security force had never seen anything like it.

The oficial de turno said, "What's the matter with the heavens? They seem so . . . patterned. And what are those lights? They look like pale green and pale blue curtains in the sky. And that dark-red glow from the north?"

Dr. Caso y Casas experienced the same ineluctable feeling that had awakened him earlier. He remembered the character played by Truffaut in *Close Encounters*. What had he called it, "an event sociological"? The historian turned to the officer. "This is remarkable! Technically, it's called the aurora borealis. But they are almost never seen in Mexico. The most historically significant sighting was by the emperor Motecuzóma II and his Aztec people of Tenochtitlán in 1519. They had just learned of the landing of Hernán Cortés and his men in Veracruz, and in their aeromancy they took the aurora borealis to be an exceptionally evil omen. According to Aztec historians the only previous recording of the lights had occurred in the year 1-Rabbit of the previous sheaf of years, and that sighting had presaged a period of great starvation. In essence, for the Indian world, the aurora borealis of 1519 became the augury of the end of the world as they knew it and the beginning of the colonial age. Now, it seems in 1992 the lights have reappeared to enlighten the Indians."

The security party moved to the south. Suddenly, in the dark they saw several great poles swing up into the air, and, for a moment, shaken Caso y Casas thought they were enormous crucifixes. Then he noticed that they had ropes attached. He whispered to the oficial, "The Voladores are here, as you said. Setting up for the dawn." They moved on. Close to the headquarters of the Banco de México there already was a tumulto. Thousands of indios were chanting and bailando indio in the form of a great serpent that wove its way across the Zócalo.

The licenciado had one young indio removed from the queue. "Are you from Anenecuilco?"

"Cómo no, patroncito, de puro 'Nenecuilco, birthplace of Zapata and the Mexican Revolution of the South."

"What are you chanting? Tell me in Spanish, I don't know your language well enough to understand by myself."

Last Sun was called 4-Water; for 52 years the water lasted.

And those who lived under this fourth Sun, they existed in the time of the Sun 4-Water.

It lasted 676 years.

Thus they perished: they were swallowed by the waters and they became fish.

The heavens collapsed upon them and in a single day they perished.

The date was 4-Flower. The year was 1-House and the day 4-Water.

They perished, all the mountains perished.

The water lasted 52 years and with this ended their years.

This Sun, called 4-Movement, this is our Sun, the one in which we now live.

And here is its sign, how the Sun fell into the fire, into the divine hearth, there at Teotihuacán.

It was also the Sun of our Lord Quetzalcoatl in Tula.

The fifth Sun, its sign 4-Movement.

It is called the Sun of Movement because it moves and follows its path.

"Why are you here? Why are you so happy? Have you been drinking?

"Drinking? No, patroncito, for alcohol is the bane of los inditos. Happy, oh yes, patroncito. For we have returned to the center of el mundo and I am told that tomorrow brings the dawning of the new sun!"

"But this is like a carnival. Everybody's having so much fun!"

"Isn't that so, patroncito? Why not join us? We are inviting mestizos like yourself to our celebration of the New World. Esta es la noche de carnaval. ¡Mañana el día de divinas palabras! The annunciation of a new sun!"

Caso y Casas staggered around the Zócalo for a little while longer, confused and disoriented rather like the bull in the corrida that's received the mortal wound but lingers on wobbly legs. In the meantime, los indios had a great time dancing in the form of the great serpent and chanting and making merry in the pitch dark. Then something clicked with Caso y Casas, and he felt this alignment between the heavens and his own mind. It was the center. That had been the fundamental notion of his dream earlier, of many ineluctable dreams about humankind and the cosmos that he had been experiencing for years. The ancient Amerindians, that is, his own people, his own ancestors, had five directions, did they not? Above the four cardinal points and prime vectors of the Western world they had known the fifth vector, the center. It was the direction that was missing in the Western world and to the Amerindians it was sacred. Together with the cardinal points, it completed one great circle: Cem-Anáhuatl. The Anáhuac. The valley of Mexico in the center and the surrounding lands and waters. The Amerindians had returned to the center of the empire, which was at the same time the beating spiritual center of the human self.

With this epiphany which Caso y Casas experienced as a phenomenological click, he fell to his knees and, looking at the heavens, wrung his hands. He was not praying, but he was rapt. The military entourage felt profoundly uncomfortable. They tried to rouse him but tears streamed unimpeded from his eyes, and they judged that he was in some kind of daze or rapture of the deep. The military's only recourse was to form a protective ring about their commandant and chief guarantor of national security. The soldiers, puros indios all but dressed in uniforms, circled their leader, puro indio, but dressed in fine European tweed, as he kneeled in the middle of the dark Zócalo at ground zero in Anáhuac, while indios dressed in traditional indio garb bailaban estilo indio and raised their dancing poles and celebrated the coming figuration of the imminent dawn.

While all this went on, Caso y Casas, his eyes fixed on the heavens, thought that he was one of the privileged few to experience the inner and the outer harmonized, both in the world and in his own educated indio self. He thought that it had been a long time since the human race, still in its infancy, ignorant, susceptible to the marvelous, easily astonished and terrified, saw the whole world as full of mystery, inexplicable, peopled with deities, spirits, jinns, and demonic forces, a world in which magic was a must for life. Nothing in that world was profane, nothing was secular. Everything was sacred. When the sun god warmed the earth and the nature god fertilized it and the rain god moistened it, corn grew. The first young corn was mediated by the young corn god and later the mature corn god appeared, for elotes in the husk were governed by yet another sacred deity. Of course, Caso y Casas did not lament the passing of that time of fear and terror and most majestic and gruesome human sacrifice, nor even the rise of the scientific and technological West, nor even the conquest and colonization of Amerindia and the racial and ethnic intermixture that was one result. Yet, in our own scientific and technological time, apogee of Western advances, in which everything seemed to be explicable, where science had seemed to have reduced the ancient verities and even the ancient questions to pointlessness, where everything had become profane and secular—was it not the return of a time of fear, of terror and anxiety, faced as we were with the appalling forces of human technical knowledge that seemed unable to be held to the service of humankind? No talisman, no magic seemed to protect humanity against the insanity of the technocrats, nothing except a return to a concept of the genuinely sacred.

Caso y Casas's self- and world revelation consisted of suddenly realizing that those early inhabitants of the planet were right. They were expressing their human quality to the fullest in affirming the existence of the sacred, in seeing something sacred, some mystery in everything. Corn was still sacred, the rain no less glorious, the earth no less hallowed, the fertilization of the earth no less revered by a detailed understanding of their nature, principles, or mechanics. The only mistake of the early humans, in their ignorance, was not to know that the sacred exists in the natural, everyday world, not just a quickening to account for lack of knowledge, not merely a provision of trolls for every bridge, deities for every joint and transition, not an external acceleration of events by spirits.

With that, Caso y Casas got up and brushed himself off. He felt like a new man, more reasonable, open, heightened in his expectations. Naturally, for no other reason, the great bell in the National Palace above the porch of the office of the president of Mexico began to toll. It was the original bell that had been used by Father Hidalgo in his Grito de Dolores and was now normally used at midnight each September 15th to commemorate the beginning of the Revolution of 1810. Then the bells of the great cathedral came on line, and soon apparently the bells of every church in Anáhuac joined in unitary clangor. Fireworks shot up into the sky over the Zócalo, harmonizing with the novel spectacle of the aurora borealis in the Mexican heavens. The Voladores de Papantla threw themselves headfirst into the air, lit up by cascades of red, white, and green flares just as sparkling tableaux were triggered on the Zócalo: the eagle perched on nopales with the serpent in its mouth; Indians cultivating maguey plants; Padre Hidalgo, José María Morelos, Emiliano Zapata, and Francisco Villa making revolution; la Malintzín and Hernán Cortés procreating "la raza cósmica"; the last emperor, Cuauhtémoc, bearing his final agony at the hands of the Spanish torturers with infinite dignity. From the center, arcs of lights spread out until it seemed that every public and private bulb in Anáhuac blazed, and Alfonso smiled with an understanding of the destination of all of the missing electricity.

Alfonso embraced the oficial de turno and said to him, "Happy Anniversary!"

The oficial was confused but he replied in kind, "Happy Anniversary!"

Then Alfonso said, "¡Feliz Cumpleaños!"

The oficial responded with confusion, "¡Feliz Cumpleaños!"

Finally, Alfonso added, "¡Feliz día del santo!"

The oficial waited for his orders.

Alfonso explained, "What is occurring now is a natural phenomenon, the closing of the current cycle and the opening of the new order. Tomorrow should be the most intensive and productive workday of our lives. We'll roll up our sleeves tomorrow, bank on it. Because it begins a new day, and a new era. Tomorrow is the first dawn of the new sun, the new road. It's the right road now. We've got our vector, and it directs us back to the origin! With tomorrow's dawn we regain the center and we move out to . . . ¡un nuevo mundo revolucionario!"

Acknowledgments *(continued)*

In addition, the first four stories in this collection comprised the volume *Tales of El Huitlacoche* (Colorado Springs, CO: Maize Press, 1984). "The Raza Who Scored Big in Anáhuac" was later reprinted in *Best New Chicano Literature 1989*, ed. Julian Palley (Tempe, AZ: Bilingual Press, 1989).

ICL 4760   3/31/93

PS
3561
E 3854
Z 3
1992